A NOVEL
BY

Eduardo R Casas

... ya can't please everyone, so ya got to please yourself
Ricky Nelson

(Referring to creative works, not other things)

Registration No. TXu 1-683-571

ISBN 978-0615436807

ISBN 0615436803

LCCN 2011920422

Published in the United States
2011

Available at Amazon.com and other retailers

Original author

Eduardo R Casas

Writersblock5000@att.net

A WRITERS' BLOCKS PUBLISHED WORK

La gache boin a boinin, le gach leabhar a leabhrum
"To every cow her calf and to every book its copy."
Irish King Dermot

To my most loyal fan and confidant, Mayling
(My daughter says the correct spelling is Mei-Ling,
Mayling has never complained so I don't believe she
cares); if she had hands instead of little paws—and could
read, she would have contributed to the novel.

PREFACE

AUTHOR'S FOREWORD

This book is predominantly a murder/mystery, however, if you saw WALL STREET–MONEY NEVER SLEEPS, this novel will answer questions raised but never answered. This novel will go behind the scenes to explore, not only the issues of what caused the meltdown, but also critical things that are hardly mentioned; mainly the inactions by the watchdogs and the systemic faults in the vetting process used to provide assurances to the public. This story explores the schemes devised to hide the fraud, and depicts the unsolved murders committed to hide it.

This is a story about the first, the largest, and most insidious financial crime of the Twenty First century. This is also a tale of a man unwittingly caught up in a major financial scandal of global proportions, and the many murders committed to hide its secrets.

Much like Upton Sinclair's "The Jungle," a novel that captured the realities and exposed the abuses and crimes in the Chicago meatpacking industry; this novel similarly captures, through this fictional expose, the realities, and exposes the abuses and crimes of the financial mortgage industry.

This novel depicts and renders, through the experiences of one man, the particulars of this compelling crime story. Although not at all dark, gloomy or disheartening as that great original novel; nonetheless, and in contrast, this sometimes darkly humorous, tongue-in-cheek, whimsical, ironic, even flippant novel, based on observations of real life cases, captures the essence of this current crisis.

This fraud has caused the largest illegal transfer of funds in U.S. history, by taking money from the pockets of the average American, and transferring it into the pockets of the wealthiest bankers and security brokers in this country. Not since the great depression has there been such pervasive and deep loss in asset value. This is the most sinister fraud to have ever been perpetrated on the American public, and a crime, which has permeated all aspects of our economy, one that continues to affect us all.

Although primarily designed as a murder/mystery to entertain and not preach, it also illuminates and educates. This story focuses and exposes the absurdity of the cynical, hypocritical, and ineffective aspects of the vetting process established in this country, which is utilized to substantiate the suitability and quality of investments offered to the American public. This state sanctioned process operates under an indefensible self-serving structure that ultimately is used to influence the financial decisions of the unsuspecting investing public.

PLOT

A lone man; an internal auditor, discovers the massive fraud during a routine review. His relentless inquiries and persistent questioning ultimately lead him to unearth mysterious and unresolved murders; some committed to hide the original crimes of fraud, others of a more personal nature, involving the oldest of motives--revenge, while still others are attributable to the unexplained insane compulsions of a serial killer.

Hired for a simple project; requiring a mere three-week audit of the Chandler bank's internal controls over mortgage securities and foreclosures. Little did Castillo suspect that a routine review, described to him as "Needing only your rubber-stamping of the process," would result in the exposure of a major worldwide financial scandal. This was to be an investigation, which would disclose billions of dollars in fraudulent financial transactions, dirty dealings, and insalubrious financial business relationships, fraught with a multitude of conflicting interests.

While unraveling the myriad of layers in cover-up schemes, and untangling a "Can-of-worms" in illicit transactions used to conceal the fraud, Castillo discovers that these schemes were not only used to conceal these crimes, but were also used to conceal mysterious murders. These crimes would ultimately implicate members of an elite group of unscrupulous men at the highest echelons of international financial power. This would be a case of intrigue, suspense, scandal and investigations of yet unresolved crimes of murder, that would challenge Castillo's skills; not only those of his chosen profession, but also those of his avocation… solving mysteries.

***

I sincerely hope that my little fairytale helps you question the reliability of statements made by "The masters of the financial universe," and that you enjoy the journey discovering clues that identify… or red herrings that misdirect you as to who the killer is.

PROLOGUE TO MURDER AND OTHER HIGH CRIMES

"Oh what a tangled web we weave, when first we practice to deceive!" Sir Walter Scott

As he sat quietly in the beach chair, sinking ever so slightly into the sand, he listened motionlessly and attentively, straining to hear the barely audible soft murmurs of the happy couple as they exchanged their wedding vows. He then casually glanced over at the expansive blue sea, allowing his mind to drift as he looked intently at the hypnotic rippling waves, listening silently to the softly lapping water as it caressed the nearby shore. The harmonious mesmerizing rhythm of the breaking waves, in the relative silence of the ceremony, created a peaceful and serene atmosphere that altered his state of consciousness, making it easy to zone-out his surroundings and freeing his thoughts to wander. While under this temporarily tranquil Zen–like trance, he was able to focus his thoughts on the events that had transpired only a few weeks ago.

It had all started one morning, when the manager of one of the firms that provided Ed with sporadic projects, had called him to engage his services in a simple routine audit, which was anticipated to last a mere three weeks. He accepted the offer without hesitation, thinking that during these difficult times, any work was welcomed, regardless of how limited, objectionable, or poorly paid it might be.

This ostensibly routine assessment of the Chandler bank's mortgage underwriting process had opened up a Pandora's Box of illicit transactions and insalubrious associations, leading to crimes of unprecedented fraud, both in scope and in magnitude, crimes that ultimately culminated in murder. The schemes devised to cover up these illegal acts had created a maelstrom of undercurrents and quagmire, a whirling eddy of undertows that would draw in all of the world's economies into a vortex of uncontrollable tumultuous events. These swirling and turbulent whirlpools of economic woe would soon also swallow the innocent and the unsuspecting. This tragedy would be reflected in terms of the human suffering of millions of individuals, who, as a consequence of these illegal and profoundly immoral acts, would lose their jobs, their savings, and their homes. The results of this debacle would ultimately be reflected in the unprecedented rise in the murder-suicide rates throughout the world.

Ed Castillo's inadvertent and unexpected stumbling into the plot had disclosed the cunning secret plans, and now his queries delving into past-unresolved murders were threatening to unravel the web even further, revealing additional cover-ups and exposing the high-level "puppet-masters" hiding behind the veil. There was no limit to the culprits' evil and no bounds to their wickedness; the perpetrators of these heinous and egregious crimes were not about to let a lone man ruin years of plotting and planning, and were more than readily disposed to unleash their more "hands-on" accomplices against him and his family.

Gabriel had vowed vengeance.
The happy occasion that had brought Ed, Manny, and their girlfriends, Katy and Manny's latest "squeeze"

Maria, to Key West, was the wedding of their cousin. Although a festive and frolicsome mood imbued the ambiance, Ed, however, was not at all at ease. Gabriel had not only threatened to kill him, but all members of his family as well, and although being threaten was not new, unusual or unsettling to Ed, as he had been menaced with failed acts of violence many times before. This new threat, however, was somewhat disconcerting, as Gabriel had the record of accomplishments to back it up.

Ed's cousin, Luis Roberto, was getting married that afternoon. The wedding was to take place at Ft. Zachary Taylor State Park, on the west side of Key West, outdoors and right on the sparkling white sandy beach. It was Nature's own al fresco cathedral and a great place to perform one of the world's oldest and most primitive tribal rituals (One which Ed had been avoiding, for almost as long as it had been in existence). The site was an idyllic setting, and the day a perfect one. A balmy 76 degrees registered on the thermometer and a soft tropical breeze gently stroked the skin as it lightly rustled the palm fronds on the nearby coconut trees. While seagulls softly soared towards the clouds, gliding through the sky as though dancing in the wind. (Hot-damn, that's poetic).The sun was brightly shining high in the sky, with not a dark cloud in sight. The warmth of its radiance felt good on the face. Ah! Yes, it was good to be alive--and to be living in South Florida during mid-winter; if you liked piña coladas, this was your kind of day.

Calypso island music, played on steel drums by a Bahamian musician set the mood. He briefly stopped playing and paused for a moment, when he began playing again, it was to perform a beautiful and unusual rendition of Mendelssohn's Wedding March on his drums, announcing and welcoming the arrival of the beaming bride. Then pleasantly and unexpectedly, as if released on cue, a cloud (a rabble to lepidopterists, and fans of collective nouns) of migrating white Pieridae butterflies, delicately fluttering their wings, swarmed around the bride; surely a good omen of things to come. It is said that when a white butterfly crosses your path, or enters your home, it will bring good fortune, it is also said that it is a sign that you will have a good life. Some believe they symbolize angels watching over you. Disappointingly, no white doves showed up.

The wedding party on the bride's side included the maid of honor and three bridesmaids all dressed in aqua blue, harmonizing with the brilliant color of the sparkling and shimmering turquoise blue sea. They stood to the left of the beautiful bride, dressed in all white satin and holding a bouquet of tropical flowers. While the groom, the best man, and the ushers on the right, were all wearing white Cuban guayaveras.

A breeze softly blew the bride's veil, fragrantly perfuming the air with the distinct bouquet of a nearby Ylang-Ylang tree, the sweet delicate scent drifting from the folds of its fragile flowers, permeating the surroundings. This tree, although ubiquitous in Costa Rica, is not as common in Florida. Katy loved that scent, who wouldn't, its essence being the source for Chanel No. 5 perfume. The sunlight reflected blinking sparkles off the tiny pearls sewn onto the brides dress, mimicking the reflection of the sun upon the shining granules of sand. Ed's only concern in all this was that Katy, in her beautiful clinging tropical dress, was going to outshine the bride. The happiness the couple felt reflected from their faces, it was a contagious joy, a joy that the guests absorbed and shared, a joy that created a mood, which could only be described as a day in paradise.

The site of all those young men in guayaberas, for some unknown reason, flashed brief and passing thoughts in Ed's mind about its origin. The guayabera, a pleated shirt, woven of fine linen or cotton that is worn loosely over the pants and often associated with formal affairs such as weddings, is a totally Cuban creation, designed by a seamstress named Encarnación Núñez Garcia, in the city of Sancti Spiritus, Cuba, in the year 1709. Originally, it was known as a yayabera, named after residents that lived near the river Yayabo, who had made it popular. Later, after farmers began using the large pockets to carry guayaba fruit, it then morphed into its current name. The guayabera, like the Scottish kilt, became a symbol of patriotism, and just as the British would do to the Scotts, the Spanish did to the Cuban independence fighters … shoot them on the spot if caught wearing one.

The casual and relaxed ceremony continued with the "Dance of the sugar plum fairy." The little flower girl, all dressed in white chiffon, tranquilly strolled down the sandy aisle while softly tossing flower petals left to right from her little woven basket, she wore a diadem of flowers around her head, looking more like a little fairy from a Disney movie or a pixie from A Midsummer Nights Dream, rather than a little girl. All that was missing was a pair of gossamer wings. She was the niece of the bride, and the cutest, tiniest, redheaded little girl you ever did see; she was a bit shy at first, but quickly got over it, when her mother, the maid of honor, coaxed her over towards the bride with a candy bar (What a great trick! just like my little dog, Ed thought). The little ring boy was part of the complementary set of bookends, just as cute and animated as the little pixie. He walked down the sand aisle holding a starfish or sea star. The two wedding rings had been placed on the legs of the starfish, as if they were fingers. Everyone at the wedding wore colorful Hawaiian shirts, richly decorated with Hibiscus and other tropical flowers, and everyone was smiling and laughing. It was an ideal day for a wedding and one of the happiest of occasions for his cousin and family. Manny mentioned that he loved getting off from the plane in Hawaii, his new girlfriend then asked why (She was yet too new to really know Manny well enough, if she had, she wouldn't have asked). He then said, "Because Hawaii is the only state where you can get a Lei as soon as you get off the plane." The ceremony concluded after the officiating priest, father Jose, or "Padre Pepe," as he was known to the family, declared them man and wife. The best part was yet to come ... free food! ... and an open bar with top-shelf liquor, hors d'oeuvres, canapés, stuffed pastry, steak, roast beef, and sushi quality tuna, all free, at the reception.

Ed, Katy, Manny, and Maria were all staying at the Westin Resort Hotel on Green Street, directly on the waterfront. The wedding reception would follow in the open air on the boardwalk in the Mallory Square area, behind the hotel near the pier where the Carnival cruise ships docked. The cruise ships had long gone out to sea, leaving a wide panoramic vista of the sea and sky; perfect for viewing the lovely Key West sunset. The hotel staff had greeted them at the entrance with Champagne and Margaritas; they had a large section of the pier cordoned off for the extravagant party. The party was complete with a musical band and that night's surprise, a mariachi trio with a roving violinist.

This branch of the family, like the other branches, had emigrated from Cuba and dispersed throughout the Caribbean and South America. These cousins had grown up in Mexico, speaking perfect Castilian Spanish, but with a pronounced Mexican accent.

The night's festivities went on with a great deal of drinking, conga lines, and mariachi sing-a-longs. The most popular song was, "Cielito Lindo," since the American side of the family knew the chorus by heart…it was not too difficult to sing Ay! Ay! Ay! Ay! Especially after a dozen or so Margaritas and Mojitos had removed any inhibitions to making fools of themselves.

If Gabriel were to make his move, it would surely be tonight, as the opportunity was certainly there. A huge crowd had gathered all around the party on the pier, the gathering primarily consisted of tourists, anxiously waiting with eager anticipation the famous and world-renowned Key West sunset. Ed thought that the surrounding crowd encircling the party would be an ideal cover for an assassin, as the killer could easily hide amongst the multitude, fire his shots, drop his gun and calmly walk away unnoticed in the wake of the panicking crowd.

Ominous dark clouds, briefly glowing with intermittent flashings of dry lighting, suddenly and unexpectedly appeared, hovering menacingly in the sky above the celebrating guests, the looming tropical storm threatening the festivities and abruptly changing the mood. It crossed Ed's mind that perhaps this was an evil portent of things to come; but just as quickly as it had appeared so did it dissipate … welcome to South Florida! He thought. The night's celebration continued unabated and fortunately ended uneventfully; as Ed had hoped for, but had not counted on.

After the reception, the party continued. They did the rounds on Duval Street, and after having several

Daiquiris at Captain Tony's Saloon on Green Street, (the original Sloppy Joe's as they proudly claimed) and then sitting on Ernest Hemingway's "original bar stool," Manny asked if the indentations on the stool were in fact those of Hemingway's ass-cheeks. They proudly proclaimed it so, adding that it was an exact molded replica of his posterior. Then Manny, in his celebratory haze, demanded that a scientific study, similar to the one performed on the Shroud of Turin should be performed to authenticate the claim.

The group moved on to Sloppy Joe's Bar, at the corner of Duval and Green Street. Ed asked for a "Margarita Key West Sunset," (formula available upon request) but Eddie, the bartender, had no idea how to make one, so Ed gave him instructions. Eddie managed to make a half-decent one for him. Tourists around the bar then began noticing the surprisingly colorful and flavorful margarita and began ordering them. Eddie was reluctant at first to making them, as it was not his concoction, and you know how obstinate some of these professional "mixologists" can be when it is not their creation. Nevertheless, he finally gave in; reluctantly and halfheartedly, he began mixing them when the requests mounted. He made quite a bit in tips that night. And had he not been so adamant about not making them, he could have made even more.

They then ordered an original Sloppy Joe's sandwich. The original sandwich was made of Cuban Picadillo, a mixture of ground beef, green peppers, olives, and onions in a light tomato sauce on Cuban bread; legend has it, that along with daiquiris from the Floridita bar in Havana, this was another favorite of Hemingway's.

The origin of the Conk Republic, the fictitious name given to Key West by mock separatists during the tongue-in-cheek protest secession of the city of Key West from the United States on April 23, 1982, is not a well-known story. It goes back to the original inhabitants whose most prominent family was the Cobos, a Cuban family, Cobo is the Spanish word for Conch, and they were the ones that ruled Key West back then, hence the birth of the Conch Republic name. (I know, I know, I'm beginning to sound like the father of the bride in that movie "My Big Fat Greek Wedding,"… everything is better with "Cuban invented Windex").

Later that night everyone walked over to Harpoon Harry's on Carolina Street, near the Key West Seaport for a midnight snack of Mahi-Mahi, grilled "dolphin" sandwiches. Ed told Katy they'd be having a piece of Flipper in every bite. And she believed him. After telling her not to worry, that Flipper was a porpoise and a mammal, and this was a fish, he added that porpoises were very promiscuous animals, and one of only a few animals known to have sex strictly for pleasure. Katy then asked," How do you know that? Have you asked each and every one of the porpoises huh?"

Ed: Well no, but you can tell by that big grin they always seem to have on their face.

The next morning Ed's uncle and the father of the groom had arranged a wonderful evening cruise on two 60-foot catamarans, run by Sebago tours in Key West. Ed thought that it would be very difficult for Gabriel to attempt anything there, not that any difficulties or obstacles of any kind had ever stopped Gabriel from completing his assigned tasks. However, the thought comforted him, and that set his mind at ease.

The celebration was scheduled to end with a great feast for close members of the family; the hotel had just hired a famous French chef, Phillip Gaston Pépin Appétit, (known as La bouche & langue Française). And as a special gift to the bride and groom, he was going to treat the happy couple and their family to his specialty signature dish, Florida Red Snapper Flambé, while his assistant Jack Strape's specialty was to be the Blue Balls Provençal. _____

CHAPTER 1
THE MAN THE MYTH THE LEGEND

€duardo Paladino Castillo was born in Havana Cuba; he had immigrated to the United States after the Castro revolution. He had arrived much later than the earlier groups of Cuban kids that had fled the island in the sixties. His uncles and some cousins were sent to the U.S. soon after the Castro revolution, when their parents, fearing the worst for their children, placed them on a Pan Am airplane, on what was called a Pedro Pan (Peter Pan) flight to the USA. These flights were established with the help of the Catholic Church, to carry the children of Cuban families, quickly and quietly away from Cuba and the indoctrination of the Castro government.

He lived temporarily with his uncle, ultimately to be housed at the St. John Bosco School, an orphanage for semi-delinquent and wayward boys, located in Marrero Louisiana. The school was established mainly for the care of poor white male orphans, until the gang of Cubans arrived. This school was also the dumping ground for disturbed and damaged priests that the Archdiocese had removed from the "better parishes." These priests had been transferred here, because they had been accused of violence, or had been accused of performing unsavory acts and displaying undesirable behavior. They had been removed from the general catholic population and "warehoused" at St John Bosco, only to be unleashed on these young innocent and unwitting poorer members of the Church. This was a true hell on earth, where the acutely religious and overly pious did not pray, but rather preyed on poor little sinners.

In this asylum like environment, he remained for two years, awaiting his parent's arrival from Cuba. It was here young Castillo developed the tough skin and sardonic humor necessary to survive in neighborhoods filled with hardened delinquents, and ultimately with the hard-nosed unscrupulous executives that he would later encounter in life.

He was "released" after two years, some of his classmates, however, remained until they were of legal age and were considered adults. This meant that they had to remain in this environment until they turned twenty-one. They could not be released, because their parents had never arrived in the USA to claim them, as many of the parents had died in Cuban jails at the hands of the Castro government. God only knows what permanent damage some had suffered under the caring hands of the St. John Bosco priestly staff. This is not to say that others had not flourished, one alumnus went on to become ambassador to Spain under the Bush administration.

He would jokingly tell his cousin Manuel (Manny) that one day he would tell him the stories of his stay in detail, so that Manny would appreciate more the pampered life he had lived as a little Cuban prince in Miami.

Castillo had a calm deliberate demeanor; he was a thoughtful logical man, non-aggressive by nature, but could be quite assertive when in search of the truth. He liked solving puzzles, mysteries, and finding solutions to problems. An unlikely hero, he had chosen a relatively passive cerebral profession as an accountant, more specifically he had chosen the field of internal audit, forensics accounting and computer auditing. He was certified in all three disciplines, this field was not the most lucrative branch of the profession, public accounting would have been the more financially rewarding choice, a tax practice even more so. This work, however, seemed to appeal to his nature and skills, it allowed him the opportunity to solve mysteries, albeit more of a financial and business nature rather than a criminal one. But as the saying goes "Money is the root of all evil" or is it "The love of money is the root of all evil," no matter, this line of work would eventually expose him to all kinds of mysteries, as well as all sources of evils, murder not being the least.

He had turned prematurely gray at age twenty-two, a condition inherited from his mother's side of the family; a sort of selective, concentrated, pinpoint albinism. He was six one in height and robustly built, he had above average good looks; although his sex appeal was more rooted in his personality, and it increased threefold when he spoke. His looks were more rugged than pretty, like a swarthy Latin Sean Connery or Gerard Butler type, rather than a Ricky Martin or other American teen idol. He had an athletic physique. Manny, his cousin had been a football star and gone on to play some pro-ball. Ed had played football in college, not a star but good. When not fighting evil, Ed would masquerade as a mild mannered accountant, performing audits, faster than a speeding bullet for the greater Miami employment agencies and audit firms. He was circumcised (perhaps more detail than you wanted to know), as probably was Superman, after all he was the creation of two Jewish immigrants. Although there is an ongoing debate about this fact, as some Superman scholars, such as Manny his cousin, argue that given that he was born in Krypton, and this was not a practice common to its residents; he was in fact not circumcised. This argument is also based on the fact that, although Jewish mohels or mohelim can cut a diamond in the back seat of a Lincoln Continental without a miscue, there is, however, no substance known to man hard enough that can be used to perform a Brit milah (circumcision) on Superman. Some experts argue that Kryptonite could have been focused on the desired area to temporarily weaken it, and allow the mohel to perform the bloody religious rite-- There is a bit of nerd in all of us, as you can see … Ed and Manny were no exception.

What's in a name? A rose by any other name....
He was named Eduardo, after his beloved aunt, his "tia" Edwina, who now lived in Phoenix Arizona. She had been married to Ed's uncle, "tio" Cancan; his uncle had acquired this nickname while he was a freshman university student visiting Paris with several of his friends. The story goes that they had visited the Moulin Rouge cabaret one night, and his uncle had been so impressed and excited by the fact that the dancers wore no panties that he would yell out can-can, and the girls would then oblige him by kicking up their skirts to expose their charms. He was able to woo one of these beauties that night, his friends in turn, were so impressed and excited they began calling him Can-Can, and it stuck.

Ed to his closest friends, Castillo to his acquaintances and business associates, only his older sister called him Eddie, only his mother called him by his formal Christian name, and when he was in real trouble, she would yell out his entire first, middle and surname, all at once, in a loud stern tone.

He disliked the nickname Eddie; this nickname had acquired a negative connotation during recent times. Eddies had become the stereotypical petty criminal of the movies; it seemed that in every movie an Eddie appeared in, he was characterized as a cheap, weak sniveling petty hood. Eddies are the nonassertive, geeky, nerdy, dirty runt, in the movies. They are the ones who would surely betray you, the one that was not so respected by the other members of the mob. Eddies are often depicted as drug abusing junkies, dirty cops, or cheap bottom feeding private detectives. At best, Eddies are the loser brother of the pretty heroin. Eddies are usually tortured; I don't mean they are emotionally tortured souls, I mean they usually are physically tortured by other hoods. Eddies, just like the guys that wear the red shirts in all Star Trek episodes, are the first to die, many times in a most unpleasant manner. They are interchangeable characters with the likes of the Italian version, the Pauli. Eddies are the type of guys in the movies that would be crying out to the hero, "They took my thumb Charlie ... they took my thumb" or other part of his body, just before he is gruesomely murdered by an extremely sadistic villain. While the hero; trying as hard as he might, is unable to save him. Eddies are abused constantly and mercilessly. Even Iron Man is sensitive about his middle name Edward; I believe he is afraid that he will be called Eddie. As far as TV tropes go, Eddie's are the king of the "Butt-Monkey's" bordering on the "Jerkass" ... a character that is destined to die.

One consolation to the hero in movies with Eddies is that he gets to bang the pretty sister. Next time you are at the movies, and there is an Eddie, you'll see what I mean. "Eds," on the other hand, are like Georges, reliable, boring, honest plodders ... he could identify with that. While names like Edward, Edmund or Edgar, and Edwin, seem to carry a regal or royal connotation, like that of a prince, count or other member of the aristocracy. It seems also that wealth or the appearance of wealth, accompanies the use of this full formal first name too. This probably explains why the country club set, call their offspring named Edward, Edmund, Edgar or Edwin, a Teddy or Ted and never ever Eddie. Case-in-point, Senator Ted Kennedy--I rest my case. Ned, by the way, is reserved for New England farmers, and Eduardo of course is too ethnic.

The name Paladino was passed down to him by his father, in homage to his grandfather and other past ancestors, his business card had been humorously imprinted "Have Pentel will travel." This in turn, was in homage to the gunslinger cowboy detective of the nineteen-fifty's TV show that went by the English version of the same name.

The story goes that one of these ancestors had served on Charlemagne's court as one of the twelve paladins or knights that were the guardians and protectors of the faith, the kingdom, and the king. They were perceived as a form of warrior cleric, not unlike the knights Templar. (You may have read that some knights Templar were burnt at the stake for having relations with other knights, that was an isolated case were the "Don't ask don't tell" rule was broken and they foolishly told). They were reputed to be gallant chivalrous knights, always disposed to protect the weak and disenfranchised. It is also reputed by family history that one of these paladins was a knight serving the Spanish king along the side of El Cid in battles against the Saracens.

Some describe the paladin as a "Warrior of the Holy Light." According to legend, they uphold all that is good and true in the world and revile all that is evil and sinister, especially the undead (They have something personal against them). They offer succor to the beleaguered and smite their enemies with holy fervor. They are particularly potent against the undead. They are a sort of zombie killer. The paladin's holy light can burn them terribly, perhaps because they are too slow or dumb to put it out. The presence of any evil is reprehensible to the paladin, but he focuses his efforts on destroying demons and the undead (I think they were obsessed with the undead). These warriors uphold the tenets of the Holy Light and defend the innocent. They must have spent a lot of down time sitting in recliners around the Paladin station house, cooking chili (much like firemen) as documented cases of the roaming undead are few and far between, probably because they are inherently shy and tend to make rare appearances and when they do, its usually at night. Frankly ... this name was just a little bit too much to live up to, Ed always thought.

Fuck Jean de la Fontaine!
Ed had grown up following the golden rule, working hard, keeping his nose to the grind. He made a decent living and was relatively happy, but as it is in life some do better than others. Many of his friends who back in high school had pursued easier paths, not requiring education, were now immensely rich. Don't get me wrong, compared to many he had a terrific life, but sometimes he would read in newspapers about friends who had done remarkably well and sometimes the ugly green-eyed monster of envy would surface and raise its ugly head, he would then say aloud, "Fuck that Jean de la Fontaine!" Manny hearing him say this then asked, "Who is that and why fuck him?" Ed told Manny that he was a big fan, and had been greatly influenced by the fable of the ant and the grasshopper. In this story, the ant works hard, and when winter comes, he is all ready for the harsh weather, while the grasshopper that had spent all of the other seasons idly playing the fiddle was now freezing his butt

and starving. Ed would say that many times it seems like if you pursue what you love, you will become rich in many ways, but if you pursue an endeavor you dislike, just for the money, you may get the money but you will never be truly rich and happy. He figured someone should have told him that, he imagined that the grasshopper in real life would have gotten a lucrative recording contract, playing along side of Charlie Daniels, and living in a waterfront mansion on Miami Beach, driving a Ferrari, and doing what he liked, as many of his friends were doing. He blames the author that popularized the original fable for misguiding him. … So fuck Jean de la Fontaine!

_____1

CHAPTER 2
THE LOVE OF HIS LIFE, HIS BEST GIRL FRIDAY, KATY

Ed referred to Katy, his girlfriend, as his beautiful "jariya" or concubine, as they were not married. She was a brave hearted lassie and a nice pretty girl with flowing red auburn hair down to her shoulders, very fair complexion and beautiful skin, she was tall, well proportionate, with all features perfectly symmetrical, large blue eyes with long eyelashes, full lips with a confident aristocratic nose, the waist of a wasp and the hips of a real woman. When excited, or drank too much wine, her face would take a rosy hue; the few freckles on her face made her look cute and younger than she really was. She was very sweet and caring. He would say that her eyes were the first thing that attracted him to her, this of course was an outright lie told for public consumption, it just sounded better in polite company, the reality was that it was her boobs.

Katy was of Scottish-Irish-German descent. A branch of her family was descendent of Sir Roderick Mackenzie, Earl of Cromartie. She had developed an interest in exploring her ancestry and had traced her lineage and heritage back to the Earl.

Ed would tease her because she was so nice that all of their acquaintances, friends, and family, on either side, as well as her coworkers, absolutely loved her, while many were lukewarm towards him. His own sisters and brothers liked her better than him. He would say to her "Everybody loves Katy," in that sarcastic, slightly envious

tone of voice used by big brother Robert in the show
Everybody Loves Raymond.

The only time she would get mad was when Ed had done
something she didn't like, and that was often. He just
bugged her too much; bugged her to the point where he
would get a rise out of her and she would react.

Lately she had begun to ignore him, going to her tea
parties, ladies luncheons, book clubs and get-togethers,
where she, along with the other attending ladies would
sell their gold jewelry at giveaway prices then
repurchased cheap new ones at an inordinately
excessive cost, thereby losing money on every
transaction. She started taking overnight wilderness trips
with her girlfriends, not unlike Oprah and Gail, (that had
started to concern him a bit). They had an on and off
relationship for over ten years, mainly on. The critical
times in their relation occurred during holidays; on
Valentines Day, her birthday and Christmas, she would
receive from Ed a necklace, a pearl ring, diamond
bracelet, or emerald pin. Then shortly afterwards the sad
face and the torrent of tears would come out.

Being the man that he was, at first he did not understand
and asking directly was "verboten." He had learned this
the hard way. It was out of the question, as it was an
unwritten law of male/female interaction, a woman riddle,
a female enigma if you will, one that he had to solve
indirectly, asking any direct questions was forbidden, and
led to anger and frustration, and statements like "You
mean you don't know?" And "Well you should know!" And
if you asked the follow-up question, "No I don't know
please tell me? " That invariably led to, "I don't wish to
talk about it now."

It was a catch 22 scenario devised by a woman, there was no way out under these circumstances. Any outward show of anger by the male, due to his frustration, would be manipulated by the female in such a manner that any pseudo-psychologist walking in on the argument would automatically assume that the male was an insensitive monster; a crazed angry animal, a beast that was on the verge of violence; a beast with no apparent reason to feel, or act that way towards such a frail and delicate creature. These casual observers (Padre Pepe would be one) would soon be drawing comparisons to Mel Gibson or Charlie Sheen and demanding that he either attend anger management classes, or apply to be a guest on the Dr. Phil show. He knew that if he allowed this to happen, she would have turned the tables on him once again, and would have won a total scorched earth type victory. It was best to stay calm.

Ed believed that the source of all political correctness emanated from the female, and then later it was disseminated in cryptic code form to all males around the world; very much like instructions from Oprah to the female populace. It was up to them to decipher this strange code and carryout the instructions. A chauvinist at heart, he believed that there was a worldwide plot to effeminate, or figuratively castrate all men; he used the attempts to pass prohibition laws, and the establishing of many other similar laws and social rules as support to his theory, rules and laws that were aimed at curving vices found primarily in men. The tradition of teatime in England, for example, was in fact a plot to stop men from drinking alcohol.

Ed was a firm believer in the "harm principle," as articulated in John Stuart Mill's essay, *On Liberty*, simply stated:

"The only purpose, for which power can be rightfully exercised over any member of a civilized community against his will, is to prevent harm to others."
"His own good, either physical or moral, is not sufficient warrant. He cannot rightfully be compelled to do or forbear because it will be better for him to do so, because it will make him happier, because, in the opinion of others, to do so would be wise, or even right. ... The only part of the conduct of anyone, for which he is amenable to society, is that which concerns others. In the part, which merely concerns himself, his independence is, of right, absolute. Over himself, over his own body and mind, the individual is sovereign."

This principle has been distorted, extended, convoluted and strained by feminists, so that they can stretch and over reach, and thus portray all male vices as harmful to others, bringing the power of the law to bear and thereby limiting, restricting and ultimately obliterating what they consider to be undesirable behavior in men.

One Valentines day Ed had given Katy a beautiful emerald ring, this had brought a smile to her face, Ed thought that finally he had given her something she liked, and more importantly something that had not made her cry. When suddenly, from the oldies radio station, out comes blaring "This Diamond Ring" by Gary Lewis and the Playboys. And just as suddenly out came a torrent of tears. The only good thing that came out of all of this was that he had figured it out; he had solved "The riddle of the Sphinx." After many trials and errors he had finally broken the code; It was the unmet expectations that made her cry, the nonexistent engagement ring, the ring that was not in the box was the cause of all this suffering.

He had solved one more riddle and broken one more cipher of the female Enigma Machine.

Ed knew that someday he would marry her, she was his soul mate, he could not live without her, and he could not function without her. But just not right now, as he felt that by marrying her, he would be exposing her to the dangers of his work.

The crisis brought about by these holidays was becoming more pronounced every year, one day he would have to act or lose everything. Armed with this knowledge Ed devised a strategy to deal with the puzzle and the obstacle. It would be an overwhelming pincer movement; an attack on several fronts.

Hercules ninth quest.
He dreaded anniversaries and the romantic holidays, Valentines' day in particular, he knew that the horrible head of unrequited expectations would surface again. The ring was the solution, other jewelry would not suffice, gold, if not in the shape of a ring would provide no guaranties, "Diamonds may be forever," but if not on top of a ring, would only mean forever misery, anguish and pain to him. Expensive perfumes would not help him reach the pinnacle. Chocolates and candy were dandy but not a ring. She did love lingerie, he thought. If he could not provide her the one thing she wanted, he would dazzle, confuse her, and overwhelm her with as many luxurious alternatives that he could think of, the least of which would be undergarments that were sensual, alluring, but also elegant and in good taste. This last task would take him from Victoria's Secret to Neiman Marcus in search for the perfect bra or other lacy, silky undergarment or negligee he could find. If Hercules' ninth labor was the obtainment of the Amazon queen's girdle,

Ed would make this his quest too, making Hercules's mission finding the Amazon's girdle a "walk-in-the-park." Heck! He would outdo Hercules; he would do him one better by combining the search for the Golden Fleece and the queen's corset … Ed would search for a golden-fleeced bra. He pondered as to what Hercules or Eurystheus, the king that had sent him on the quest, would want with a corset. Perhaps Eurystheus or old Herc put on some lipstick, then put on the girdle and danced around in the basement to the tune of q. lazzarus's "goodbye horses," like Buffalo Bill in the Silence of the Lambs-- It's possible. (This issue with the ring had begun to affect Ed's thinking; it was disturbing to him that he was beginning to sound like Stewie from Family Guy).

Ed had a selective memory, he would lose his keys, forget to pay bills, didn't know the difference between Britney Spears and a Pop-Tart (Perhaps there was none) had no interest or cared in what nightclub Paris Hilton was spotted in. He didn't know what day of the week it was, forget directions to places visited a dozen times, failed to renew his license, don't even mention birthdays and anniversaries, he didn't even know how much money was in the bank. No idea of the balance, not how much he owed on credit cards or the amount due on the mortgage, if it were not for Katy, the check book would be out of balance and the checks would be bouncing all over the place. You know how the saying goes, "In the house of the cobbler, the kids have no shoes." He was an accountant and auditor, for cripes sake!

He would say that his brain was like a computer, and he did not want to overcrowd it with unnecessary detail that would slowdown his CPU and clog his Hard Drive. He would say that Einstein would make a conscious effort not to remember things, so he could devote his total brain capacity to the problem at hand … and where would we be without $E=MC^2$.

Tinkle, tinkle little Eddie.
Katy: You were in my bathroom weren't you?

 Ed said, "I was not, you didn't see me, no one saw me, you can't prove it." (With women, you have to deny, deny, deny; admitting anything will open the floodgates to further and relentless everlasting harassment and humiliation).

Katy: Oh yes, I can.

Ed: How?

Katy: It is very simple, only two things are ever different after you have visited my toilet, the seat is not up, and you peed all over it; her powers of observation were keen, he thought.

Whenever he visited her house uninvited, she knew, she knew because half the milk in the carton was gone, she could also tell he had been in a hurry, because the presence of (although miniscule) … telltale pee droplets on her toilet seat were clearly visible to her keen eyesight. He never lifted it when in a hurry.

No fury like a woman scorned.
Now here was a human being, that when angry, you could literally say could consume you with fireballs from her eyes and bolts of lightning from her ass. Or, is it the other way around? Ed would ask, "Why do you get so mad?" She would say to him, in her best imitation of

David Banner … Oh this isn't mad … you don't want to see me when I am mad.

She would get very angry when he was late. He had written a little poem for her, which he threatened to change from the original, because of how mad she got when he was late.

The original went like this:
If you should pass before I die, let it be my fate
For then a cheerful welcome would greet me at the gate.

The revised version would go like this:
If you should pass before I'm dead … let it not be my fate
For then a pissy welcome would greet me when I'm late.

He would say, "Why can't you be more like Mayling ... she greets me at the door with a wiggling and wagging tail and then she licks my hand!" Her answer to that was … "That'll be the day!"

The relationship after all these years was getting to be like an old comfortable pair of slippers, although the sex was still great for both of them, the embers, however, were slightly waning, when compared to the days they were both eighteen. Ed was trying hard to revitalize their relationship. He was trying to make the times they spent together more exciting and loving, but Jeez! It was hard; it was really, really hard.

Katy had given Ed a new lighter for his birthday. He had many bad habits, the smoking of a pipe or cigar was one of them. He would smoke a pipe-full or two after lunch and dinners; it relaxed him and took the edge off after a tense day. Smoking the pipe seemed to allow him to think clearer. This lighter was silver, monogrammed with his initials, it was designed specifically for pipes, with a fire nozzle at right angle to the body of the lighter, making it easier to light a pipe without contorting the wrist, it had a jet blue, extremely hot two-inch flame, it even sounded like a jet when flicked. Ed loved that lighter, he kept it with him and by his nightstand at night, and it always reminded him of her.

He was telling Katy one day how he wanted to try other avenues, invest in some new business.

Katy: Please not another new business, remember Ducky Wucky Pool Bingo?

Ah yes, Ducky Wucky Pool Bingo, Ed had invented, designed and manufactured a game which he thought would be a terrific game for Florida and other southern states. He had invested large amounts of both time and money and had tried marketing the game himself. He had a strong start; sales by word of mouth and sales on the Internet had gone well. Then he approached this sleazebag toy agent who promised him he could get valuable information that would turn his little game into a success story. He had gotten the guy's name from a list of toy agents recommended by the largest toy manufacturers, so he thought it was legit. It was called NewFunier. He took Ed's money, and after repeated attempts at contacting him, all the guy had to say was that he had called around, and the feedback was that the economy was so bad no one was interested in a pool game; and that was it. Ed contacted the Better Business Bureau; they tried to help, but "doing the right thing," they said was all on a volunteer basis. Ed had no more money; he kept the proof of the cheating and chucked it up to experience. He had considered private investors, but they were sharks who wanted controlling interest for a fraction of what it was worth. It was a shame, as it was a beautiful little game, which combined water play with bingo. Little ducks with letters that spelled "Oh! Duck!" floated, and when a letter was called out, the kids would have to find the duck with the letter on its bottom. There were thirty-four ducks, some were decoys, no letters on them, some were wild, like in card games (not actual wild ducks, silly) the first team that spelled "Oh! Duck!" Would yell out the phrase and win. Ed ended up saying "Oh! Duck!" and put the idea in a drawer.

It seemed to Ed that he had spent his entire life trying to impress Katy, and she did not impress easily. Even now, if he walked through the door and said to her that he had just been awarded the Nobel prize, or had just been elected the president of the United States; she would probably say something like, " That's nice dear, today is Friday you know? Did you remember to take out the trash?" _____2

CHAPTER 3
CASTILLO FOR HIRE
♪ ♫ **A three-hour tour, a three-hour tour ♪ ♫**

Castillo was an independent consultant; he was only hired for difficult projects when the accounting firms could not figure out the answer to their problem, did not want to be directly involved, or had some political ax to grind and wanted to deflect attention from themselves, while blaming someone else. He was their firewall; sometimes their Judas goat, luring out those who committed fraud, more often though, he was their sacrificial lamb. In any case, they always took credit for the big improvements and big findings, while blaming the consultant for the time delays, the excessive cost, and for any screw-ups, whether his fault or not.

As perplexing as it may seem, many times they didn't want to know the answer. When deniability was at a premium, Castillo could be the perfect patsy for them; he was cheap and expendable. He needed the money, they needed deniability; it was a symbiotic relationship that he could live with. This business was full of traps; you never knew whose toes you were stepping-on. Castillo was the cannon fodder, and a human minesweeper forced to use himself as the probing rod. Fortunately his competence and tenacity, or as most would say, his pure luck, had saved him more than once. If you needed a scapegoat, he was your man. So he became the go to guy when a resolution was required at all costs, and plausible deniability was a necessity.

The pay was fairly decent, although he was often underpaid. One thing is for sure he would never get rich on these wages, but, as they say, it "covered his nut." What really burned his ass was when the agents took a thirty three percent cut off the top; they said the client company was paying for this, so why was he worried. These SOBs' seriously thought Castillo was a stupid fuck; that thirty-three, you could bet came out of his end.

That morning he got a call ... he thought as he answered it, "I hope it isn't an agent and what am I being set up for this time."

Denis Flannigan was at the other end; he was one of the firm's managers that Ed had worked for in the past. "Castillo come to my office, I have a new assignment for you, I need you to go over to the Chandler bank's headquarters on 5th street and Biscayne and meet with Mr. Johnson the Controller. We need to complete an internal audit of the mortgage transactions of the bank and issue a report on the controls, this should be a slam dunk project and should not require much time, maybe three weeks max, a no-brainer of non eventful proportions ... right down your alley, so make sure the report finishes up uneventful. I don't want excessive hours on this job and make sure they are all billable, and don't start going off on tangents like usual. All I need is for you to rubber stamp the process."

It appeared to be a routine, run-of-the-mill, pat answer type review, designed to produce a feel-good comfort letter for creditors, stockholders and the feds. The boss's emphasis on time and his insistence on it being uneventful, however, were as though he was telling Castillo how the audit should or must end ... a forgone conclusion. Not a good sign if an independent review was the true objective. "Why should this one be any different, you never know what ulterior motives these guys have for hiring you, as long as it is not too objectionable and is defensible I'll take the job," he thought.

There was something familiar about the Chandler bank. Something Castillo had heard or read recently in the news and something from the past too, but he could not recall exactly what it was … so he put it aside because he thought it could not have been too important.

At the bank, Mr. Johnson turned out to be a personal friend and crony of one of the firm's senior partners, and as his name implied, a real dick. Less than forthcoming, he attempted to impede the process of the review at every turn. Johnson used his connection with Castillo's superiors to remind him continually (through a thin veil of threats and intimidation) that an unacceptable report on Castillo's part would lead to his dismissal from the project.

He thought that the political pressure being exerted appeared disproportionate to the importance of the job, which was to be a routine review. This alone was a red flag suggesting some major issues resided in the books of this bank. Issues that this firm did not want to touch "Not even with a ten-foot pole and a Trojan prophylactic at the end."

Cognizant of his employers implied commands and the controller's not so subtle implications, it was beginning to appear that this engagement might pose a dilemma in which choosing either alternative could lead to a premature career ending choice. Castillo was not one looking for career suicide, but he was also not one to look the other way on important issues. The proverbial tiger by the tail scenario was developing. He was being placed between two horns of a dilemma, both sharp and unappealing. He had determined early on in his career that, only the truth and nothing but the total truth could stand up against the blinding light of sunshine. He was a "Tell it like it is" sort of guy in a world of political correctness and rampant euphemistic terms. The truth, he believed, would always turn out to be the best CYA (cover your ass) strategy one could have in these situations. _____**3**

CHAPTER 4
I AM THE LAW
A polemic discourse; I am right you are wrong, the end

Many of us know that the audit conclusions reached and the auditors' opinions given (opinions upon which we rely upon) as a result of many recent financial audits have been analogous to a doctor telling the family (just before the bill is paid) "The operation was a total success" ... only to be told later, after the bill is paid ..."Unfortunately the patient died."

Audits are allowing "Creative Accounting" to present financial statements that are more fiction than fact. The oligopoly comprised of a mere eight firms, which had been fostered, nurtured, and reared since inception on self-serving inflexible rules, would soon be reduced to four, as it would be unable to protect itself from the economic fallout of the financial realities that would soon hit the fan. An unfortunate consequence of this situation may be that a greater level of incompetence is now concentrated in the remaining four. Their incompetence would not be an issue if they restricted their evaluations to only certifying the voting ballots at the Oscars.

Although the Emperor in the tale of "The Emperor's New Clothes" may have been a total, complete, and utter idiot, it was his ministers and advisors; however, that convinced him that his none-existing clothes were exquisite. They were ultimately responsible for his embarrassment and demise. The public accountants of these failed firms and the officers of these banks are equivalently responsible and are remarkably similar in character to the slobbering advisors who lauded the king with praise. The senior partners at the firm that had engaged Ed were such type of advisors.

Ed always found it odd that financial auditors are called certified public accountants, yet they certify nothing, they "issue an opinion" with so many disclaimers and loopholes that in comparison make Swiss cheese seem like the densest of heavy metals. The term "opinion" in itself is a weak indicator of the confidence placed on the level of assurance they provide, otherwise a stronger more direct word, such as certify, or attest would be used. It is curious how the PCAOB (Public Company Accounting Oversight Board) the regulatory body over audit practices and reporting to the public, explicitly uses the word attest to describe the responsibility of external auditors in their reporting of management assertions as to the effectiveness of controls, this is a no-nonsense word that is a synonym for certify. There is no equivocation on the part of the PCAOB as to their intent and expectations from the audit. And as far as "public," they are paid by the very companies who hire them, and at very handsome rates, I might say; a bit of a conflict wouldn't you say. Where in the end would one conclude their allegiance lies, to the public or to the paying client?

The assurances provided by public accountants in their clean opinions have been riddled with disclaimers and caveats that exemplify little confidence in their work or provide little comfort to the investor. They merely attempt to deflect responsibility unto management in the event of lawsuits. Auditors now want to institutionalize their insulation from accountability to their clients, by lobbying for a law that will cap their liability to the shareholders, with a policy of claiming that they can't afford it, that their number is too few to pay such large sums, a variation on the theme of "Too big to fail." This of course, like the dry cleaners' disclaimers on the laundry tickets, did little to protect the then eight and now four largest public accounting firms from legal responsibility due to negligence and fraud. In the past when they did issue an adverse opinion, it was rare and not sufficiently comprehensive to reveal anything of consequence.

The recent world financial woes can be directly traced to the collegial and cozy relationships, cemented by the exorbitant fees, corporations pay to public accounting firms. The size of these fees provides direct influencing pressure on the amount of independence auditors agree to maintain or are willing to exercise during their audits. Others argue that paying too little for audit services is instrumental to the decay of effective audits, because the audit firms in turn hire and assign cheap and inexperienced recent college graduates. These "interns" then are camped out in the company's conference room where all they are doing is learning to "tick and tie" on their client's dime. Their experience having been gained with little oversight or supervision by more seasoned members, thereby reducing the audit firms costs and effectiveness. This was one of the many accusations leveled against Arthur Anderson just prior to their demise.

This new SOX law (the Sarbanes-Oxley act) was intended to require a truth in reporting, that should, if applied as intended, mitigate this common practice. Before the passing of the SOX act, his services were not so much in demand; this act had changed the mood and the demand for his services and given him a little more leverage in negotiating fees and the extent and nature of the required work to ensure compliance. There is nothing faster to light a fire under a high-level executive's ass, than threatening him with jail time, for him to ensure that the required internal controls are in place and effective.

Although SOX included many improvements, Ed believed that government might have altogether missed the boat or at least a good opportunity to provide even greater protection to the public. He concluded that the reports that the public, investors and analysts expect and need, must not only provide them with assurances of the reliability of the reported numbers, but must also reasonably alert them of the portent of impending disaster.

Here is a parable to understand the significance of why this new law was necessary and what this new law is designed to achieve. There is a little Spanish ditty- of- a-song, "La Chivita" (The Little Goat) that is sung to small children (although I do not know why to small children, since it implies the need for violence, and just prior to the ending it becomes a bit morbid) It is a story or fable; a cautionary tale with a moral lesson. It is also an allegory of today's apathy by government and institutions. It does end with a happy ending (a fairytale happy ending … not the massage type).

It starts with a little goat that refuses to come out of a cave. And then describes the attempts to force her out; by eliciting the aid of a series of helpers, which due to apathy or whatever selfish reason never made quite clear in the little song, are reluctant at first and must be compelled or coerced to coax her out.

The story continues along, requesting help from animals, a number of inanimate objects and the forces of nature, all of whom refuse. In succession, each refusal is met with an attempt to elicit an appropriate motivator or prod, perfectly suited to motivate the preceding one. (For example, water is asked to put out the fire, fire is then asked to burn the wood stick and so on).

The request eventually reaches man, the penultimate link in the sequence, but he also refuses … until finally, the Grim Reaper is called to deal with the reluctant human, and of course, Death has no qualms in taking man away. This gets the ball rolling immediately, and in rapid succession everyone previously summoned is more than willing to perform the tasks, the end-result is that the goat comes out of the cave, and is ultimately saved. Of course, the goat would have never gone into the cave in the first place had the shepherd exercised adequate oversight over his flock. This parable is a metaphor for financial reality in America and it should be heeded well.

SOX was the death knell to audits that are indifferent to economic reality, the civil and criminal sanctions provided in the act are the equivalent of death in the little ditty. It was designed to be the "End of Days" for the management lobbying tail, wagging the legal and regulatory standards setting dog.

This was to be the impetus for the public accountants to perform the required assigned function, for which they are well qualified, but nonetheless have been reluctant to perform. The same applies to internal auditors, management, executives, and company boards. The objective is to induce action and save our collective "goat" if not their own, or should I say save their ass or what ever other animal is in the farm.

"Physician heal thyself" … if not others will.
Many in industry and in auditing circles bitched and moaned about SOX, they forget that in the past, several

other acts have been enacted to monitor and control abuses. The 1933 securities act being one; hell! physical inventory taking practices did not become a standard audit processes until a major fraud case in the nineteen hundreds occurred, that had duped auditors into issuing a clean opinion of a company that had reported millions in nonexistent inventory. This caused a kicking and wailing congress to pass regulations that required all auditors to observe and verify the physical inventories, as well as confirming the title to the inventory. Was this a good thing? Duh! Of course. By the way, this is one strategy allegedly used by "Chainsaw Al" of the Sunbeam Company to pump up the stock, during his pump-and-dump days. He actually encouraged the recording of ostensive sales (they were not because title had not passed to the buyer), that were in fact consignments, with a right of return, thereby overstating sales and profits. It was rumored, that although Al had not succeeded with this scheme at Sunbeam, he had managed to dupe the buyers of Scott Paper with a similar one. This rule and many more, were single stopgap measures, while the SOX law is a holistic approach to the basic problem.

Unfortunately, not only did the law come too late, as the sub-prime mortgage failure was already brewing and beginning to fester, but the government has for years nullified and defanged many laws through numerous reversals or deregulation of other protective measures, such as the cancellation of usury laws. Lobbyists for banks and credit card companies have made sure that protective measures over the years got eroded one by one. ...There was a new sheriff in town, but his bullets had been taken away, and his actions, having been reactionary, as all law enforcement is, may have come too late to save the town.

They say to make your god your religion and not your religion your god. By focusing on the loopholes in the "accounting rules," i.e. "The religion of accounting" and not the god, i.e. the "economic reality" they were designed to venerate. The current accounting framework has allowed the drifting of focus away from what is truly indispensable, which is the fair reporting of economic substance in financial statements, towards the more mundane, looped-holed rules of accounting. In the past, conservative fundamental accounting rules would not allow revenue recognition of income that was not earned, but only recently the floodgates were opened to any voodoo accounting that the client wished. Many new accounting rules over securitization of assets magically converted liabilities back to assets. The allowing of the off-balance-sheet "non-reporting" of liabilities, as well as other GAAP witches brews allowed for the recognition of earnings based on estimates that were more of a fairy tale than even a guess, further adding to the illusion of real value and wealth that did not exist. These were all permissive accounting standards that allowed, no, more than that, encouraged creative accounting that was more a fantasy than it was economic fact. Add to this the "look the other way" or complicit auditing that allowed the frauds to continue and build year after year, and you had a recipe for disaster.

Deregulation, Ed thought, *now there's an awesomely euphemistic word for what should be called in reality, dismantling, the definition being "the taking apart of something in a way <u>that causes it to stop working."</u>*

Deregulation? Or lack of regulation?
The birth of this crisis can be traced back to the times when the laws and regulations separating commercial

banks, brokers, and insurers from those of the savings banks were eliminated or diluted to the point that differences were blurred beyond recognition. This allowed, no, more than that it encouraged the taking of greater risks and eliminated the "lofty" objective of affordable mortgage loans from further consideration; once the primary goal of the Savings and Loans.

"Teacher says every time a government official farts ... a devil gets its pitchfork."
In real life, George Bailey's dream of making home ownership more affordable was replaced by the nightmare of Henry F. Potter's vision. The part of Uncle Billy, having been played by Uncle Sam.

Did anyone notice that Mr. Potter was never caught, never held accountable for the theft. He kept the money from uncle Billy's misplaced deposit and never paid it back! ! Somewhat reminiscent to the U.S. bankers' relationship with the U.S. government ... wouldn't you say.

The creation of the government sponsored, unregulated and exempt mortgage-backed securitization process supported by collateralized debt obligations gave rise to the growth of the sub-prime industry, and the basically "junk' mortgages that underlie, and inflated the housing bubble. Higher returns require higher risks; the impetus for this is unbridled greed. By providing mass bailouts, the government was the enabler that led to the "moral hazard" that drove the greed, because there was no downside for the lenders.

The government was not the only accomplice; also complicit in the debacle were rating agencies like Moody and S&P that continued issuing "AAA" ratings, equivalent to high-grade investment paper to companies in precarious financial positions, like the Chandler bank; companies that securitized sub-prime mortgage investments.

Strong cohesive lobbying associations like the AICPA, which rivals the AMA and the insurance industry in its power to influence government, stands ready and willing to ensure the interests of its members. This was the environment and the atmosphere under which the massive financial crimes of this decade were born and nourished. This is why foreclosures are rampant, this is why a new industry has been created just to manage the thousands of foreclosures, and this is why you may be losing your home.

Here is a relevant quote that covers the result of all these blunders: "As our own day's story of stupid policies and lax regulations, of great moneymen, free-market hucksters, White-collar thieves, and self-serving politicians unfold and banks foreclose on millions of families' homes, workers lose their jobs and life savings disappear." A very current statement that covers what is occurring today; this quote, however, is by Elliot J. Gorn and it was made about the 1930's depression. The attitudes expressed by statements of laissez-faire, let them eat cake and no holds barred business tactics are views of yesterday, views, that must give way to a gentler, albeit, more government intrusive type of capitalism, where business leaders take a more holistic social view of their responsibilities. _____**4**

CHAPTER 5
LET THE GAMES BEGIN

This audit was beginning to reveal the tip of the iceberg, and beginning to unearth the festering that lay below the surface, as well as the lengths a group of greedy men will go to hide their greedy acts and avoid doing the right thing.

While researching some of the larger and more numerous transactions, Ed noticed that the initials HA, approving many of the loans, appeared and reappeared on the documents, it turned out that they were the initials of the VP responsible for the loan and mortgage securities department, a Mr. Herbert Afortunado. Ed had that nagging thought that this name was familiar and that he knew he had seen it somewhere else, but he just could not recall where.

The job was straightforward enough; determine the validity and accuracy of the reported asset value of the mortgages and the controls that ensure that they were being processed and approved properly, and that the controls were strong enough to prevent any errors or manipulation of these reported amounts. The approval of the mortgages was to be based on criteria established by the board of directors, requiring certain certifications supported by verifiable documentation as proof of the existence of a real borrower with verifiable income, a strong credit history, proof of employment, supported by pay stubs, audited business financials, tax returns, and other independent documentation. The market value of the property had to be supported by an appraisal prepared by an independent certified appraiser. This was of particular importance for jumbo loans over a million dollars.

Preliminary findings indicated that some documents were missing or never requested. The same appraising company, the Deltona Appraisal Company, appeared and reappeared on many documents. Some documents were illegible and appeared forged. He also noticed that after a certain date, the more recent handwritten initials, "HA," approving the loans, seemed to differ from prior ones. All this information was critical, as assets on a balance sheet needed to be substantiated. They had to meet the criteria of value, occurrence, and validity. If none of the facts leading to the issuing of these mortgages are true, then the assets, (the value of which is supported by the underpinning of facts) are not accurately and properly stated, they are, in fact, artificially inflated, as these surely were. The stockholders then are being lied to, the government is being lied to, and the general investing public is being lied to.

Millions of these inflated value sub-prime mortgages, totaling billions and billions of dollars were then being combined into financial instruments called mortgage Pass-Through Certificates. Moreover, bundles of this marketable investment paper, through a process called securitization, were being issued by brokers like Goldman Saks, Lehman Brothers and others to unsuspecting individual investors and institutional investors like pension funds, all around the world. Even the Bank Medici of Austria that claimed to have "The world's most sophisticated financial and technological, experts" bought $2 billion of these certificates. Ed thought, "There but for the grace of God go I," as he often thought of investing in these securities.

If the court appointed firm that handled Madoff's case charged $700 an hour for a whopping total of $15.5 million, then surely, the lawyers who will handle this mortgage debacle will more than double that. The churning by reselling old and new individual mortgages and the bundled securities would create an artificially inflated market in the trillions of dollars (greater than the economies of most countries). When combined with usurious interest rates, that were scheduled to kick in, because many were not fixed rate mortgages, but rather variable rate ones, this would increase their reported inflated value even more. The dollar volume of these fraudulent transactions was enough to destabilize the economy of any country. Once the defaults that were surely to occur were reported, the world economy would be in serious trouble. The potential for a catastrophic economic meltdown was looming. This was voodoo economics at its worst.

None of this would faze the merchants of finance who orchestrated all this, any collapse would have little effect on them, as the millions of dollars paid out in fees, commissions, and bonuses had been siphoned off right from the top. If they had been bookies, one could say that they had taken their piece of the pie in advance, or their "vig, overround fee."

A liquidity crisis. The lubrication of the engine that drives our economy is cash, loaned at fair rates it keeps it chugging along. These schemes reduce the flow and amount of cash available, they also added unnecessary costs that made the lubricant a thick gooey mess, which eventually brings it to a halt … and we all know what happens to an engine that ceases up … the friction eventually causes it to burn up. Ed thought that most bankers and brokers in this situation would seriously consider anything to keep this secret ..." Hell! I would kill to keep this quiet."

Testing the limits ... of greed.
He began to test the individual documents supporting mortgages and found fictitious borrowers, inflated incomes, less than stellar credit reports and what could only be described as out right bogus appraisals. Additionally during the review of disbursements, there were numerous checks for related mortgage expenses to individuals. He recognized many names of high-level influential people including, financial Czars, ministers, and treasures of many international banks, he knew that fees normally go to a department, not to an individual, so why were these paid to individuals. Some of the names he recognized as being murder victims that had been killed by an international serial killer, a few years back.

He knew he had serious credible findings; some of this could be attributed to error perhaps, but not all. He needed more, he needed the smoking gun of evidence that would not only prove that this fraud occurred; but would also identify who was directly responsible and who pulled the strings behind the scene. He felt he had to put an end to this practice, even though thousands if not millions of people were already hurt but didn't know it, perhaps he could save the retirement nest, and the homes of many others.

How could this have occurred? Where was management in all of this, "Asleep at the wheel?" Moreover, what happen to all the fail-safe controls? He thought that only collusion on a massive scale could have allowed this to occur and continue undetected, or was it just acquiescence stimulated by greed? A case of follow blindly the yellow brick road, ride the unimpeded gravy train of wealth and at the end claim, "We were only following orders."

A pattern began to emerge. You needed collusion by appraiser, mortgage originator, loan officer, securities broker, real estate agent, mortgage broker, and bank approver to perpetrate this fraud. This was not an isolated case by one rogue bank officer.
The approving investing officer that arranged the deals and packaged the sale of the securities, The VP with initials HA, Herbert Afortunado was the last link in the chain; He must have known; he could have put a stop to this, he must be implicated in all this, and what about the audit firm, these frauds went back for years. These deficiencies were so obvious that even the most casual of observers would have found them, let alone a discerning one.

The appraising company turned out to be a subsidiary of the bank. Dewey Chaney and Howell were the designated watchdogs, as they were the auditors that should have caught any irregularities in the bank lending practices. Bank officers in the mortgage department unit had been hired; hand picked and promoted by Ms. Du Poi the bank president's wife and a senior VP of the bank. The principal real estate agent was a Haitian national with ties to the bank branch in Haiti and to Ms. Du Poi; brokers must have known but seemly out of greed tacitly acquiesced. There were at least ten high officers in the chain of individuals involved. But where were the bank examiners? And where in the hell was the SEC?

This fraud had all the elements of predatory securitization practices ... these mortgages were products that were created with lax underwriting standards and improper due diligence. Products that were fueling the mortgage bust. Products, which had been created through predatory lending practices, which in turn would ultimately lead to the predatory mortgage servicing practices of today.

He knew that if he dug further, he would get answers, and as the fraud grew, more and more would be revealed. Greed has the effect of a drug on an addict, and Ed knew that the ones behind the acts would soon tip their hand, or some other part of their body, and expose themselves--"Doth like the ape the more it climbs the more it shows his ass" (Quoted from Alexander Pope).

This fraud had some of the elements of a Ponzi scheme, in that proceeds from the mortgage investments were being used to pay off those involved, in the form of fees, commissions, and kickbacks. The payments were processed by clerical personnel in on the scam. This would be easy enough to prove, and prosecute, and once squeezed, these low-level culprits would squeal and rat on their own mothers.

The past is repeated; heed the warnings of history. He was no stranger to illegal banking practices, having worked on another significant fraud case, the case of the Bank of Credit and Commerce International (BCCI) a scandal that had recently rocked the financial world. Founded by Agha Hasan Abedi, a Pakistani financier, this bank was a leading international bank. The Bank was registered in Luxembourg. Within ten years BCCI had reached its pinnacle, it operated in 78 countries, had over 400 branches, and had assets in excess of US $ 20 billion, making it the 7th largest private bank in the world by assets. Capital from Sheikh Zayed bin Sultan Al

Nahyan, the ruler of Abu Dhabi in the United Arab Emirates financed the bulk of the venture. A twenty-five percent interest was held by Bank of America. BCCI became the focus of an intense regulatory legal investigation during 1991, the media referred to this incident as a "$20-billion-plus heist."

The bank had established itself, purposely, only in banking jurisdictions that by law fostered secrecy of operations, such as the Cayman Islands. Its procedures were designed and contrived to be complicated as part of their strategy. The banks officers were experienced international bankers, with a primary goal of ensuring that all transactions were conducted in secret. As their activity was primarily the commission of fraud on a worldwide scale, they operated in a manner that would avoid any detection of their true activities.

The primary control weakness, from the perspective of the regulatory agencies, was that the bank was structured so that no single country could oversee thru regulation all of its parts. A "three blind man" regulatory theory of regulation was in effect. Its two holding companies were based in Luxembourg and the Cayman Islands, two jurisdictions where banking regulation was known to be extremely lax. Add to this the fact that none of the countries it operated in had a central bank and another perfect storm of financial calamity was formed. It was a brilliant scheme.

This points to the importance and need for globalization of regulations to constrain the abuses of globalization, something that as of today has not been achieved. Many renowned financial experts have been advocating for these reforms. Most notable are the recommendations by

George Soros, as described in his book, *The Crisis of Global Capitalism.*

The bank was a participant in soliciting deposits from drug traffickers and money launderers. The Medellin Cartel was one of their clients that deposited drug proceeds for laundering. Most seriously, BCCI had made a staggering $1.48 billion worth of loans to its own shareholders, who used BCCI stock as collateral. Standard banking practices these days dictate that a bank not lend more than 10 percent of its capital to a single customer.

Deregulation by monitoring agencies around the world had allowed BCCI, the bank, to invest in highly risky commodities and financial markets, investments that caused it enormous losses. Their schemes soon required a Ponzi type payment practice where the bank began paying expenses and profits to its shareholders from customer deposits.

F. Lee Bailey was a director of CenTrust Federal Savings Bank in Florida, a failed satellite of BCCI; His involvement would eventually lead to Bailey's disbarment. BCCI's customers included many notorious individuals. It handled money for such dictators as Saddam Hussein, Manuel Noriega, Hussain Mohammad Ershad, and Samuel Doe. Other customers included the notorious Medellin Cartel and Abu Nidal. The banks rivals assigned it the moniker of "the Bank of Crooks and Criminals International." Even the U.S. Central Intelligence Agency held numerous accounts at BCCI, according to William von Raab, former U.S. Commissioner of Customs. Oliver North also used and held multiple accounts at BCCI.

These bank accounts were used for a variety of illegal covert operations, including transfers of money and weapons related to the Iran-Contra scandal. The CIA also worked with BCCI in arming and financing the Afghan mujahedeen during the Afghan War against the Soviet Union, using BCCI to launder proceeds from trafficking heroin grown in the Pakistan-Afghanistan area.

He had uncovered that the bank was not only financing Noriega's drug deals but was also complicit in hiding drugs on its own premises; the floor of the Tampa branch had numerous bags of cocaine cleverly hidden below the beautiful wooden floor boards.

After the trial in Tampa, bank officers with detailed knowledge of the crimes, who had elected not to cooperate were convicted and received long prison sentences. But after having experienced a significant measure of unpleasant jail time and a sampling of prison food, they began cooperating with authorities in order to obtain a reduced sentence. Eventually they revealed many crimes that were not known to the authorities.

Despite these problems, Price Waterhouse signed BCCI's 1989 annual report. BCCI had also applied the "The Three Blind Men theory "of auditing to its business, this was accomplished by hiring different accounting firms and preventing them from talking to each other. By the time regulatory agencies had decided to order BCCI to change to a single accounting firm, the harm was done. The BCCI scandal even caused intra accounting firm legal fights, the liquidators, Deloitte & Touche, filed a lawsuit against Price Waterhouse and Ernst & Young - the bank's auditors –for $175 million. Eventually leading to the dissolution of these limited partnerships and the formation of new entities that were needed in order for them to survive. Issues like these have caused the Big 8 to become the Big 4. BCCI came under the scrutiny of regulatory bodies and intelligence agencies in the 1980s. Back then, the bank was accused of failing to comply with federal regulations.

BCCI's downfall started when a US Customs undercover operation led by Special Agent Robert Mazur infiltrated the bank's client roster. The US Customs Service started an investigation that ended with the contrived wedding of undercover Special Agent Robert Mazur. The wedding planners had invited as special guests not only BCCI officers but also drug dealers from all around the world, who had created accounts at the bank. This made it relatively easy to arrest the culprits all at once. This was a variant of the "Lottery sting," where crooks receive notice that they have won the lottery and are asked to come to a specific address to claim their winnings.

If this account of a bank's demise was not sufficient to institute stronger regulations and require international regulatory oversight of international corporations I cannot imagine what would. The BCCI strategy was the blue print employed by the power brokers, the Chandler bank officers, and the audit firm that monitored its controls to carryout their deeds.

Ed was amazed how naive five out of the nine members of the supreme court were, when they ruled recently that the status of corporations equaled those of the individual, when it related to freedom of speech. What fools he thought, don't they understand that unlike the individual, corporations not being human have unnatural and excessive powers to exert undue influence over our democratic system. How can you possibly equate the rights of entities, with the rights of an individual. Haven't they heard of the old proverb "Power corrupts and absolute power corrupts absolutely." Only time will tell the effects of this vote on the political and ultimately the economic structure of this country.

The structure that was the imposing edifice of the sub-prime mortgage market had begun showing dangerous fissures in its foundation. The whole bank's reputation and wealth was nothing but a house of cards, the knowledge of this, closely guarded by its own "gang of ten." The gleaming glass and steel sky scrapers towering over every major city with the big shining silver letters that spelled out Chandler Bank, had been built on a sand foundation, while the giant granite gods of finance running it were nothing more than false idols with feet of clay. The pressures building between the financial faults, would cause a financial seismic tremor, the size of which would cause a massive economic quake never before felt throughout the world. He thought that any one in the chain of transactions could have put a stop to this before the quagmire spilled over unto the worlds markets, but why had no one tried. On the other hand, maybe they had. _____**5**

CHAPTER 6
♪ STIR IT UP LITTLE DARLING ♪
Or I never met a hand I didn't bite

When you throw a rock at a hornets nest, as any curious and overly active little boy will tell you, the hornets will fly right after the one who threw the rock first, stinging him relentlessly and without compassion. They just seem to know, they have a built in honing system that identifies the offender, some passersby may be stung inadvertently; but they are just unintended collateral damage. Not a fool and not a precocious child, Ed always worked under the assumption that "He who pays the piper calls the tunes." This was a case where he would be stirring the nest of the hornets that paid the piper. "Here we go again," he thought, "having to put my ass in a sling and having to bite the hand that feeds me." Nevertheless, he had to; yes, he had to blow the whistle on this, before the lid blew off. But how was he to do it, without getting caught in the quagmire. He was running out of time and snappy proverbs.

He would go through channels first and see the reaction. However, he knew the times and conditions did not favor him, as looking the other way and political correctness were the order of the day. If that failed, he would bring this to the attention of the SEC or FBI; but he thought how whistle blowers are not always well received, they are sometimes thought of as stool pigeons, snitches, and none-trust-worthy cowards. In Cuba, the practice was to hang them by the neck with barbed wire. The saints, he remembered reading, weren't burned at the stake for prophesying, witchcraft, or performing miracles, but for speaking the truth (not that he was a saint by any stretch of the imagination). How many whistle blowers have been fired, and discredited for being the so-called "disgruntled employee."

To Mr. Denis Flannigan, the firm's manager, "denial" was only a river in Egypt.
"He is a crackpot! I have an utter contempt for him. He is hysterical, unbalanced, and untruthful. Three-fourths of the things he said were absolute falsehoods. For some of the remainder there was only a basis of truth, intentionally misleading and false, willful and deliberate, misrepresentations of fact, and utter absurdity"... No, those were not Flannigan's words; they were the words of Theodore Roosevelt and his inspectors, talking about the author Upton Sinclair and his reported abuses of the Chicago meat industry, as related in his novel, "The Jungle." ... So you see there was precedence to support Ed's fears.

When Ed first brought his concerns to the firm's engagement manager, his reaction was swift and as anticipated, it was one of denial. He could not or would not accept it; he would not even acknowledge his concerns, apparently, Flannigan suffered from some form of auditory dyslexia that allowed hearing, but not listening.

Flannigan: Why do you always have to read more into things than there is, why can't you follow the program, do what you're told and stick to the script? What is it with you ... you think you're some kind of Dick Tracy or Inspector Gadget? I told you before don't make waves ... what part of don't rock the boat is it you do not understand. Why can't you just do what you're told?

"God he sounded like my mother," Ed thought.

Flannigan: You're just a bean counter not a detective! Crunch the goddamn numbers and let it go!

Ed thought "just a bean counter" hmm! Well it was an accountant who brought down Al Capone, you ignorant bastard you ... you stupid fuck!

Flannigan: Do you want to continue receiving those nice big fat checks, well, do you? ...You know your demeanor has been noticed, you know that?

As Flannigan spoke the words, a phrase from the movie Dr. Zhivago, spoken by a diehard communist party member, flashed in Ed's head, "Your attitude's been noticed, comrade, oh yes, it has! Your attitude has been noticed, you know."

Flannigan: The best financial minds of our time were in charge of that department, people of unquestionable reputations ... hell! Herbert Afortunado was an expert and legend in the field of securitization of sub-prime mortgages. He also helped develop the use of derivatives too, he was in charge of the mortgage investment department, he was a VP at the bank, and you mean to tell me you're smarter than him, you are questioning his competence and integrity.

Ed thought derivatives? Hell, nobody understands them; you might as well gamble your life's savings at a Miccosukee casino or bet on the ponies at Hialeah or the greyhounds at the Flagler dog track ... that goes for heating oil futures and options too. You're better off betting on Jai Ali games and bribing one of the Basque players to throw the game at the Dania Beach Fronton.

"He was … he is no more?" … Ed asked.

Flannigan: Yes, he died in an unfortunate diving accident a few weeks ago.

Just then, Ed remembered what had been so familiar about this bank. He remembered now … the Herald's obituary section a few weeks back, Herbert Afortunado apparently had been involved in a diving accident off the Delray Beach coast. It may have been an unrelated coincidence that a major fraud had occurred and the VP overseeing the department responsible had died in an accident. Ed, however, did not believe in coincidence, when it related to money and death.

He was mulling around in his head what Flannigan had said about the bank's VP. He then recalled the initials HA and how the more recent ones differed from the older ones. He had noticed that some loan approvals were relatively recent, but how could that be when the VP had died several weeks before, "I have it, I have the smoking gun, he thought. "

Castillo then also remembered something unusual, another employee of the bank, an assistant VP, she had worked under Afortunado, and she also had died in an accident only a few days ago. Susan Boyl was found dead just before the assignment was given to him. He had assumed then that it was just another unfortunate coincidence. But not now, if you counted Manny's brother's death, there were three deaths associated somehow with the Chandler Group; too much of a coincidence.

His past experience with the SEC had indicated that they operated under a variant of the "Ostrich Strategy." The Ostrich, a very large bird with a very small brain, when it panics and is confused, will stick its head in the sand, apparently the darkness and silence there, gives him a sense of security, a warm fuzzy feeling if you will. While the SEC's variant methodology, for the most part, is to place their heads firmly and snugly wedged up their incompetent "could give a shit" collective asses. In this position, they apparently enjoy the same degree of warmth and fuzziness that the Ostrich experiences. This wasn't just Ed's beliefs. Harry Markopolos CFE, a certified fraud examiner had proven that there was no legal or economic way that Bernard L Madoff's firm could produce those exorbitant returns on investments that Madoff claimed. He had reported this to the SEC back in 1999 and had followed up with additional evidence during the subsequent eight years; He had not received even an acknowledgment that they had received the information.

You don't know, what you don't know.
Fissures in the intellectual edifice of sub-prime mortgage developed but were unnoticed by the mathematical computer models of the risk "mismanagers." The SEC, the credit rating agencies and the general public placed more credibility on reported financial information by a computer than on a man of integrity and competence. We are now experiencing the effects on blindly relying on these financial models, a cataclysmic meltdown of our economy. Computers and their models, you see, give all of us a false sense of security; many, including the SEC, have actually suspended independent thinking and have deferred this to the computer. What must be understood is that computers tend to compound everything, whether it is good or bad.

The old adage, "garbage in, garbage out" certainly applies. Financial models with even a small error will magnify the error a thousand fold; they are in fact a complex guess supported by dubious facts (garnered from the irrelevant past ... of all things) about the financial future which are then used for predicting it. The facts themselves come from a statistical wasteland, a geographical space devoid of relevant data.

Here are some statements made by the so-called mathematical experts **after** the failures of these wonderful statistical models known as VaR or value at risk models:

- "At the very least, the risks that VaR measured did not include the biggest risk of all: the possibility of a financial meltdown. "
- "Risk modeling didn't help as much as it should have," a former risk manager at Morgan Stanley said:
- "VaR is a very limited tool; the VaR models were relatively useless as a risk-management tool and potentially catastrophic when its use creates a false sense of security among senior managers and watchdogs."
- "This is like an air bag that works all the time, except when you have a car accident." Many are now simply calling these models "a fraud."
- Wall Street risk models, no matter how mathematically sophisticated, are bogus;

....everyone is an expert ... after the fact. "If past history was all there was to the game the richest people would be librarians." --Warren Buffett, he also said, "In the business world, the rearview mirror is always clearer than the windshield."

The Madoff scheme succeeded because the last line of defense, the independent public accounting firm that audited Madoff's books was a one-man-band, the firm of Friehling & Horowitz, performed the audits, but Horowitz was dead. David Friehling the only living member of the firm did the audits, and as any competent auditor will tell you, it would be impossible for a one man firm to meet the professional standards required to perform an audit of such a large institution, but he did. It is also pertinent to indicate that Mr. Friehling had invested $14 million of his own money in the Madoff scheme, a slight conflict of interest one would say.

In the trading circles an unforeseen unplanned event of catastrophic proportions but with a miniscule statistical probability of occurring is referred to by some as either a "fat tail" or a "black swan" this mortgage debacle was to be the mother of all fat tailed black swans, and the infinitesimal probability was now a reality.

Oh no! Ed wasn't bitter … his 401k had been cut to less than half overnight … but he wasn't bitter.

The award for the grand prize of incompetence is a tossup between the FDA and the SEC; one is suppose to watch out for our physical well being while the other for our financial well being (their interpretation of the scope of their responsibility would be much narrower of course) neither one however is doing a very good job. _____**6**

CHAPTER 7
THE CHAIRMAN OF THE BOARD

He decided to pay a visit to his friend Pierre, the Chief Examiner for Dade County first, and later pay a visit to the FBI. But before he could act upon his last thoughts, Castillo received a very unusual telephone call, the man at the other end identified himself as the chairman of the board and chief executive officer of the Chandler Group. He said it was urgent that they meet, adding that it would also be very lucrative for Castillo. He indicated that it was not safe to discuss the matter over the phone and asked Castillo to meet him at Bayside Park; he would then explain the details once Ed arrived. He told Ed not to try to trace the call, as this was a throwaway phone, which he would discard right after the call. Intrigued and happy to hear the words "Lucrative and Castillo" together in one sentence, he headed to the designated meeting place.

Chairman Randolph Chandler III: Thank you for coming, I see that you're both skeptical as to who I am and puzzled about the reason for our meeting, and why we are meeting here and not at my bank's offices.

Ed: You're right on the second and third count but not the first. I know who you are.

Chairman: Of course, I am an old man and forget we are in the age of the Internet, you probably googled my image. Well, let me illuminate you on the reason for my call-- first let me ask you, are you familiar with the Bible's admonition by Matthew 19:23-24, Mark 10:24-25 and Luke 18:24-25.

Ed: No, I can't say that I am.

Chairman: I'm sure you have heard of the saying attributed to Jesus when he said "And again I say unto you, it is easier for a camel to go through the eye of a needle, than for a rich man to enter into the kingdom of God."

Ed: Yes, I have heard that saying before.

Chairman: Actually, you know, it's not an accurate translation, although it captures the implied meaning. You see the word camel in Greek is Kamelos, while the word for the thick heavy ropes used to moor fishing boats ... a sailor's rope, is Kamilos. You can see how a minor error in translation can lead to a confusing statement, and why the saying sounds a bit weird. The use of the latter word makes more sense in the context of what Jesus was trying to convey.

Ed: Yes, I can see that, but what is your point?

Chairman: My point is that I am a dying old man that has done many semi-illegal things in this life, but would like to honor the memory of his ancestors who established this bank ... before passing. I would also like to save the reputation and good name of Chandler. I would like to leave a legacy to my children that they can be proud of, and hopefully beat the odds against me as relayed by that saying. Finally, I would like the murder of my good friend Herbert, avenged. If you find the killer, I would like you to bring him back to me personally.

I have suspected underhanded dealings at my bank for quite some time, but have not been able to get to the truth; my office, my phone, and my home have been bugged. There have been illegal transactions and then cover-ups, and now I suspect murder. I want you to find out who is responsible and why. I gather from your initial findings that you already know what is going on and how it was perpetrated. I asked Dewy to get an outside consultant because I suspected that his firm had dropped the ball, apparently I was right, as you seem to have struck a raw nerve. Some of those auditors at that firm couldn't find fraud if it bit them in the ass, how could they, some can't even tell the difference between their own ass and a hole in the ground. (That phrase had reminded Ed of some of the SEC examiners on the Madoff case). I'll get Dewy to get Flannigan off your back; I will pay you very well for this service. No strings attached, all I want is the truth about everything, and I mean everything."

As he was stepping into his white Mercedes stretch limo he added." You can talk to Marta Gutierrez, she is the VP of public relations; she knows were all the bodies are buried and where the closets are."

Ed: Closets?

Yeah! Where the skeletons are hidden, she knows this because she helped me put them there. Talk to her ... ask her to help you.

Ed thought, *I hope the burying part is not literal but figurative too.*

Castillo immediately accepted, as the goals of the chairman were the same, and the word lucrative was attached to the project and his name. Now he had the resources, backing and influential support he needed to search for the facts. _____7

CHAPTER 8
EVERY "BODY" HAS A COUSIN IN MIAMI

Manny was Ed's cousin and childhood friend, he was Ed's right hand man in their informal partnership, a wingman who always had Ed's back. Armandito was the hanging-on little brother of Manny and Ed's little cousin, he had been murdered a few years back, and his murder had never been solved.

Manny was bigger than Ed, a Leonidas on steroids, he looked like Jose Canseco, he could have passed for a third brother. He was what Cubans referred to as a "Cubanaso," the Cuban equivalent of "A perfect specimen of an American Male." Cubans on occasion were tall, but for the most part of average height. Manny's theory was that ever since arriving in the USA and eating all that meat with hormones and steroids, some had grown pretty big, while others had developed beautiful breasts, the females that is. Manny has the neck of a Miura Spanish fighting bull, the big black ones seen in the Spanish Corridas. He also has a big heart to match his big stature. He exhibits an unbridled exuberance for life and displays the uncurbed enthusiasm of an eight year old, even now as an adult. Although not necessarily a quick wit, he is quick to laugh.

As a young teenager Manuel had the use of his father's sailboat, a 40 foot Catalina, Ed and Manny would take it over to Biscayne Bay's Dinner Key or to the Sonesta hotel on Key Biscayne. They would anchor the boat so that the stern would face the east, and the bow the shore, then they would let out the spinnaker sail leaving the bottom untied from the mast. They then placed a little wooden seat at the bottom of the sail, the kind found in a swing at a park, and attached the ends of the sail rope through a pulley and then to the seat. The trick was to sit down on the little seat, while in the water and then even out the rope lengths on either side, by pulling on the rope and having it slide through the pulley and brass rings attached to the ends of the sail. This would make the spinnaker sail fill up with air, and in seconds, the Atlantic breezes would jettison the rider high into the air, by making the ropes uneven it would have the opposite effect, deflating the sail and sending the rider crashing into the water. They referred to this stunt and the sail as "The Magnet" because it attracted so many girls. Every time they set the sail, a bunch of girls would swim up and ask for a ride, males were discouraged and doomed to swim back … if they could make it.

They would say "Sorry guys this is an invitation only party, we do have some good news and some bad news for you ... the good news is that if you are not tired and a good swimmer you can swim back, you'll reach land in about three minutes. … The bad news is that if you can't, you'll reach land in a matter of seconds."

Early on Manny had become aware of another beneficial side effect of this pastime. It turns out that the rapid ascent towards the sky caused the bathing suit of the rider to fall down, exposing their butt. Manny, Ed and Armandito would await the precise moment with anticipation … and a camera, one would be the gunner's lookout giving directions, while the other took the photos. You had to, wait … wait for It. … "Wait until you saw the white of their ass …. wait for it … wait for it. … Ready now ... shoot!" They had a great photo collection of many a German tourist's rear ends who had their bikinis partially removed by this stunt. They thought, if only there where a market for this crap, like a version of "Girls Gone Wild" for rear-ends, they would be rich. What can I say; it didn't take much to entertain teenage boys living in Miami, and it beat tipping over sleeping cows in Oklahoma.

They never knew exactly what Manny's father did for a living. He had no visible means of support and hadn't filed a tax return in years. Once Manny asked his father how he could afford to give him that very expensive boat and his father simply replied ..." You want me to take the boat away."... Needles to say Manny never asked again.

They say a friend is one that will not rat on you when you commit murder but a really good friend helps you bury the body. Manny was a good friend and a good guy, he was a streetwise no nonsense kind of guy but not the brightest or sharpest crayon in the Crayola box. And it didn't help that he would swig down mojitos all day long as if they were milk shakes. His most common saying was "It's got to be 5 O'clock somewhere on this earth."

Ed tells some stories about "Manny-isms" that had occurred in the past.

Ed recalled how during a guy's-night-out camping trip he had brushed against some Poison Ivy and was beginning to itch like crazy. Manny then said, "I think you have to pee on it or something, who's going to do it?" No replies by the other guys in the group, "I guess it's up to me" said Manny as he begun unzipping ... Ed had to correct him right away ... "Oh no! No, no-one has to genius ... that's for Man O' War stings at the beach."

Manny had three main vices, women, drinking and gambling. Manny's nick name was Thumper, not because he looked like that famous cute little rabbit, and not because he could knock just about anybody on their ass, but because he would fuck like a drunken rabbit on Viagra with anybody.

Always the comedian never the groom.
When things got too serious with a current girlfriend, Manny always had a unique, clever, and always crazy way of braking up with each of his girlfriends. The basic formula required that the girl get so mad that she would do the breaking up. Here's what happened with the last one: Manny walks into the bedroom with a sheep on a leash and says, "Honey, this is the cow I make love to when you have a headache."

The girlfriend lying on the bed reading a book looks up and mockingly says, "If you weren't such an idiot, you'd know that's a sheep, not a cow." ... Manny then replied, "If you weren't such a presumptuous bitch, you'd realize I was talking to the sheep." Drum roll ... param ... pam, that's it, they had broken-up; he was free to continue with the current girl he was cheating with, without fear of being caught.

Manny could be jealous of other men's conquests. Once a roommate who had gotten a divorce stayed with him, Manny had encouraged him to date. Feeling bad for the guy he made the apartment available and prepared a lavish meal to aid with the seduction. The guy brought the girl over one night; she was a knockout. Next morning Manny woke him up at 4:00 AM after his date had left, Manny was visibly upset, then shaking him violently, he said "Me cago en ti maricon!" (Its something said by a Cuban buddy to his good pal, roughly translates to, "I love you man") … Here I think that the poor schmo needed companionship and found some fat ugly girl to keep him company. So I go and prepare this great lobster dinner and it turns out she is a gorgeous woman (she was, she looked just like Trumps second wife Marla Maples the one after Ivanka) you don't need any help from me you bastard."

Manny always tried to outdo Ed, it was a friendly competition, and Manny always wanted to show that he too had great skills of observation and memory. Ed recalled a recent trip to Hollywood, where Ed and Manny ran into the actor that plays the mentalist on TV, Ed started by complementing the actor on his great role, Manny had no idea who he was but nonetheless started by saying. "You were great in that show, Gilligan's Island, and the movie Attack of the Crab Monsters, but how did you stay so young." The guy did look a lot like the actor Manny had alluded to, the one who had played the professor, but he would be over eighty today, eighty six I'd say. Good old Manny … always a barrel of laughs.

Once, Ed asked him about his latest conquest, a one-night stand.

Ed: Well, did you make love to her?

Manny: Hell yes … (In typical Manny-talk) … Banged her like a screen door in a Miami hurricane.

Ed: Felipe the super says she was a bit fat, how fat was she?

Manny: …"Well, lets put it this way, this very night … right now somewhere in East Asia, there's a mahout frantically looking for his long lost elephant"… leave it to

Manny if it had a skirt he would chase it, I feel sorry for any Scotsman that bends over in front of him. For Manny, it was quantity not quality.

Manny and Three Card Monty or "Greed is Good" but knowledge is better.
The guy was a card shark and cheap hood who had learned his skills on the streets of NY City. He'd taken Manny's money, it had been relatively easy because Manny was a habitual gambler with little concept of this trick. Ed said to Manny that he would get his money back but this was to be the last time, after that he would be on his own. Ed was familiar with this type of easy simple con, from his audit experiences in NY City. As an auditor, you must be highly observant and a good listener, the word auditor comes from "audio" which means to listen while observation is just part of due-diligence.

The set up, the fleecing trick and the sting.
His observations of this con first took place on the sidewalks next to the Empire State building. A guy sets up a makeshift table with two boxes, a few people gather around, he then lays out three cards on the table, and asks those that wanted to bet to pick the queen from the three cards, several selected correctly and won the bet, soon the crowd grew and the bets got bigger. After awhile the pot got even bigger and every one began to lose, I mean everyone. After the last huge bet the dealer gathered the hundreds of dollars he had made, and then someone in the back of the crowd yelled out "cops," Ed didn't leave, as he was not betting, the cops never came, it was all a ruse to disperse the crowd and leave with their winnings. Ed managed to follow the guy, witnessing the splitting of the loot between the "plants" and the lookout.

The set up.
This was the set up and trick, the guy at the table works with a "plant" or "plants," as the accomplices are known. They appear to be making bets and winning big, yelling loudly to attract unsuspecting marks. The marks may be allowed to win the one-dollar bets, but once the bets grow and hit about twenty dollars, sometimes higher, they begin to lose in rapid succession. Once a good amount has been fleeced, another accomplice in the back of the crowd, the look out, yells "cops." This disperses the crowd and in the confusion, all escape with the money.

The Trick.
The queen is shown to all, at the bottom of the two-card deck, which is held in the right hand, for all to see. A third card is held in the left hand, the cards are dropped on the table one by one, the queen first, then the card in the left hand and finally the card that was on top of the queen. Shuffling of the cards is done in the fashion of the old nutshell con, played on unsuspecting kids at the carnival fairway. It is relative easy to follow the queen's positioning in all of the shuffling, this is done purposely … so at first there are many winners.

Here's where the power of observation comes in. When the bets are at their peak, the dealer, with a little legerdemain or slight of hand, actually drops the card above the queen first; to the unsuspecting victim it appears as though the queen has been dropped first on the table. At this point, the game is lost, as he will be following the wrong card throughout every shuffle and will surely lose. The dealer knowing that the mark thinks the first card hitting the table was the queen, shuffles, but not very fast, as he wants to make sure the mark follows this card and picks up this card after the final shuffle.

There are other variations but this is the basic trick. Any huckster can learn it in a few hours.

The sting.
Ed went on to make a sizable bet, knowing that the queen was the second card hitting the table. It was easy to follow. He won the money back, and with Manny yelling cops from the back of the crowd; Ed was able to walk away with the winnings without being pressured to remain.

The Caveman Chronicles, "Good Feces make good neighbors."
If Ed was a paternalistic, chivalrous, chauvinist, then Manny was a card and club carrying prehistoric cave man, a Neanderthal who was not quite yet a troglodyte, more of a troglodyte in the making, a cave dweller with a man cave. He believed that if something had tires or tits it was destined to give you trouble.

Manny began his diatribe on male/female relationships by applying his own perverse philosophy. He theorized, based on his extensive and expert experience obtained as an avid and loyal viewer of televised nature shows, that animals that use piss and feces to set lines of demarcation and mark their territorial boundaries, did so, for more than just a means of establishing territorial dominance. They did it to avoid confrontation, prevent or minimize aggression and ultimately avoid violence between males. Something that Neo-feminists do not seem to understand, they are oblivious of, or ignorant about this basic law of nature. Some violate it knowingly, willfully and willingly. They cross the invisible piss line of the male and then when the male reacts, they cry out abuse, they fall back on this female defense and may retaliate with extreme violence. Violence that has become an acceptable and justified means of defense against the abuser, ever since "The Burning Bed scenario" was popularized by the 1984 movie of the same name (Don't misunderstand, he abhorred and condemned abusers and their violence against the innocent and defenseless, but he also could not condone burning them alive). This is done in their ongoing pursuit of equality and independence. They perceive male aggressive tactics as being a necessary means of achieving their goals. They believe that in the process, they will become "more equal" to men. During this process; however, they also acquire the less desirable traits of men, becoming manlier in their demeanor, making them less attractive as women and as human beings.

Men have unspoken rules that govern this process. Manny quoted Dirty Harry and said, "A man must know his limitations." Whenever men gather for any social activity, whether it is to play sports, watch sports, play video or board games or simply hang out at a bar , they are cognizant of these invisible rules, rules that set boundaries or piss lines, lines that every man knows he must not cross, as this they well know will inevitably lead to violence. They know at what point they must stop, unless they intentionally wish to participate in a physical altercation, women just don't know or choose to ignore these invisible lines. There is a point where assertiveness becomes aggressiveness. As example, Manny referred to the news story where "Snooki" the diminutive and vocal female member of the MTV reality show "The Jersey Shore" was assaulted. This incident recorded in the show became the center stage story in all major networks. An inebriated male gym teacher, while in a bar at a Jersey seaside community, had punched the also inebriated Snooki in the face. What the news did not elaborate on was the fact that witnesses and the video of the show clearly indicated that Snooki had become aggressive, screaming and putting her face within inches of the drunken teacher's face. While there is never an excuse for violence, this man was obviously provoked into violence. Had this been a male, self-defense could have been used as an effective argument. If it had been a man, it probably would not have happened at all, as he would have known when to back off. Manny said perhaps Dirty Harry should have said" A woman has to know her limitations." Ed could find some validity in this straw man's argument, but reserved the right to hold back his conclusion until a feminist had the opportunity of presenting an effective side to this argument.

_____**8**

CHAPTER 9
MURDER SO VILE
Friends, Romans, Murdered-men, lend me your ears

Manny's little brother, Armandito, had died several years ago under mysterious circumstances, he had been a victim of the so-called Alphabet Assassin. He had been a good student, and a hard working young man, with a bright future. Only a few years before his death he'd secured a position as a bank loan officer, with one of the cities major banks. He was doing well and had been tapped to become the Assistant Vice President of the Mortgage loan department at the bank. The bank that Ed now recalled had been a prime target for acquisition by the Chandler Group. The Florida International Bank, it was a major player in mortgage lending, and Armandito's employer. The Chandler bank had acquired this bank only a few weeks after Armandito's death.

Armandito had been acting rather strangely just weeks before his death; he appeared to be nervous and uneasy, and although he had not yet confided to Manny the source of his stress, he had mentioned that he would discuss everything with him after he had checked out some facts. The night before his death, he had called Ed; they were to meet the next day, as he wanted to discuss some accounting control issues relative to the bank. He never made the appointment.

After years, the trail of the murderer had gone cold, originally it had been established that the murderer was a serial killer. After Manny's research, the profile was amended to that of a highly paid contract killer, a sociopath with sadistic serial murderer tendencies and habits nonetheless. This was determined after one of the clients had been identified, he had revealed under questioning that he hired this killer to murder his partner and had paid the assassin thousands of dollars for this service. Based on this new theory, the police developed further leads. It was puzzling, however, to both the police and Manny, as to who would want to hire such a highly paid assassin to kill Armando, and why was he targeted. They were also puzzled as to why the killer had burned a letter of the alphabet into the skin of his brother ... while he was still alive.

Manny was an ex cop from North Miami; he had been a very good cop but not necessarily a great detective. It was, however, through his connections, his experience and bulldog tenacity that the killer's profile was more accurately compiled. Prior to Manny's work, the descriptions by the police were like that of three blind men describing an elephant, the one at the trunk saying he was like a large snake, the man in the middle saying it is more like a large truck while the one at the tail end saying it is like a large worm.

Manny's inquiries with the Mexican FBI the AFI's General David Cabeza de Vaca. (General Cow's Head ...Man you cannot make that name up) and the Federal Police in Brazil, (their version of the FBI), Interpol in Europe, and other agencies in three other continents had made it possible to compare the details of the crimes and form a composite view. Soon a pattern of obvious similarities and exact methods surfaced. It was then that the media gave the pseudonym Alphabet Assassin to the killer. As his methods, appeared to be somewhat suggestive of the Alphabet Murders that had occurred back in the 1970's, in the Rochester NY area. Some say the media gave the killer this moniker, because of the similarities between this case and the murders in the novel The ABC murders by Agatha Christy.

Here is where the similarity to these other past cases ends. In this case, the initials of their name did not play a role in the selection of the victims, nor did the towns they lived in; they were selected because someone with lots of money wanted them dead. The primary reason for the moniker given, was that the victims found were all physically branded with a letter. Presumably corresponding to the order or sequence in which they were killed.

This killer also had additional serial killer habits or compulsions; in this case, he kept souvenirs... the right ear of the victims. He always branded them with a letter, usually by the neck, using a small-customized branding iron, the letter size small enough to fit on the surface of an average sized monogrammed cufflink. He started with the letter A and has continued consecutively for five years; he is now up to T. At the rate he was going, this year will be a milestone year, and the police are watching to see how he continues, hoping it will provide clues towards his capture.

The press had reported twenty known branded victims, because the letter T was the 20th letter of the Alphabet. As mentioned, it was determined that he was a contract killer because in some cases, a motive for profit was uncovered and the hiring client arrested. The clients were all very wealthy men and institutions. The identity of the killer, however, was never known, and his method of being hired did not provide many clues. The South American police knew him as "El Angel de la Muerte," or angel of death, because his code-name when hired was Gabriel, the avenging angel.

Gabriel's clients that had been arrested were telling all. They said that Gabriel would meet them at the North Miami Memorial cemetery, hiding behind a mausoleum wall made of marble; no one was buried near by because locals believed that the veins on the Carrara marble resembled the face of the devil, and it did. This area provided a considerable degree of privacy. Although the trail was cold, Manny never was too far from the scent of this killer. He wanted to plan a trap. He put an ad in the paper to meet at the cemetery, but no one bit. The many newspaper articles that had revealed details about the crimes had spooked the killer. _____9

CHAPTER 10
OTHELLO THE BLACK QUINCY

One would think that any institution located at One Bob Hope Road in Miami Florida would be a happy and fun place, where jokes and high-jinx would be the order of the day; instead, here is where one will find the quietest and deadest place in the county. At this address, you will find the Miami-Dade County Medical Examiner's Department and the office of the Miami Dade County chief examiner, Dr. Pierre Othello De Baptist.

Dr. De Baptist was of Haitian descent, although his immediate family had immigrated to America several generations ago, he continued to maintain close ties with his extended family back in Haiti. A medical doctor and honor graduate of the Harvard Medical School, he specialized in anatomical pathology and sub-specialized in forensic pathology. He was a renowned toxicologist and expert in the study of poisons, toxins, and venoms. He often performed or assisted in autopsies, his opinion on cause and manner of death at a post mortem examination was highly valued throughout all the Florida counties. Tall and distinguished he had the look and manner of a younger Morgan Freeman.

He had attended Belen high school in Miami along with Ed and Manny. They were all close friends and often collaborated on difficult cases. Pierre was indebted to Ed, as he had pulled the good doctor's ass out of the fire many times before. Not that Ed would demand money or anything in return. In the Miami underground social and cultural circles, it was a well-known fact that a favor for a favor was expected in the future. It had always been the currency "du jour" and of choice. The doctor was renowned in medical circles as a world expert in the field of toxicology. Coroners, and medical examiners in other counties and countries often called him in to consult on difficult cases. He had just returned from examining the body of a recent drowning victim suspected of having been drugged.

They say it was an accidental drowning.
Being a medical examiner from Florida had exposed Dr. De Baptist to many an accidental drowning. He also had personal experience with drownings that had been portrayed as accidents. As a young child, he was told that his grandfather had died in a drowning accident, in a small town in Georgia. Then as a young man, he was told the true story.
After work, his grandfather was always very hungry, so each night he would take a short cut by swimming to his home across the pond; it was shorter than having to walk around it, and contrary to myth and racially stereotyped urban legend, he was an exceptionally strong swimmer. This day, his grandfather had an altercation with several of the white workers. It was a well-known fact that the supervisor was a bigot who hated his grandfather and had tried to fire him many times before, but had failed, because the owner liked, respected, and was in debt to his grandfather for having saved his only son from drowning. They knew his routine well. That night they had lined the section of the pond, where his grandfather used to dive in, with barbed wire, they set the wire just below the surface of the water where it would not be seen. When he dove in, he was snagged on the submerged wire. His overalls catching on the barbs, he was quickly snarled in the lines of wire; the effect was like being entangled in seaweed. As he struggled and gasped for

air, he tangled himself more and more and then cut himself badly, attracting the alligators. He struggled and fought until exhaustion got the better of him, and then he slowly sank below the surface. Official cause of death was accidental drowning while swimming, aggravated by alligator attacks. No mention of the barbed wire, He had drowned all right! But the cause was homicide. This incident would be the impetus to Pierre selecting a career as a medical examiner and coroner.

Every year hundreds of tourists and Florida residents die from drowning. Many are unattended toddlers swimming only feet away from shore, of those, many drown at the beach or in canals, but most drown in the family pools (300 annually under the age of 5) of which there are thousands in South Florida. Florida loses more children under age five to drowning than any other state. Annually enough children to fill four preschool classrooms do not live to see their 5th birthday. Florida overwhelmingly has the highest unintentional drowning rate in the nation for the 0 to 4 year old age group with a rate of 7.39 per 100,000 population (Arizona was second for this age group with a rate of 5.41). This does not even account for near-drownings that may leave children with severe brain damage.

Manny had seen his share of children drowning during his career as a police officer and had formulated very strong opinions on the subject. Every time a child drowned, he would go into his diatribe on his "Monkey-Mother" theory of child rearing. He believed that all the pool fences and pool alarms in the world were no substitute for diligent supervision and oversight. As support for his theory, he would use the example of a monkey's mother, borrowed from his extensive experience in watching TV nature programs on PBS. The mother monkey he would explain, has her baby tightly strapped to her back or belly, never ever leaving him out of sight or out of reach, she knows the dangers that lurk in the world and the risk of leaving her offspring unattended. How many accidents scenes he had investigated where the grieving inconsolable parents, grandparent or other relative or baby sitter would say, "I only left him for an instant to answer the door, answer the phone, to put the laundry in the dryer, turn off the stove or look for something. It was only a moment, how could this have happened." Well it happens. We should all be more like those monkey mothers he would say. Ed being a logical thinker could appreciate the theory. He thought that, even as crazy as Manny is, and as macho and chauvinistic his thinking was, perhaps he had a point there. The guy had a soft spot for kids, dogs, and he guessed monkeys too.

Pierre was very sensitive to criticism, especially if he felt it was racially motivated. He had traced his roots back to Alexander Dumas's father. He said that many don't know that he was a brave general who had fought along side Napoleon, but after the French revolution in 1802 racist laws were passed that had all men of color removed from their army positions.

Pierre was also a bit sensitive, due to all the second-guessing he had been subjected to over the years from white doctors and patients, based solely on his race. Although he had it relatively easy compared to his uncle who had also been a doctor. His uncle had experienced many humiliating moments throughout his career. Pierre told a story of one such incident.

Only a country doctor.
Pierre's uncle had retired after many years of practicing
medicine up north, he then moved to a small southern
town where the pace was a bit slower, although he
continued to practice as a country doctor and
moonlighted as a part-time coroner.

A difficult capital case developed, in which a rich,
prominent, and powerful white man had been charged
with murder; the doctor as acting coroner had performed
the examination of the victim and the related crime
scene. Because of his findings and presentation of the
forensic evidence, it was certain that the man would be
found guilty. The high-powered expensive lawyer
(nonetheless a shyster in moral character) hired by the
defendant was a southern red neck with the same
prejudices and resentments held by his client. The lawyer
thought that it was going to be easy to discredit this "Old,
inexperienced, dumb backwater nigger doctor." The
lawyer began by framing questions that would show the
old doctor's inexperience with criminal cases and in
particularly murder cases.

"Tell me doctor, could you tell the court if you have
performed … say ten autopsies in your career?"

The doctor answered, "Yes I think I have."

"That's good; well can you tell the court if you have
performed say one hundred autopsies in your lifetime."

The doctor hesitated a bit, but still answered yes. The
hesitation in the doctor's voice appeared to the shyster
lawyer as a lack of confidence on the part of the doctor.
The lawyer had been carefully laying and setting his trap
all along, waiting only for an opportune time to spring it

shut, he knew that the time had arrived. He would close and easily win the case with a question he knew the doctor could never, in a lifetime, answer with a yes. He would humiliate and discredit the doctor with his next question; the lawyer now smelled blood in the water and readied himself to go for the jugular and the kill. He went ahead and with a contemptuous self-assured tone in his voice (and a smirk on his face that begged to be wiped off with a swift right cross) asked:

"Well then my good doctor, can you swear that you have performed twenty thousand or even ten thousand autopsies and examinations in your entire career?"

The doctor hesitated again, the lawyer now began salivating, as he was sure he had the doctor cornered, snared and hogtied.

The old country doctor calmly and deliberately, yet still hesitating then said ... "Why ... I believe so ... yes ... I think so ... you see ... as the chief examiner for the city of New York for over forty years and at an average of five hundred murders per year not counting suicides, and other deaths that required investigation and autopsies. I can safely say that I have performed over twenty thousand examinations of murder victims." The lawyer's strategy had backfired; he had definitely lost the case.

_____**10**

CHAPTER 11
FUGU –MERCURY IS THE LEAST OF YOUR PROBLEMS

Ed eventually freed up some time and arranged to meet with his friend Dr. Pierre. Although there were some preliminary indications that Mr. Afortunado may have died of respiratory arrest, this hypothesis was not immediately confirmed, as there were after all many more obvious signs for the cause of death. Like the repeated shark bites and the other gaping wounds to the head, this had to be further explored. A note by the coroner of Palm Beach County stated that according to the police report, the body, carried by the Gulf Stream, was found north of the accident. The body had some cuts that appeared to have been made by a tool or blade. The county coroner had indicated that the cause of death was first assumed to be due to exsanguination caused by the numerous shark bites, then after noting the other wounds by the blade, and subsequently casting the wound and examining the angles, length, width, and depth, it appeared that a blade … a propeller blade, caused these wounds. Once an accidental cause involving others, or possible foul play was suspected, additional, and extensive tests of the body were performed to determine cause of death. These tests indicated that the man had not died from the shark bites nor had he died from the blade cuts.

The shark bites were determined to have been inflicted postmortem; this was easily discerned from the pooling of blood and in the discoloration of the wound area that had occurred during lividity. Although the cuts by the blade were very serious, and definitely occurring while the victim was still alive, they ultimately proved to be none lethal, there were, in fact, no mortal wounds of any kind on the body.

The fact that little or no water was found in the lungs was puzzling to the coroner at first, especially given where the body was found and under the circumstances in which it was found.

The autopsy later revealed that the body showed signs of respiratory arrest. Such noticeable signs as the bluing around the face and neck and fluids in the lungs were present, however, no saltwater was found in the lungs; the lungs of a man found in an ocean of salt water.

Dr. De Baptist was called in for his expertise. In his preliminary report, the doctor had been factual and included only objective observations of facts that he could substantiate. However, to Ed in private he revealed that he suspected toxins. Later, tests by him showed that toxins were indeed found in the body, they did not appear to have been injected but had in fact been taken orally. Additional tests of body fluids designed to identify possible drugs and other toxins performed by Dr. De Baptist and an independent lab, conclusively established the cause of death … Mr. Afortunado had died of poisoning; manner of death was changed from accidental to homicide. The tests had revealed the presence of significant amounts of a toxin known as tetrodotoxin a powerful neurotoxin. This compound in even small amounts is known as a deadly poison. In highly diluted amounts, it was being used as a painkiller for victims of neuralgia, arthritis, and rheumatism. The tests identified other drugs and compounds but could not determine their effects.

Dr. De Baptist also told Ed that the medical history of Mr. Afortunado did not indicate that he suffered from any of the ailments the drug was designed to treat, nor had it been prescribed by any of his doctors. The toxin compound along with the mixture of the other chemicals and plant extracts created a distinct potion … a potion the good doctor had seen only once before in his life, in Haiti. And, although he suspected that the potion he observed being administered in Haiti included a mixture of that toxin he could not identify the other components, he could only explain what he had observed. He went on to explain in great detail the source and nature of tetrodotoxin.

Fugu, is not just for breakfast anymore.
This toxin is commonly found in the Caribbean puffer or blowfish, known in Japan as fugu, and in some octopus. They use it as a form of defense against predators. The puffer has it in its skin and sharp quills, but primarily in its liver and ovaries. The fish carrying this deadly toxin ironically is also widely thought after as a culinary delicacy in Japan, where it is known as fugu or torafugu i.e. tiger fish. It has long been praised in Japan as the most delicious of all fish. It has also been feared, as improper preparation may cause fatal poisoning. Even during the Meiji period, the period (1868-1912) and the period of shoguns and samurai, the sale of fugu was prohibited in some districts. The city Shimonoseki in Japan is one of the most popular cities that have restaurants specializing in this delicacy; this city is where the largest catch of these fish is taken in Japan each year. The poisonous parts of the fish, such as the ovary and the liver, have been identified, and health authorities have exercised strict supervision over its preparation.

A pinch of the tetrodotoxin white powder or puffer poison, about the amount found in one prime-sized tiger fugu is enough to kill more than 30 persons. The estimated lethal dose for an adult, a mere one to two milligrams, could be put on a pinhead. Puffer toxin blocks sodium channels in nerve tissues, ultimately paralyzing muscles much like curare. Since a fugu's poison can lead to instantaneous deaths of diners, only licensed cooks are allowed to prepare fugu. You must have special skills and knowledge about fugu to be licensed. Poisonous parts of fugu differ, depending on the kind of fugu. Although the strict regulations over its preparation have significantly decreased the number of deaths, eating fugu continues to be the gastronomic equivalent of Russian roulette. Because of this, fugu is the only delicacy that cannot be served to the emperor.

Respiratory arrest is the cause of death. There is no proven antidote, perhaps because the toxin has a molecular structure, unlike anything previously known to organic chemistry. Pierre said that because of its potency, it is 1250 times deadlier than cyanide, "It's a terrible death. Although you can think clearly, you cannot speak or move and soon cannot breathe," --this may be the cause of death for Mr. Afortunado, and explains why no saltwater was found in the lungs.

Professor Hashimoto of the University of Tokyo and his colleague Noguchi have confirmed the existence of the neurotoxin but could not explain the presence of the other drugs or compounds …"But I can, I think I know now where the other compounds came from, I had seen this mixture before, as I mentioned in Haiti. It is not too common, only the high priests know how to mix and create this potion; it is a concoction made up of Rhododendrons, Indian peas, fugu, herbs and other plants such as the deadly nightshade. The toxin is relatively inexpensive in Haiti and in South American countries where they say, "All you need is ten centavos to poison a cat."

Ed: Why didn't the killer use strychnine as a poison, or arsenic, cyanide, or Ricin for that matter?

Pierre: They are all easily detected, if you want to try to hide a murder through a suicide or accident, they are not the best, Strychnine is one of the bitterest substance in the world easily detectable by a potential victim in their food. Arsenic poisoning symptoms and its telltale signs are common, so the cause by arsenic can be determined in less than 24 hours. Cyanide same as arsenic; it also has the distinct taste and odor of bitter almonds. Ricin is also a poison that could have been used, it is a poison found naturally in castor beans. One can make it by mashing the beans, if castor beans are chewed and swallowed; the released Ricin can cause injury. Ricin can also be made from the waste material left over from processing castor beans. It is very potent, only a dosage the size of a grain of sand can cause death, but again, it would not be the poison of choice if you want to portray the murder as an accident or suicide, it can be messy. If someone swallows a significant amount of Ricin, the symptoms would be vomiting and diarrhea that may become bloody. Inhaling it would probably also cause the symptoms, but also fluid in the lungs. I think an assassin would not want to have a victim in the back seat that is vomiting and has bloody diarrhea, as he is transporting him to stage an accident scene. Poisons can be found in all types of edible plants as well as in many potted plants and flowers; I think that if you are a modern poisoner your best bet is to be trendy and go "green and natural."

Ed: As I've said before, you doctor, have been hanging around a little too much with Manny.

Pierre: Eating fugu is a source for many Japanese traditional senryu verses, this is a form of verse or poem somewhat like a haiku, but more morbid, for example, here are some in reference to the fugu:

> *Those who do not eat fugu are fools*
> *While those who do are also fools.*

> *Last night I ate fugu with my friend*
> *Today I carry his coffin at his funeral*

That's really clever ... Ed said sarcastically.

The doc then said, I didn't say they were good, just morbid.

This explained why there was no salt water in his lungs, as Mr. Afortunado's lung muscles had been paralyzed before he entered the ocean, but it didn't explain how and who had provided the fugu poison.

Anti-dote--Not Uncle Dote's wife.
There was no known scientific medically formulated antidote for Fugu poisoning, but the voodoo priests back in Haiti that had developed the potion from native herbs and tree leaves had. Pierre had developed an equivalent, it was an anti sodium blocker; he had already tried it on some rats and it worked. He had gone beyond that and had developed a blocker that if taken in advance would coat the victim's stomach and protect them from absorbing the poison.

Ed: Great, after all this will sell it to restaurants and customers in Japan and the world that insist on eating Fugu.

Pierre told Ed, just to remember that the antidote is in the bottle with the black top, while the blocker is in the one with the white top and the poison is in a jar with a red top.

For a moment there, Ed felt as if he was in an old Danny Kay movie ... you know ..."The pellet with the poison is in the flagon with the dragon; the vessel with the pestle has the brew that is true." monologue.

Ed: Well Doc that was fascinating, you are a wealth of information and a great historian.

Pierre: Inspector Tradeles called, he wants me to come to a crime scene, and he wants you to come along.

Earlier Ed arranged a meeting with Inspector Tradeles from the FBI, and detective Matson from the state police out of Tallahassee. Tradeles had some financial investigation experience and grasped the situation immediately, and with Pierre's forensic information, they where able to convince them that something was going on beyond the financial fraud. Matson would be working on Florida murders by the Alphabet Assassin, while Tradeles worked on national ones and on the financial fraud.

Detective Matson was an affable man, but seemed to show a noticeable dislike for Latin Americans. This had not always been the case. As a young man, he had married a Mexican girl, after the wedding they had moved to Mexico to live in a large rancho, after being there only a few weeks his bride was abducted. Although Matson had paid the ransom, they still killed her; it seems that when he saw Latin Americans and heard Spanish-speaking people it reminded him of his loss.

The Inspector general and the case of the Ernest Hemingway impersonator.
Inspector Tradeles was a competent enough man, but with little imagination, skeptical at first of an accountant meddling in criminal affairs, he would soon be won over, and in fact, would welcome Ed's input, as Ed would always allow him to take the credit, and Tradeles did so love the exposure in the media. Ed had met him through Manny. His first encounter with the inspector had lead to Ed assisting the Inspector in an unusual case that had occurred in Key West. A man with a unique story had approached the inspector. The man, Antony Hare was the manager of a small souvenir shop in Key West. His assistant manager had pointed to an ad in The Key West Citizen, advertising for Ernest Hemingway look-alikes. The Society of Ernest Hemingway impersonators League was searching for one man to star in several commercials promoting the association. Hare looked like the famous author, and had entered several of the look-alike contests before; this one paid very well for six days, Monday through Saturday less than a week's work. Mr. Hare was an unusually thrifty man that never took vacations, his assistant convinced him to take a vacation and apply for the position, and if he got it, he would be earning three times his weekly salary in one week. When he arrived at the offices of the association there was a long line, but he was quickly whisked to the front of the line, as the man in the office thought he was the best look alike of all (he was not).

He was hired on the spot. His duties were to read from a Hemingway novel into an unmanned camera, a task that he found strange, but one he did not question. All went well until Friday morning. On that day as he approached the offices where he had been talking into the camera, he noticed the signs were down, inside there was no camera and the office desks were empty, he made inquires from the landlord who then informed him that these were offices rented by the day and the tenant had moved out.

Mr. Hare went to the FBI, as he feared something was wrong; Tradeles suggested that he call the local police, but said that he would need to wait twenty-four hours before filing a complaint about missing persons, he then suggested Manny, who was a private eye, as an alternative. Manny then called Ed, as he could not make heads or tails about the incident. Ed and Manny then traveled to Key West and met the man, he said, "call me Red," then realizing Ed and Manny's reaction as his hair and beard were salt and pepper gray, said "Oh! I used to have bright red hair a long time ago but everybody in Key West still calls me Red." They took a quick tour of the shop and attached buildings. Ed noticed that the building on the left was the Key West Community Bank, and the shop had a small locked stockroom that faced that side. He told Red and Manny to walk out of the shop, talk loudly, and mention they were leaving, and then told them to slam the door. Ed stayed behind quietly and put his ear to the door of the storeroom, then walked out and then said, I got it.

Manny and Mr. Hare said, Huh!

Ed said that Mr. Hare should call the police and have them go in the bank next door that very night and wait for the bank robbers to break through the wall, and since it was a federal crime, he should call Tradeles of the FBI.

He did, and the two men who broke in that night were promptly arrested. The two who were arrested turned out to be the man at the Societies office, the man who had enlisted the look-alikes, and the second was Mr. Hare's assistant manager at the shop. It had all been a ruse to get Mr. Hare out of the shop so both could dig faster and without being questioned or heard by the shop manager. They were nearly done, and Ed thought that it would be easier to arrest them and convict them if they were surprised as they entered the bank.

_____11

CHAPTER 12
THE FIRM'S PARTNERS
"DOWE, CHEATEM AND HOW"
The good, the bad, and the incompetent

At Dewey, Chaney, and Howell, he never quite seemed to fit. He was too direct, his humor for instance was too sharp, too sarcastic, even too dark and sardonic at times, and most definitely too ethnic. It was good he thought that he worked as an independent consultant and not as a hired employee. This crowd was made up of stern bureaucrats devoid of any humor, they spent so much time with their sight on the trees they never saw the forest. They had to be politically correct at all-times, this in turn, allowed little wiggle room for any kind of real humor or creativity. The main purpose of bureaucrats, any kind, is to interfere with the creative process, and yes, effective audits require creativity of which this crowd had none.

"Esta vida es un relajo, en forma de gallinero, los que suben arriba se cagan el los de a bajo" (This life is a joke, a farce in the form of a chicken coop, where those who climb to the top defecate on those below).
This firm's world was analogous to a chicken coup. On the highest perch of the hierarchy where the partners, at this level they were the best fed, hence the ones who were the fullest of shit. Followed by the lower ranking chickens on the perches below, who in turn progressively received on top of their heads an ever larger and larger portion of the recycled droppings, with those at the lowest rung receiving the largest; outside consultants were a step below this. These were directors, managers and

supervisors, senior members and the kiss- ass-staff. …
you had to be … if only to survive. These were Yuppies,
or as some were known in Miami in later years, Yucas
(Young upper mobile Cuban Americans) … they were
upper crust wannabes, a pretensions lot that called
themselves and their children Buffy, Muffin, Muffy and
Pookee, (cutesy nicknames more suited for puppies).
They were waiting in line for their turn to sit by the pool,
next to the tennis courts, sipping Perrier, and admiring
their BMW's, Porches, Mercedes, and Jaguars. They
hoped to gain a seat at the country club table and a place
at the communal troth, as full-fledged members of this
exclusive private club.

Manny seemed to have a joke for every occasion; he
would ask Ed," What's the difference between a
porcupine and a BMW?"

Ed: What?

Manny: A porcupine has all the pricks on the outside.

Ed knew what to expect from and what to deliver to the
paying partners, and although most of the staff were very
nice and competent, there was a small group of
treacherous Machiavellian little shits that primarily
concerned him. He never knew what kind of
backstabbing scheme these prep school junior-pricks
could conger-up. He had to be careful disclosing his
thoughts, as these little shits were not below stealing
them and then presenting them as their own. These were
also the same guys and gals dressed in identical
charcoal grey suits sitting around the conference table
(imagine the scene in Blazing Saddles) that would shoot
down your ideas and then immediately begin to cheer
when the boss at the head of the table rephrased or

regurgitated them back as if they were his own. Not an original thought in their heads, if they had one it was surely destined to die of loneliness. These were cookie-cutter men in cookie-cutter suits, with cookie-cutter brains. Their lack of independent thought, together with their inbred group instinct of lemmings, made them the ultimate tool for performing mindless audits, the types of audits that had allowed the economy to fall over the precipice.

The firm was also made up of the biggest cheaters in the world, second only to lawyers and bankers that is. Still way ahead of agents and used-car salesmen, who in comparison were amateur grifters to these guys. Their main function and job title was that of executive meddlers, but even with all the losses they had allowed to occur and the unearned exorbitant fees charged, they still seemed to be able to fly just below the media and the public's radar, never noticed, and never held accountable. That is, until this mortgage debacle shit hits the proverbial fan.

They would look the other way, fudge, distort, bend and stretch the facts and manipulate them to fit their clients' wishes, while padding their expense accounts and charging exorbitant fees for their inflated reports on work not actually done. Ed believed they were actually charging by the word, and when you are a bull-shit-artist charging big bucks, you can be assured that words will flow like diarrhea from a man who has just eaten a half-dozen dangerously undercooked bean and chicken burritos with all the super spiced condiments on top. They would charge staff out at anywhere between $150 and $300 an hour and pay them $30 to $40 for the actual hours, while the number of billable hours charged the client were always padded.

Although lip service was given to uncovering significant financial audit findings, in truth what was held most highly was discretion and mediocrity. A mediocrity that would not raise pertinent questions, one that would not make any waves, one that in turn would not disturb the flow of fees into the partnership's coffers. The dichotomy and contradictory responsibilities of uncovering significant financial reporting errors in the financials, and keeping the clients happy always seemed to give way and deference to maintaining the collegial relations that would ensure the retaining of the clients' benevolence and their lucrative contracts. Enthusiasm and competency in performing ones duties did not figure into the master plan nor into the partners' ultimate objective, they took a back seat to appeasement; they were dampened and curved. These attributes in a staff member were looked upon with suspicion ... very close to disdain.

He would have to suffer the barbs of disparaging words from many of the firm's members. (Bullshit, he would get pissed-off and threaten them quietly and out the sight of witnesses) as they were always eager to minimize and discredit his work, because the name-of-the-game was appease and kiss-ass and not necessarily determine the truth.

Conversations were safe, predictable, trite, and boring; they did not go past saying "How about those Dolphins" or "Go Canes or Gators or Seminoles." Most of them were geeks who had never even thrown a football in their lives or had accomplished anything of any significance in life; instead, they were trying to live vicariously through the players and the team's success. They were much like effeminate roman aristocrats at a gladiators fight. They all drove luxury vehicles, even though some lived in

appalling conditions; appearances were of paramount
importance. This mindset affected every aspect of their
lives influencing their professional decisions and even the
way they lived their personal lives. Ed and Manny would
laugh, because, although some had broken car air
conditioners, they refused to let on, and would actually
drive with all the windows up in the Miami heat, at least
while they were still within eyesight of the office. After all
the lying they did to themselves, the lines between reality
and fantasy had blurred and they became the phonies
that they pretended to be. _____**12**

CHAPTER 13
THE PARTNER– BP, THE BRITISH PRICK

Lanky and tall, with angular creepy facial features, he had a long bulbous nose, more of a proboscis than a nose. He had a skinny long neck with defined sinewy neck tendons and a protruding boxy Adam's apple that seem to bob in his neck. He looked like an aging Ichabod Crane, the schoolteacher in the Legend of Sleepy Hollow. He had a weak chin to complement his similarly weak character. His skin was sallow, pale, clammy, and bumpy as a prickly pear. His fingers were long, bony, and wiry. His gangling frame and gawky manner caused him to ambulate with the ungainly awkward gate of an aging giraffe. His yellow, crooked, chipped, and cavity riddled teeth were what one would expect from the British socialized dentistry system.

His chain smoking had aged him beyond his actual years, leaving deep-seated wrinkles in his face, as though he had been overly exposed to the Florida sun. His arched eyebrows, made him look like a demon, had he had a goatee and horns he could win the Halloween prize for best devil at any party. He wore round wired rim glasses over his beady little eyes. His bespectacled face gave the appearance of a mad-scientist. He had huge ears, the kind seen on old farmers; he looked more like an old wino or bum than a senior partner. He reeked of stale cigarettes and alcohol. The whisky bottle, which he kept in a file drawer, was no secret. He once made a big stink at the airport because they would not allow him to bring his half-open bottle onboard. He grew up in a working neighborhood of Liverpool. All his life he tried to distance himself from whence he came. He worked hard at developing a patrician bearing to no avail, and although he wore the most expensive designer suits he could buy, they did little to enhance his appearance and nothing to improve his manners, proving once again that "You just can't make a silk purse out of a sow's ear."

He was one of those limey snobs who believed, while looking down his nose, that any other life style was, as he put it "going native" and beneath him. He was vain, insecure, ambitious, and overly anxious for recognition. The only reason he was hired and made partner was that he was married to one of the partner's daughters. She was the daughter of Rhodri Howell the third. Howell had traced his ancestry to Rhodri the great king of Wales. He in turn, was one of those misguided American anglophiles that is easily impressed by any British accent, the type that tends to confuse, and still believes that if you speak with a British accent, any one of them, you're more intelligent and sophisticated than the rest. Ed always thought that if you got a dull documentary, slapped a famous British voice to it … Voila! You'd have a hit.

He had an effeminate manner about him; his mannerisms were those of an aging bitchy queen, even his name was somewhat like the British version of a "Boy named Sue." Ed always seemed to forget his name, a mental block of some kind. He remembered it by thinking it was one of those slightly ambiguous androgynous English names or by using a mnemonic devise and associating it with something else … was it Lauren, Leslie, Marion, Nigel … sounded like vanilla, that's it; it would always come to him … Neville. He had a cold and sneaky personality, if anyone could be qualified as reptilian in looks and nature, Neville was it. He thought of himself as being clever, in reality he was more cunning and furtive than clever, his favorite ploy was that of omission—"the sin of the coward." He favored omitting critical facts to confuse and achieve his goals. He tried to give the perception of confidence and self-assurance; he accomplished this, mainly, by not speaking and acting as if he understood everything and knew everything. Ed however could notice that he was uneasy, guarding, or hiding something from his past, a deep dark secret no doubt. His outward persona and composure would scream out "I'm rich, powerful and in control" and a "Don't you even think of crossing me" attitude. However, to Ed, Neville's manner and demeanor would only remind him of the man in that poem, Richard Cory, a fake, and a fraud, who outwardly exuded confidence and success while inwardly he was nothing but a fearful coward, an imposter, who eventually blew his brains out.

In British culture the backhanded compliment is considered to be a genteel or polite way of expressing disdain; Neville had elevated it to an art form. His insecurity led to a defensive attitude that he would always turn into passive aggression. He was the type of insecure man that when introduced to a subordinate would immediately make a subtle, indiscernible, almost covert, derogatory comment, one purposely designed to belittle, condescend and cut the individuals confidence; it was always made sufficiently ambiguous and evasive enough so as not to make it obvious to, or defendable by the recipient. Although intended to be furtive and imperceptible, thereby fooling the listener, Neville really didn't care if it did or not, as long as the slight and the insult was delivered. This was his "shot across the bow," delineating the piss line of his authority. Neville had the means; inherent in his very being, you would also find in him the acrimony and the inclination to ruin careers--as he often did. He was an abuser who reveled in his hubris, "the pride that blinds," experiencing great pleasure and gratification from the shaming and humiliating of his victims. He would have made a perfect literary critic, publisher, editor or agent … (If he had decided not to sign-you-up as a client) in contrast, if you wielded great power, and exerted authority, he would kiss your ass from here to eternity. The vagaries of his actions, attitude, and demeanor fluctuated wildly, and were totally dependent on whether you could further his ambitions.

His position of power at the firm and his extreme arrogance blinded him, and caused him to overestimate his competence and capabilities. He knew little about, or paid attention to, the old admonition that "Pride goes before the fall."

Neville had a deep, pervasive, and enduring hatred of any lifestyle different from his own, he was particularly enraged by the Latin culture of Miami; why he chose to live there was a mystery. He was often away from his office in Miami, defending his absenteeism on the grounds that the climate in South Florida was not apposite to his "English constitution."

He was socially inept, aloof and removed from his family, friends, and his staff; every cell in his head and in his whole being devoted to making money. His most enduring trait was that of independent, individualistic, selfish greed. Neville would complain that his height had prevented him from having a career as an RAF pilot; he claimed that he was disqualified because he could not fit in the cockpit … So he said. Ed thought that there's got to be more to it than that; Ed questioned his judgment, his imagination, his guts, and his loyalty, hell! He questioned everything about the man that constituted and made up what one would consider attributes of an honorable man. Ed thought for sure the RAF did too ... Neville was well qualified for his role in life, and his profession fit him well. He bragged how he had been a big dog in the company British Petroleum; everyone started calling him BP behind his back--short for British Prick.

Ed would say, "You know, in this world; I can think of only two men I personally met that I can say were truly evil, and that was El Che and Castro. However, I have met an awful lot of little prick weasels in this world; too many in fact, Neville was one of these. This is a guy that would as soon betray you and throw you to the wolves as easily as blowing his nose and discarding a tissue. (Ann Frank would have survived only minutes on the streets of Amsterdam, had Neville been her neighbor). He was the antithesis of the swashbuckling English hero, no Earl Flynn, no David Niven, nor James Bond type here.

Only in his mind did Britain continue to be a powerful empire. Neville always complained about America imitating Britain by trying to build an empire. Ed reminded him of what one of his fellow citizens, the Archbishop of Canterbury, had said to Colin Powell while at a large conference. The Archbishop In a loud condemning tone, said to Mr. Powell, "Aren't your plans for Iraq nothing but an example of empire building by George Bush." Powell answered by saying, "Over the years, the United States has sent many of its fine young men and women into great peril to fight for freedom beyond our borders. The only amount of land we have ever asked for in return is enough to bury those that did not return." That shut him right up.

To Ed it seemed like the current atmosphere that promoted the excessive use of over refined euphemisms, (with the express purpose of minimizing or eliminating offensive terms that would assail the sensibilities of selected groups), had served to rob men of their more vigorous qualities, such as veracity. Sapping their moral strength and replacing it with the weakness of political correctness, a sort of "Effemination of America" that was supposed to make us more civilized, more genteel, but had instead given rise and had helped to foster and nurture this type of spineless, sneaky individual-- the Neville's and Madoff's of our society.

Neville was a master of minutia with a firm grip of the obvious, a schemer, and a plotter, a true Machiavellian disciple. The only human thing about Neville was that he liked to care for his tropical fish and never allowed any one near them. He did not even hire one of the many companies in Florida that take care of large home and business aquariums. These fish tanks are difficult to maintain clean; the salt-water ones are a particular challenge. Once Manny tried to get close to look at the fish, Neville got extremely angry and told him to move away because the fish were very sensitive to intrusion and would go into shock and die. They had never heard of such a thing, and could not find any experts to confirm this.

He bragged of British culture and Shakespeare's contribution to literature; Ed said to him that Shakespeare was a plagiarist who had stolen the story of Othello from Giovanni Batista's "Un Capitano Moro" A Moorish Captain, written in 1565 while Shakespeare wrote his version in 1603.

He bragged about English culture, but failed to mention that when Spain was a cultural mecca of learning, the English were savages painting their faces blue and living in huts made of sod, they had no alphabet and no written language. The queen is the queen only because her ancestors beheaded the opposition. An adulterer, who wanted a quickie Tijuana like divorce, founded the Church of England, because the Pope had refused to give him that divorce. This I am sure was not the only or even the principal reason for establishing a separate and independent church. A more compelling reason for any autocratic ruler would be the removal of the pope's authority and interference over his country's economical and political affairs. Although the Spanish, as well as other Europeans, enslaved, tortured and drove the indigenous population of the Caribbean Indians to near extinction, it is also true that considerable efforts by padre De Las Casas and others were taken to protect the Indians. Ed told Neville that all those English movies that portrayed Spaniards as the killers of the poor Indians, simply ignored that in Spanish ruled countries, the indigenous population today is a large percentage of the total population and it is integrated very much so in the total. While in the English ruled countries like America, the native population has been disseminated to the point of extinction. In these countries, they had been confined to reservations, which were the equivalent of Jewish concentration camps and ghettos, comprised of the most undesirable lands. And God help the poor Native American, if anything of value, like gold or oil, where to be found on these lands. The only lucky ones are those running casinos.

While the prissy Englishmen shunned the native women, the Spaniards married them.

There is a saying that there are three principal innovations of the Spaniards: the Beret, which is neither a hat nor a cap, the Alpargata (a type of espadrille) which is neither a shoe nor a sandal, and the Mulata, which is neither black nor white.

Neville's tastes ran expensive; he wore New & Lingwood Russian Calf Shoes, preferred by graduates of Eaton (the school he claimed he graduated from, but could provide no records to substantiate his claim) the shoes are really made of reindeer leather, which has been cured in baths of rye, oat flour and yeast, and then hand-finished and soaked, in wood liquor. The leather is then hand-curried while still wet and then soaked in seal oil and birch tannig oil, which gives it a distinctive scent. They go for around $1,550 a pair. He knew little about them other that than they were British and worn by those who had attended Eaton. As far as the skill and quality of the material that went into making these shoes, he was ignorant on all counts; he just wanted to impress his audience and cared nothing about them.

Shitty Coffee.
Ed had brought Manny along while he met with Neville. Neville was nouveau riche and ignorant about the items he bought, he often bought the most expensive items in the world with the sole purpose of showing off, even though he knew little about what he had purchased. Status, prestige, power, and pomp were probably inscriptions on his coat of arms. He would brag, with immense pride "I only drink the best coffee in the world, Kopi Luwak Coffee," as he drank his cup.

Ed: Hate to burst your bubble, but you do realize that's shitty coffee.

Neville: What the hell do you mean! This is the rarest and most unusual coffee in the world; I will have you know!

Ed: What I mean is that this coffee, the coffee you are drinking right now, the coffee passing your lips this instant, came from a cat's ass. That's why it is so rare (or should I say rear) and unusual. The source for the coffee you are drinking is a bean that has been eaten by the Luwak or civet cat, a close relative to the skunk, with which it shares the ability to excrete a noxious odor from scent glands near its anus. The same anus, by the way, the coffee beans of the coffee you drink pass through. Once eaten, the beans go through the animal's digestive path, eventually passing in the animals droppings. Farmers then collect the droppings. The coffee is then cleaned, (as much as you can clean something that has just come out of the ass of a cat). That's the straight poop on your coffee, Neville.

Neville was furious, "He was angrier than a white shopkeeper's dialogue in a Spike Lee movie." ... "Get out and take that other Cuban hood with you!" He shouted.

Manny made things worse by saying, "Now is that nice, and I just finished standing up for the British. They were just saying at my favorite local bar how the English were not fit to eat with pigs ... and I said you certainly were. Oh and by the way, Lord Admiral Horatio Nelson was gay ... at his deathbed during the smoke filled battle he said to his second in command, "Kiss me Neville, kiss me hardy."

Neville now in a rage, said, "He did not, he said, "Kiss me Hardy." And they were just close friends you idiot."

Manny: Same difference… oh yes, and his nickname was horn blower, he must have gotten that nickname for some reason. Where there's smoke there's fire … in the eyes.

Neville: Get out … get out right now!

As they were leaving his office, an exceptionally large man was coming in; he wore a custom suit that although surely expensive, was also quite a bit garish, the kind MBA players, and pimps used to wear. I guess there is no substitute for taste.

Manny: You know who that is.

Ed: No why?

Manny: That's Ozzie the "Columbian Bear," he said, and went on to describe who and what he was.

His friends knew Clemente Oziago as Ozzie, the victims of loan sharking knew him as El Oso Colombiano (the Columbian Bear). He worked for the Columbian Drug lords who had diversified and expanded into extortion, kidnapping, the protection racket, and their core business, which was loan sharking. The Cartel's business was booming during these times of economic woes, it also helped that the interest rate they imposed was in line with the credit card rates being charged by legitimate lending institutions; making them highly competitive.

The Dunning process is a long established methodical process of communicating with customers to ensure the collection of debt; it varies and escalates, from gentle reminders to threatening letters and phone calls, as accounts become more past due. The word stems from the 17th century verb dun, meaning to demand payment of a debt. The Columbian cartels had a similar process. Ozzie was their last step in the dunning collections process, if you will. He was the equivalent of the action taken by creditors after the last dunning letter is issued, i.e. the legal actions of repossession, foreclosure, and wage garnishment. The only difference was that, in Ozzie's world, there were no laws against the harassment or the threatening of consumers (not that they were being observed in the legal world either) in his world everything was allowed, with no limits on the degree and extent of pain a collector could inflict on his victims. Ozzie's specialty was the broken leg and the broken kneecap. This treatment was reserved for those that did not perform manual labor in earning income. His tool of choice was a sawed-off baseball bat. As a debtor, you surely did not want to see Ozzie on the steps of your home or business. Nonetheless, here was Ozzie, of all places, in the office of Neville Fox.

The Bear did a lot of work for Tonio, (his real name was Antonio Medebes) he had made millions if not billions as a member of the Colombian drug Cartel. He got out before the drug wars had started between Pablo Escobar and the rest of the gang. If there were a Forbes' list of all the richest men in the world that included those that made it through violent crime, he would be in the top one hundred. The rumor was that he is heavily invested in legitimate businesses; has controlling interests in several banks and that he continues to be an "independent lender." He uses The Bear to collect these loans.

Manny: The guy can be a bit of a sadist, he enjoys his job a little too much; I wonder what the hell he is doing here? … Ed: So do I. _____**13**

CHAPTER 14
MR. HOWELL'S LITTLE BOY, THE LITTLE ELITIST SHIT

Ed and Manny were true epicureans, in search of modest pleasures, such as those of gourmet dining, tranquility of mind and freedom from pain. They would find some of these the next morning when Ed and Manny visited Wolfie's Deli in South Beach, not the original Cohen Rascal House in Miami Beach, that one had fallen victim to the pasture eaters. They had bagels with cream cheese, locks, and chives. They were also able to get their Cuban coffee, a Cuban "colada," which is like a pot of regular coffee, only smaller and more potent. Afterwards, they bought two Cuban seed cigars made in the Dominican Republic and relaxed. Ed later headed to the firms office for a meeting with Tradeles.

Chris Howell was the product of Mr. Jonathan Howell's (one of the rich partners of the firm and Neville's father-in-law) lucky little sperm. Chris was blonde-haired, with perfectly manicured looks, he was particularly neat, actually too neat, he was either gay (not that there is anything wrong with that) semi-gay, or at a minimum metro-sexual. He did not have the expected preppie look of a rich banker's son, but more like that movie character Bruno. He had failed in school, and in every job, his father had ever bought for him; and as one would expect, he was not a source of great pride to his father. Due to the good fortune of his heredity, ancestral pedigree, and accident of birth, he was now a very wealthy trust baby.

He worked as a staff member, but got paid like a director. He would soon be kicked upstairs where he could do no harm and where he could spend his idle time, which was the whole day, at the golf club. He was a Trust baby after all, so eventually his days were destined to end up there. I'm sure the fall of Tiger Woods was of considerable pleasure to his type, as golf was one of the remaining bastions of sports in which white elitist businessmen still reigned. There in the comfort of the club lounge, large black men could not threaten their manhood. For the same reason, it probably burned their asses when Tiger ascended to the top.

Chris had been one of the key players approving the financial audit reports of the Chandler bank. He was an unwitting participant in the cover up. Neville had placed him in that position deliberately and with a purpose. With this assignment, the fox, Neville Fox that is, was literally placed to guard the chicken coup. And although Chris was up to his ass in Florida alligators, he did not know it. Ed thought that this shrimp was being set up to be the fall guy for Neville.

Ed was in the firms offices when Inspector Tradeles came in looking for him. When the inspector asked for Ed, Chris said, in his wise-ass ignorant manner, typical to these self-absorbed prima donnas … I don't know, how would I know … ask the Albanian.

.
Inspector Tradeles: Who's the Albanian?

Chris: Pop's over there with the white hair … the little punk replied.

"Goldilocks" means me, Ed retorted, adding … I 'm neither an Albanian nor an albino, which is what the ignorant little shit is trying to say.

The inspector together with Ed and detective Matson began questioning Chris Howell about his role in the mortgage frauds, it was obvious he didn't understand the consequences of his actions and had been rubber-stamping everything. He did know the names of those involved but was hesitant to divulge them. The inspector said to him, "You'd better start talking or you'll find that prison is just right for you goldilocks. It won't be too soft for you, and for your type … it is never hard enough." He spilled his guts immediately afterwards.

Tradeles: Maybe we can meet for lunch in Broward tomorrow and catch up. I'm building a case against some of these characters, and I'd like to pass some ideas by you.

Ed: That's on the other side of the border; you can't get proper Cuban food there!

Tradeles: What do you mean border.

Ed: Any place north of Dade County.

Matson then made a bit of a derogatory comment about minority Spics.

Ed told him to be careful of what he said because in Dade County, he was the minority.

Ed and Manny were planning to head to the bank next and try to track Afortunado's movements on his last days, but first they stopped to have lunch with Pierre to discuss

the case over a large serving of arroz-con-pollo. Ed then started one of his diatribes about the economy, and political correctness." What was needed in this world to correct all the financial evils, was a return to the direct, in your face, negative terms of the past. What we need in today's society is the old fashion calling a spade a spade … no offense Pierre."

Pierre: None taken.

He then went on (and on, and on) "The understanding that the public receives of the recent economic upheavals; leading to the current recession is clouded by politically correct terminology. Few have used the best terms to describe the causes leading to these events, in terms such as usury, or perhaps a term such as government sanctioned loan sharking ... Oh! That's right, he forgets that recent laws have made the term usury obsolete, as the new laws make the charging of exorbitant rates legal ... so in practice there can be no usury, there can be no loan sharking. Instead, many couch all that is negative and unpleasant by explaining them in newer, less direct, awkward and ever more politically correct sterilized euphemisms. We are, as someone said, 'Going on a downwardly sloped euphemism treadmill' that continues to dilute unpleasant terms. A perfect example is the word cripple, even as far back as the early twentieth century, it was an apt and descriptive term of a condition, perfectly acceptable, but now thought to be offensive. This term has been euphemized down, first to handicap and now to physically- challenged. Soon, a man that is bald will not be called bald, but follicularly challenged."

He recalled one audit at a large cement production facility in Roanoke Virginia, where one of its customers had

racked up a balance of accounts receivables that was past due. Over a million dollars and over 120 days past due, this was not only at variance with company policy, but a terrifically bad business practice, especially in these uncertain times. When he reported the customer in question, the controller, began to expound a number of excuses, for a moment Ed thought he was going to call this deadbeat a "credit-challenged debtor. "However, he went beyond that, he actually said, "The customer is not a bad credit risk and is not really passed due; he simply has taken a more aggressive repayment stance, besides he had agreed to sign a promissory note." A note not worth the paper it was printed on; it was not signed, it was not witnessed, nor was it dated, it did not meet Interstate Commerce Commission rules, and it had not been filed with the courts. It was in fact, totally unenforceable. What a beautifully constructed euphemism, Ed thought that he should frame the email and hang it in his office. When Ed defended his position to the CFO, he was immediately and severely chastised.

This reminded Ed of the Romans and the Spaniard joke, which he proceeded to tell: A captured Spaniard was told he was being given a chance to live; all he had to do was kill a lion. A hole was dug in the middle of an arena and the Spaniard was buried up to his neck, the lion was then released. During the struggle, the Spaniard somehow was able to get his mouth on the lion's testicles; he bit down hard, castrating and killing the lion. Three Roman soldiers, Gluteus and Maximus were ordered to run with Mucus to the middle of the arena. The Spaniard thought he was about to be released. Then the three men suddenly started kicking him in the head while screaming, "Fight fair Spick!" (This was years before the Rodney King case). Life had given him the fickle finger of fate. "Fight fair Spick, "the story of his life, Ed thought.

His mother always used to say "When life gives you lemons make lemonade," she left out one thing, however, she failed to tell him how many lemons had to be squeezed throughout one's life and how hard they would need to be squeezed.

Ed continued with his tirade. "If the economy and its financial institutions were a criminal organization, the term skimming from the top would be apt terminology to describe what bankers and brokers have done to the cash flow of this economy and continue to do so." However, these transactions at the bank went beyond government-sponsored usury and normal every day law approved skimming, they were outright crimes of fraud and of staggering proportions. Here! Here! His buddies clamored; the meal then finished in typical Cuban style ... lots of arguments and disagreements over politics and as to who had been the best Cuban baseball player to have ever played the game.

Rub my head and tell me everything is going to be all right. After a tense meeting with the executives and managers at the firm, Ed always needed his ego stroked; it was time to visit his amateur analyst, Katy. Ed took Katy to La Carreta restaurant that night for a big Cuban dinner, he had ropa-vieja, (old clothes) it is a mixture of stringed shredded beef with tomato, onion and sweet green pepper sauce; she always ordered the roasted pork sandwich, her favorite. She was wearing a form fitting little black dress that accentuated the curves of her body, it was cut elegantly in the front so that enough cleavage would show, making her alluring, yet not so low as to give her a slutty appearance. Unlike many American women, she had a Cuban like ass that was both round like an apple and outstanding (it stood out).

Her legs were long, with shapely calves that tapered beautifully at the ankles, while her tiny waist accentuated her well-formed breasts. She wore the pearl necklace that Ed had bought for her birthday. It had cost a mint, but still brought on a deluge of tears. She also had the matching earrings, a gift from Ed from the previous Christmas; they too had brought on a river of tears. Apparently nothing but a ring would do.

At the restaurant, every skirt-hound in the place was looking at her boobs or at her ass. And Latinos as a group are not shy about it. The men were staring and the women were pulling at their ears or grabbing their chins and turning their heads back towards them; Ed didn't know whether to puff his chest out with pride or to kick their asses.

Ed: This project is turning into a real can of worms.

Katy: How so?

Ed: Well there are so many people on this illegal gravy train; many are well-connected powerful people in Miami. There are so many layers of cover-ups, so many fraudulent transactions, so many illegal business arrangements, so many forged documents.
This kind of crime is difficult to prove if there is no way to trace the trail of documentation, and even if there is, some smart-ass lawyer can use the laws to prevent their use in court or maneuver so it appears as if it was just an honest mistake, the judge will then throw it out. Then there is the fact that there are more people with power interested in making sure the investigation fails than those that want to see it succeed. On top of that, is the fact that people are being killed too.

Katy: Who?

Ed: Well there is Herbert Afortunado and his assistant, just to mention two. Pierre and I are sure that one killer murdered the VP and his Assistant VP, and there may be more killers. Once they know of my involvement and they feel threaten, they will act against me.

Katy: How?

Ed: They will try to kill me; that's how!

Katy: God no! Make sure Manny is always with you and call either Coco or the Kid.

Ed: That's not a bad idea, but it's too soon, let me see what develops.

Katy: By then they will have taken a shot at you. ____**14**

CHAPTER 15
LEAD ON

𝕿he killer was an equal opportunity assassin. He murdered all types of people, from all races, genders and socioeconomic status, short, tall, skinny or fat and by any means, shooting, stabbing, strangulation, you name it. He also had killed in many other countries.

Manny, always on the case of his brother's murderer, had arranged a phone conference with a sergeant of the national police of Finland. A murder attributed to the killer had been recently investigated in Lapland. At first, it was thought it was a suicide, but later deemed murder. It seems, as Manny put it, the guy had taken a "Louganis" (that would be a dive to you and me) out of the 14th floor unto the payment below. Later it was determined that it had been involuntary, or as Manny put it, he had been "Louganised" against his will.

Ed: Haven't I've heard that term before.

Manny: You couldn't have ... I just made it up, you are probably thinking of "Take a Brody," after the first guy to jump from the 135-foot high Brooklyn Bridge and survive; made famous by George Raft in a movie, and later mentioned in a Robert B. Parker book.

Manny: My term is named after Greg Louganis the famous high diver. No sir this one I made up myself!

Ed: Yes Manny, you should be very proud!

"Anyway, there had been a witness, a local girl, who the sergeant said was visiting Miami, and we may want to talk to her." They took the number and arranged to meet her.

♪ ♫ **All the single (Lebanese) Ladies oh, oh, oh♪ ♫**
When they met her at the La Cote bar of the Fontainebleau hotel, on Collins Avenue, Manny was drunk and disoriented. She was sitting with a girlfriend, they had been kissing, as she was an important eyewitnesses and Ed needed her cooperation, he knew he'd better give Manny the heads up so he would not say anything offensive. He told him, before introducing them, that they were lesbians, "So refrain from making any politically incorrect off-colored jokes." But what does Manny do, he immediately asked them ... "How's Beirut these days ladies?"

Ed whispered sternly in his ear ... they're lesbians Manny, I repeat lesbians, not Lebanese you idiot. Thank God, they had a sense of humor.

Talk about your reindeer games.
This woman was Scandinavian, from Finland, her name was Helmi; she had a huge mouth with extremely large and numerous teeth, looking into the abyss that was her mouth one could swear she had twice the number of natural teeth. She mentioned that she was from Lapland. Ed remembering the old Mondo Cane film series and the Faces of Death series of sensational documentaries, wondered if she was one of those women whose duties as a reindeer herder was to castrate deer with her teeth, she certainly had the chops for it. Her sexual proclivity also would tend to add to her motivation in performing her duties, as probably she had not outgrown her "Electra Complex,"... Jung's theory, or Freud's penis envy

theory. Then again, these thoughts may have been stimulated by Ed's own "castration anxiety."

According to Dr. Beatriz, Ed's cousin, the psychologist, these theories are outmoded and have been replaced by studies that are more current. (Ed didn't care; Freud's were more fun, because they always had connotations of sex).

She said that she saw a man being tossed by a medium build man with a goatee, sunken cheeks, and angular features. "He looked like either Lance Henriksen from the Hellraiser movies or more like one of the bad guys from Kill Bill, (Ed immediately thought of David Carradine) but then she said, "or was it the guy from Robocop, Peter Weller." She couldn't make up her mind.

Ed: Who was the victim?

Helmi: He was Sven Jorgensen VP at a large international bank, had just returned from America, he said he was meeting another bank executive from a bank called Challenger or something.

Ed: Could it be Chandler?

Helmi: Yes, that's it.

She added that when the killer ran he had a significant limp. ...They were beginning to get a picture of the guy.
_____15

CHAPTER 16
MADAME PETIT DU POI

She was a petite woman with a greenish-tan complexion; not unlike a pea, not the fresh frozen but more like the overcooked version that comes in cans. She had little beady piercing eyes; wore way too much mascara and had long fake eyelashes, like spider legs attached to her eyelids. She looked a lot like the cartoon character version of Eartha Kitt in The Emperors New Groove. Her lipstick was bright fire engine red and smeared, as though she had applied the lipstick while on a jerky Disney World ride; she even had globs of it on her teeth. The ends of her mouth curved downward, giving her the look of an angry grouper, who had just missed his last minnow. This grimace remained on her face throughout the interview. Apparently, this permanent scowl on her countenance was due to a severe case of consistent and everlasting state of PMS. Ed was startled when he first met her, he winced and slightly recoiled at the sight of her face, he almost said yikes and eek!--Man she was scary looking; she had a devious evil look about her. She also reminded him of that scary blonde-haired woman on the religious TV channel, not Tammy but another platinum blond, the one with all the blue eye shadow and black eyeliner on her eyes … like Cleopatra. The one with the sixties teased up beehive hairdo … you'd know if you were religious. Madam Du Poi's hair was as stiff as that of an Alabama waitress at a truck stop coffee shop. She had enough spray on it to withstand a category five hurricane.

She met them at the door with her face blotted in heavy powder, giving her the look of a cadaver. She was wearing a garishly loud vibrantly colored African dashiki, with a green and yellow bandana on her head that looked like a hodgepodge of Aunt Jemima's head bandana, the Chiquita banana girl's hat and Carmen Miranda's assorted fruited headdress. She looked like a voodoo priestess or an exotic palm reader from a carnival.

Her stern character and demeanor was intimidating, hers was a cross between that of his teacher back in grade school, Sister Marion Joseph, the principal and mother superior of St. Patrick's Cathedral, nurse Ratched, and Martha Stewart. If she were to write a book, Ed thought it would surely be called "How to Serve Man"… the cookbook. If Neville was the image of a reptile, she was the image of an arachnid … a spider, a black widow more precisely. One could sense the evil in her, and just like Frau Blücher, Ed could swear that at the mention of her name he could hear horses neighing in the background.

Ms. Du Poi had married for money, same as Neville; to the son of the chairman of the Chandler Bank (his wife had died under suspicious circumstances) she kept her maiden name and now was one of the biggest shareholders of the Chandler Group. Kitty to her friends, she had more the personality of a witch's black cat than a kitten. After meeting her again later, Ed would still cringe. Even the thought of her face would make him flinch. The shock never wore off.

Ed thought that, although there was no apparent connection, this had to be a plot devised by Neville Fox and Du Poi. If she were to dump that stock now, before the scandal broke, she would make a killing, after the scandal, she would lose everything, and if implicated in the fraud, the cover up, and the murders she would be going to the big house for a very long time. Cagey and defiant in her responses, she divulged nothing of any importance during the interview; but she was definitely hiding something. _____**16**

CHAPTER 17
THE BODIES OF EVIDENCE WERE MOUNTING....
EEK! IS IT SAFE?
♫ ♪ Or one of these things <u>does </u>belong with the other ♪... but is missing

𝕸anny and Ed arrived at the crime scene, along with the assistant coroner Dr. Cornelia. Pierre was working on other cases and had assigned Dr. Cornelia, a very young but very competent forensics pathologist with superb investigative instincts.

Although in an average city this scene would seem horrific, for a large city like Miami this scene was not atypical at all. The victim was a one armed man, his genitals, to be more specific his penis and right gonad were missing; they had been surgically removed. The body had a chloros yellow green hue. He was missing a tooth, the right upper cusped; it had been freshly pulled out with pliers during the crime. The initial X burned into his neck. The jagged cut suggested he had been stabbed with a broken sword and then his throat was slit. This was the typical overkill of a sadistic serial murderer.

The doctor said that had his throat not been cut he could have survived, she said it was a "Condito sine qua non, "for his death, even though his penis and testicle were gone.

Ed: How long has he been dead?

Inspector: there is a broken clock by the dresser that shows it stopped two hours ago; it must be the time of the struggle and murder.

Doctor Cornelia: Based on the stage of rigor, the postmortem body temperature, and lividity, as well as degree of putrefaction, I can roughly estimate the time of death at around over thirty hours earlier. Later, during the autopsy I will be able to examine more closely the information and give you a more accurate time. After I perform further forensic pathology tests of the stomach contents, measure chemical changes within the body and inspect for any insect activity, I will also perform blood analysis and other clinical test. This will provide me with better and more accurate information.

Ed: The broken clock, stopped at only two hours ago, was a feeble and obvious attempt to hide the actual time, perhaps to confuse or create an alibi.

Doctor: It gets even more grisly and gruesome; when I flipped him over to insert the rectal thermometer, I noted a sizable amount of flesh had been carved from his Gluteus-maxim muscle; by the shape and size, I would say equivalent to a pound in weight. His Achilles tendon was also severed.

Manny: Rectal? Now I remember why I didn't go into medicine.

"Like that was the only reason," Ed thought.

Manny had been a cop for many years in Miami. He had seen many gruesome and sad crime scenes. He was a good catholic boy, taught to respect his elders, women and the dead, but his experiences had hardened him a bit; many people thought he was insensitive because of comments he made. What they did not know was that he used humor to cover his true feelings; this helped him cope with life's tragedies. He had seen Columbian necktie murders, hanging with barbwire; machete slayings, people set on fire, decapitations, you name it; the most disturbing of all, always, was the murder of small children.

Ed: The tendon was probably cut to bring him down or incapacitate him. It looks like he may have been lying on the bed then got up to go to the dresser.

Manny: Maybe a killer dwarf did it.

Ed gave him a disapproving look.

Manny: It's possible. Say he hid under the bed and waited, then slashed the guy's tendon as he walked by ... it's possible. It was hard for Ed to believe Manny was ever a detective.

Manny then said, "You know I was thinking ... yeah, sure he could have lived, but who would want to ... by the way, what's a gluteus! And this condiment stuff."

Ed: His ass Manny ... I think the removal of that amount is symbolic, it looks like the killer extracted his "Pound of flesh," and the other is just Latin for a "Condition that must exist." Ed then said, "For example, in solving crimes it is the thought process that counts, it is necessary to have clear thinking, it is a "Condito sine qua non," while some CSI techniques are important, they may be only contributory and not necessarily ... necessary."

Ed then exclaimed, very impressed with himself ... "Hey that's deep!"

Manny then said …"Yeah and so are the holes for outhouses … Poor guy … I guess he wouldn't have been able to count his change at the bus stop any more, had he lived … or sit on the bus for that matter!"

What do you mean; Cornelia started to ask … just before Ed could interrupt her question.

Ed said …"Damn it I am too late … You had to ask … now he's going to visually and graphically demonstrate it."

Manny then went on to perform his imitation of a one-armed-man counting his change in front of a bus stop. He pulled out his right arm from his jacket, rolled up his jacket sleeve to give the appearance of having just one arm, and then hid this right arm inside the jacket. He then put this hand down his pants; he opened his zipper, and with his left hand pulled out two fingers of the hidden hand as though it was his penis. Then, with the left hand he got out some coins, he placed them in his cupped hand in front of his unzipped pants, in front of his exposed "penis like fingers," he then proceeded to count the change with his imitation faux penis.

Dr. Cornelia made a face, but also laughed.

Manny occasionally did have his moments of clarity, at these times, he'd point out something significant; he had been in the Navy Seals, and when it came to effective ways to kill, he knew his stuff. "This was a professionally trained killer," he said, "I could tell that by the way he cut the throat. In the movies, the killer comes from behind, and if he is right handed he stabs the victim on his left side, then in a sickle half-moon motion cuts the throat, this plays well on camera as it provides a very dramatic effect. A professional, however, takes the knife and holds the point at the victim's right side, off the neck just behind the jaw point and below the neck bones, a straight line back from the chin. With the sharpened cutting edge facing forward, he then plunges the blade into the jugular vein and pushes straightforward, getting as much power from his shoulder as he can. The other way is awkward; pulling is not nearly as forceful as pushing forward. For a fast and quiet kill, you need a knife that is long and sharp, a knife that can sever both, the internal and external jugular veins, the carotid artery and the trachea too, preventing the victim from crying out. …This one was textbook on! The trace evidence left by the blood splatter indicates blood must have spurted out of his neck. He must have bled out in seconds."

In the bureau dresser, the Brazilian passport of a Fernando Guarano was found hidden. It was stamped, showing entry into several countries. The guy traveled a lot but only stayed short periods in each location; he had even visited Finland recently. Cancelled flight tickets to Tahlequah, Oklahoma were also found.

Inspector Tradeles: I guess it's another of the Alphabet Assassin victims. We sprayed the area with luminal and used the ultraviolet lights searching for any trace evidence, but only the victims blood came up, we also dusted for latent and patent finger and palm prints, but again all we found were the victims. His wallet was missing; I don't think it was a robbery, but more an attempt at hiding the identity of the corpse.

Ed: Yes, I agree inspector, but this one is more personal, you can't get any more personal than this. There's a great deal more anger in the commission of this crime. The killer knew and hated the victim, the physical parts taken were more personal and significant, and they were more violently taken. In fact, the excising of the ears during prior crimes was like taking home a souvenir, while this is more like taking home an anatomical trophy.

There is a precision to the deliberate malice in the mutilation of the body, the extent of which is much more pronounced than the mutilations inflicted on any of the other victims found thus far, this was very, very personal.

The guy is expensively dressed in an Italian designer suit, the shoes are also Italian, custom made I'd say, and very expensive, possibly Ferragamos, and he is wearing a Patek Philippe watch, makes me wonder why he is living in this dump. ... The tooth removal is puzzlingly too.

Dr. Cornelia placed a bar coded tag on the big toe, just like the meat at the local Publix super market.

Ed then said, "Death is not the end it is only the beginning."

Inspector Tradeles said, "Now that is deep, where'd you get that ... Aristotle, St Augustine?"

Ed: The Ghost Whisperer, I forget which episode.
_____17

CHAPTER 18
♪   ♫   **A TOTAL ECLIPSE OF THE HEART** ♪ ♫
Or what doesn't kill you will definitely eat you ... alive

Several days later Pierre called, "Ed, guess what ... we have another."

Above, hovering over the body was what Manny had called a flock of crows. Ed corrected him and said it is called a murder of crows ..."What are you talking about?" said Manny.

Ed: Well it's just the correct term, like a pack of wolves, a herd of cattle; it's the correct term, that's all. Oh, never mind.

The day started with all the accoutrements of a hot summer day in the everglades of Florida, heat, humidity, haze, stagnate swamp water smell, horse flies, mosquitoes, lots of saw grass, the occasional cotton mouth, anaconda and alligator, king fishers hooting and those annoying sticking little balls with needles ... Ah yes ... this was paradise. Ed thought a national park ... "Yeah right! The river of grass, my ass, how poetic it all sounds in the tourist pamphlets, nothing but PR euphemism for swamp," If Flagler had lived a few more years, we'd have a nice subdivision here now. All he could think of was that little melody and lyrics "Pave (the so called) paradise and put up a parking lot" ... and why someone wasn't doing it faster. No majestic Yellowstone here, I think our Florida legislators may have had park envy when they pushed to have this swamp declared a national park.

The body had been found partially digested in the stomach of an exceptionally large African Python. Every bone in his body had been crushed; heart missing, surgically removed post mortem or post "crunch time" as Manny would say, how the guy did it, Pierre couldn't figure out. Apparently, the killer wanted to watch the victim suffer. He was found with a sizable yellow diamond (I guess there was a majestic yellow stone here) that had been cut into the shape of a tooth, molded to fit as a cusped or eyetooth in the upper right jaw. There were signs of obvious attempts at removal with pliers, as the tooth was three quarters of the way out. His hands were tied behind his back. A gold ring with intricate ornamental filigree and the Ace of spades engraved on it was on his ring finger, a very distinct and expensive piece of craftsmanship, Ed noted. He had been stabbed with a broken sword, as was Fernando Guarano.

Dr. De Baptist: We were fortunate to find the body in such good condition, a few more days or a week at most, and all the flesh and most of the bones would have been consumed by the gastric juices of the snake's stomach; there isn't much of a face I'm afraid. It was only discovered because of the cold spell that had swept South Florida this winter, causing the premature death of the snake, as they are not native to Florida and not equipped to survive cold weather for any extended period.

Manny: Tell me about it, that cold spell was enough to freeze the balls on a brass monkey.

Ed: I know you're purposely trying to sound crude, that's just you, but the source of that saying is not. "Brass monkeys" was the name given to the square metal pieces attached to the ships floor that had large holes cut into them to hold cannon balls. They were an improvement on the old iron ones that would rust to the balls, however in cold weather, because brass reacts faster and contracts more rapidly than iron in cold weather; it causes the balls to wedge or "freeze" in the holes, hence the saying.

Manny: You know Ed, sometimes you bug the shit out of me, no wonder Katy gets pissed.

Pierre ignored them and continued with out missing a step, "It is very possible the victim was still alive while he was being eaten, or at least warm, as snakes like their food warm, preferably fresh, and alive. This African Python is unusually large; it has had time to grow. There are no predators, other than alligators, that can eat them, and they are only a threat when the snakes are less than six months old. This one is several years old, and unusually large, it is significantly over twenty-five feet, with a girth larger than a telephone pole, over thirty inches around, expandable to accommodate a large man. They can also unhinge their jaws, allowing them to eat deer or other large mammals whole. The African Python is more ferocious and extremely more aggressive than the Burmese Python. They are known to be man-eaters back in Africa, and unlike the relatively more gentle Burmese, it will strike faster and harder; they are extremely aggressive. There is documented evidence of them eating ten-foot alligators. A large constrictor can exert about 90 PSI or over eight thousand pounds on one's body; this is equivalent to having a school bus sitting on your chest. It's like having a giant blood pressure cuff exerting ten thousand times the pressure on your body; this causes blood vessels to burst and your heart to stop, hopefully just before you're eaten. In 1993 in Colorado, the family's python attacked a fifteen-year-old boy weighing ninety-five pounds. The snake was only of medium size being eleven feet long and weighing fifty three pounds, yet was able to kill the boy, though it did not attempt to eat him."

Manny: In all the years in the force, I've never seen anything like this, I remember this guy, Jake, who had broken into a home in one of the gate-guarded communities, the alarm had gone off, and the police were at the front door. He decided to escape by jumping in the canal behind the house, but there in the dark lay waiting a twelve-foot gator, old Jake became Jake tartar.

Dr. Cornelia asked "What?"

Manny: You know Gator Grub, Cayman Candy, Alimiento de Alligator, Comida de Cocodrilo. Should I go on?

Ed examined the body too, paying particular attention to the hands and shoes.

He looked at the neck and there was a faint burn scar, it could not be made out clearly, because snakes start eating their victims by the head first, the stomach acids would have started to eat at the flesh in this area first, within six days the hydrochloric acid and peptic enzymes would have consumed the bones.

His right forearm had the traces of a faded tattoo, looked like an old anchor, the word Antwerp slightly legible below.

Ed: He was most likely Brazilian, a diamond miner, or at least he was one at one time, perhaps an owner, most likely rich, he had expensive tastes, undoubtedly a jewel cutter, but only on a part time basis. He had very likely traveled to Europe, probably Italy very recently. He may have been a sailor and diamond merchant or smuggler. He also enjoined gambling. I'll leave the discussion of the taking of the heart to the doctor but it may be related to a vindictive act of vengeance or a more personal souvenir of a serial killer.

Doctor: The surgical removal could be by a doctor, surgical nurse or experienced repeat killer with surgical knowledge. Voodoo priests often use the heart in Haiti for rituals of revenge and for what is believed to be power transfer, could be a reason for removal.

Manny: Ed, how can you possibly know all that to be true?

Ed: Well its common knowledge that yellow diamonds, although relatively scarce in many of the countries where diamonds are mined, are known to be found in relative abundance in Brazil. The practice of replacing a lost tooth with a diamond is typical to many miners who have struck it rich in the Brazilian precious stone mines, it is their not too subtle way of showing off wealth and letting everyone know they are rich. The physical development of his muscular body particularly the forearms indicates a man that worked at one time, very hard with his upper body and arms, possibly using a pick.

Manny: What the fuck! What about the rest?

Ed: His hands are strong, nails highly polished and the telltale sings of fading calluses remain, indicating he has not performed heavy manual labor for some time. There is a particular distinct one on his left thumb, typical to diamond cutters. It is more pronounced, and therefore current, the callosity however is not as deep as you would find in a jeweler that has worked consecutive extended periods of time cutting diamonds. He still does it currently, but only on a part time basis. The legible label on his clothes and the real silk threads of his clothing indicate he purchased European designer items found only in high-end boutiques. The shoes that he wears are brand-new, exclusive, and very expensive; they can only be found in Italy, as they are not currently imported. By what's left of these labels, I can tell you that this guy shopped at the same stores that the one-armed man, Fernando Guarano shopped at. The polished nails indicate that he had a great deal of idle time, and could afford a high-end manicure. Anchors are common tattoos for sailors, and Antwerp is the diamond trade capital of the world. It is located on the banks of the river Scheldt, with access to the North Sea. It is a port of call for many ships going to Europe; his ring is common to gamblers whose hands are always visible at the table, so they try to make them attractive by polishing their nails and by displaying jewelry, which exemplifies their pastime.

Manny: Ok, I'll buy that, but why could he not have bought the shoes through the Net? What are they Salvatore Ferragamos? You know they make a pair out of python, wouldn't that be something huh! Mine are Manolo originals … made by my tio (uncle) Manolo.

Tradeles: Are they Prada?

Ed: No, compared to these, Prada are peasant shoes … they are hand made custom Berluti's … or Louis Vuitton Manhattan Richelieu, these are very exclusive shoes. They are maybe ostrich or alligator; we'll be able to tell once all the swamp mud and snake gastric juice is removed … or simply look inside for the label.

Manny: Alligator shoes … probably what attracted the snake … Ok … Ok, but he could have been working part time, as a carpenter or shoe repair guy.

Ed: The skin build up would be on his right hand.

Manny: What if he was left handed?

Ed: He wasn't.

Manny: Again, how the hell do you know for sure?

Ed: Easy, based on the manner in which he tied his shoes, more specifically the direction of the knots and loops. A right-handed man makes a loop with the left side lace that has ended up as a loop on his right after the first snug tie. The right sided lace that ends on the left … after that same snug tie, he uses it to go over the first loop to make the knot, and then makes the second loop by sliding it through the knot. A left handed man ties it in the opposite way.

Manny: Fuck me! How in the hell do you know all this shit. Fuck man I'm the fucking ex detective you are only a bean-counting accountant.

Ed: The Internet Manny, the Internet-- I can also pop an egg out of its shell, wana see.

All the time Tradeles was taking notes and said nothing. Then he said, "It looks like robbery they took his wallet and were trying to get the tooth."

Ed: No, I don't think so; the killer was trying to hide the identity to slowdown the police from making any connection to other crimes. The diamond removal I'm beginning to think is a personal matter. The removal of the heart also indicates it was personal. That ring is near solid gold, very expensive, just based on the price of an ounce of gold at today's prices, underneath the duct tape there is also a very expensive antique Patek Philippe watch, worth well over twenty thousand dollars. He wears it on the left wrist, as would a right-handed man … Manny.

Manny: The Internet, right?

Ed: No, actually, it was PBS, the Antiques Roadshow.

Manny: I think the deadly dwarf that cut the other guy's Achilles tendon did it.

Ed said, "Ok Manny," and then asked the park ranger who was present, if tourists visited this desolate area.

Park ranger: tourist no, but lots of hunters, this is alligator season, and on top of that special permits to hunt and kill none-native imported snakes have been issued; and there is a boat ramp just down the road. This is terrible, being killed and eaten like this.

Pierre: It's worse than that, this was being alive, while being eaten.

Ed: So the killer could have been interrupted while removing the tooth.

Ranger: Very possible as there are lots of fresh tire and foot tracks by the ramp.

Manny: Say ranger, are these anacondas or pythons.

Park ranger: Could not say I never get quite that close enough to find out.

Manny quickly stepped back.

Manny: How come you always seem to know more than Tradeles and Matson?

Ed: It's easy, you know what they say, "In the land of the blind, the one eyed man is king."

Inspector: As soon as we determine his identity and time of death, we will try to trace his whereabouts during his last day. We will then establish a time line and see who he met, to narrow the possibilities.

Pierre was gathering samples and other forensics; he told Ed that he would run DNA tests and get back to him. "Based on the length of the Diptera larvae I will guess he has been dead for over twenty hours. During the autopsy, I will perform clinical pathologic tests such as the potassium eye test to see if I am able to approximate a closer estimate of the time of death, one that is more precise. Some parts of the body maybe beyond putrefaction and testing of chemical changes may not be possible. There is still one more method; I will try to determine time of death by applying detailed forensic entomology."

Manny: How's that work?

"It is common knowledge that death attracts insects. What is not common knowledge is that through forensic entomology estimating time of death can be achieved simply by knowing which insects are generally the first to arrive, and at what stages of decomposition it is that other insects will begin to arrive. Then, by estimating what stage of life the insects that inhabit the body are in, Entomologists like me can determine a close approximation of time of death. "

Manny: Yeah like that moth in Silence of the Lambs.

Pierre: Not quite, you are referring to the Death's-head Hawk moth, they actually raid beehives and eat honey, in the movie the killer introduces the moth into the victims' throats; he had some fascination with morphing, something moths do, he wished to have a transsexual operation to become or "morph" into a woman. These moths are called by this name because of the unusual pattern on their backs that looks like a skull. In the movie poster these markings are actually Salvador Dali's painting called "Voluptas Mors" also known as "Naked Ladies" it is that of seven naked women posing in positions that give the illusion of a skull.

The insects that usually arrive first are the Diptera, commonly called "Blowflies" and Sarcophagidae, or "Fleshflies." In temperate regions, they will usually arrive within fifteen minutes of death. The female blowflies will lay their eggs on the body, especially around the natural orifices. Eggs will also be laid in any open wounds. Fleshflies do not lay eggs, but…

Manny, interrupting: Natural orifices? You mean ass too.

Ed: Yes Manny, what's your obsession with that anyways?

Pierre continued … will deposit larvae. Blowfly larvae have three "Instars" or stages. The first instar….

Manny interrupting; Oh Yeah! That really bad comedy
with Dustin Hoffman and Warren Beatty.

... is approximately five millimeters long after 1.8 days.
The second instar is approximately ten millimeters long
after 2.5 days, and the third instar is approximately 17
millimeters long after 4 to 5 days, this man has been
dead over 2 days. A more accurate way for forensic
entomologists to determine age of larvae and eggs is
called "rearing." The entomologist raise a test group of
the same blowflies for comparison to those found at the
crime scene. They record the time it took for them to
hatch, and can determine the time it took the hatchlings
on the body to hatch. This is just one example of the
many ways forensic entomologists can estimate time of
death. The succession of various organisms on cadavers
happens in a fairly predictable sequence. As stated
earlier, blowflies and fleshflies arrive first, and as
putrefaction develops, more groups arrive at the scene,
with most groups present just before the body dries out
due to seepage of liquids. There are other insects which
will show up after the body has dried out, which can
provide fairly accurate time of death estimates, three to
six months back, possibly even more. However, the
potassium eye test is the definitive test." _____**18**

CHAPTER 19
WHO WAS IT THAT WHO DONE IT

The phone rang, it was Pierre, "I examined the DNA of the man in the snake and compared it to recent victims; it turns out that Fernando Guarano, the one-armed victim and this man, are related to each other. The letter on his neck appears to be Z." He also added that someone broke into the morgue and had stolen the yellow diamond tooth.

Ed: How related? ... Ed had begun to theorize that there was a connection between the attempt to steal the tooth from this man in the everglades and the fact the victim Fernando Guarano was missing one—"The letter Z, huh! ... Guarano was marked with the letter X; the killer has been a busy boy. There must be another victim In between the two, marked with the letter Y, I wonder why it hasn't turned up, because the killer seems to always make it possible for the police to find them."

Pierre: That I don't know, but a 99.9 match makes him a close relative, too young to be the father too old to be a son, my guess, only for your ears, I would guess his brother.

Ed: Have you told Manny.

Pierre: Not yet.

Ed: He's working on the Fernando Guarano family information, profession, background stuff, he has talked to the Brazilian police, and he is getting ready to brief me.

He killed her in a "Rit of fealous jage."
Inspector Ruben Crusoe had been a gendarme and
detective in the French Sûreté, he had many years of
experience in criminal investigation; now semi retired he
was inspector in the island of Martinique. As far as crime
activity he would say, "Things were so quiet here it felt as
if he was on a deserted island," except for the one
sensational crime not too long ago, nothing was
happening. He had been one of the investigators trying to
identify the European fences that were dealing with
Murph the Surf to sell the Star of India sapphire. He was
a good friend of Manny's father.

He was the one who had called Manny to discuss the
murder of a young woman who had been dating a
Brazilian national in the island of Martinique. Little more
was known about him, he was designated as a person of
interest after the girl had been found dead, her body had
some of the markings of the alphabet assassin, brutally
killed, based on the castings of the wound area, with a
broken sword, but no letter on the neck. She had been
dating this man, but then abruptly broke it off (not the
sword, not his member, the relationship); neighbors had
heard them arguing the night she died.

The description given of the man was that of a limping
David Carradine or a Lance Henriksen from the X-Files
and Hellraiser. Ed thought that the killer was also
suspected of wearing many disguises, so how accurate
could this be. The murder, the inspector suspected, was
committed by an ex-boyfriend who **had killed her in a fit
of jealous rage.**

Ed had a theory that the killer was crazed with
vengeance and was in search of specific targets; he had
been able to combine his search for the persons he

sought, with his chosen profession of contract killer. Nevertheless, why were some marked and others weren't?

He was a serial killer that was also a paid assassin or a paid assassin that was also a serial killer, with a very personal agenda. The killer had turned down lucrative contracts at many locations all over the world, this was known because the clients who had been arrested had indicated that they had asked him to kill again; upping the fee several times, but he had refused. It appeared to them that he was in a hurry to leave and follow someone.

Ed theorized that the killer was following the trail of his prey from Brazil to Miami, to all over the world, including Tahlequah Oklahoma. He also theorized that the Guanaro brothers were the killer's primary target; the others paid the bills and were nothing more than a means to an end. "If we could narrow the search by identifying where and when they traveled and could match it with the itinerary of Brazilian Nationals that met the description of the killer maybe we could find him faster."

The subterfuge of the serial killer's profile and his signature e.g., taking the ears and branding, was a great cover for a killer-for-hire, the police would be looking for a crazy man not a meticulous planner. _____**19**

CHAPTER 20
♪OH! TAHLEQUAH, OUR NATIVE SACRED LAND♪
Sung to the tune of Oh Canada

𝕸anny, through his Brazilian connections, had traced the past of the victim, Fernando Guarano. He was a wealthy Brazilian who had made his money in the precious stone mines of Brazil, he and his brother Alfonzo had gotten very wealthy; they had mansions in Miami and cattle ranches in Oklahoma. Why he was living where he was found was a mystery, although rumors have it that he and his brother Alfonzo had betrayed their partner and stolen the rights to his claims in the mine; all his money and even his fiancé. Perhaps they were trying to hide from family members who were seeking revenge, as the third partner was presumed to have been murdered. Although no body had been found, a bloody shirt and trousers belonging to him had been fished out of the river where he is thought to have drowned.

Ed and Manny had to confirm it, but they were pretty sure it was Alfonzo in the belly of the beast.

The Guarano brothers had left Miami in a hurry, just about the time the Alphabet Assassin started killing there. They traveled extensively all over the world, apparently not wishing to remain fixed for any extended period of time in any one place. They had been known to be living in their ranch in Oklahoma in a little town named Tahlequah.

They decided to schedule a trip to Tahlequah and follow up on the known facts. At the airport entrance, discreetly dressed Hare Krishna's followers greeted them. Ed bowed and said, "Namaste" and told them that he already belonged to the "Khajuraho Temple" religion (a made up sect, it was really an ancient temple adorned with stone carvings depicting various erotic sexual positions) and said that he was a fervent follower and practitioner of their teachings, as found in the Kama Sutra. He then asked if they would be interested in hearing more, he said he had pamphlets he could provide them with on all the details; this little act was sufficient to dissuade them from any further conversion attempts. In fact, they actually scurried away, running from whom, they surely thought was a religious fanatical nut.

Ed and Manny took a flight from Miami to Tulsa. They then took a connecting chartered flight on a small airline, Pilgrim Airways, to Tahlequah; at first, they could not find the gate, so Manny said to the pretty ticket agent at the counter "Where did you park the Mayflower sweetheart?" She smiled and directed them to the gate. This airline had a reputation for crashing, or near crash landings. Because of this, it was commonly referred to as the "Vomit comet." The airline's reputation, together with Manny's inherent fear of flying made Manny more nervous than normal. Manny tended to sing when nervous, his nervousness in turn made him forget the words to the songs, and when in a panicked state of fear he would just makeup lyrics. Ed thought that, perhaps it might be some form of Tourette's syndrome, brought about by stress … or maybe Manny was just crazy. He started singing to the tune of the musical Oklahoma; the lyrics were a bit fractured and quite twisted. Oscar Hammerstein's words "Oklahoma where the wind comes sweepin' down the plain," became "Oklahoma where the wind comes blowing up your skirt." Oscar must have been spinning in his grave.

The stewardess on board was an old, aged "flight attendant," she had logged one too many miles on her "life's flight plan" and because of union work rules she didn't have to retire and could be just as rude as she liked to, in fact it was a requirement. Manny and Ed longed for the old days when stewardesses were female, young, beautiful, kind, and susceptible to the advances of dirty old men. When deplaning, her "bab-by's" at the doorway seem to have an attitude, sounding more like "get out and get off." One could only hope that someday she would be on one of those deadhead flights, that crashed, where the rest of the crew survived but she had been forced to bend over and kiss her ass goodbye.

Tahlequah's only claim to fame was the small state university campus, the cattle and of course the burial place of Mr. Ed, the palomino star of the show by the same name, I say palomino and not blond because, for those who don't know or recall, Mr. Ed "was a horse....of course, as everybody knows of course." I kid you, there is a lot more to Tahlequah, the town was the capital of the Cherokee Nation and is located in the midst of Indian Territory. What was very intriguing about the town was that alphabet assassinations had actually occurred in this sleepy little town. Manny had found out through his police contacts that the Guarano brothers had been contributors to the Tahlequah hospital, the former Rosamund House and to Northeastern University as well as other local institutions, they were in fact model citizens.

Only a few weeks before their arrival, the body of Fernando's wife, Francesca, also a Brazilian, had been found in the basement apartment of the Franklin Castle. She had been mutilated and stabbed with a broken sword, the infamous letter affixed and deeply burned into her neck, it was a "U," together with a large scarlet letter "A," which had been also burned on her chest and colored bright red with blood. Authorities believed the killer knew her, and the murder was possibly the result of jealous rage by an ex-lover. She apparently was killed before Fernando. Two unidentified partial bloody prints were found and sent to inspector Tradeles at the FBI. One was a partial print of a left thumb, the second print was that of the killer's ass. Police concluded that the killer had removed all his clothed prior to the slashing mutilation blows, as this much blood spatter would have surely gotten on his clothes. They surmised that he had killed her while he was nude, then slipped, fell on his ass, and although he wiped the palm prints, he however, overlooked his ass print. Possibly because this large blotch appeared like a random splatter, this oversight on his part would provide positive identification as he had a distinct horizontal scar on his (as Forrest Gump would say) buttocks. The partial thumbprint could not be matched but it would come in handy if and when he was captured.

Alfonzo Guarano's girlfriend, Adsila (Blossom in Cherokee) had also been found murdered. She was a Native American of Cherokee and European heritage. She had been mutilated, although not to the extent that Francesca had been. Her body was found at the bottom of Bailey's Falls; the letter V burned on her neck. Three other Indian girls and their teacher had also been killed; the police believed they had been unsuspecting witnesses that had inadvertently walked in on the killer while on a class hike to the falls. They however were not mutilated or branded. Ed wondered why, and why the letters U, V, had been used, while no victim with a W has ever been found. That should have been the letter before Fernando's X, and why no victim with the letter Y had ever been found after him. It seemed like he had skipped it and had jumped to Z, the letter used to brand his brother. It didn't make sense, unless there were other yet to surface victims.

Trails of blood were everywhere. The tribe mothers and wives as well as the local school paper, the Cherokee Rose Bud, were referring to these murders as the new "Trail of Blood" killings, in reference to the long arduous trip forced on the Cherokee Nation. When the U.S. army had forcefully removed them from their homelands back in 1839, and had made them march without resting to their new relocation site. The police were able to sort the blood types, and after DNA testing, they matched them to the victims. There was one small droplet of O positive blood, which could not be matched; police conjectured that it belonged to the Killer.

Manny turned to Ed and said in a mock Indian parody, "Many long knives come … kill women … rape buffalo."

Ed said in a stern tone …"Not now Manny!"

Manny's eldest sister, Beatriz, was a professor at Northeastern State University for many years, she had a doctorates in psychology (Ed used to call her the Alienist, prior to the twentieth century, persons suffering from mental illness were thought to be alienated, not only from the rest of society but from their own true natures. Those experts who studied mental pathologies were known as alienists) and Manny thought, as did Ed, that it might be a good idea to speak to her about the murders and get some insight into the mind of the killer. She said that she had a personal interest, because the girls that had been killed at Bailey's Falls had been chaperoned by her good friend Emily Lawford, and she had been killed too. Emily was British, and was married to a colleague of hers, a Dr. Lawford, professor of linguistics at the university.

Ed: Had any new visitors arrived just prior to the murders?

Dr. Beatriz: Why yes, a stranger had come into town, said he was a professor on sabbatical from the University of Florence, and was doing some research, he asked many questions about the Guarano brothers and their family and friends. The Guarano brothers were out of town on business; after the murders, they never returned. The stranger said his name was Dr. Azreal; he then left just after the murders.

Ed: What did he look like?

Dr. Beatriz: He had a goatee, thin sharp features, long blondish hair combed back, deep wrinkles, looked a lot like that 1930's scary actor Boris Karloff, or was it John Carradine, no more like Stephen McHattie. Ed showed her all the evidence and Manny filled in the details. She was able to confirm the profile and add important information about the killer's persona.

Ed: Azreal is another name for the angel of death. This killer is unbelievably brazen; he is flaunting himself, and saying, catch me if you can.

Dr. Beatriz: I believe this man is a psychologically disturbed individual, all serial killers demonstrate some form of antisocial personality disorder, along with other psychiatric conditions which cause them to have a distorted view of the world, a view which is fundamentally different from that of other people. There are serial killers that are "organized" serial killers, who put their high intelligence to use when planning their crimes, and "disorganized" serial killers, who strike out in a much less disciplined way. They may possess an intelligence level that is below the norm; this one is definitely in the first category. Some, like Jack the Ripper, are "missionary" serial killers, using their deeds to send a message, and some kill for a sense of power and control. A serial killer is someone who kills at least three victims one by one in a series of sequential murders. They seek this as a form of psychological gratification, which is their primary motive. Psychological gratification distinguishes serial killers from other types of murderers, who usually murder for things like profit or revenge. These killers are compulsive, and always need to perform some form of ritual, or ceremony that must be performed in a certain sequence, this is necessary for them to achieve the maximum gratification from the act. This killer is definitely a sadist, and he maybe sadomasochistic, in that he may also derive pleasure from having pain inflicted on him.

Ed: This case is unusual, as the killer has also murdered for profit.

Dr. Beatriz: Although uncommon, he may be the three types combined, a true "organized" serial killer, a killer for profit, and a "missionary killer," one with specific targets of a personal nature, his mutilation pattern may be his personal message. This killer has special and specific compulsions, as he only brands and mutilates specific targets. The girls and Mrs. Lawford appear to be accidental witnesses and not on his warped agenda, while Francesca and Adsila, Fernando's and Alfonso's wives, were definitely personal murders with a message. Francesca was a perfect example as to what ritualistic killers do, the scarlet letter infers that the killer had a very personal hate for her.

Manny: You know sis I used to be schizophrenic.

Dr. Beatriz: You were?

Manny: Oh Yeah, I used to be schizophrenic but I'm not any more … and neither am I.

Dr. Beatriz: Funny Manny, but what you mean, is dual personality disorder.

Manny: That would never work in the joke … it's too long.

They were staying at the Hard Rock Cherokee Casino Hotel. This was quail hunting season in the Tahlequah region, so they decide to go to lunch at the Echota House Restaurant; it was serving bobtail quail, a common plate for this area, fresh, as it was caught locally. The more adventuresome were having mountain oysters, listed on the menu as balls of fire, or bull's balls … but after the recent crime scene that Ed and Manny had witnessed, where Fernando's testicle had been removed; they thought they would pass. The guys at the next table were a bit more daring, and were having them, one asked, "How come the balls on my plate are smaller than his"… pointing to his buddy's plate. The waiter, a Mexican guy, then said half jokingly and half seriously … "Well ju see señor some times the bull fighter wins and some times the bull wins." Everybody laughed.

Many told the story how one Indian chief would name his kids after the memorable event that had occurred during their conception. The chief went on to tell his children why they were named as such … Rainbow Star, we

named you this because of the rainbow that appeared
after the starry night, your mother and I made love …
You, Thunder Cloud; because you were conceived during
a storm. He then went on like this until the ninth child,
and then he said … and as for you Broken Rubber….

Later that night at the Cherokee Casino Hotel, they had a
drink at the bar; the bartender in a friendly cowboy like
accent asked, "Are you boy's strangers in town?"
"I can give you a guided tour, anything in particular you'd
like to do?" Trying to pickup some extra cash, Ed
guessed. Manny ever the comedian, started doing a very
feeble imitation of John Wayne's walk and talk, he then
said, "Why yes partner I'd like to kiss me an Indian and
wrestle me a pretty girl." Laughing, the bartender said
well I could arrange that too, if that's what you really
want. _____**20**

CHAPTER 21
YOU SAY ZOMBIE, I SAY DRUG INDUCED SEMI CATATONIC STUPOR

Back at home, Ed and Manny were back to following the leads Pierre had developed, by first finding more about Herbert Afortunado's life during the days preceding his death. They went to his office at the bank to speak to his assistant. Mr. Afortunado's assistant, Maggie, had indicated that Herbert Afortunado had been acting strangely during his last days. A man, who was identified only as a Mr. Smith, an acquaintance or friend of the bank president's wife, had accompanied him on his last day.

Maggie: She's Haitian you know … the president's wife.

Ed: Yes, we heard, but tell us, how was he acting strangely?

Maggie: Well, he would not answer a question directly but seemed to require assistance or prompting by this Mr. Smith before he answered; it seemed like he was being led to answer in a particular way.

Ed: Was he being coerced? Did he show signs of fear?

Maggie: No … not exactly, more as if he was being coached in what to say.

Ed: What did this Mr. Smith look like?

Maggie: He was black, very black in fact, I thought that he was unusually black, he was very tall, six-four or five, broad shouldered, looked like a bigger meaner version of Seal. He looked like a bouncer or football player, not the type Mr. A usually would hang around with. I noticed that the passport he had in his pocket was not from the USA. He also had an unusual accent I could not place it, perhaps French, actually now that I have heard the doctor's accent, seems to be faintly reminiscent to that accent, but his was much more pronounced.

Ed: When did this all start?

Maggie: It started a few weeks ago, after Mr. A had returned from lunch with that man.

Ed: Where did they go?

Maggie: Well, Mr. A would often go to lunch at a local bar and grill named the Lucky Leprechaun, a few blocks away, they never came back, and I don't know where they went afterwards, the next day Mr. Afortunado was found dead.

Ed: Thank you Maggie. This Mr. Smith appears to have been speaking Creole; he could be a Haitian National. We'll have to visit the Lucky Leprechaun, and say hello to our good friend Aonghus. Pierre, do you know if a man can be hypnotized to do something against his will?

Dr. Pierre: No, I don't believe so, but I know what can, as I mentioned, I have seen this before, I told you there are some things I can't explain, but I believe that Mr. Afortunado ingested or was injected with what is known throughout Haiti as zombie poison.

Ed thought awhile before questioning the good doctor, recalling his sensitivity issues.

Ed: Come on Doc, now you're sounding more like a witch doctor than a scientist, don't you think this is a little farfetched?

Doc: Not at all, I know that there is a logical explanation for everything; it's just that some things, given the available knowledge, can't be explained. It does explain, however, Mr. Afortunado's passive attitude and submissive behavior. This is why he was willing to follow all leads by this Mr. Smith, whom I now suspect is a Houngan high priest.

Ed: Let's say it's true, so what is the potion?

Dr. De Baptist went on to tell Ed the story, prefacing it by telling Ed that although he is a man of science there are some things that he has not been able to prove or explain by science alone.

Pierre: As I mentioned earlier, a mixture of tetrodotoxin extracted from the fugu fish liver and ovaries and then mixed with other drugs and vegetation found on the island, like rhododendrons and Indian peas; combined they can be made into a potion only known to Voodoo priests who are members of the Bizango secret societies of Haiti. This compound causes zombification when ingested or injected. This causes a person to fall into a death-like trance, which is both drug and culturally induced. Without these additional drugs or herbs, unlike in the movies where the subject is maintained alive even after ingesting a strait dosage of Tetrodotoxin, the subject would die, as his breathing capacity operates on muscles, which would be affected along with the other muscles by the toxin. Only a mixture that dilutes the toxin and enables the breathing function to continue would allow the zombie to function.

Manny: Yeah like that movie a Perfect Citizen or Law Abiding Citizen or something like that, the guy on the operating table would have stopped breathing on straight Tetrodotoxin.

Pierre: Exactly, you need additional drugs that dilute that effect, but still maintain the subject alive and conscious. Zombies do exist, Voodoo priests create them, they are maintained in a death-like trance, or semi-coma, then revived and kept under the control of the Houngan priest by the use of other drugs. There are actually very few of them, zombification is the ultimate punishment, this fate is usually reserved for someone who has seriously violated the law of the Bizango secret society and has betrayed their members. Bizango societies constitute a very secret and hidden other government, operating beneath the surface of Haitian society. People who betray one of the society's members could be subject to this punishment. The bank president's wife is from Haiti, and she is known to be a direct descendant of a prominent and famous, or infamous depending on your point of view, line of Houngans of the Bizango society, it is rumored that she is one of the high priestess or Mambo, the female version of high priest in this society.

Pierre: It is common in the Caribbean to have these Afro-Christian sects. You in Cuba have the Santeria religion where strange rituals' combining the worship of saints with African gods is carried out, the sacrificing of animals, the smoking of cigars by the priests and priestesses, and the indulgence in trances that alter the state of mind is a common practice. These mixtures of religions are sincretic, they meld various types of beliefs and rituals, they came about when the white owners and Christian priests forbade worship of their gods, so practical people that they were, the slaves substituted the saints for their gods, and combined their African Yoruba rites with the Catholic. Chango the most powerful god became St. Barbara, for example. The Catholic priests found it a good process as well, since it eventually led to the gradual conversion of the slaves. These native priests practiced geomancy, like the American Indians, they tossed up bones, pennies, entrails, and other stuff, and then read the future from their pattern and relative positioning on the ground . You know that before the Internet and the evening news, everybody, including Europeans used to do this to forecast the weather and predict the future.

Manny interrupted. They still do a variation of this; my priest draws a circle and throws the money he collects up into the sky. Whatever falls inside the circle he keeps, my Jewish friend said his rabbi does the same thing, but he keeps all that comes down, as he figured that if God wanted it, he would have taken it while it was still up in the air.

Ed: Thank you Manny, for that illuminating insight.

Pierre continued. Now you can find these churches in the Internet, there's even a directory to find you're local Santeria group, it's just like a Tupperware party, where you can buy the latest and the greatest charms and amulets , you could probably by one of the containers to keep the leftover sacrificial goat parts. You can even attend rituals at the established church of Lukumi Babalu Aye, you can sing along with the priests, known as babaleros or fathers of Orisha, right here in Miami. Get them to perform a "babalao" at your home and on yourself, to rid it and you of evil spirits; a babalao is a kind of exorcism. I think they use cigar smoke instead of holy water … you should like that Ed.

Ed: Funny Doc …You, my friend ... have been hanging around Manny, way too much. With all this talk of zombies i.e. the undead; Ed was thinking this would be a good time to have the powers of a real paladin.

Ed: I am beginning to think Afortunado was not in on the fraud after all; we'll go to his house right after we visit the latest crime scene.

Ed went on. "Let's say this is all true and possible, what happened then to Susan Boyl the assistant VP?"

Dr. Pierre: I am glad you asked, because the body has not been released for burial, so after you informed me of the related deaths, I proceeded under the assumption that foul play may have been the cause of her death too.

At first, it was reported as another accidental death due to suffocation from carbon monoxide poisoning, as a result of using a gas grill to warm her house. But again, just as in Mr. Afortunado's case, none of the supposedly causing agents, water in Mr. Afortunado's case, and carbon monoxide gas in this case, could be found in the lungs, proving that the victim had stopped breathing before she had a chance to inhale the gas. Then the rope was found and the damage to the throat noted, no ligature marks by the rope could be identified, death had occurred before hanging. I performed the same test on Ms. Boyl and again large amounts of tetrodoxin were found.

Inspector Tradeles has the rope, he believes it is a slam-dunk, open and shut case of suicide. I do not believe this; the killer I think was staging a suicide, In fact, as noted in my autopsy I do not believe she hanged herself but rather was hoisted up by the murderer, maybe you can convince Tradeles, because he was not convinced, and has asked for you, he is expecting you.

Ed: We'll go to Miss Boyl's house to check it out.

THE ROSE- A prostate exam by any other name would still not smell like a rose.
Pierre: You know it's that time of the year again.
Ed would soon be getting a rose by UPS. Pierre was not only a good friend but also Ed's doctor, what he meant was that it was time for Ed's annual checkup. Ever since his first prostate exam, the Doc had sent him a rose as a reminder, this came about because of Ed saying to Pierre, after that first exam: "You know Doc the least you can do after you have gotten so personal and intimate with me is to buy me flowers and take me out to dinner!"

Pierre would say during the exam. "Now this is going to hurt you more than me. Turn your head and cough … just kidding that's another examination."

Ed: Take it easy Doc; after all, you're not digging for gold down there.

Pierre: It's either this or a colonoscopy, what would you rather have, my two small delicate fingers or a long rigid pole up your rectum.

Ed: That reminds me of a joke. A witness in West Virginia is describing an accident to a cop; he is surrounded by women and small children, as he said,

"The truck smacked the guy right in the ass," the cop noticing the small children, corrects the man and said, "You mean rectum." The guy then says ... " Rect-him, hell! Damn near killed him."

Ed: I hate to say this, but your intromission and extensive probing is beginning to stimulate me; does that make me a player for the other team?

Pierre: Not at all, is only natural, didn't you see the movie; I'll Sleep When I'm Dead, with Clive Owens?

Ed: I can't say that I have.

Pierre: Well, the guy's brother gets raped and he unintentionally, you know ... activates.

Ed: That is sick.

Pierre: No, that's physiology.

Pierre: You know Ed, looking at your physique reminds me of the Naviwang legend.

Ed: What's that Doc?

Pierre: Well, it's the real reason why humans resent the Navi, and why they wear such long loincloths.

Ed: What are you talking about Doc?

Pierre: The Navi are a very well endowed people, and this embarrassed the humans, this is why the humans really resented them, and it is also why they never wanted to shower with the Navi in gym class. They are also the only ones in the camp that could carry two cups of coffee and a dozen doughnuts at the same time.

Ed: I didn't know you were a sci-fi geek Doc. … By the way, that is a racial stereotype Doc.

Pierre: Is it?

Ed: You know Doc, you are beginning to worry me…you are really, really sounding way too much like Manny.

A fart ripped through the room, and Pierre said to Ed ... "You shouldn't be embarrassed Ed, that's Ok too, that too is also natural."

Ed: But I didn't fart, it was you who farted!

Pierre: I know ... I picked up that little subterfuge from a TV doctor show.

A tradition was born, after the exam Pierre would invite him to a feast of Cuban pork sandwiches and beer. He picked up the tab, after all the cost of the exam was exorbitant and the insurance company was paying for it.

With everything now in good shape, having played hand puppet to the good doctor's hand, he could now continue with the matter at hand.

Sizzle, thistle, poison, or strangulation.
They asked the building superintendent, Ramon, to take them to Miss Boyl's apartment, he then said, "Oh jes its dee big laydee with the pig face." Ed, not whishing anybody to speak ill of the dead, was a bit offended by this comment and went on to defend the dead lady's honor…(when he wanted to speak with authority he

would use his best American Dad's tone of voice). He then said … "Ramon, although it may be accurately descriptive, it's not a very nice thing to say about a deceased lady."

Ramon: Oh no señor, ju do not understand, I meant she had a pig face on the wall, ju no … a jabali; her husband was a good hunter ju no!

As they entered the burnt apartment, they could see the partial remains of a mounted boar's head on the floor. Inspector Tradeles was leaning towards suicide as the cause of death. She had been found with hemp or thistle rope around her neck that had been flung over a wooden beam, parts of a toppled chair were found on the floor as well as a broken glass; the room had then been torched.

Ed examined the photographs of the scene and the rope, noting the positioning of the rope and then he examined the rope fibers. He noticed that the direction of the loose ends of the rope fibers, not unlike hair, were raised against the grain, un-matted and sloping in the opposite direction, towards the hangman's noose … and not their normal way of laying flat and matted . They were scuffed and forcibly pushed in the opposite direction. He concluded that this had been a homicide.

Inspector Tradeles: What can possibly make you reach that conclusion?

Ed: Elementary my dear Tradeles. The reason the fiber ends point towards the hangman's knot, is that the body, with the noose around the neck was hoisted up rather than it falling down. The scraping of the rope was caused by it being pulled across the beam, when the body was being raised up. This caused the fibers to lean in the opposite direction of their normal position as the body was raised. Had she hanged herself the weight of her body falling downward would cause the fibers to lay flat matting in their normal position.

Inspector Tradeles: Yes, I can see that, but how could any one lift a woman that big while she is struggling?

Doc: I already examined the body for toxins and I also examined the broken glass, there were residues of a toxin. This drug most likely rendered the victim unconscious; he then killed her by strangulation, prior to her body being lifted. This person practiced overkill, as there is evidence of ligature strangulation, not with the rope but with panty hose.

Inspector Tradeles: That's what I'm saying she was hanged.

Doctor Pierre: Well, it's not exactly the same, though the mechanism of strangulation is very similar to hanging. Strangulation is carried out by the use of some form of cord, or as in this case stockings, which were used by the killer to squeeze the neck, while death by hanging is caused by the weight of the body. I believe, based on the marks around the neck, he used support stockings first. The strangling force, as Ed has pointed out, did not come from the bodyweight, as she was already dead. The rope was used merely to stage the suicide.

My autopsy concluded that complete occlusion of the carotid arteries caused by the hanging was post mortem. Ligature strangulation is distinguished from hanging in that the method does not use the victims body weight as the source of the strangulation, as Ed and I believe is this case. Cases of ligature strangulation are common in homicides of women, children, and elderly persons. She was drugged, then strangled, and finally hanged for effect; the fire was another cover-up.

There was significant lividity above the ligature mark on her neck and pronounced lividity in the extremities of the arms and legs, due to hanging. After the six-hour mark, lividity is fixed as blood vessels begin to break down within the body. Ms. Boyl has been dead more than six hours but less than ten based on the degree of rigor. Rigor Mortis is the rigid stage; it is the stiffening of the body after death, caused by the loss of Adenosine Triphosphate (ATP) from the body's muscles. ATP is the substance that allows energy to flow to the muscles and help them work, without this, the muscles become stiff and inflexible. Rigor normally appears within the body around two hours after the deceased has passed. It normally lasts anything from eight to twelve hours after which time the body is completely stiff; this fixed state lasts for up to another eighteen hours. Rigor Mortis begins throughout the body at the same time. However, the body's smaller muscles-- such as those in the face, neck, arms, and shoulders are affected first and then the subsequent muscles. Those which are larger in size, are affected later, this is why I can say from experience that she has been dead more than six hours but less than ten based on the degree of rigor.

Contrary to common perception, the process of Rigor Mortis actually does reverse and the body returns to a flaccid state. Total reversal occurs … well in reverse, where the last larger organs become flexible first; and so on. This process takes a total of 36 to 48 hours to reverse in total. The doctor went on; the teacher in him just could not be silenced. Lividity is the process through which the body's blood supply will stop moving after the heart has stopped pumping it around the body of the deceased. What normally happens is that the blood will settle in direct response to gravity. Lividity displays itself as a dark purple discoloration of the body. It is also referred to as Livor Mortis or Post Mortem Hypostasis.

Ted Bundy used support stockings, I believe his preference was the brand Hanes, he had stated calmly and matter of fact like, as though he was talking about a cooking utensil used by Julia Childs, that it had a stronger tensile strength than others did, and that it made the ideal garrote of choice for ligature strangulations. We found a knotted panty hose in a hamper, examination of the epidermis particles on it will determine if it was used on her throat.

Manny said, so the woman had been killed, and then hung.

Ed jokingly corrected Manny by saying pictures are hung people are hanged. The fire, he went on to say, was a distraction, sometimes a killers motto, like Prometheus is, "When in doubt, set something on fire."

Manny: Unless it's me, I haven't been hanged but I'm really hung.

Ed: Real funny Manny, real funny.

Manny: Let's go get some black beans and rice and some Cuban Palomilla steaks or maybe a Churrasco.

Ed: I'm game! _____**21**

CHAPTER 22
THE QUEEN OF POLITICAL CORRECTNESS

Ed had arranged to meet with Marta Gutierrez, the Chandler Bank Vice President of Public Relations. The Lettuce-Entertain-You bistro, as one would expect from the name, was like a high class grassing pasture, no eating of real food here. The crowd was made up of skinny women and metro-sexual men chomping down on leaves, drinking diet colas and imported bottled water, Perrier seemed to be the liquid of choice; how much more snooty than that could you get; after all Zephyrhills was better, cheaper and local.

These excessively tanned Lady Madonna's with designer gym bags and dogs at their feet, had made a solemn vow that," No meat shall pass these sacred lips." Their goal, apparently, was to live forever, and if this was not possible, then leave a healthy looking corpse that could be cryogenically frozen, to be reanimated at a later date when science would allow it. If only they could afford it, this was their dream, the eternal life of a god. This was the generation of the impossibly thin and the impossibly healthy. Just as this "me-generation" had accepted the cult of the outward appearance of wealth, they had also accepted the cult of impossible health, while ignoring conscience and real self-development.

All you could hear was the crackling of the crispy lettuce all around you. It sounded, in the relative silence of the place (as this wasn't your typical Cuban restaurant where you couldn't hear yourself think, let alone hold a conversation) like a swarm of the three-year locust clamoring in a sea of green that was being devoured by YUPPIE grasshoppers. I would have said a herd of cows, but they were so skinny, I mean so skinny! Every rib of their ribcage was visible, every vertebrae exposed on their necks, if one were to look up anorexic or bulimic (or is it "Nourishment challenged" now?) in the dictionary or googled images on the Web, a photo of one these gals would surely pop up. It was a virtual runway of leathery-skinned emaciated model wannabes; apparently, the withered and gaunt look of a starving Ethiopian Kate Moss was back.

What they didn't know or cared to know, (As they were mostly into themselves and primarily interested as to what they looked like in a dress to other women, and not necessarily how attractive they appeared to men) is that an abundant and soft woman, not unlike the women in Dali's Voluptas Mors painting, always looks, and feels better naked.

Here, sitting like the queen locust (if there is such a thing) was Marta Gutierrez the VP responsible for the Chandler Bank PR department. She had a master's in business from Harvard, and was currently working on her PHD at the University of Miami; she was renowned as a master spin-doctor in the PR circles. She had a reputation for being smart and charming, but it was also said that if you got on her bad side, man or women she could figuratively castrate you (if that were possible for women) with a stare or a verbal retort.

The grass diet had served her well; she was slim but curvy. She was also an exercise freak, so no moss or green of any kind would grow under that shapely ass; it was tighter than a drum, and outstanding like a shelf, you could place two margarita glasses on it without fear of a spill. Her rock hard abs were cut like a washboard, while her large and firm breasts defied gravity. Although obviously enhanced, that is to say "the big valley" between them was more of a man made "silicone valley" rather than a natural formation; the deep cleavage created was nonetheless attractive. Surely, she had laid down a few thou for that improvement. The protruding nipples threatening to pierce her tight T-shirt were as round and long as that of the first knuckle of my pinky. They seemed to be the first part of her body to enter a room. She knew they aroused men, and played them for all they were worth.

Miami was a throwback city, going back to before the feminist movement, and she, like most Miami Latin girls had never gotten the feminist memo on how to dress for the movement. Although she had adopted the castration of men part, in section two of the little red book of Mao-feminist readings, she had chosen to disregard the section on fashion. She still wore the blouses that showed ample cleavage and the semi miniskirts and high heels that accentuate her long legs, typical to the dress code for all Miami women. The Miami female newscasters and weather girls (Or should I say weather meteorologists) on Telemundo were the sexiest dressed media people in the country.

She said, "You do look a bit like the early James Bond"; Ed had described himself as younger looking Latin Sean Connery or a Gerard Butler. "You know ... with a beard, you'd look a bit like he looks today."

He said, ... in his best imitation of Sean Connery," Why thank you Mish Money-Penny."

"Now you spoiled the illusion ... whose voice was that you were imitating anyways ... Holly Hunter's?"

Ed: Sorry.

Ed said that Mr. Chandler had recommended that he speak with her so he could get some sense of the bank's staff ... and of course the skeletons.

He asked about Susan Boyl.

She said, "Mr. Afortunado's assistant VP; she died, and they say it was a suicide."

Ed: I'll have to update you on both Mr. Afortunado and Susan; the Miami medical examiner has performed some follow up tests and determined they were both murdered.

Marta: Murdered?

Ed: Yes.

Marta: By whom ... why?

Ed: I am working on the whom... him, her or them and the who, he, she or they-- the why ... you as a portrayer of favorable images, will want to know, appears to be the need to hide corruption at the bank. The FBI is currently conducting an ongoing criminal investigation on this matter.

Marta: I suspected something was going on there.

Ed: Do you know if anything out of the ordinary occurred just before their deaths?

Marta: All I can tell you is that Ms. Du Poi, the president's wife and VP of the bank, had taken an interest in the department Mr. Afortunado managed. There had been some arguments, the details I do not know, but shortly after Ms. Du Poi introduced Mr. Afortunado to a strange black man, a Mr. Smith, I had heard he was asking many questions and he too argued with Mr. Afortunado. Also, I have been following these alphabet murders and I can tell you for a fact that many of these victims were individuals that had dealings with her; I met many of them at the bank. Are you a detective?

Ed: No, not really I am an internal auditor.

Marta: What's the difference between that and a regular?

Ed: About fifty thousand dollars more, just kidding, I audit institutions to determine that the internal controls over their financials, administrative functions, systems and operations are working properly … a combination of compliance, efficiency, effectiveness and security check, if you will. As financial auditors, the CPA firm members, the "regulars" are primarily concerned with the reliability of reported financial information and regulatory compliance. They spend a great deal of their time ticking and tying of balances.

Marta: Oh, they certify the financials.

Ed: Not exactly, they issue an opinion. Sometimes, I do a little extra internal auditing type work and forensic accounting, for special clients like Mr. Chandler.

Marta: Why do they need auditing I thought banks were honest?

Ed: They are honest, audits just keeps them that way.

Marta: I'll keep my eyes open and inform you on anything that will help you, as per Mr. Chandler's orders. Lets get together sometime and have sushi, I know how to roll a California roll, come over, and you can have some of my homemade Australian sushi or a roll.

Ed: Australian sushi, never heard of it, what's that?

Marta: You know … way down-under.

Ed: I'd love to have some of your fresh sushi, and a roll with you would certainly be pleasurable, but at the moment I'm tied up with this case, I'll have to take a rain check on that. For some reason thoughts of her in tight leather pants, stiletto heels and a whip by her side, while he was literally tied up, flashed in his mind, something he had never experimented with before but was game to try.

Surprisingly they sold a damn good piece of fudge there, he had bought a piece and offered it to Marta. She refused it at first, until Ed, in his best imitation of Max von Sydow, picked it up, and using it like an exorcist's cross, said, "The power of fudge compels you, the power of fudge compels you," so she took a bite. This apparently did the trick of exorcising the most dreaded of demonic entities (even more dreaded than Pazuzu or was it Isuzu) that seems to take possession of many a young American female –the much feared demon, "Anorexia Verbose," also known as the ancient one; father Merrin and his sidekick, father Damien would have been proud.

After munching on the rabbit food, Ed called Manny,

"Man I am hungry, lets go to Los Ranchos and get some of those Argentinean steaks," I'm game said Manny.

_____**22**

CHAPTER 23
AN EPIPHANY, NEITHER A MEDICAL PROCEDURE NOR A GREEK PASTRY
A Mexican forecast, chili today, hot tamale
The day shimmered in the sun!

Mayling softly growled then snorted several times as she did when she was being ignored, and then barked, stood by the side of the bed and licked Ed's face, then she bit the sheet and pulled it off Ed's sleeping body. This dog refused to be ignored, she was always there wagging her tail to say good morning, greet you at the door, and say good night. "What a loyal creature hath God thus created," he thought. Manny would say that if your wife and your barking dog are outside, you should only let in the dog, because he at least would stop bitching once inside.

Ed lovingly said, "Damn you, you little Shit ... Sue, why can't you let me sleep."

He opened the window glancing at the bougainvilleas he and Katy had planted; they glowed with a crimson iridescent hue in the Florida sun, going from purple to violet to red. The sky glistened, the sea shimmered the ... GRRRRSSSSHHHHHHH!

Ed: Ah! Shit what now.

His dog, or I should say their dog as he and Katy held joint custody, had just bumped in to the nightstand where Ed was playing an old record LP (long Play) on one of those new fangled machines, (He was over thirty and thought it was time to start talking like an old codger) that allow you to play and convert the record to a CD. The arm with the needle had run across the record making that noise that disk jockeys purposely make at a disco party. She was a little "Shit … Sue" as he called her, weighed only twelve pounds but the table was wobbly.

As a devout bachelor, he thought the most difficult thing when families with kids, as well as regular couples break up, is … who is going to get the dog, as far as he was concerned the woman should keep the kids, the custody of the dog on the other hand he thought, would be the biggest, well … bone-of-contention. Heck! With the kids, she can keep them!

I'm glad the dog interrupted my soliloquy he thought, I was beginning to sound to myself like a tourist, they seemed to overuse adjectives like glimmer, shimmer, sparkled, gleamed, glistened, glowed, glittered and the like; for cripes sake! This is Florida, the sunshine state; every free-ken thing does that. The sky, the ocean, the sand, buildings, glass, car hoods, stop signs … cripes! Every piece of metal shines, glows, reflects, glimmers, even the sun lotion soaked rear ends of the German and Canadian tourists did that. You ask how he would know if they are tourists, well, acclimated Floridians, similar to a vampire's aversion to light, can only tolerate water temperatures that are over 80 degrees; as such, you will not find them by the ocean during the winter months.

He thought of the dog transfer day. This transfer usually would take place on the weekends, when Katy would come and pick up the dog. She'd come in and pick Mayling up, then sing her a made up little song, to the tune of the Mickey Mouse club theme --"Whose the best doggy in the world that's made for you and me, M A Y…

why, because we love you, Maylingy, Wingy, Dingy." She had another when she would put the dog in the pool, this one was to the tune of the Flipper TV show ..."They called her Maylingy Wingy the wonderful dog"...You'd have to be there.

He listen to the weather report on the TV, the announcer said is going to be another shimmering day in Florida, a little bit chilly today, but hot tomorrow. He then poured a big Cuban coffee and toasted some Cuban bread.

Epiphany 1 confusion 0 .
Ed was already formulating the theory that two different killers were involved. He knew that the Alphabet Assassin was the killer of Armandito, his cousin, while the other was the killer of Herbert Afortunado and his assistant Ms. Boyl. He speculated that the second was the one that somehow was associated with Haiti, Madam Du Poi and the bank, the one who would have the knowledge of the paralyzing drug, the zombie drug.

He also speculated that his cousin's murder was arranged at a time when the Alphabet Assassin was still a very mysterious man, an unknown quantity, and murders were being attributed to a serial killer rather than an assassin. The killer had been profiled at first as a sociopath serial killer, a good cover to deflect attention from casting him as a contract killer. This ruse made him more valuable as it would redirect the police's attention away from his true motives and related leads. However, the killer's value as a contract killer had diminished a great deal once it became common knowledge that he was paid for the murders. This awareness would cause prospective clients to shy away. This is most likely why the poison killer had been engaged, because as a member of a clandestine society, to which Madame Du

Poi belonged, he could be trusted with secrets and not attract undue attention. One string was beginning to tie it all together; many of the victims had a direct relationship to the bank and the mortgage investment scam. Armandito, Afortunado, Boyl, and the bank executives killed around the world all had connections to the Chandler Bank.

The Alphabet Assassin wore disguises; apparently, he was a master of makeup. He would alter the way he walked and talked, he could pass himself off as a doctor and sometimes as a professor. Eyewitnesses were describing him as a middle aged David Carradine or Boris Karloff or Peter Weller or Stephen McHattie or Lance Hendriksen. Shit, they all look alike; if you were a casting director, any one could substitute for the other, except the dead ones. All of this deliberate and by design, He wanted to confuse the police and make it more difficult and time consuming for them to catch him.

————————————**23**

CHAPTER 24
THE AMERICAN DREAM, TO HAVE FRIENDS IN LOW PLACES

Manny and Ed decided to visit Umberto Afortunado at his father's home. Umberto was Herbert Afortunado's son, Berto as he liked to be called, had telephoned to discuss the investigation of his father's death, and mentioned that he may have a lucrative opportunity for Castillo. This was the second time in several weeks he had heard his name associated with the word lucrative.

Berto was a YUCA (Young Upwardly-mobile Cuban American) lawyer and successful real estate venture capitalist, a good line of work for Florida, only owning an amusement park or a gold mine was better, real estate investments a close third, unless you were a Miccosukee Indian who just happened to own a casino. They had gotten so rich that they were hiring white men to do the alligator wrestling. Apparently, after several unfortunate incidents of alligator wrestling, many of the tribe Indians had unwontedly acquired the nickname of lefty, and because of this, they felt that this particular dangerous display for tourist should be left to the hired help. They, however, did continue the erection of Chikee huts, because according to Florida law only native American Indians were granted this right.

They met at his father's house in Delray, a beautiful seaside mansion on the intracoastal. He took them outside to talk, it was a beautiful day and the ocean view was spectacular, the water shimmered (yes he knew what he had thought about these adjectives, tourist and

Florida, but it really did) the house was none-too-shabby, built on a point lot; it had water on three sides. Umberto then gave them the grand tour.

The mansion had Carrara marble floors and columns, library, media room, one hundred inch TV, top of the line sound system, directly across this wall was a gigantic Oolite fireplace set in a sixteen-foot high wall made of bright white and highly polished Oolite. The bathrooms included Jacuzzi tubs, multi head showers, Chinese Honey Onyx tile on the walls, floors and ceiling, marble tub, steam bath and sauna spa. The gourmet kitchen had cherry cabinets, French door oversized Kitchen-Aid refrigerator, professional gas and induction stoves. There was a separate room for massages, the schedule was on the wall, and poor Herbert had missed his last one. This guy would get daily full body massages followed by the hot tub and a quick splash in the eternity edge pool that seemed to merge with the ocean behind it ... Manny of course wondered if a "happy ending" was included in the massage service.

Next on the tour were the sculptures and statues, Picasso drawings and Wilfredo Lam oil painting. Ed recognized it because his grandfather, a Basque immigrant back in Cuba had one of the San Sebastian coastline and the Bay of Biscay hung by the bar. This was a realistic painting, before Lam started painting modern abstractions. Ed had discussed the painting's dimensions and detail with a dealer at a Miami art show and found out that it was probably worth more than half a million dollars, even more if sold through an auction house, some place like Sotheby's. If the Castro government had discovered it, it now surely hung in one of the bastard's many homes. Ed was going to mention it to Umberto, but since he didn't have it, it was not something he could gloat about. It wasn't just the wealth and the good taste of his family he wanted to convey, but more importantly their power and influence. In the study's library were several collectible and valuable first editions, while on the walls hung photographs of Berto with his father, Jimmy Carter, Reagan, the Bushes, the Clintons, and the Obamas. They weren't your typical assembly line posed-for-pictures taken at political rallies. They were more personal, as many where taken in the patio of this house. Berto added "We contribute to both parties; you got to cover all your bases you know." There were pictures with foreign heads of state, other dignitaries, and powerful people from the media, computer companies, and other industries. You name them, and they were there. Ed thought, no wonder rich people have their bodies or heads cryogenically frozen, so one day they can come back, and continue to enjoy the best, life can offer.

Berto showed him a priceless Pre-Columbian urn, for a moment he thought about asking how much it was worth, but thought it would be impolite, and besides as the saying goes … If you have to ask.…

Manny Asked, what's a pre-Columbian urn?

Berto: About one bushel of corn an hour … just a little pre –Columbian joke.

Manny: You know what I would do if I won the Florida LOTTO?

Ed: No, what?

Manny: I'd spend half on wine, women, and song.

Ed thought, and why should it be any different from the way he spends it now.

Ed: What would you do with the other half Manny?

Manny: Oh, I'd just piss it away.

Berto talked of his grandfather and the tree nursery he had started that had made all this possible. He pointed to the sixty-foot plus high palms that encircled the patio; they made the backyard look like some palace from the Middle East. "You know what kind they are," Berto asked; Ed said, "I am not sure but they could be Canary or Sylvester," Berto--"That's right, they are Canary island date palms or Phoenix canariensis, you can tell because of the pineapple bulblike top, the Sylvester is more slender and shorter with a blue green hue. My abuelito (his grandfather) planted these palms over forty years ago. These palms, if you were to buy them at retail would run you about $30,000.00 or more each, if you can find them in this size." There were twenty planted semi-circularly around the patio, another twenty lined the driveway. "The first crop he planted he used to buy a house, the second to put my father and his brothers through college, the third was for his retirement. It was a great capital investment as the value increased annually, faster than the consumer price index, better returns than Wall Street." The palms were a living growing piggy bank. These were over sixty feet, they take from ten to twenty years to mature and sell for about five-hundred dollars per foot.

"Did you know there are no canaries in the Canary Islands, well the name really was meant to be the "Dog islands." When the Romans first landed there, the islands were full of dogs, and Canare means dog in Latin."

Ed: Did not know that.

Berto: My father bought this house, helped my grandfather plant these palms; he was hardworking, honest, and unlike me, he was not born with a silver spoon in his mouth. They were sugar brokers back in Cuba, had their own firm, abuelito told me the other day that based on world sugar prices and the volume he used to move, his commission would have been over two million dollars, not too shabby huh Ed? Ed nodded his head in agreement trying to remain agreeable and build camaraderie in between Berto's itemization of his assets. Ed said, "My grandfather … my "aitona" … that's Basque for grandfather, was also a sugar broker."

Berto was fit, tan and trim, looked like a fortyish Julio Iglesias. He asked for Ed's help, because he felt the private-eyes and police were spinning their wheels, and he had heard good things from good sources of his work.

Berto: I have it on good account from reliable influential sources in high places, that you are tenacious and resourceful.

Ed said, "Really what sources? I only have friends in low places!"

Berto: Well Mr. Castillo you seem to have a friend in a high place now, a very influential friend … Mr. Randolph Chandler called me and recommended you.

Ed: I'm already on that project … eh … case.

Berto: That's Ok, we both agreed to pay you because we know its going to take time and you'll have to look into the other murders associated with my father and his assistant VP Susan Boyl ... as well as others I'm sure. In addition, I know that you're looking into financial issues for Randolph. We want you to succeed, find the bastard, and bring him to us first.

Ed thought about that last sentence, Old-man Chandler had said the same thing. It appeared to Ed that these rich self-made men were readily disposed to taking matters into their own hands and not leaving it to the police or chance.

Berto: You know, my abuelito was a trained sniper and is an expert marksman; he trained with the Cuban forces that invaded the Bay of Pigs. He is quite a sharpshooter; with a mounted telescope, he can still shoot the balls of a fly at 1000 yards, without disturbing its pecker. Last year he bought a fifty caliber BMG (12.7 mm) McMillan TAC-50 bolt-action rifle, same gun used in the longest sniper kill ever, by Corporal Rob Furlong, a sniper from Newfoundland. The longest range recorded for a sniper shot currently stands at 2,430 meters (2,657 yd, or 1.51 miles),The second longest was by Carlos Norman Hathcock II, I think he was Cuban.-- Ed didn't think so, that guy, Hathcock, was born in Arkansas, another sergeant York. Berto continued, "My abuelito practices once a week, you know." Berto gestured pointing to a little old man pruning the flowers nearby ... "there he is now." The little old man with the straw hat looked just like the rest of the Latin American gardeners feverishly pruning the magnificent gardens.

"Not only do Randolph and myself have a personal interest in this case, but I also have another friend, Edward Kerrigan, a very wealthy man, makes me look like a hobo, his family was victimized by this assassin too. I don't know if you are aware but his brother was murdered too, he was a board member at the Chandler bank. Teddy thinks of himself as some sort of captain courageous, he even bought one of the old sailing ships used in a past Americas Cup race.

Ed: You do know; it may not have been the Alphabet Assassin that killed your father.

Berto: Doesn't matter, just find the bastard! Maybe we can go out some time on my yacht I have a 55 ft Talaria and … Ah! Here he is.

Kerrigan: Hello, I see that you are my "tocayo" (Spanish for namesake) I am Teddy.

Ed thought, of course you are, if you were not rich you'd be Eddie.

Ed had heard his name before, he was richer than God, had cleaned-up as a lawyer, getting a huge chunk of the class-action lawsuit against the tobacco companies. As is more often than not, the only ones who benefit in large legal disputes are the lawyers; they always reaped the juiciest plums of the financial harvest. Kerrigan had an enormous house in Palm Beach on US 1, rivaling Trumps Mar-a-Lago, the former home of Marjorie Meriwether Post, the cereal heiress. Both houses had frontage on the Intracostal and on the beach side. You could moor your 100 ft yacht on one side and dip your big toe in the Atlantic on the other.

Ed said, "I'd like you to meet my associate Manny."

Kerrigan: Oh! I know Manny very well.

Ed: You do?

Kerrigan: Manny's father and my father were yachting buddies, made lots of trips to Colombia, mainly to Barranquilla and Medellin. You may not remember, Manny, most trips were in the dead of night.

Manny: Oh, I remember … How are you doing Teddy.

Kerrigan: Nice to see you again, nice shirt by the way, mine is a Kenneth Cole what's yours?

Manny: Mine is a Pen'ey original.

Kerrigan: Don't think I ever heard of that designer; have to ask the wife, see if she can pick me up a dozen or so.

Ed, as an aside to Manny: I think he let the cat out of the bag on the source of some of his wealth, same as your dad's was … and a Pen'ey original, come on Manny!

Manny: Sure a JC Penney original … I didn't lie. My pants are from Tar 'get.

Kerrigan: You guys have to come fishing with me sometime, on my boat the Lucky Lady, it's a 160 footer Christensen, and It's bigger than Tiger Wood's 155 footer.

Ed thought about that old adage −"The difference between men and boys, is the price of their toys," but didn't say anything.

Manny said that Tiger had a new sponsor.

Kerrigan, Who?

Manny: Trojan Condoms, their slogan under Tiger's image says "for those who are tired of playing the same hole, over and over again."

Kerrigan laughed, "Good one Manny," ... Kerrigan's bragging then went on.

Ali with the Large Member.
Ed was getting a little resentful about all this macho bragging as to who had the biggest ... boat, so out of the blue he said, "You know leading world physiologist agree that the size of a man's yacht is inversely proportionate to the size of his penis." He wasn't sure of these statistics but it sounded good.

A long pause ensued during which no one said anything.

Ed could see a bit of annoyance on their faces, his next thought was "What kind of idiot am I, I'm going to lose these contracts. "

Manny, always the wingman, tried to break the ice and save Ed's ass. ..."Yeah! You got to consider this is coming from a man that only owns a dingy." --No reaction from the crowd.

Ed quickly and in an unbroken flurry of words added in rapid succession:

Billionaire Nasser Al-Rashid owns The Lady Moura, a $210 million 344-foot mega-yacht.

The Octopus, owned by Microsoft co-founder Paul Allen, is the world's eighth largest yacht at 414-foot.

The Rising Sun, a $200 million dollar yacht co-owned by Oracle's Larry Ellison and media mogul David Geffen, is 453 foot long. The Dubai is a $350 million yacht that has a new name; the Platinum, is a 525 footer, owned by some sheik. The Eclipse will be $1.2 billion super-yacht and at 560-foot a real monster when completed, it is owned by Russian billionaire and Chelsea football club owner Roman Abramowitz.

Ed: Now you know these guys really, really have a real serious problem with the size of their dicks!

They all laughed loud and long. Kerrigan then said, "You're Ok Ed, you're Ok" ... It sounded to Ed a bit condescending like "That'll do pig-- that'll do"... Ed had saved his own ass!

Kerrigan: I want you to investigate my brother's death, I'll make it lucrative for you! We , my father and I, need ... what's that ephemeral euphemistic politically correct term Ah! Yes ... closure ... more importantly we want vengeance!

Ed: I love the sound of that word ... lucrative and I like the way you think!

Ed thought I'm beginning to like these rich guys, I guess it's true what they say, "How can you soar with the eagles when you are surrounded by turkeys?" Manny came to mind when he had this thought.

Manny said, "Man you pulled your ass out of the fire, how'd you know all that shit?" ... That's right! I forget the ... Internet."

This beautiful Bo Derek look-alike girl walked out onto the patio, Kerrigan introduced her as Catalina Calor. This nymphet could not have been more than twenty, She said hello and something, something, about parking her "carr," they really weren't paying attention to what she was saying … too busy just ogling her body.

Catalina walked over to Ed and said, "Hello I'm Catalina Clarice Calor."

Ed: Guess your friends call you Cat or Kitty.

Catalina: Nope.

Ed: CC?

Catalina: Wrong again.

They call me Pussy, because friends of mine… real James Bond fanatics, said that in one of the old movies there was a character that reminded them of me.

Ed: Were they guys?

Catalina: Yes, how did you know?

Ed: Just a hunch, what are you studying?

Catalina: Forensics, I'm doing an internship at the Miami city morgue, I supplement my income by doing exotic dancing at a club in South Beach.

Ed: You must know Dr. Pierre.

Catalina: Why yes! I often run errands for his assistant.

Catalina: Hey, you know, you look a little bit like that guy in the old James Bond movies.

Ed: Some people say that.

She was from Boston, Ed could tell by the accent and the way she pronounced words like car, she would say "carr."

He said you're from Boston aren't you.

Catalina: How'd you know?

Ed: By the accent and the way you pronounce certain words, it's a very charming accent (he really thought it sounded more like a speech impediment but wasn't about to tell this gorgeous girl that). Spaniards also seem to have an accent that is close to a speech impediment. They seem to use the sound of the letter z a lot, sounding a great deal like a Spanish speaking Sylvester the cat, you know "Zuffering' Zuccotash."

She was flirtatious and very forward … damn dirty he thought. Ed happened to be alone with her and she made a very aggressive and forward comment, she said, "You seem to be a very healthy and … a very large man too," as she looked down at his crotch.

Ed tried to make light of it, he was thinking --don't blow it, think lucrative, (as she was obviously "Uncle Kerrigan's protégé") and said, "You know, I really am quite flattered, and I like the way you think … but it's just a roll of quarters."

She giggled and laughed.

She said something about being late because the census guy caught her at the door when she was leaving and started asking her a bunch of questions.

Ed said he had the perfect way of avoiding the census, and she would appreciate it, with a middle name like Clarice, and being Latin.

She asked, how.

Ed: You open the door with your lips and chin covered with ketchup, and then say, "A census taker once tried to test me. I ate his liver with some black beans and a nice Corona."

She giggled and laughed out aloud, and laughed some more, and said: "You're funny"…"I wike you" (she had started talking baby talk … a sure sign of interest).

She sounded a bit like the vaguely desperate girl in the Progresso soup commercials that were running on the TV. The one where the girl is flirting on the Progresso soup can phone with the soup cook at the other end. She had the potential of being a persistent stalker, he thought. Catalina asked many questions, where did Ed live, when he would be home, and his schedule. Ed thought that she must be interested in him, but also thought that she seemed like someone who was casing a joint before a robbery.

Manny was quite the skirt-hound and attempted to get her to go out with him. She finally agreed. Manny later told Ed that she was very fickle, played hard to get; he said that he was never able to get pass first base with her. This would eventually prove to have been lucky for him. She told Manny that she wanted to get "weighed" so he took her to the local amusement park and she got on the scale, every time he asked her what else she would like to do, she would say she wanted to get weighed. It turns out she did have a slight speech impediment, because when she got home her mother asked if she had a good time, and she just said, "I had a wousy time."

As she walked away Ed stared, his look was far away as he contemplated her beauty and fantasized. Manny saw him and made a fake gun with his hand, stuck it at Ed's side and said, "This is the dirty-fantasy police, you are under arrest, any thoughts you have can and will be held against you."

Ed: Then the only thing I can say is Eva Mendez, Sofia Vergara and that girl; oh ... can I add another.

Manny: It's your dirty fantasy!

Ed: Ok then, the three previously mentioned ladies and add the 2010 playboy centerfold of the year. If Ed only knew, what he had wished for.

They asked Berto to take them to his father's boat. They walked over to the pier to examine the yacht his father had used on his last dive. Manny immediately noticed something. As a Navy Seal Manny had been a trained expert diver, he was also a PADI certified SCUBA instructor and had gone on many dives.

They asked Umberto "Was this the exact way the boat was found."

He said yes, the only difference was the buoy was in the water.

Manny, knowing that he would have something over on Ed, said, "Notice something wrong?"

Ed said, "No … why?" Then Ed noticed the international signal flag attached to the diving buoy …"Oh yes!"

What? Manny said, hoping to get Ed in a misstep.

Ed said, "I am not an expert like you are Manny, but I'd say that, this flag is the international signal flag for man overboard, the letter O."

Manny: And?

Ed: Well, an experienced diver like Mr. Afortunado would have had the "Divers down flag," which is red with a diagonal white line running from the left upper corner down to the right lower corner. While the "Man overboard flag" is the signal for the letter O, a flag divided in half diagonally forming a yellow triangle on the lower left-side and a red triangle on the upper right-side.

Manny: Damn it!

Berto then said, "I should have noticed that!"

Ed theorized that the killer had put Mr. Afortunado on the boat, and then dumped him in the water with the wrong flag; he then ran him over with the boat to make it appear as if an accident had occurred, Mr. Afortunado then suffered paralysis from the drug and died. Later on sharks bit the body.

Kerrigan took Ed aside and said lets take a walk. They strolled through Berto's backyard. As they walked, they came up on a cluster of banana trees on the property.

The trees had hanging bananas all over. Kerrigan was saying how his family and Berto's were close and that they often did favors for one another. Kerrigan hesitated and said, "Hello what have we here," he then took a small empty glass jar from his pocket, it had a lid that had little holes punched into it, he cupped what appeared to be a spider with the jar.

Kerrigan: Are you familiar with insects, Castillo?

Ed: Just spent some quality time with a bunch of mosquitoes in the everglades, does that count.

Kerrigan smiled.

I am a lawyer by profession, my avocation, some people would say is yachting or polo, but it isn't, my real passion is the study of insects. They fascinate me, as a child I could watch ants and bees for hours and hours, the ant colonies are like little cities, mini societies; they have their own hierarchy, they have worker ants, army ants and queens; they are great engineers too. The insects are my passion.

Ed thought huh; "Wonder if the queens have a Fire Island or South Beach too."

He showed Ed the captured beast.
Kerrigan: Well this is the infamous Banana Spider, I found a couple in my banana trees one day, and began breeding them, they are a most interesting creature, technically an arachnid not an insect. She is known to hide among bananas shipped to the US (Probably how Madame Du Poi got in, Ed thought as he cringed). It is really called the Brazilian Wandering Spider. These spiders are aggressive, very venomous and not at all

intimidated by size, they have no qualms in attacking people, and they do not back away, but will actually chase you if threatened. (If Ed didn't know better, Kerrigan could be describing Ms. Du Poi) ...The odd thing about the Banana Spider is that studies indicate only thirty three percent of the spider bites actually contain any significant amount of venom, a strategy designed to save venom. That is why, if one wishes to kill a human being, and ensure a high success rate of death, numerous spiders may be required to bite at once. Those bites that successfully inject venom are a very serious danger! ... Ed, do you know what you will find in the Guinness World Records book of 2007 when you look up the world's most venomous spider?

Ed: A picture of Madame Du Poi? ... Kerrigan laughed, as he knew her well.

Kerrigan: No but I know what you mean. No, it will be the Banana spider. (Not to be confused with the relatively harmless species of the genus Nephila ... not that any one is going to look that closely to find out).

Ed: Did not know that sir ... Ed was being McMahon to his Carson, Kevin to his Leno.

Kerrigan continued; they belong to the genus Phoneutria, the Greek word for "Murderess." The Brazilian Wandering Spider not only has a potent neurotoxin, but it is also said to have one of the most excruciatingly painful spider bites of all spiders, due to its high concentration of serotonin. I would think that this alone would make its venom the poison of choice, if revenge were a primary motive. P. nigriventer is the most venomous species. Its venom contains a potent neurotoxin, known as PhTx3. At deadly concentrations, this neurotoxin causes loss of muscle control and breathing problems, resulting in paralysis and eventual asphyxiation. In addition, the venom causes intense pain and inflammation following an attack due to an excitatory effect the venom has on the serotonin 5-HT4 receptors of sensory nerves. This sensory nerve stimulation causes a release of neuropathies such as substance P, which triggers inflammation and pain. Aside from causing intense pain, the venom of the spider can also cause priapism in humans. Erections resulting from the bite are uncomfortable, can last for many hours and can lead to impotence. A component of the venom (Tx2-6) is being studied for use in erectile dysfunction treatments. Do you know where the word comes from ... it comes from the Greek god, Priapus, In Greek mythology, Priapus or Priapos, (Ancient Greek: Πρίαπος) was a minor rustic fertility god, protector of livestock, fruit plants, gardens and male genitalia. Priapus was best noted for his large, permanent erection, which gave rise to the medical term priapism. So Castillo, if you ever come across a "stiff with a stiffy" it may well be that he died from a spider bite.

Ed: Livestock? And protector of male genitalia? Mmm! ... I guess if you get it, priapism that is, and you have an erection lasting more than four hours, you should of course call your doctor ... and your friends, neighbors and girls you have been trying to impress. I mean, this is a memorable event, I would think, one which should be witnessed, documented and put to good use ... It carries big bragging rights wouldn't you say.

Kerrigan laughed.

Ed: Well Kerrigan that was an impressive lecture, you sound like Dr. De Baptist back at the coroner's office.

Kerrigan: Oh, but I am a doctor, I have a PhD in Arthropodlogy, specializing in arachnology, the study of spiders.

Kerrigan then invited them for a boat ride; they cruised down through the Fort Lauderdale intracoastal waterways, he pointed out the house of the waste disposal magnate and part owner of the Dolphins. He showed them the old homestead of the actor who had played the part of the six million-dollar-man on TV. He then pointed to one of Al Capone's old houses; he had one in Miami too. He took the boat up to Pompano Beach and then pointed to one of the most spectacular mansions on a point lot; this house had a pool that meandered under a bridge and a gazebo, enough waterfront for a 300 ft yacht. It was the house of Screw magazine's owner. The most outstanding and shocking feature was an eleven-foot sculpture of a giant hand with its middle digit extended, giving the neighbors and all passersby the finger. It had become a famous local landmark. They saw flying fish and dolphins, close to shore they spotted a manatee swimming towards fresh water. Manny seizing the moment, went into joke mode.

"A manatee takes his car into the shop and the mechanic says he needs an hour to check it out. The manatee decides to waddle across the street to a Seven-Eleven to kill some time and get an ice cream. Because he has no hands, the poor big guy gets the ice cream all over his mouth and whiskers. He then waddles back to the shop; the mechanic comes out from under the hood, turns towards the manatee, and says, "Looks like you blew a seal." The manatee, somewhat offended, then says, "No, that's just a little ice cream.""

They took a similar tour through the Miami waterways. Kerrigan pointing out the homes of Gloria Estefan, Julio Iglesias and the house Celia Cruz used to live in, and Al's other house; they say the real secret vault of Capone's is still hidden some where's in that mansion, on the left he pointed to the Shaffer mansion, one of the homes of the pen maker tycoon.

They were tearing down two huge mansions to make one huge lot; this seemed to be a shame. Kerrigan said, "Do you know whose house that's going to be...the Dell guy," owner of the computer company by that same name. Nearby was another monster of a house, owned by some German guy, who was trying to bring Las Vega style gambling to Miami. He was being financed by a bank in the Cayman Island, a Banco de Sicilia, Kerrigan then took his index fingers and flattened his nose and bent one ear, "You know who backs them don't you? ... the syndicate guidos. They already run the Casinos down there."

They went by this bar on the waterfront. All these college guys were standing by the porch railing on the second floor, as the Jungle Queen paddle boat went by filled with old lady tourists, a signal was given and all of them in unison took down their shorts and displayed their asses, they formed a mooning chorus line that rivaled the Rockettes in NY City. Manny wondered if there was a Guinness record for most people mooning all at once. They then heard a loud gasp, made in unison by all the passengers, and then loud laughter was heard.

They parked the boat by the Bayside mall and had a couple of six packs of Coronas. Kerrigan ordered what seemed like the largest seafood buffet they had ever seen, it started with oysters on the half shell, continued with shrimp cocktails and lobster, stuffed Red Snapper.

Manny told a couple of Pepito jokes; Pepito is the Cuban equivalent of the Little Johnny jokes.

Pepito is in class and the teacher asks, "I would like each of you to tell me a fact about some scientific truth."

Maria: The moon revolves around the earth and the earth around the sun.

Very good, the teacher said.

Jaime: Light is faster than sound.

Very good Jaime.

Pepito had been raising his hand, waving it frantically, but the teacher was trying very hard to ignore him, as his answers, questions, and comments had always been of a prurient nature. When she had run out of extended arms to pick, she finally and very hesitantly called on Pepito; She was always in fear of what he would say.

Pepito: I know that light can be eaten.

Teacher: Why Pepito that's not true!

Pepito: Sure it can, last night I was going by my parent's room and I heard my dad say, turn off the light and put it in your mouth.

The teacher fainted.

That night Kerrigan was having a big function, he had
rented out the Vizcaya mansion on Biscayne Bay, it was
a benefit dinner with all the trimmings and all the local
dignitaries, the mayor of Miami was there, he was good
friends with both Kerrigan and Umberto. They had all
attended Belen high together. He introduced Ed and
Manny to all. The fundraiser was to establish college
scholarships for local underprivileged children so they
could attend local and international universities, the funds
were established to encourage students to learn to speak
other foreign languages. Kerrigan mentioned to Ed that it
was going to be an opportunity to meet other family
members that had suffered a loss to the Alphabet
Assassin. Kerrigan also said that his European police
sources had told him that they suspected that the
Alphabet Assassin moved within these social circles
freely.

At the function there was a group of professors
representing local colleges and universities; there were
also several professors from several international
universities. Kerrigan introduced them as distinguished
guests, there was professor Redrum from the University
of Glasgow in Scotland, two Japanese professors and
their sponsor, a big shot from a major electronics
manufacturing company, a Mr. Kyoukou Hitogoroshi.
Also at he party were professors Satsujin Kyoukou, and
his companion, Professor Satsu Satsugai from the
University of Tokyo; the most prestigious university in
Japan, It ranks as the highest in Asia and third in the
world in 2009, according to Global University Ranking.
Ed talked to them about campus life and the cherry
blossom season, sushi and the fugu delicacy. Now that
Ed was a semi-expert, he felt comfortable about
discussing its pros and cons, and although it was not

their field, they were very knowledgeable about the subject.

There was also a French professor from the Sorbonne, a Monsieur Tueur Buteur Le Meurtrier. He came from a wealthy French family; his father was Count Buteur. Professor Tueur Buteur was hesitant, as though he did not wish to engage in conversation. But nonetheless Introduced himself and said he was a professor of linguistics at Florida International University and an expert in etymology, the study of the history of words. He said he had several classes teaching various languages, Spanish, Portuguese, French, and Italian. Once he warmed up, he said to stop by some time. It appeared to Ed that the man was disingenuous in his invitation, even while he tried to appear casual and nonchalant as he expressed his pleasure in meeting him. His acting was not convincing at all, in fact, it was right out of the Chuck Norris School for thespians. Ed noticed that the professor was missing part of the tip of the little finger of his left hand, and he was moving it stiffly. The professor said it was from a kitchen accident, he never bothered to get it fixed because it was so minor, and the stiff movement was from arthritis, caused by a motorcycle accident when he was very young. The professor had known about one of the Alphabet Assassin's victims; he said that he was in France at the time a French industrialist, a Daniel De Paradox had been found murdered, and the initial F burned on the neck; one of Gabriel's first victims.

Ed's sharp nose had detected that the professor, as well as all the other professors, were wearing a very distinct cologne, later he was told that it was a party gift from Kerrigan to all the male guests, and there was one for him in the vestibule by the front door. Ed asked what was that wonderful cologne he was wearing, he said it is

Canoe, French cologne of course. Ed said, of course, I like your tiepin too, Ed then noting that all the professors were wearing tiepins, added, "They must be making a come back."

Tueur: They never left France.

Ed: Mmm ...Tueur, unusual name ... is it French?

Tueur: Of course it is monsieur, look it up in Google.

He bragged about France, Ed recalling how these shits had not allowed America to fly its warplanes over their air space during recent wars, then reminded him of a story, how the French general De Gaulle had demanded, after the war, that all Americans leave. Dean Rusk the then secretary of state said, "All of the soldiers, even the sixty thousand plus soldiers from world war I and World War II that are buried in your soil?"

De Gaulle walked off without answering and so did professor Tueur.

Ed invited professor Seamus Redrum to come to the Lucky Leprechaun, meet Aonghus the Scottish proprietor, and have some Haggis. He said he hated the stuff but loved Cuban food and Spanish Paella; he did say he would take him up on some Scotch whisky. Ed mentioned that his great grandfather was from Scotland, a Joseph McCoulloch. He owned sugar mills in Cuba. Ed asked where he could get a hold of the clan's tartan; he wanted a kilt to wear to Aonghus' parties. This guy was a look alike of Lance Hendrickson. He lived only two miles away from the Alphabets Assassin's Scottish victim, Ed put him down on his list of potential candidates.

Kerrigan walked over to Ed and Manny and said he
would like to introduce them to an individual, another
member of his small, sad, and unfortunate club. He was
a family member of one of Gabriel's victims; he too was
the brother of a murdered victim. Felipe Artimori had
been a professor of philosophy at the University of
Florence. To this day, his murder remained unresolved,
the motive in particular was a mystery, as he had no
great wealth and did not fit the profile of the victims, in
that he had no one that would want him dead, no one to
profit from his death as many of the Alphabet Assassin's
victims had.

Dr. Seraphim A. Artimori was the victim's brother; he, like
many of the guests was also a linguistics professor, he
taught at Florida International University. Artimori
appeared to be a very pleasant and charming man. Now
this guy did look like the actor that plays the Mentalist,
and somewhat like the professor on Gilligan's Island. He
dressed a bit more elegantly than your average professor
did. He wore a beige Italian designer suit by Brioni, and
A.Testoni shoes, by a Bologna Italy designer, they were
custom made. The pants fashionably draped over the
shoe, almost touching the floor at the back of the shoe.
He wore an imported white silk shirt with a wide brown
silk tie. Affixed to his tie was a very distinct and elegant
tiepin. His hands were impeccably manicured, long and
elegant, perfect fingers like a pianist or a surgeon. This
guy had big bucks, no way could he afford such elegant
and expensive clothes on a professors' salary.

Ed discussed his brother's murder. The professor told in
great detail how his brother had been stabbed. He told
how the doctors tried everything, including performing a
blood transfusion with his blood. However, in the end

they could not save him. The professor then broke down, excused himself, and walked away.

The mayor went on to give a symbolic key to the city to Kerrigan.

Manny danced with his new girlfriend and Ed with Katy.

There were editors from the Herald, CEOs' of all the major corporations in Florida and many bankers, Ed noted, after speaking to many of the bankers, that all of them in one way or another, had a banking friend or acquaintance that had been touched by the Alphabet Assassin.

One beautiful Panamanian girl approached Ed while he was in a corner and momentarily alone, Katy was off talking to some of the guests.

Hello, she said I am Elena De Trolla; I could not help but notice you in the room.

Ed: I could not help but notice you, that is an unusual name, isn't that the same as Helen of Troy? You certainly have the face to launch a thousand ships.

The one and only, I am the one Homer wrote about in the Iliad.

Ed: Homer Simpson?

Elena said, "You are funny," then walked away.

Manny walked over and said "Boy she looks a lot like Eva Longoria; you know I was in a movie with her."

Ed: Oh yeah that B or C or D rated movie that went straight to video before she was famous.

Manny: Hey don't knock it, it paid the bills, and I got to meet and be killed by her, I only wish I had a part where I kissed her, oh well.

Elena overheard and said, "I didn't know that. What was the movie and what role did you play, I'd like to take it out."

Manny: I am glad that some people appreciate an artist. The movie's title was a kind of knock–off, of the Al Pacino movie "Carlito's Way," this one was called "Carlita's Secret." I played the Latin American drug dealer, Miguel Diez. My best line was "Money … money never disappoints me."

Elena: Manny would you like to play tennis with me tomorrow?

Manny noticing his girlfriend coming over said, "I can't, I have Vitas-Gerulaitis of the elbow."

Elena: "Oh, I am sorry, that must really hurt," as she walked off again.

Ed: Manny, you do know that's not a sport's injury, but the name of an old tennis player.

Manny: "Gosh, I didn't know that." Manny tended to invent things when under pressure.

Ed: You do know she's a hooker.

Manny: I'd still do her.

Ed: She's a high-end hooker.

Manny: I'd still do her.

Ed: She charges one thousand dollars an hour.

Manny: In that case ... I'd still do her, but she better fuck like the original Helen of Troy-- with her ass on fire.

Katy had just returned, and asked if she was interrupting; it was enough to chase the beautiful girl away permanently.

Kerrigan strolled by and invited Ed and Manny to lunch at his private club in downtown Fort Lauderdale, the Tower Club on the penthouse floor in a Las Olas Boulevard office building. Ed said, "Yes, I know it well; my friend Angelo Lacuona plays piano there." Angelo was a Cuban Italian who had worked in clubs in New Jersey's Union City, a Cuban enclave. Angelo had been playing at clubs owned by Benito the Bull Macereti, and at the end of his gig, he was told that he had to pay kickback to Benito, money he didn't have. This was a way for the mob to get its talons into an artist so that he would become a serf in their fiefdom. Without paying tribute or "payola," artists just could not work in the New Jersey clubs. Kerrigan had helped Angelo escape and had gotten him the gig at the Tower Club. Ed knew him from social gatherings; his wife was good friends with Katy. Angelo was keeping a low profile, as this club catered to an exclusive clientele of mostly blue bloods in South Florida's social circles, there weren't too many Italians in that group.

Ed brought Kerrigan up to date; he mentioned that he was certain the killer of Berto's father was a different man from the one who had killed Manny's brother. The one that killed Armandito had probably killed Kerrigan's brother too. He told Kerrigan that he was closing in on the identity of the killer, and would have some more news after he traveled to Brazil. There, he suspected the killer of his brother had gotten his start; there he was sure that he could piece everything together and get a good description of the killer and his real identity. He told Kerrigan to tell Berto that he was planning a trip to Haiti also, and there he was sure he could identify the killer of Herbert Afortunado, Berto's father. _____**24**

CHAPTER 25
LA MONA, MONKEY GIRL

𝕹ext morning Ed ran into a creature from the past, Shauna "La Mona," (Spanish for female monkey) as she was known in school. Shauna Gomes had been a reporter for the Herald, she now worked for a sleazy scandal mongering paper; she was basically a gossip columnist. At times, she would sell stories to the lowest of the low bottom feeders in the industry. Manny had said to her that she was more of a bottom-feeding muckraker than a reporter, this got her all riled up and she began stuttering ... " A muck, a muck." Manny told her that she sounded like Sara Jessica Parker, when she played the witch in the movie Hocus Pocus.

She was what you'd say today "very sexually active," she had gone through half-dozen cub reporters at the Herald and now had "dated" half the police force in Miami. She had made several passes at Ed, but he had shown little interest.

It is said that beauty is only skin deep, but ugly goes all the way to the bone. As far as Ed was concerned, there were only two types of redheads in this world. The ones that looked like Katy with rich deep auburn hair and skin like alabaster with hues of pink, (Ed had to explain alabaster to Manny, he just said its like DuPont Corian countertops) Manny then said, "Oh yeah! ... that's really nice, and of course big boobs are nice too."
The other type was the ones that at best looked like Carrot Top or the marionette Howdy Doody and at worst, the ones that looked like Chucky the killer doll, Shauna

was the latter. She looked like a redheaded combination of Glenn Close and radio talk show host Imus.....closer to Imus and even closer to Chucky. Although thin faced she had thick ankles, more like cankles or table legs. She liked to wear Reeboks with the white ankle sox and the little pom-pom balls at the back, just like those worn by hefty New England girls in Hartford as they take their lunch walks around the state capitol grounds. Manny would unkindly refer to them as Hartford heifers because of their thick and bulging ankles. Her witch like features, had boys hum the theme of the Wicked Witch of the West as she scurried by, you know, the little tune played as she peddled her bike. Boys can be so cruel don't you think. Beauty may be in the eyes of the beholder, but ugly was always on her face. She had the infamous reputation of screwing like a wild monkey. Even back then, one knew she had the potential of becoming a very good stalker. Once she asked Ed out and all that flashed in his mind was the picture of Glenn Close standing in front of that sink holding a bloody white rabbit in her hand…he bowed out gracefully and said no thank you.

Shauna: I heard you got hired by some big shots to look into the Alphabet Assassin murders.

Ed: Where'd you here that?

Shauna: I am a reporter I got sources, come on Ed! You can tell me details, I am the soul of discretion, you can tell me anything in confidence, secrets of any kind, and my mouth is zipped. (As a high school student, her mouth had been anything but zipped), Ed thought, "Yeah right!" Telling anything to Shauna and expecting her not to reveal it, was like yelling through a police megaphone and expecting nothing to come out of the other end.

Ed: Shauna, have you heard the fable of the frog and the scorpion.

Shauna: No, I have not, but I'm sure you are going to tell me-- she had known Ed for many years.

Ed: Well it goes like this: One day, a scorpion stood on the side of a stream and asked a frog to carry him to the other side. "How do I know you won't sting me?" the frog asked. "Because if I sting you, I'll drown," the scorpion said. The frog thought about it and realized that the scorpion was right. So he put the scorpion on his back and started ferrying him across. Midway across the stream, the scorpion plunged its stinger into the frog's back. As they both began to sink below the surface and drown, the frog gasped, "Why?" The scorpion replied …"Because it is my nature."

Shauna: I get it, you are the frog, and I'm the scorpion…. you're not still mad about that job I got you where I was paid a sixty-six percent commission are you?

Ed: I thought you said it was forty.

Shauna: Never mind … But seriously, let's get back to business ... come on Ed! Was Afortunado humping his secretary, was he buffing her huh? Give me something.

Ed: What finishing school did you attend? Is that how the nuns at Immaculata high school and Biscayne College taught you how to speak? I'll tell you what I'll do, when this is all finished I'll give you an exclusive, but you've got to help me dig up facts, Ok.

Shauna: it's a deal!

Ed met Manny the next day and told Manny about the meeting with Shauna.

Manny: Oh Yeah! La Mona, she was my first success with the "Manny's, typical nasty weather strategy."

Ed: Ok I'll bite, what the hell is that?

Manny: Well in high school I'd sit behind a girl, and you know how those seats are, I would rub their ass with my knee, if they turned around and gave me a nasty look I'd stop, but if they smiled I made a date.

Ed: Jeez Manny even for you it sounds sick, but why do you call it that?

Manny: Well, Its named after the joke were the guy walks up next to a pretty girl at a bus stop and say's "Tickle your ass with a feather," and then if she smiles he would make a date, if she sounded offended he'd say "Typical nasty weather" and she then felt embarrassed for thinking the worst.

Ed: You are one sick individual … you know that! There were only seven periods and you sat behind a lot of guys, so what was your success rate.

Manny: Well, Shauna was the first … and only one.

_____**25**

CHAPTER 26
AWAKEN THE KRAKEN

𝕸anny's inquiries in Brazil about the Guarano Brothers must have gotten back to those interested in stopping further investigations. A big white Mercedes S600 was following Ed. Unlike New York, the preferred color for luxury cars in Florida and many southern states is white. White is the black of Florida, as black cars can reach an internal temperature, as much as 8 degrees or more, higher than white cars. Besides, they look cool in a tropical setting. He could not think of a more conspicuous car, oh, there were many luxury cars in Miami, Boca, and Palm Beach. Still, this was a $160,000 car, a car, which was taking every single turn Ed was taking. He could not see the driver, because of the illegal dark tinting; he must have enough money to keep paying the fines Ed guessed. Ed sped up, took some back alleys, and thought he lost the Benz.

Ed had started getting threats in his mailbox, on sheets of paper that had letters cut from newspapers and magazines, saying "Stop looking into the bank's business and the murders, we know where you and Katy live."

He hated the dog next door, Princess, what a name he thought, "loud bitch" was more appropriate, always barking and growling when he went for the mail or paper. This one night, Ed had been by the kitchen window when the dog barked unusually loud, Ed looked out, in the darkness he could see a shadowy figure holding a gun. He instinctively dove to the ground, a shot was fired; the round got imbedded in the back wall, which would have surely gotten him in the heart. …He loved that dog ever since.

It looked like Ed and Manny were getting too close. Someone wanted them to back-off. Ed was wondering who could have known he would be home that night, as he spent time at Katy's, and some times at Manny's, and was traveling too. His phone is unlisted, no one was lurking around, and he had lost the tail that was following him, so he thought.

Police confirmed, through measurements of angle and height, as well as his position in front of the window, that the bullet would have been dead on Ed's heart. A 9mm slug, from what was presumed to be a Glock semi automatic was found imbedded in the wall, its corresponding casing by the window. They went outside, took castings of shoe prints. Manny's police buddy said to him that he would get back to him ASAP, before the official report was out. This was good, as the police information officer, the PIO, tended to be tight lipped and kept official information on crimes close to the vest, only releasing it after the chief had approved it.

The morning after, Manny came over with a box of Cuban soul food, "cangrejitos" (little crabs) flaky slightly sweet croissants filled with meat, and other "pastelitos" of guava and cream cheese.

Manny: These are from the "La Gran Via" bakery in Miami, (named after a famous bakery in Cuba, which in turn was named after a famous avenue in Madrid Spain) you know these are made with real lard, that's what makes them so crispy and flaky, just like the ones made in Cuba in the old days. Ed did you ever watch that show on PBS "Spain On The Road Again," the one where they are at the bakery and this baker makes this great big round thing, with layer upon layer of lard, well these are the same thing, only little ones.

Ed: This is good, you know Manny I was in Massachusetts, on the Cape once. Friends asked me to try this bread called Anadama bread, it wasn't that bad, but there is nothing like Cuban bread. They said the name came about when a fisherman, angry with his wife, Anna, for serving him nothing but cornmeal and molasses, one day adds flour and yeast to his porridge and eats the resultant bread, while cursing, "Anna, damn her!" They had some café-con-leche, and finished a dozen in one sitting.

Ed: After last night, it reminds you that life can be very short and one should enjoy every day as if it's your last one.

Manny: Amen brother … gulp!

Manny asked Ed if he had a gun, Ed said yes, a Model 1903 Pocket Hammerless ACP.32 caliber Colt semi automatic pistol. Then Manny in an Australian accent sounding more like the crocodile hunter, but imitating Paul Hogan as Crocodile Dundee, said "That's not a gun," and pulled out a colt .44 magnum revolver and said "Now that's a gun."

Ed: You know Manny, a gun's caliber, just like boats, are inversely proportional to a man's penis.

Manny: You are just saying that because you own a .32, by the way I own a .22. But seriously, the best thing at close range is a shotgun. Preferably a sawed-off one, but now there's this gun called the Judge, uses .45 caliber and shotgun shells, this will stop an elephant in full charge and with the shot gun shell you can hit a couple a guys at once, it's a good defensive weapon. We should probably get one---or escalate; I think its time for the Holy hand-grenade!

Ed had inherited the Colt handgun; it had been passed down from his great grandfather, a former Pan Am pilot. At that time, it was standard issue for not only army officers, but also for Pan Am pilots. They would carry them on the planes as a side arm in a holster. Gangsters liked them, mainly because they were relatively small, and they could be hidden under a suit coat. Al Capone had one concealed in his coat pocket; Bonnie Parker used one to break Clyde Barrow out of jail, after smuggling it into the jail by taping it to her thigh. Today the pilots union is vehemently oppose to carrying weapons as they feel flying the plane should be their only concern, while security should be left to the air marshals. It was not the most powerful of weapons, but it never jammed and he could quick fire it and empty the clip in seconds, just like a machine gun.

I guess he could have been more faithful to the Paladin name and added to his business cards "Have Pentel and gun and will travel," but he was the brains of the partnership, muscle and action was more Manny's gig.

The gun was in perfect condition, all the bluing was intact; Ed took it out to the firing range every so often to keep sharp and to relax, as concentrating on your shot made it impossible to worry about anything else. He would practice, the now most popular, tried and true firing stance, the Weaver stance. This was not always the preferred stance; in the 1950's L.A. County deputy sheriff Jack Weaver developed the two-handed shooting stance that still bears his name today. He developed the Weaver Stance, with only one purpose, winning Jeff Cooper's "Leatherslap" competition in Big Bear, California. At that time everyone shot from the hip or one-handed from the shoulder, which is a style know as "point shooting." This worked well on television and the movies, but in real life competition, it was a failure. After all the blazing of guns by several competitors, it was embarrassing to see the targets unscathed. When Jack came up, some people laughed, but his not quite-a-quick draw hit every time, no one laughed after that. The ultimate endorsement to this stance came in 1982 from the then assistant director of the FBI James D. McKenzie, who had just completed a yearlong survey of handgun shooting techniques; in his report, he explained how the accuracy of this technique would make it the FBI's official training stance.

Ed would swab his Colt 32 gun with gun oil as he reminisced on the good times he had spent with his dad at the range.

Manny: You know I tried teaching one of my girlfriends the Weaver stance; she wasn't too bright and thought it was just one more position of the Kama Sutra. So I took advantage of that.

Ed: You would Manny.

After the attempt on his life, he would keep it loaded and holstered, full magazine clip, one round in the chamber, a total of nine chances to hit his target, being a semiautomatic he kept it cocked, slide pulled back and safety off. An additional two magazines in the drawer of his nightstand, if it came to this, he knew it would mean a big shootout. Although not taped to his thigh, he did use duct tape to fasten the slip-holster to the back of his nightstand. He would practice a semi quick draw, while lying on the bed, and got to be pretty fast at it. Speed would be of no use to him if he missed the target, so he maintained a very tight pattern on the hearts of the practice silhouette targets, this was a winning, and killing combination.

Ed was telling Manny how he had met a quick draw champion back in his high school days. The guy had showed him some techniques on drawing a gun from a holster and some exercises to increase his dexterity and speed. He would take three quarters, place them on the back of his hand while he extended it horizontally in front of him, then toss them in the air, and catch them all one at a time before they hit the ground. He was up to four at one time; the champion could do five or six. "My reflexes have slowed down a bit and three is all I can manage, pretty much the number that my sex prowess was at these days. "

Manny: Yeah if you took a dozen Viagra!

Ed: That reminds me, I wrote a limerick I was going to try out at Aonghus' place.

There was a Chinese woman named Jill
Whose husband had taken one thousand blue pills
They found her yellow vagina
In her hometown in China
And her blue tits in Beverly Hills

Manny: I like it, but it's not very politically correct, I am sure Aonghus will like it.

Ed: And when have I ever been politically correct! __26

CHAPTER 27
THE LEVELING OF JUSTICE
Bring in all the unusual suspects

Reports on murders that included a description of the killer, varied and were inconsistent. The height was pretty much on, but some times, he was fat, sometimes he was thin, sometimes he had short hair, other times long hair, and still other times he was bald. Witnesses could not agree as to whether he limped or not. Some of the witnesses had described a man with a very pronounced limp, they said it could not be faked because they could tell that one leg was shorter, while others swore that he didn't limp at all and his legs were quite normal.

The man that had shot at Ed had left a distinctive shoe print outside his kitchen, one was slightly more indented, deeper into the ground than the other, a logo could be barely made out, after taking a cast and some extra forensics work, police were able to identify the brand as an unusual orthotic one. Manny traced it to a manufacturer named Evenup, and later to a local dealer in Miami, who said that they were custom made shoes manufactured to correct short leg syndrome or Leg Length Discrepancy. He had a list of all his customers' names, none recognizable, he did mention a name of an old customer who wore the same size, a fellow from Brazil, an Angel Du Mort; his parents had brought him here from Brazil to fit him with a pair. Ever since then he comes back every year or so to be fitted with a new pair. He was due for a fitting, as he seemed to wear them out after a few years. And this is about the time he is due.

They asked him to describe the customer, he said he had been a handsome young man but now seemed to have changed, looking more haggard, like the actor Glen Scott.

Ed thought, shit not another actor to describe the killer, why can't these witnesses make up their minds.

They asked "Anything else you remember?"

Yes he said, a few years back when Mr. Du Mort had stopped by as an adult, I noticed he was missing part of his left little finger tip.

Ed: Was he a French man, did he speak French?

Shoe man: Well his father was French ... I am sure he did.

They left a number where they could be reached, warning him not to mention anything about this meeting as it could mean his life, and to act naturally as always when he fitted the shoes. After the customer had made the appointment to pick the shoes up, he was to call the number immediately. ____27

CHAPTER 28
EARMARKED FOR TOO CLOSE A SHAVE– I'M READY FOR MY CLOSE- UP MR. GILLETTE

𝕿hat evening, as Ed was opening the door to his townhouse, he was suddenly hit in back of the head, when he woke up he found himself with an excruciating headache and tied to a chair, in what appeared to be one of those rental warehouses, the size of a two-car garage, about 400 sq ft. They are found in an area common to the Miami commercial warehouse district. A bright light was shining in his face through his blindfolded eyes.

A dark figure dressed in all black and wearing a ski mask was looking at a TV security monitor, apparently directly pointing towards the outside at the entrance to the complex. The man started talking through a device that altered his voice, he said, "Good afternoon Mr. Castillo, welcome to my lair. I gave you several warnings to stay away from the bank and the alphabet investigation, but you didn't listen, I failed the other day, I missed my shot, and I never miss, you were extremely lucky that dog barked. I'm not making that same mistake again," and then he said, "But first, we are going to have some fun, you and me, Hey!"

"You know that one of my crime signatures is that I remove an ear from my victims before I kill them. But no one really knows why, they think it's a compulsion of a crazy killer … but really it is not. You probably don't know that I am a great admirer of Quentin Tarentino's work, I just love that movie Reservoir Dogs, have you seen it?

Great movie! I especially like the character Mr. Blond
played by Michael Madsen, you know he didn't want to
do that scene; he was too sensitive an actor. In this
scene, the cop tied to the chair is pleading for his life and
mentions he has a child, Madsen had just become a
father, you know, and this scene struck a cord. You know
the scene I am talking about, the one in the warehouse."

Ed thought, shit, I know the movie very well, you sick fuck
… where the fuck is Manny when you need him.
Although his eyes were covered, if he raised his head up
Ed was able to get glimpses of small parts of the room.
Suddenly, from a CD player out comes blaring "Stuck in
the Middle with You" by Stealers Wheel. Not a good sign
as Ed remembered the movie. The dark figure begins
dancing like Mr. Blond in the movie, he dances, brushing
against Ed's arm, Ed then gets a whiff of the strong scent
of his cologne, a scent Ed had smelled before, an
expensive cologne but in this state of mind he could not
place either where he had fist smelled it or its name.
Then it came to him it was Canoe, his new favorite, the
assassin has the same taste, who would have imagined
it.

The dark figure pulled out from his pocket a sheath and
then from it he pulled out what appeared to be the
biggest, shiniest, sharpest straight razor or scalpel Ed
had ever seen. As the man starts walking towards him,
Ed remembers that this is the guy that had cutoff
Fernando's penis. His sphincter muscle tighten so fast
and so tight he could have used it as a slicing mandolin
to cut cucumbers or cutoff the tip of his cigars… he
thought of this mind flashing analogy he had just had ; It
was a bad one. He then prayed, "Please let it be the ear
only, please let it be the ear." He even thought of telling
the guy that if he were to remain true to the script he

could not go beyond the ear ... He then panicked a bit, actually quite a bit, and hoped the guy <u>was</u> following the script word for word, as he had been doing thus far, because losing an ear would be the least of two evils. He then felt a lump in his throat; and thought, surely his balls had gone so far up his body that they were now lodged up there.

Dark figure: This isn't crazy, you see what I do is homage to Tarentino my idol; today in his honor, I'm doing a double homage!

Ed thought, "Thank God it looks like only the two ears. I hear that they are doing wonderful things with pig DNA, reconstructing realistic ear cartilage ... and a homage? Come on! Isn't that just a euphemism for plagiarism; why the hell am I thinking this shit at a time like this."

The booming American Dad like voice in his head had lost its deep base resonance (Suggestion: If you must have a voice in your head, make sure, it has the reassuring tone of an airline captain's voice) it was telling him he should have worn depends. He thought of his earless body and the pee stain, God how embarrassing. He had worn clean underwear as he always listened to his mother's advice." What if you're in an accident and they have to take off your pants," why in this moment of crisis he thought of these things he could not understand. What about all that shit about your life flashing before you? Was this the extent of his life's memories?

Dark figure: Perhaps I'll improvise and do some Fernando like work on you.

Ed thought, "Shit, don't improvise, you'll spoil the movie, and the censors are sure to take the scene out. Why the fuck am I thinking this shit—there are no censors." The formerly deep reassuring American Dad voice in his head was now sounding more like that of a shrieking little girl's voice, screaming at him to do something. Ed thought it might be a good time to start praying to the god Priapus … the protector of male genitalia.

Then a loud noise, a bang, the sound of metal hitting metal, sounded like a car accident right outside the front door of the warehouse. The dark figure runs to the monitor and yells shit. He sheathed his razor and runs out the back door. Within seconds, you hear the sound of an engine and squealing of tires. The front door drops to the floor and there is good old Manny holding a police battering ram, "Sorry I'm late, lost the guy, and the GPS signal I had on you was not working until I got closer."

Ed: Thank you Mr. Orange, and thank God and GPS, (he thought that would be a good title for a country western song) one moment later and I wouldn't have been able to wear my sunglasses or have a place for my Bluetooth. And worst of all there would be no little Eddies to carry on my good name … By the way, when did you place a GPS tracker on me?

Manny went to the back door gun in hand. "The other day I put a tiny tracker in your wallet … It looks like he's got away."

Manny said, "I think we should bring in Coco and have him stay with you." Coriando Corridas, Coco to his friends was a small muscular guy, had been a cop with Manny, an expert in Kung Fu, a black belt in Karate, had sparred with Bruce Lee and held his own. He could shoot the balls off a fly at fifty paces. A master with the katana, the Japanese samurai sword, he had studied this deadly art in Japan and had ordered and brought home a custom made katana made of Tama Hagane (Jewel steel) This is the hardest steel in the world, able to hold the sharpest edge in the world. He ordered a four-body katana, the standard rating method used by the Japanese sword makers to rate the finished sword, this means that in one swing it can cut through four human bodies. Although they could not be tested like the old days, because of the many consumer complaints and the fact that killing four people or mutilating four bodies would be frowned upon, they did however tested on bamboo trees and hanging sides of pork.

This guy knew a thousand ways to kill, he knew every vital organ and pressure kill point on the human body, and he was always anxious to try a new one out. He had a long way to go before he finished this very special and personal "bucket list."

Ed: Yeah, will bring in Coco … but not for me … for Katy.

Next door, there was a little old lady sitting by the window. They walked over to see if she saw anything; she started by introducing her cats. The nice old lady began naming them, that's Tom-Tom, then there's Kathy Ketchup, she loves ketchup, Dandy Danny, always grooming himself, Peter Peck … oh, I can't tell you why I named him that, as she giggled. Harry Houdini, he escapes from the house no matter what I do.

Ed: Obviously, she's a compulsive Alliterate.

Manny: What? She can't read or write?

Ed: No, she can't control using the same starting consonants for every name.

She said that a man in a big white car pulled in but she
didn't know what kind. Her description sounded like a
Benz. _____**28**

CHAPTER 29
COCO AND THE KID

They called Coco; he said no problem, but needed to pick up his car because it was in the shop. Coco said, "Mind if I bring a backup."

Ed: Who?

Coco: The Kid!

Ed: Sure.

Gerardo Gomez, Kid Gavilan (Kid Hawk) was a Miami local hero, he was a black Cuban kid who had taken the name from a great old Cuban champion, a fighter that fought in the same weight class, the welterweight division. He had been pretty good, but had suffered a detached retina and had to quit the game. He now was a part time bouncer and bodyguard, Ed and Manny new him well as he had grown up with them.

Ed: Good, the more the merrier, as they sped to find Coco, they went over the speed limit.

Cop: Where's the fire guys?

Manny: In your eyes officer, in your eyes!

Cop: Oh, A wisecracker huh! As he looks inside … Manny, you old SOB! Haven't seen you since you left the force.

Manny: Nice seeing you Ralph. Listen we're in a hurry, trying to get help to protect my cousin's girlfriend.

Cop: Ok, but take it easy there's a couple more speed traps ahead and some of those guys haven't made their quota, like I have, just kidding , I'll call ahead and let them know it's you, one of them is Fred the other George, they'll let you fly by. Manny said, "Say hi to the guys for me." They picked up Coco and the Kid. They were both packing, Ed then drove them up to Katy's place. She was none-to-happy, but accepted the situation and put Coco and the Kid in the guest room.

First stop afterwards was the local fishmonger, Manny ordered two pounds of Halibut steaks; the fish guy said "Anything else Manny?" ..." Yeah throw in two pounds of shrimp...just for the Halibut."

That night after calling Tradeles and detective Matson with details, Ed stayed at Manny's place. He was cooking "Camarones al Ajo," Spanish Garlic shrimp, and was cutting the garlic super thin with a shaving razor blade. The garlic would melt immediately into the olive oil giving off a terrific smell.

Manny: You know how I learned this trick, he said ... from Pauli in prison.

Ed: Pauli who? ...You've never been to prison.

Manny: Yeah, you know, in the movie Goodfellas, Pauli has to go to jail but they still manage to live large inside because they were able to bribe the guards and get all the good Italian food they want ...You know this really works. He added some onion, olives, some flat Italian parsley, some dry white Spanish wine, an Albariño, butter and fresh lemon, hot sauce to taste, poured it all over some Mahatma rice, "I think I'll skip the green peppers," they polished-off a six pack off Corona beers and called it a day.

Ed: You know you could add some capers too.

Manny: Maybe next time.

Manny: Hey Ed, have you ever smelled mothballs.

Ed: Sure, I kept my wool sweaters in them, to protect them, when I lived up north.

Manny: How you get their little legs apart?

Ed: Good one Manny. There is nothing like a good meal with a friend, a good drink, and a good joke, especially after an attempted murder on your life, to end a day.

Ed: Doesn't get better than this.

Manny: Amen Bro! _____**29**

CHAPTER 30
THE KEEPER OF THE GATES TO THE TOWER OF BABEL

𝔑ext morning Ed and Manny drove over to Wolfie's Deli on South Beach, not the original Cohen Rascal House in Miami Beach, that one had fallen victim to the pasture eaters, they had bagels with cream cheese, lox, and chives. They were able to get their Cuban coffee, a Cuban "colada" or strainer, which is like a pot of regular coffee, but smaller. It's the amount that passes through the colander and comes out off the espresso machine from one cycle. They bought two Cuban seed cigars made in the Dominican Republic and relaxed.

Flannigan, from the firm, had called late Friday night. He said he was working late at the firm, had a check for Ed, and if he wanted it today he should come in at twelve midnight, otherwise it would be mailed on Tuesday as Monday was a holiday, and he would not get it till Thursday , Ed needed the money so he went.

As he past Fox's office, Neville was walking out with a visitor.

Neville: Castillo, what are you doing here, (appearing surprised).

Ed: Picking up a check.

Neville: Oh!

Ed said hello; the visitor was Professor Tueur Buteur, he carried a large yellow envelope that appeared to be stuffed with small papers. Ed could see the outline of the bulge showing on the creased surface. The professor made a halfhearted invitation to have Ed come to FIU (Florida International University) and to bring the documents Ed had mentioned that needed translation.

Ed took his check and mentioned to the professor that he may just do that, as he had some documents in French that he may need translating. Ed was curious as to why these two were meeting, as they seemed like "Strange bedfellows."

Ed had Manny do a background check on Tueur. Manny said that he was a professor that had quit a job at the Sorbonne University in Paris. He had taught linguistics at the university. They say he quit abruptly and only left a resignation letter. He failed to mention that he personally knew the French industrialist that was killed by Gabriel, in fact, the police were about to question him just before he left France.

Ed: Did you get a description.

Manny: No but I'll call my connection in the French police and try again. The French police system not unlike the U.S. was made up of many different police forces and just like the USA; they didn't speak to each other, every group guarding its independence and political status. I am afraid not much has changed since Nine-Eleven.

Ed took up the half-baked invitation. He got to FIU before the professor's class was over. He noticed professor Artimori was teaching, so he peeked in the classroom window and the professor waved him in. He sat in the back, auditing the class. The professor was asking questions and making critiques of certain homework papers. One student had submitted a paper that included several incorrect statements about English literature; he had used improper grammar, and had misspelled several key words in his essay. The professor said that it was not a good example of English grammar or the use of the English alphabet. Ed had some time until he met Professor Tueur Buteur so he stayed back to chitchat with Artimori. Ed admired his monogrammed tiepin, simple, not quite as elaborate as Dr. Buteur's tiepin, nevertheless very elegant. He said it was a gift from his mother, he liked to look sharp when he gave seminars, "A tool of the trade you know, must look good for the audience." He still looked more like a dandy than a professor. He also had added a new and unusual key chain or pocket watch chain to his wardrobe ensemble, which had three silver-cupped settings. Ed mentioned how he and Katy had visited Florence and the Uffizi Museum, where they saw the Birth of Venus painting by Sandro Botticelli. He said, yes it's a beautiful and original painting. He told Ed that he held a PhD in linguistics and was an expert in entomology; the study of the history of words, their origins, and how their form and meaning have changed over time, and went on about graduating from Oxford and Cambridge with a Suma Cum Laude and a Magna Cum Laude. To subdue some of Artimorie's bragging Ed interjected that although the painting was original it had been greatly influenced by the Greek artist Apelles, who in the 2nd century painted the mural in Pompeii depicting the Venus Anadyomene or "Venus Rising from the Sea," she too was depicted in a sea shell. Talk about Florence had brought bittersweet memories to the professor and his face saddened as he recalled the death of his brother at the hands of the assassin.

Ed later met with Professor Monsieur Tueur Buteur and provided some non-important documents to have the professor translate them. He offered to pay, but the professor said, "Don't worry it's on the house." The professor mentioned that he was a consultant for the bank and for the audit firm Ed had been doing contract work at. As he walked away he limped, Ed asked him about it and he said he pulled a hamstring muscle while playing tennis at the university with some much younger players that ran him ragged on the courts. Ed noticed in the parking lot that the professor was driving a very new and expensive white Mercedes Benz, an automobile that usually could not be afforded on a professors' salary. He did come from a wealthy family so this was not a surprise. He then noticed that professor Seamus Redrum was pulling out of the parking lot … in a big white Mercedes Benz … I must be in the wrong line of work he thought. _____30

CHAPTER 31
THE LUCKY LEPRECHAUN

€d and Manny were very familiar with this bar, they knew the owner well and frequented it often, they decided to visit and follow up on Afortunado's last days, which had included a stop at this bar.

Aonghus Argyle Aberdeen Malcolm McGregor (that was just one guy) owned the pub. He had obtained the down payment by winning a contest that was being promoted by the O'Doul Brewing Company for the best limerick. He proudly had it hanging on the wall; the little ditty went like this:

On the breasts of a barmaid from Yale
Were tattooed all the prices of ale
And for the sake of the blind
Upon her behind
You could find all the same but in Braille.

He purchased the Pub from an Irishman, and since the name was so well known and the clientele consistent, he thought that to change the name would spoil a good thing. Every time he saw Ed, he would say stuff like "Hoot man you make me tremble in ma boots lad" and "Is that a gun under yar kilt or are ya joost happy to see me." Aonghus was a drinking buddy; Ed, Manny, and Pierre were invited during St. Pattie's and especially during the feast of St. Andrews to drink with him. Actually, any day was a good day.

Never judge a song by the company it keeps.
He would bring out several bottles of Johnny Walker
Black; then in Gaelic, he'd yell here it is lads, "Uisge
Beatha!" "The water of life." They would tease him and
say you're saving the real good stuff for yourself, the blue
label Johnny Walker, and the expensive single malt
Scottish whiskeys Ay!

They would sing songs like, "My Bonnie Lies over the
Ocean," "The Bonnie Banks of Loch Lomond" and Irish
ditties too, like "Mollie Malone" and "Oh Danny Boy."

Aonghus was a great storyteller. He related one of
several versions about the song, Loch Lomond. You
know, "You take the high road and I'll take the low road"
etc, etc. He said legend has it, that this song is about two
of Bonnie Prince Charlie's men, captured and left behind
in Carlisle after the failed rising of 1745. The song
appears to be written by one young soldier to his
sweetheart. He was to be executed, the other released.
The spirit of the dead soldier traveling by the "Low road'
would reach Scotland before his comrade, struggling
along the actual road over high rugged country.

Manny said, "That's not the story I heard, the one I heard
was the song about these two very stingy Scottish eye
surgeons that were arguing over a patient, then finally
agreed on a compromise and sang this song ...'"You
take the right eye and I'll take the left eye and we'll
operate on your Glaucoma!."

Aonghus: Very funny lad, very funny.

Manny: Hey Aonghus why don't you play the harp for us
… you know Ed, Aonghus not only plays the bagpipes,
but he's also a really good harp player.

Ed: Lyre.

Manny: No really, it's the truth.

After a few shots, no one would remember the words, a verse to Mollie Malone became "Her hair was so pretty and so were her titties. "

Aonghus was skilled at rhyming and ever since he won that contest, reciting semi-obscene limericks had become a tradition at the Lucky Leprechaun; one of his favorites was "The man from Madras":

There once was a man from Madras
Who was born with balls made of brass
In bad stormy weather
He'd bang' m together
Causing lightening bolts to shoot from his ass

He said to Pierre, "You know what the world's three shortest books are."
-The list of Polish geniuses
-The list of Italian war heroes
- Niggers I met while yachting

Oh boy! ... Ed was watching Pierre's face, he thought, "Now you've done it Aonghus," across his mind the sketch on Saturday Night Live with Chevy Chase and Richard Pryor flashed, the one where Chevy gives Pryor a word association test that starts with innocuous related words escalating and ending with Chevy saying nigger, and Pryor saying dead honky!

Surprisingly Pierre didn't get mad, he simply said, "What we lack in numbers we make up in size and quality.

Some time I'll take you to see Tiger Wood's yacht and then you'll know what I mean, maybe I'll even ask him to let you step aboard, maybe you don't know this, but I am his personal physician."

Then he said, "Hey Aonghus you know why Scottish men's pants only have buttons on their fly?"

Aonghus: No Why?

Pierre: It's because Scottish sheep can hear a Zipper a mile away … Zing, Pierre got him good.

Aonghus: But that's never been a problem … why do you think we wear kilts?

Manny was sporting a mustache at the time and Aonghus said to him, "Manny you know why young Latin boys grow mustaches?"

Manny: No, but I am sure you are going to tell me.

Aonghus: Well, they do it because they want to grow up looking just like their mothers, don't you know!

Manny then asked Aonghus, "Do you know the words that are said by every Scotsman's first love?"

Aonghus: No, but tell me lad.

Manny: Bah, Bah, Bah!

Aonghus: Good one Laddie! Now, if a graduate from Smith and graduate from Mt. Holyoke College, girls with same personality types, hard workers and good looking, applied for a job at your company who would you hire?

The one with the biggest tits, said Manny.

Ah! You know that one lad.

Aonghus: One last one, what are the world's three biggest lies?

The check is in the mail. The French government will support America against Iraq. Don't worry baby I won't come in your mo....

Aonghus' girlfriend had just walked in and he stopped stone cold in mid sentence.

Aonghus was applying for citizenship and Ed asked him if he was ready.

Aonghus: I surely am lad; I have a full proof method-- I wrote answers on the waistband of my underwear.

Ed: Let me quiz you.

How many states in the union?

Aonghus discreetly rolling the waist of his pants said 46.

Ed: What's the name of the first president?

Aonghus: Same sneaky peak, Mr. Haines.

Ed: What's the color of the American flag?

Aonghus: Brown and white.

Ed: One last one, who is Samuel Adams?

Aonghus: Why that's easy lad, that's the man that makes one of me most favorite beers.

Ed: Hate to tell you Aonghus but you had better start studying right away. By the way, you have your underwear on backwards.

Ed: I think you've had your fill Aonghus.

Aonghus then said, Ahg! Laddie, I can table you under the drink any time … and then collapsed.

After polishing the bottles down to the last drop, Aonghus had fallen asleep. Manny lifted his kilt and tied a blue ribbon from one of the bottles to his penis, finished his last mojito and left.

Next morning Aonghus wakes up looks down and says –I don't know where you've been little Aonghus laddie boy, but it looks like you won first prize!

The day Ed and Manny came to the bar in search of information, Aonghus asked Ed for a favor. He told Ed that his bar sales were unusually low and that he couldn't figure it out, his inventory he said, was never short, in fact it wasn't going down that much, and he could sense, based on drinks being served that there should be more sales for booze, he just could not figure it out.

The bar inventory closet in the back was under lock and key and Aonghus had the only one.

Ed: Does your bartender bring in a bag or wear a coat when it's hot.

Aonghus: Mickey brings his bag for the gym every day.

Ed: Any others bring bags or wear loose clothing.

Aonghus: No.

 Ed: I think I know what's going on; this one bartender has "gone into business for himself."

Aonghus: What? How?

Well, it's a common practice at bars where cash sales occur frequently. The scam is carried out by the bartender bringing his own bottle, he pours from his bottle and pockets the cash without recording the sale, the inventory doesn't go down, and an audit of cash against booked receipts will balance, while the amounts gone down from inventory will also square. He may have served more drinks, but they came from his own bottle.

Stamp all your bottles with large red letters that are visible when you walk in the back of the bar, stamp them with, say … the bars name, do it tonight. Don't tell anyone, let him bring his bottle in, and when he places it on the lower shelf; where he hides it, it will stand out like a sore thumb; If you watch him, you can catch him in the act.

Mickey the bartender was a wise ass.
I'd like a beer and some information Ed said.

Bartender: The beer is cheap but anything else will cost you a hundred.

Ed then gave him a hundred.

Ed: Any one here knows a Mr. Afortunado.

Bartender: Don't know, but Katrina would.

Ed: Who's that?

Bartender: She is a Polish girl that is a part time dancer here; she hangs out with all the customers.

Ed: When will she be back?

Bartender: Don't know ... she is an exotic dancer, works in this traveling circuit of dancers.

Ed: That's all I get for a Benjamin?

Bartender: Maybe the Russians over there can help you.

Ed knew that someone there had the answer but he would have to become one of them and infiltrate their culture.

A group of Russian guys were in a corner gambling, one of them was using cheap bar tricks to fleece all of the rest out of their cash. Ed approached the men and placed a one hundred dollar wager on the table, and promptly lost. He then set a challenge of one thousand dollars, and said to the guy " if I can place this toothpick tip on top of this other toothpick tip making it stand end to end without falling, all I'll want is two-hundred dollars and information, If I can't and it falls, I'll give each of you one thousand dollars."

Manny: What the hell are you doing we don't have that kind of cash ... and you just lost two hundred. This is a sure way of getting beaten to death by a gang of hoods with Louisville sluggers.

Ed: Don't worry they are Russian ... they don't play baseball.

Manny: Yeah but an ax handle or Billy-club will have the same effect.

It sounds fair enough the Russian guy with the money said, but you can't use glue or spit, and it has to stay up for a full minute.

Ed: I'd say at least a minute but no banging on the table or blowing on it … Ok.

Russian guy, Ok, is bet!

Ed got a wine bottle cork, two forks, two toothpicks, and one bottle of wine. He stuck the forks into the sides of the cork, making an airplane like composition with forks for wings and the cork as the fuselage; creating a perfectly balanced structure. He then continued and inserted the tip of one toothpick into the bottom of the cork of the airplane like structure. Then he took the tip of the other toothpick and inserted into the cork in the bottle. He then placed the exposed tip of the one toothpick sticking out of the cork on the other toothpick tip sticking out of the bottle. Then if by magic, the structure balanced itself on the very tips of the two toothpicks. A cheap barroom trick that won him back his two hundred bucks and the answers he was looking for.

Russian guy: The girl works next door at the tattoo shop.

The Russian guy then said double or nothing for two minutes. Ed would have taken him up on the bet, and won again, but they were in a hurry. Actually, the toothpicks could have remained like this indefinitely as long as there was no wind or vibrations. Ed had performed this trick many times, some times with needles. The guy just could not wrap his mind around this simple physics display of balance.

Manny: How did you know that trick ... never mind!

Aonghus walked over and gave Ed the money the bartender had taken, he said, I'm the owner and only I can fleece my customers. Well thanks, Ed said, I'll return the favor some day.

You don't have to, you already did, I fired Mickey; I caught him bringing a bottle into the bar from his gym bag.

Ed said, "Nostrovia," drank his beer, scooped the money from the table, added "Spas Ibo" and headed for the tattoo parlor next door.

Manny: What's this nostrovia, spas Ibo crap?

Ed: Just whishing him good health, and thanking the man.

Tattoo lady.
While they waited at the tattoo parlor next door to the Lucky Leprechaun, called Tattoo Blues, a girl came in and asked for a "tat," the owner asked what kind and where ... she said a heart over my breast.

How original, Ed thought.

Tattoo artist: Which one?

Tattoo lady: The red one.

Tattoo artist: No, I mean which side.

Tattoo lady: I want it on the right ... over my heart.

Ed thought sarcastically ..." Ah! Pretty and smart."

Manny, noticing that she already had several tattoos there, including the ubiquitous butterfly, said, "I guess that's her preferred tit-for-tat" ... the humor was lost on them.

Ed asked about Katrina, and was told she would be coming in soon.

The Polish pole dancer.
Katrina's stage name at the Lucky Leprechaun pub was Erin Go-braless. She was only an occasional pole dancer at the pub, most of the time she worked at the Pussy Cat Club or the Platinum lounge, two stripper clubs owned by the Russian Brotherhood. They were everywhere in South Florida, there was even a section of Miami that was being called little Odessa II, after the departing point for many Russians, also after the ethnic neighborhood in New York City.

Herbert Afortunado frequented the bar and often socialized with Katrina. She came over to Ed and Manny's table and sat down. Ed thought that she was a nice enough pretty girl, who some times had a little difficulty understanding English. She was saying how she had first met Mr. Afortunado at the Chandler bank where she would make her deposits, sometimes thousands of dollars at a time. Ed jokingly said to her "You've been hording haven't you?" She paused for a moment and then said in her broken English, "Well yes, but my sister helped me whore half." Manny and Ed almost choked trying not to laugh in her face … just as Ed thought a nice girl.

She went on to say that the last day she had seen Mr. Afortunado was on a Wednesday. He had come in for lunch accompanied by a tall black man; this was a few weeks ago on the day he went diving. At first, Mr. Afortunado seemed angry and upset as they argued, but then after a couple of drinks and eating, Mr. Afortunado became very quite, "he didn't even seem to recognize me when I said hello. After that, they got up and left."

Ed: Anything else unusual?

Yes, when Mr. A went to the men's room, the man added salt; and what looked to me like salad dressing to Mr. A's food. Later the man was holding Mr. A's arm and pulling him as though he was taking him somewhere. Herbert seemed like he was staring into space and acting like a robot. I overheard them say they were going to Delray Beach to go diving on Mr. A's boat.

Ed: Four weeks ago, Wednesday was the day of the accident; he must have slipped him the full dosage of the drug during lunch. Pierre had said that too much would kill a person, but in small dosages it could be used to control a man, making him mind-numb and catatonic, he also said it had to be re-ingested periodically to maintain that state.

Ed: Spasibo Katrina, YA lyublyu tebya.

Manny: Again, with the frickin Russian, what did that mean?

Ed: Just thanked her and told her I love you.

Manny: Were do you get this shit? ... I do have to remember the Yaki lulu part; it may come in handy some day.

Ed: The Internet.

Manny: I should have known by now, but I'll have you know it was a rhetorical question.

Ed: Pretty big word for you, Manny, where did you pick it up?

Manny: The Internet

Ed: Touché!

Manny: I'm trying to learn ten new words every day as Churchill did. _____31

CHAPTER 32
♪ ♫ FLY ME TO THE MOON, IN EVER SO LIGHT GOSSAMER LOAFERS ♪

Shauna Gomes called Ed one morning.

Ed: Hello?

Shauna: I have something for you, come over in an hour to my apartment.

Ed: Now Shauna, you know I like you ....

Shauna: No, No, it's about your case.

Ed: Case?, Oh yeah , yeah. He could not think without his morning Cuban coffee, and besides, Ed thought of these as contracted projects, after so many years as an accountant, he just accepted the unsolved murders and other crimes he was looking into as just another form or extension of the audit project.

He was a CFE, Certified Fraud Examiner too, and although this usually involved forensics accounting, the criminal investigation, and prosecution was up to the cops and prosecutors. He would serve as an expert witness and did interview the criminals he had identified through the process, mainly to confirm the crime and elicit a confession, if he could. He usually had so much and so detailed and strong incriminating evidence that the suspect cracked and confessed. Once he completed his part of the forensics investigation and identified the criminal, the police and prosecutors would take over and establish a case.

His information technology (IT) experience combined with fraud investigation was critical in many "cases," it was important for instance, to make a copy of all the files in the suspects computer to protect the original evidence and document the trail of events and the audit trail of the work. This process is critical so as not to disturb the original evidence. It is important in any civil or criminal investigation to maintain the "chain of custody" intact, this is vital to any successful fraud investigation and prosecution. If you compromise the chain of evidence in any way, the defending attorney will tear you and the evidence apart, and the judge will surely throw it out.

Ed arrived at Shauna's apartment about a half hour late. He thought, "heck she is always late, this is not a free-ken movie, he didn't miss the beginning and besides this is Miami and everybody is on Cuban time."

Shauna introduced Ernesto, a recent arrival from Cuba. Shauna had many sources on all levels of Miami society, mainly at the sub basement level. There may be no real subbasements in Florida but they did exist at the human level. She said Ernesto has some important information.

Ernesto was a slim, almost delicate individual, very pleasant, more pretty than handsome, and very, very gay. He was a steward or a flight attendant back in Cuba and is now looking for similar work, but for now, he was dependent on the kindness of strangers. He wore a bright tight yellow polo shirt with the collar up, a soft pink cashmere sweater wrapped around his shoulders, like preppie's wear when playing tennis, fashionable Ray-

Bans and off-white tennis shorts. Looked like the gay guy who had won American's Idol recently.

Ernesto: Helo, señor Castillo.

Ed: Helo Ernesto.

Ernesto: Oh! Call me Enerstico or better yet Ernie (then in a singsong manner) we are in America, after all!

Ernesto: Chona said I should tell ju about my Mr. David Flynn, he said he was a CPA, I see him a lot at one of my Miami hangouts, Azucar, the club near South Beach, ju know the building that looks a lot like the one in the movie the "Bird Cage"... Ju know his name was not real!

Ed: How do you know?

Ernesto: Well I tink he forgets his name, the next time we meet he say it was Earl Niven.

Ed: Oh, I see, but how does this relate.

Shauna: Let him finish!

Ernesto: We got to talking, he say he was rich and a big shot partner at his firm. I knew he was English, very ugly man ju know, look like a skinny bird like Homer Simpson's boss... ju know, and very nasty too. I did no like him, but gave me lots of money. He gave me a diamond ring and kissed me ... ju know " Every kiss begins with gays."

Ed: I believe that's every kiss begins with Kay's ... never mind ... it sounds like Neville Fox... where did you meet?

Ernesto: We met at the Marlin's game, I just love baseball and baseball is been very, very good to me.

Ed: How so? I didn't think you would be a person that would be into sports (Ed was not trying to be disrespectful, he knew of many great athletes that were homosexual).

Ernesto: Oh! Jes, I into baseball a lot, hee! hee! Well I met my first novio (boyfriend) he was a baseball player ju know, so cute in his tight spandex pants, I love the atmosphere, all that fanny spanking stuff, and the sweaty muscles. That reminds me I also like gladiator movies, I don't like the spitting of tobacco though. I love the way they hold the bats and crouch down, I love when the gang runs in the field and, what do they call it … jes … they huddle, and then they have a group hug … some times they kiss ju know, I imagine myself in the locker room and then I….

Ed interrupting, "Yes that's interesting Ernesto, I think they only huddle in football. I've never thought of baseball like that before, you have etched a very vivid image in my mind about the game that I will never forget. Every time I see a game I probably will be thinking of this, even though I'll try putting it out of my head."

Ernesto: Ju welcome.

Ed: Tell me more about Mr. Flynn or Niven did you know he was gay?

Ernesto: Gay–Dar, darling, I knew. (Ernesto saying it in same singsong tone).

Ernesto: Ju know he was bipolar.

Ed: You mean bisexual.

Ernesto: No man! Bipolar, ju know he takes the pole…

Ed: Abruptly interrupted, Shauna was no prissy lady but Ed was getting embarrassed, even in front of Shauna.

Ernesto: Jes he was you know a pitcher and a catcher, he was AC/ DC too, more AC than DC….ju know… bisexual, but only because he had to be.

Ed: What do you mean?

Ernesto: He said he marry a rich lady for her money and she was, ju know his mustache.

Ed: Mustache? … you mean his beard.

Ernesto: Jes man! His makeup disguise, his cover-up. He said he would be leaving the U.S. soon with lots of money and diamonds, said he would have to, once the "Shit was out" … I guess he was, how ju say, constipated or something, and then he said he would take me with him. He said he owed mucho dinero and someone was after him, but he did not have the cash, so wanted to leave early, He was scared of animals too, he say the bear was after him. He spends mucho time at the Miccosukee Casino, played the ponies too and Jai Ali.

Ernesto: That reminds me, Mr. Castillo do ju know why the pony could not talk.

Ed: No Ernesto, please tell me.

Ernesto: 'Cause he was a little horse, funny no?

Ed: Very funny, I see your adapting well to life in the US.

Ernesto: I adapt very well, at least twenty positions … He said he had firewalls to keep his way of life hidden.

Ed had recalled the rumors that had been circulating around the office a few years back. Rumors that Neville had been arrested at a small Coral Springs park, called Sherwood Forest. He had been charged; it is said, along with several other men, for soliciting sex for money. The headline of the local paper read "Merry Men arrested in Sherwood Forest." However, his name was never mentioned and he was never tried.

Ed: So he was not openly gay.

Ernesto: Jes man; he was in the deep end of the closet and then that closet was inside another closet.

Ernesto: He said he mentor boys, I said ju mentor them in the morning and mentor them in the afternoon, and mentor them at supper time.

Ed: When?

Ernesto: When, what?

Ed: When is he leaving?

Ernesto: He don't say, but my friend DongLover, ees a mechanic at the Miami airport, he said he saw heem checking out a private jet.

Ed: Really … that's interesting … that's also an unusual name … Dong Lover.

Ernesto: No silly! It's Don ... Glover.

Ed: Thank you Ernesto, by the way, what's your last name?

Ernesto: Is Enola.

Ed: How befitting ... and you're gay?

Ernesto: Jes I am very happy and very proud too, is good to be in America, in Cuba I would be in concentration camp. My middle name, I never use, its Guevara, my father loved the communists, he was in the party, and got to work at the meat packing plant. He stole a lot of meat for us. I don't like this name; I am changing it to Ernestina Genera ... once I have my operation. I've been saving ju know.

Ed thought it was time for a laugh and thought he'd try it again, one more time. He figured that if it worked with Katrina maybe it would work with Ernesto. Ed then said, "So you have been hording?"

Ernesto: Oh! Jes, I I've been whoring a lot, I whored it all by myself.

Shauna laughed.

Ed: Sounds like Neville Fox, and it sounds like he is into debt to Antonio Medebes, not a good thing for him.

Shauna: Oh yeah! Who's he?

Ed: The biggest loan shark in town.

Ed: You see Shauna, now you know why it is so hard for women to find men that are sensitive, caring, and good-looking.

Shauna: Why?

Ed: Because those men already have boyfriends like Ernesto.

Ed knew that Shauna's motto was the opposite of the Las Vegas motto, hers was more like, "What happens in Miami doesn't stay in Miami" … she would spread it all over the world; she was the bullhorn to the masses.

Ed: Please keep this confidential until we can see where it takes us. _____**32**

CHAPTER 33
SOMETHING DID NOT SMELL RIGHT, A NOSE FOR TROUBLE

The trio visited Haiti and pursued the leads there; they needed to know more and get evidence on the poison killer. Ed had concluded that two different killers were involved. One was Gabriel, the Alphabet Assassin, the killer of Armandito, his cousin, and also the killer of Kerrigan's brother, while the other was the killer of Afortunado and Susan Boyl. He would find this one in Haiti.

Manny suggested, that after all these attempts they should pack a gun for the trip, Ed said, "We can't, the airports have metal detectors." Manny then said, "Look I trained as a navy seal in covert operations, if you really want to transport a gun you can."

Ed: Are you crazy, it's a federal offense; in today's environment, they would throw the book at you.

Manny: Look Ed I am not suggesting taking it in the cabin, just in our checked suitcase.

Ed: The charges and consequences are the same.

Manny: I've done it several times.

Ed: Manny you are crazy!

Manny: All you do is put it in a plastic container add water and freeze it, then wrap it in carbon paper and keep it cold with dry ice; X- ray machines and scanners will not be able to make out the shape or detect the metal, we need it for protection.

Ed: I am not chancing it, besides Pierre's nephew is a cop, and if we need a gun, he can get it for us.

Manny: Ok, Ok, it was just a suggestion.

Ed: A very bad one and a very dangerous one at that.

Before boarding they had to go through the TSA's legal groping or "freedom pat" (TSA now stood for Touching, Squeezing and Arresting) Manny thanked the guy and told him "If you squeeze me one more time down there your going to have to buy me dinner." They took a flight to Port-au-Prince Haiti, to visit the main Chandler bank branch there. They made inquires about Madame Du Poi and found a young helpful staff member. Celine Du Mar was a pleasant girl, innocent, talkative, and very pretty, the opposite of Madame Poi. She resembled a combination Halle Berry and Beyoncé, cinnamon skin and all. When they entered her office, there on her wall hung a group picture with Madam Du Poi, she stood between a very large black man, and to their surprise Neville Fox. Behind her stood another tall white man, she went on to say that he was Madam Du Poi's first husband, he was a wealthy British man that had left his vast fortune to Ms. Du Poi, Celine added that he had died under suspicious circumstances, and that the case was still open but unresolved. She also said that Ms. Du Poi had later married and divorced Neville Fox. Back in Miami at the bank or at the firm's office, they never gave any indication that they had been married, in fact they acted as if they didn't even know each other. Ed and Manny were in shock! She went on to say that, the tall black man was Josef Matombo Mostasa; she said it almost in a whisper, "He was her lover!"

Manny then said to Ed, "So while Neville was hard at work mentoring and playing hide the one eyed British snake with young Haitian boys, she was playing hide the voodoo salami with Matombo." Manny then began to imitate Bonsai, the hyena in the Lion King, sounding like Cheech Marin, he said …"Ooh, scary name Mostasa … Mostasa … Mostasa."

Noting the fear in her eyes, Ed went on to ask her more about Matombo, but more quietly this time. Ed asked about the keloid scars that were clearly visible in the photograph on Matombo's right arm. She said those were the symbols of the Ton tons, they would burn or cut their mark into their own flesh. She said he was a mysterious man who it was rumored was a leader of the Milice de Voluntaries de la Sécurité Nationale or (MVSN) (Militia of National Security Volunteers), also called just the Voluntaries de la Sécurité Nationale or VSN. In the streets of Haiti, they were commonly called the Tonton Macoutes. Although now disbanded, they nonetheless continued to act as a secret society. They were ruthless thugs who tortured and killed anyone that opposed them. The uttering of their name was done in whispers, as they were greatly feared by most Haitians. Her voice got even lower and she added that he is known to be a high priest in the Voodoo religion in Haiti. Ed then knew they had identified the killer … Or at least one of the killers.

Little Pierre.
Pierre's nephew, little Pierre was the police sergeant in charge of a district north of Port au Prince; he was stationed in the town of Saint Marc. He had asked them to stop by as he may have information on Matombo, also

because he needed their help. Little Pierre was a towering young man, perhaps six-five with wide shoulders and a big smile to match. Ed noticed that the town's people were all smiling and genuinely happy to greet them. He thought, these people are so poor, they have little if any material goods, yet they seem happy, they don't hold grudges and have no type of inferiority complex, they are not guarded as many people are in the USA, they are open and friendly. They treat everyone as equals; they showed no outward signs of intimidation, as you get back home. Not that Ed and Manny could be easily intimidated, Manny specially, as he had broken many a man's jaw that had tried.

Little Pierre invited them to a Haitian style barbeque pig roast , it reminded Ed and Manny of the Cuban pig roasts during Noche Buena (Christmas Eve) in Miami.

The not so silence of the pigs.
The slaughter of the pig was supposed to be a quick and relatively painless ordeal. One quick stab to the heart, one loud scream, one dead pig (One quiet death that would not horrify the gawking tourists …priceless). Well this did not happen as anticipated. The expected instant death lasted minutes, instead of going silently into the night it screamed in agony like … well … like a stuck pig. As it screamed, it sounded more like a man in great anguish, until it was abruptly turned onto the opposite side, quickly stabbed, and put out of its misery. Apparently this pig had his heart on the other side of his body, the right side, they later learned that it is not uncommon for one in a thousand or so pigs to be born with this anomaly; maybe tattoo girl was right after all, maybe her heart was on that side.

After dinner, Little Pierre began relating the story of Marie's father. Marie was Little Pierre's girlfriend. Her father, who lived in a near by village, was a hard working man, a religious man that did not believe in voodoo. He refused to buy voodoo dolls, amulets and the other superstitious paraphernalia that Matombo would sell to the villagers at exorbitant prices. Matombo would scare them into believing harm would come to them if they did not buy. He then would sell them trinkets for large amounts of cash, forcing many to sell their possessions; he was beginning to demand that they give up their children to him; he would sell them as forced labor or use them to beg from tourists in Port au Prince.

She said that he is evil incarnate, "He is an evil man that is feared greatly," fear is how he maintains control over the people. Matombo had threaten her father with death and said he had placed a curse on him. Her father did not believe in curses, he was a brave man, and publicly denounced Matombo. Matombo was beginning to lose his grip of fear on the people; they stopped buying and never gave up their children, this made him furious with Marie's father and he swore revenge. Her father did take the threat seriously, he would enclose himself in his bungalow, seal everything tight, and bolted shut the windows and doors from the inside.

The night he died, he had taken the same precautions; the bungalow was practically airtight. Next morning Little Pierre had to brake down the door to get him out; there were no signs of entry, no wounds or bite marks on the body. The water in his glass next to his bed was tested, and no poison found. The coroner had checked for needle marks and poison in his food, drink, utensils, and glass, nothing was found. The coroner had not yet issued the death certificate, but told Dr. Pierre he could not find any indication of foul play, and unless Little Pierre found something else, he could do nothing else and would have to rule death by natural causes. This incident was sufficient to scare the villagers back into believing. Little Pierre investigated the crime scene but found nothing to incriminate Matombo.

Ed asked if they could look at the bungalow. Little Pierre said, "of course, this is the main reason I wanted you to come." He drove them over to the nearby village. Little Pierre introduced them to Marie, his girlfriend and her aunt Claudette; he then took them to Marie's father's bungalow. Little Pierre said nothing has been touched and handed Ed photographs of the crime scene taken by the crime photographer. Saying, "We don't have the latest and greatest of equipment, but I was trained at the FBI crime lab at the Quantico headquarters, and I do try to do everything by the book." Ed said," I'll talk to Inspector Tradeles and see if he can spare some of last years stuff. They piss away more money on gadgets in one day than the annual budget of your department. Even with all that stuff they still can't solve crimes, it seems like they think leading edge equipment is a substitute for thought. You've done a good job Pierre."

Ed walked slowly all around the room noticing how airtight the room was, barely enough air to breathe. He walked and examined everything, comparing the items and their placement to the photos. He then walked up to the bedside night table where Marie's father had a candelabrum; the four candles had almost totally melted. Ed then noticed a barely visible black mark at the base of one candle, the partial shape appeared to be a symbol of the zodiac; it was shaped like a scorpion. Ed asked Little Pierre to a take a look at the symbol. He asked Pierre if he recognized it. Pierre said "Why I never noticed that before Mr. Castillo, but I know what that is. Matombo places this symbol on the talismans and other voodoo things he sells."

Marie then said, "My father would never buy this evil thing, and I never did."

As Ed was making one last examination of the contents in the room, Marie's aunt Claudette started crying, loudly and uncontrollably, and then said, "I did, I bought the candles, I thought it would protect him, we were running out of candles anyway and Matombo offered them cheaply."

Ed: I believe I know how he died.

Manny: But how? No one could get to him; he was barricaded inside, this place is like a bunker, and you saw the coroner's preliminary report.

Ed then took his penknife, cut a small piece of the candle, sniffed it, and asked Dr. De Baptist to smell it, "What does that smell like to you Dr. … Pierre then said, "Bitter almonds, definitely bitter almonds."

Ed: By burning cyanide, you can extract hydrogen cyanide gas; in this tightly enclosed room, there are sufficient candles here to kill several men in minutes. The Nazis were able to convert cyanide into Zyklon B pellets, which were then used in the gas extermination chambers at both Auschwitz and Birkenau. The original product was designed as an insecticide that had an added scent or odor as a safety measure; the Nazis in violation of German law had it manufactured by Degesch Corporation without the odor. Ironically, the name of this poison used for extermination was prominently marked on the can; the name was Zyklon or "Gift gas." Ironically also, is the fact that this company and its name continue to live and remain prominent and prosperous. One distinct feature of this poison is that it smells like bitter almonds.

Little Pierre said I'll go to his place and arrest him immediately; I'll get a warrant for his arrest later. Unfortunately, Matombo had "Low friends in high places." By the time they arrived at his place, Matombo was gone. Little Pierre had some clues as to his whereabouts but they were contradictory, one was that he had fled to Jamaica across the channel or had taken the Windward Passage to Cuba. He could have taken a number of boats out of the ports on the Gulf of Gonâve to Tortuga or many of the other islands, the most reliable information had him heading towards the Massif du Nord mountain range and in the direction of the Dominican Republic, towards a vacation home owned by Ms. Du Poi.

Little Pierre had arrested a member of the Matombo sect, but he would not say where Matombo might be hiding; Little Pierre was certain that the man knew, but could not get him to divulge what he knew.

Ed: Let me talk to him. Ed holding a long rope and a heavy bag of sand, walked up to the prisoner, and whispered in his ear and took out a picture that illustrated something, Ed called Dr. Pierre over, who then said something to the prisoner. The man suddenly called Little Pierre and said he would tell him anything he wanted to know.

Little Pierre: What in heavens name, did you say to him, what did you show him?

Ed: It was more like what in hell's name I said. Ed then
pulled out a picture of a man hanging from his arms,
which were tied, at the back. Ed went on to describe the
torture called Strappado and gave the man three choices.
"Strappado," he said, had other names including
"Reverse hanging" and "Palestinian hanging," it is a form
of torture in which the victim's hands are first tied behind
their back, and then he or she is suspended in the air by
means of a rope attached to wrists, which most likely
dislocates both arms. It is best known for its use in the
torture chambers of the medieval Inquisition, but the
practice continues in modern times. Ed went on to
explain the man's choices, one, he will tie his hands
behind his back; and tie a rope to his wrists, passing it
over a pulley throwing it over a beam or a hook on the
ceiling. They would then pull on this rope until he is
hanging from the arms. "Since your hands are tied
behind your back, this will cause you very intense pain
and possible dislocation of both of your arms. The full
weight of your body will be supported by the extended
and internally rotated shoulder sockets. This will show no
external injuries that can be used by your defense
lawyer; it will however cause you long-term nerve,
ligament, or tendon damage." Ed called Dr Pierre who
confirmed this to the man and added, in his best
performance as Dr. Josef Mengele, "The technique will
cause you brachial plexus injury, leading to paralysis or
loss of sensation." In the second choice, Ed said, "your
hands are tied to the front. You will be hung from the
hands, and your ankles tied and a heavy weight will be
attached. This will cause you pain and possible damage
not only to the arms, but also to the legs and hips. This, if
you are interested is called "Squassation." It is believed
that Niccolò Machiavelli, during his 1513 imprisonment
after allegedly conspiring against the Medici family in
Florence, was subjected to this form of Strappado. You

know that water boarding, according to the US government is not torture. This is just a little extension (no pun intended) of an interrogation method, so I guess it isn't torture either."

"The third cho...." --This is the point at which the man called Little Pierre.

Of course, they did not intend to do any of this, but just the description of all that detail and a Doctor in a white coat using scary Latin words was enough to make this guy turn in his own mother.

Little Pierre assembled a team, they were going east towards the mountains and the Dominican Republic, and he also filed an extradition order and directed the local police to Madam Du Poi's home in the Dominican Republic.

Then later that night Manny got a bit somber; apparently hearing the story of this brave father reminded him of his own father, he then broke down, and started to tell the story of his father, Ed's uncle. A story he had never told before. Manny started telling Ed of when and why his father had resigned from the police force. During the summer of 1985, a fishing boat named the Mary C trolled up the Miami River. It had cargo on board worth $12 million in cocaine. During this period, the Miami River had become a major port for smugglers. The smugglers would bring in major loads of cocaine and marijuana into the United States from Colombia to Miami. The Miami River would be packed with ships from all over the southern hemisphere and the world, for smugglers, it was a perfect place to surreptitiously unload illegal contraband. Three miles into the river, the Mary C moored at the Jones Boat Yard. That same evening, six men started to unload the cargo into a van. At 2 a.m. that morning something happened that changed the anticipated outcome. On July 29th 1985, a special unit known as "Centac 26" was formed, their job was to carry out official inquiries of murders related to drug cases in the Dade County area. That night they were sent to the Miami River, where three bodies were seen floating in the river. The bodies had on them beepers, money, and guns. They surmised that it was another drug deal gone bad, but then they learned more. A witness, a night watchman described that a dozen police officers had come aboard the ship that night. The smugglers then started running. They were afraid of arrest or death as the officers had their weapons drawn and were yelling, "Kill them! Kill them!" … Afraid, the smugglers jumped overboard into the river. Shots were fired men were killed.

My father was driving by on his day off and heard the shots; he had his service revolver and went in to help. He witnessed the killings and tried to put a stop to the massacre, but there were too many cops shooting at him. There was no police report on the incident. 400 kilograms of cocaine had been on the ship, now it was all gone. The cops became the object of the investigation. Police were in disbelief. The officers under investigation were all green recruits of the Miami Police Department. The investigation found that a gang of cops had started by arresting drug dealers and stealing their cash and drugs. The cops all worked in the Little Havana section of Miami, and all worked the night shift; they would pay off the local bartenders to point out drug dealers to them. Later they upgraded, expanded, and started stealing entire shipments of smuggled contraband. Investigators guessed that cops were making $2 million, at a minimum. They had been doing this, way before they were caught.

This time they were careless. Moreover, smugglers were killed and clues were left. The case of the Miami River cops would quickly become one of the most scandalous biggest and most vicious cases of police corruption in Miami history. Fifteen officers were initially arrested, convicted, and sentenced to prison for up to 35 years. The FBI investigation of corruption was intense, eighty cops were sent to prison. They figured that ten percent of the Miami police force was corrupt. One of the original Miami River cops, Armando Garcia, is still running, and is one of the FBI's ten most wanted men. A snitch who had lied and traded false accusations against my father for a lighter sentence implicated my father. There was absolutely no truth to this, my father could not clear his name, over three years he struggled to maintain the family of eight together. He could not find honest work and ended up turning to the very thing he had fought against all of his life. He became very successful at it too. He put all of us through college. Nevertheless, he was still a burdened man, you could see it in his face; he never really enjoyed his life, and spent little on himself. If you saw him on the street you would think he was an average worker, no jewelry of gold, no fancy car, it was all for his family. I think this life went against all his beliefs; he died wealthy, but a broken man.

Ed then related to Manny one of his most unpleasant experiences of his childhood. He told Manny of a Brother John Deller, one of the whack-job teachers at the St. John Bosco School. He was there because of his violent behavior towards students. He had once slammed a yardstick against a boy's mouth and broken his front teeth, I am sure the Diocese paid dearly for that one. This is the sicko that was placed in charge of the boy's dormitory. He was a pudgy Irish man with very black hair, yet very white pasty skin that would flush a reddish pink

on a hot day. He was a man full of false pride, although
priests and brothers were allowed to wear summer
layman's clothing, he would insist on wearing that
cassock; heavy, long, and black, it must have felt like
being in a steam room. He was constantly dabbing his fat
sweaty neck with a white handkerchief that he kept inside
his sleeve cuff, like an effeminate nobleman or a woman.
He put on too much cologne and walked around like a
dandy. He wore a graduation ring as though it was a
bishop's ring. His violent personality would erupt
unpredictably, and in an instant, he would be all over a
kid, slapping, punching him, and kicking him if he had
fallen to the ground. On cold days he would make the
offending child put out his hands and he would hit them
across the palms with a thin wooden-switch, he felt that a
thin cane would sting more sharply, especially on cold
mornings. He was a sadistic son-of-a-bitch. He had a list
of boys he disliked; Cubans were on the top of the list.
He relished practicing his sadistic ways on this group.
Although eventually, their number and the fact that they
stuck together and that there were some big Cuban
teenagers in the group, seemed to keep him at bay.

It was summer in Marrero Louisiana; many of the boys
had gone back to their single parent homes for the
summer. The Cuban boys including Ed's older brother
remained, they had been playing all day and the
adrenaline was still flowing at night after lights-out, so
they were still a bit talkative but not loud. After falling
asleep, Brother John woke everyone up at midnight, with
the clapping of his hands, as he would do in the
mornings. He made all the boys, the oldest of which was
probably eleven, stand at the foot of their single cots.
"We were all a bit startled and scared," Ed said. Then like
a Nazi commandant, he walked down the middle of the
aisle that separated the two rows of cots. He would

violently slap each student in the face, one by one, as he walked down the aisle, I don't know why but none of them tried to run or cry or even yell out, it could have been from fear but Ed didn't think so. They were trying to give a message to that sick prick, that they did not fear him. During the ordeal, they seemed not to feel pain. It was more a feeling of humiliation which quickly turned into anger an anger that made them stronger, it had brought them closer together and from then on, all of them would speak about him and to him with disdain. Ed would go to sleep fantasizing of tying the fat fuck up, putting a hood over his head and taking him into the nearby woods and then beating the crap out of him.

Father Chick was a Hungarian priest. He was Principal and Headmaster, a very nice man but very old, he seemed to be out of touch with what was going on around him. They knew that going to him was of no use. Fortunately, for their group, an Italian priest, father Esposito had been named Precept and Vice Principal. He was relatively normal; he spoke Spanish and took the group under his wing. Brother John was soon transferred. To what hellhole they could not imagine, as they could not conceive of any place worse than the St. John Bosco School for wayward boys.

Little Pierre later took them for a ride to the coast; he told them stories of how pirates, after the revolution on the island, would lure commercial sailing ships, especially French ships, to the shore with lanterns, hoping they would think it was a lighthouse, so they would crash on the rocks and then they would plunder the cargo. The Haitians paid a heavy price for their revolt and independence, the French set up blockades and did not permit trade with them, most European nations and even the U.S. refused to recognize the Haitian government for decades.

He also said that on these very shores Black Beard and Blue Beard the pirates had hidden treasures.

Ed said to Manny, "you know Black Beard's beard was really black, but Blue Beard's beard was not really blue, the blue hue came from the blue dye he borrowed from his retired grandmother in Boca Raton."

Manny: Just like you huh Ed! _____33

CHAPTER 34
WHAT'S A META FOR?

That night, Manny was reading what appeared to be a novel, a little annoyed, he then said to Ed, "Why is it that in these stories everybody is saying one thing is like another?"

Ed: What'd you mean?

Manny: Well for example, one reads something like, "A two-ton truck hit the guy and it felt like an elephant had just hit him," then you read, "The guy was stomped by an elephant and it felt like a two-ton truck rolled over him." Why not just say it and let it go at that, what is that called … a Meta something?"

Ed: You're thinking of a metaphor.

Manny: What's a Meta for?

Ed: It's for catching metas-- just joshing with you. It's when you say something is like something else, but you don't use like or as. There may be a bit of overkill as far as their usage, by the way the examples you gave were similes, when you use "like" or, "as," that's a simile, a type of metaphor. "The truck was an elephant stomping on the guy, or the elephant was a two ton truck rolling over him." These would be metaphors, not very good ones, but yes metaphors.

Manny: Don't tell me the Internet?

Ed: Not quite … freshman English, father Donavan's class.

Manny: Oh! Yeah I skipped that class a lot.

Ed: One too many I'd say! ... It seemed at times that Manny's IQ never quite reached room temperature.

Manny took out a notebook and as he wrote he spoke aloud, "He wore a blue blazer, penny loafers and blue shirt with a yellow polka dot tie."

Ed: What are you doing now, going into men's wear or becoming a member of the fashion police?

Manny: No, I am writing a book.

Ed: But why all the fashion detail.

Manny: It adds words to the story, you know filler, fluff; that way I can write a big thick book.

Ed said, you know Manny, Mark Twain once said, *"I like a thick book because it will steady a table, a leather volume to strop a razor and a heavy book to throw at the cat."* He was trying to make a point, and that point is that a book does not necessarily have to be thick to be good. Did you know the Great Gatsby by F. Scott Fitzgerald was less than 200 pages long?

Manny went on writing and talking aloud, "The structure was a three story building, designed in the Art Deco style, the walls were an off-white color with a pink trim and Bahamas hurricane shutters, the windows glistening in the sun."

Ed: What are you doing now; you sound like your writing for Architectural Digest.

Manny: I am writing for verisimilitude.

Ed: What???

Manny: It's my new word for today, you know, writing for realism.

Ed: I Know what it means, I wasn't sure you did.

Manny: That is cruel Ed, even for you-- what do you think maybe we could write a book together, but with all the new technology, computers, CDs, video games, and e-books will anybody be interested? And traditional publishers hold so much sway over what readers get to read. And how can we write a great book?

Ed: Oh, I think so, these are just the medium or means of dissemination, in fact, I read somewhere that the new technology was going to increase demand for more content, it takes humans for that, there is no substitute for taste or imagination, and creativity. Besides traditional publishers are like "buggy whip makers" in the era of the automobile. They should be afraid ... very afraid. The democratization of the publishing process will curtail their distribution oligopoly and omnipotent power, then they will be offering incentives to you for selecting them. For too long has the concentration of the entire printing business been in the hands of too few. No more shall they sit like effeminate aristocratic Romans at a gladiator's fight giving thumbs up or down. Before the "Statute of Anne" in England…

Manny interrupted, "There's a statue of a woman named Anne?"

Ed: No Manny … a law (Ed continued) … it was the printers who restricted the wide distribution of literary works, since then it has been the publishers. Printing privileges then and traditional publishing privileges now, serve as a censorship device that it is used to limit content and does not foster the wide distribution of knowledge. Authors are at the mercy and beneficence of the traditional publisher, a group currently not known or associated with generosity.

The statute of Anne was known as "An Act for the Encouragement of Learning, by Vesting the Copies of Printed Books in the Authors or Purchasers of such Copies. … "E-publishing accomplishes the same, only better. The last chapter of this new "Battle of the Book Sellers" has not been written, and you can bet that the "Star Chamber" members of traditional book publishers will not go down without a fight.

Manny: Man Ed! You are one full of shit dude, how in the hell can you spew all that crap out in one breath. …You know this editor said I had to cut so much out of my draft that it changed the whole thing.

Ed: It seems like "surgeons" always suggest what they are good at as a solution, and not necessarily, what's best for the patient. You know what I said to one after all his excessive questioning, slashing, and testing ….

"An editor once tried to test me. I ate his liver with some black beans and a nice Corona."

Manny: You like that line don't you?

Ed: Well there are an awful lot of pontificators in this world that should have their livers eaten.

Manny: You being one--just payback for that earlier comment-- what about these "formula books?"

Ed: Just like there are diploma mills so it is that there are "novel-mills." Any one can write a cookie-cutter type novel on a Henry Ford type assembly line. This type of novel is devised through the use of templates that aid in cranking out formulaic drivel that might as well have been prepared by a copying machine for all of its originality. One could also use intellectual fraud or intellectual dishonesty by employing subordinates or hired "freelance contract players" to write creative material that is then legally plagiarized by "name brand authors," that merely stamp their name on the cover.

You could argue that this at least provides income to these starving authors and therefore it is a good thing. You could say that it's the money centric publishers that cause this situation, by not providing an outlet or venue for these new authors, or you could say it's the reading publics fault for not venturing into new territory and experimenting by reading the works of unknown authors.

Who knows, now with the invention of these "thinking" computers such as the "Watson," which recently beat the Jeopardy human champions, perhaps all novels will be written by machines in the future, that's probably all a publisher will need … no royalties will be paid, only electrical utility bills and the programmers' salary will be required for out of pocket expenses. Look out proofreaders and editors your next! And as far as a great book, many of the world's most famous and greatest authors were great and skilful plagiarists; take Shakespeare, Hemingway and others for instance. Although in defense of Shakespeare it was said, "If this is plagiarism we need more of it."

Manny: Amazing!

Ed: What, amazed at my knowledge?

Manny: No … more at your bullshit.

Manny looked down at his shirt and started writing. "He wore a white shirt with blue pinstripes. A Penn'ey original, he thought, or it could have been a Tar'get designer shirt. It draped ever so smoothly over his muscular body, the cloth was of fine polyester thread, extracted from the rare and elusive polyester-blend worm, it ruffled ever so softly in the balmy summer sea breeze, as the colors of the fine stripes shimmered in the soft blue light of the moon under the Miami sky."

Ed: I like that shirt. However, you might want to research your sources for that "rare and elusive polyester-blend worm." Remember when you wrote, "Many a little vinyl creature had to give up its life for the making of that fine leather coat she wore."

Manny: Oh yeah, there was no such animal … I thought it was leather, when my ex-girlfriend found out it was vinyl, I had to make up a little story. I should have said it was Corinthian leather. By the way, this shirt is a gift from my new girlfriend.

Ed: New?

Manny: Yeah, didn't I tell you, must have forgot; let me ask you a serious question?

Ed: Shoot … wait a minute, bad choice of words, why don't you just ask me.

Manny: Why is it you haven't married Katy?

Ed: Well Manny, I looked around at all my married friends and got scared, it just seems like most marriages start and end up like two movies by Elizabeth Taylor and Richard Burton. They all seem to start with great love and passion, like that of the characters Anthony and Cleopatra, in the movie "Cleopatra," and end up with great hatred, like the characters of "Who's Afraid of Virginia Wolf," sad don't you think; the way we have it now seems to work well.

Manny: You think we will be able to make some inroads into this new partnership of ours.

Ed: I think so, "A warped mind needs no straight roads."

Manny: What the hell? ___**34**

CHAPTER 35
OUR MAN IN RIO
The Pentimento, the peeling back of layers had begun

Ed and Manny were concerned with leaks in communications. Therefore, this time, rather than having a conversation over unsecured lines, they decided to fly to Rio and meet with the captain of the Brazilian police who had been in charge of investigating missing persons and murders. He had a police file on the Guarano brothers, as they had been "persons of interest" in several investigations.

They barely made the plane, as Manny always operated on Cuban time. They flew to Rio then Salvador, the last leg was on a small single engine Cessna plane, destined to the Diamantina region of Brazil. The pilot had several deep scars and severe burns on his face, when they inquired about them, the mechanic told them that he has had a few crashes, but they shouldn't worry because that was a long time ago. They asked about the passengers of the last crash, the mechanic was a bit hesitant to answer at first, but finally said, "They found the plane on the banks of the São Francisco River."

Ed: And the passengers?

Mechanic: You probably would have to ask the Piranhas about that.

On the plane, Manny seemed a bit nervous, he said, while looking out the window, "Look at that Ed. ... The cars look like little ants scurrying about."

Ed: Those are ants Manny ... we haven't taken off yet.

Manny: Aren't there cannibals in Brazil too?

Ed: Oh no, no cannibals in Brazil.

Manny then exhaled, "That's good."

Ed: Oh no, no cannibals in Brazil, what you do have to worry about is the headhunters, they'll take your head and shrink it, then sell it to a tourist, you never know, your girlfriend may find it hanging on the rearview mirror of a Miami taxi.

Manny: Thanks a lot Ed.

Ed: Don't thank me; you should see what they do to your balls.

Manny then started nervously singing one of his lyrically distorted songs. Before landing, the pilot made one first pass, he then blared a ship's foghorn that he had mounted on the plane to scare off the cows pasturing on the runway, and he then landed on the second pass. The area was not tropical; it was semi-arid with beautiful valleys, no Piranhas here. In the backcountry near Mato Grosso, there were alligators or jacaras, as they are known. There were also capybaras, large mammals that look like giant rats with the face of a beaver, and Tapirs, ant eating pig like animals. They traveled to the headquarters of the local police and met with the area's chief law enforcement officer and his lieutenant. First they stopped and had a few Brahma beers and a few Caipirinhas, the national cocktail of Brazil, Manny had more than a few, especially after hearing about the headhunters. They followed it by having some Brazilian cafezinho a form of Cuban espresso. They then met with Capitain Fernão de Barros and his lieutenant João Aires, who headed the local police office in the Diamantina region. This region by the Diamantina River was known for its Diamond mines. He gave a brief description of the mine's location owned by the Guarano brothers and its history and then told the story of the brothers. The mine was near Mato Grosso's capital, there are more than 50 kimberlitic veins located there, he said. These veins are the source for the region's alluvial deposits, or "placer" deposits, where at times diamonds can be just picked up on the surface. He told how the brothers had not only mined their own claim, but had also illegally entered the protected Cinta Larga ("broad belt") Indian reservation to mine for diamonds. This area along the Bolivian boarder had restricted mining. It was forbidden to mine there, in order to preserve the indigenous "Cinta Larga" people's homeland. The Cinta Larga natives were allowed to conduct small scale prospecting, as only the indigenous Indians were allowed to perform manual labor. Estimates of the value in diamonds of the region were that of over $3.5 billion annually. You can see why the brothers would kill to steal the claim. "You should be aware that bands of the Indians of Cinta Larga attacked a group of illegal prospectors recently, killing 30 of them; I would not advise going there alone." He described how the two brothers had formed a partnership with a third man, then after striking it rich, the third man mysteriously disappeared. Later one of the brothers married the girlfriend of the missing third man. The partnership was called The Amazon Gold Diamond Mine, it was established to mine diamonds in the region.

Ed showed him pictures of Fernando Guarano. He confirmed that Fernando was one of the partners. Ed gave a description and showed him a picture of the hand and ring of the man found in the Florida everglades. He had no photo of the mans face, as his face had been wiped to the bone by the snakes stomach acids, he also informed the captain that Pierre's DNA test had confirmed that that man was a close relative of Fernando; the captain said that by the description it sounded like Fernando's brother, Alfonzo. Captain de Barros said the third partner was presumed dead, although his body was never found. His bloody shirt and pants and the tip of his left hand's little finger wrapped in a handkerchief were found in a swamp. The forensics expert found skin and fragments of bone from that hand and speculated that this hand had been somewhat damaged. The captain suspected the Guarano brothers stole the mine from the third partner and then murdered him, but they had no proof and no body to support it, only a bloody shirt and trousers with a long slash on the right buttocks, which based on the amount of soaked blood, must have also been deep. The blood was identified as Type O positive, latter DNA confirmed it was that of Angel Du Mort.

Angel Du Mort had inherited the mine from his father a French immigrant, Henri Fransua Du Mort. Henri Du Mort had married a local girl who was famous in these parts because she was a makeup artist to Brazilian stars. They had only one son, Angel. He had studied medicine and wanted to be a surgeon, although he never graduated as a doctor, he was a practicing surgical nurse. The family traveled a lot; Angel spoke several languages, and attended prep school in Italy.

A local power broker named Atanas had bought controlling interest from the two brothers, shortly after Angel's disappearance, the brothers then left abruptly for America after the accident and the sale.

Treachery is all fun and games until someone loses an arm. Ed then asked how Fernando Guarano had lost his arm. Captain de Barros stated that after the presumed death of Angel, strange unexplained accidents began to occur. There was a large machine at the mine, which ground stones and rocks to expose diamonds found in the mineral aggregate. Every two months it was shutdown for maintenance, the machine could be easily shutoff. Pushing a large red button would immediately shutdown the machine. It also applied the brakes that would stop the grinding teeth in fractions of a second. Starting the machine however, required keys and two men, it had been designed with a fail-safe mechanism, in such a way that two buttons were required to start it, and they were so far apart that it required two men to start it, and this could only be accomplished by pressing both buttons simultaneously. Fernando, would occasionally stop the machine to inspect the aggregate, he would then takeout the large diamonds.

The night before the accident the machine was shut down according to the scheduled maintenance. The next day the machine was started early in the morning, Fernando came in that afternoon and stopped the machine; he would later call in one of the men when he wanted it restarted. He put his hand deep in the stopped grinder; he then heard a switch trip, in an instant his arm was eaten up by the aggregate-crushing teeth. His loud terrifying screams could be heard throughout the mine. Fortunately, for him, a supervisor was walking by, hit the red button and shut the machine down, a few more seconds and his entire body would have been eaten by the machine, leaving only a mush of ground-up flesh. This supervisor had just finished a safety course. He knew that releasing Fernando at this time would have caused massive loss of blood and probably death in minutes, so he did not. Fernando screamed like the stuck pig in Haiti, his horrifying anguished cries lasted what seemed an eternity, until he fainted from exhaustion and shock.

When the doctor arrived, he commended the supervisor on his quick thinking. The doctor had brought blood plasma, clotting agents and the blood type of Fernando. He set a tourniquet and then the gears were released, most of his arm was gone but the doctor was able to save his life.

The night of the accident the machine was shut down, and remained shut until the next day, when groups of expert investigators including electricians were brought in for a formal examination. That same evening after the accident, a night watchman had heard a noise as he looked towards the machine switches he saw a man running off. The next day the electrician investigating, thought at first that there was nothing wrong with the switch, but then he found a piece of wire and noted the brass screws on the two switches were bright and shiny as compared to others around it. He determined that someone had tampered with the switches and rigged them so that only one was necessary to start the machine. The culprit must have come back to remove the alteration, but was interrupted and dropped the wire. That proved that the incident was not an accident. The partial prints found could not be used to identify the culprit. Police concluded that someone must have had keys, knowledge of the machine, knowledge of the maintenance schedule, and knowledge of Fernando's habits.

After the disappearance of Angel, Fernando pursued Angel's fiancée, Francesca Cherenza vigorously. A year later she gave in, the wedding announcement was placed in the newspaper, the accident had occurred shortly there after.

"The layers of the onion," which was this case, were finally peeling. The layer upon layer of obscuring paint, that was hiding the true picture, were being removed. Ed and Manny took one day to travel throughout Rio de Janeiro and to visit the sites and artwork-- mainly the statuesque bodies of the women at Ipanema beach; they admired the brown bodies lying on the beach in their "tangas," one of Brazil's greatest inventions by the way, and its gift to "men-kind,"… the Brazilian string bikini.

The captain invited them over to his home for dinner; his wife, a very good cook, had prepared a lavish dish, Bacalhau ao forno, or baked codfish, white Feijão or beans and Farofa, a Brazilian stuffing. His wife was a grade school teacher at a nearby school. She had purchased with her own money a big laminated chart of the Brazilian alphabet, which she was taking to the school the next morning. She mentioned that there were big changes to come during the coming year, and wanted to keep the children current. Ed, out of curiosity, glanced at the chart, on the lower hand corner there was a smaller insert of the old alphabet chart; it was interesting to see how languages change and evolved over time.

Lead us not into temptation.
That night as they strolled through the streets of Rio, they
were approached by beautiful ladies of the evening,
although in Rio is hard to tell if they are ladies. They
spoke the international language of love for sale, and
uttered in near perfect English the international (perfectly
legal and defendable in court) phrase known to all
streetwalkers of the world ... "Honey do you want a date."
..."Muito obrigado but no obrigado" ... and "Boa noite,"
Ed said, they smiled and replied "De nada."

At a local nightclub, they encountered these four beautiful
cinnamon skinned quadruplets with gorgeous green
eyes. They looked like younger versions of a well-tanned
Rachel Welch or a Kim Kardashian. Now Ed was a
"Faithful man" the operative word being man, and this
created a bit of an inner conflict in his mind, Manny, on
the other hand, had no such inner conflicts; he was the
first to take two up to his room. Ultimately, as all men
know, "The spirit may be willing but the flesh is weak." Ed
wasn't even sure about the spirit part, it was more a case
of "The spirit indeed is willing and the flesh is too"-- I
mean it was a whole hearted team effort, the body, mind,
and soul working in unison and in harmony, they were
the three musketeers on a great adventure ... all for one
and one for all. No equivocation no buts (maybe some)
ifs or maybes, he was committed to perform at his full
potential, he could not afford any distractions such as
thoughts of guilt, that would hamper his performance,
onward and upwards, are we not men? Or are we mice?
Charge! ...It was a once in a lifetime experience that
could not be passed by ... I mean they were quadruplets
for goodness sake. ... Next day he thought ...Take that
one off the "bucket list" and five more off the positions
from the Kama Sutra checklist ..."Uhm--- lets see what
we've got left on our wish list ... Pool table, been there,

done that ... hanging from a chandelier? ... that seems a bit dangerous.

The Speedo is a piece of garment that by law should come with instructions for wearers, especially if you are an overweight French Canadian tourist, and yes, they are in Rio too. This bathing suit can be the most unsightly piece of men's wear if not worn properly, the instructions should state that ones member should be tucked in a southern direction, pointing towards the sand and neatly tucked between the left thigh and scrotum(unless you point naturally to the right) it should never, ever point upwards toward the sky. This sight is particularly disturbing when the French Canadian tourist encounters a topless German tourist in a string bikini, and becomes aroused. Some of these tourist were right out of a "Wal-Mart at the Beach" sighting, you know ... those people that insist on wearing outrageous outfits when they go shopping at their favorite store. One had to pay a price for staring at the gorgeous Ipanima girls, and that price was the occasional obstruction of the view by a fat tourist in a Speedo with a protruding awkward bulge. _____**35**

CHAPTER 36
THREE ON A MATCH ONE ON A LIGHTER

Once back home, Ed was relaxing, knowing Katy was safe. He thought that after two failed attempts on his life perhaps they had given up on murdering him. These thoughts may have been premature, as it seems that many times, terrible things, like airplane accidents happen in threes. As he lay in bed relaxing and smoking his pipe, suddenly a large figure leaped on top of him. A man had been hiding in the closet, waiting for him. The huge man with large strong hands, the size of baseball mitts and protruding polish sausage size fingers, placed an iron grip on Ed's throat. Ed brought a knee slam to the guy's groin; this only slowed him down and made him angry. As Ed struggled, he felt less and less air enter his lungs, he was about to pass out. He frantically reached for his gun taped behind the nightstand, but could not reach it. As he flopped around like a flounder, his outstretched left hand passed over the top of the nightstand. He then felt the lighter on the top; the one Katy had given him. He grasped it and plunged it into the left eye of the assailant and flicked it, a two-inch flame burst into the man's left eye. He screamed in agony, loosening his grip, he brought both hands up to his eye and stumbled backwards. Ed got on his feet, took the aluminum bat he kept by the bed and took a swing to his right kneecap. This brought the giant down like a large evergreen tree to his knees. With his enormous round head now at a perfect strike zone level, Ed took another nice smooth swing. (A home run hit Ed figured, had it been a ball) this only made the big fucker wobble; he hit him again, but the son-of- a-bitch just would not fucking fall. He actually managed to jump out of the window and run to a waiting car that had its engine running. All that was left was a puddle of blood from the guy's head on the sill and floor. What kind of a fucking monster could take a hit like that to the head and not fall, Ed just could not imagine, Ed thought, good god I never want to meet this guy again.

Ed called Manny and detective Matson. The police brought in a forensic team and gathered all available evidence, inclusive of the man's blood and gigantic footprints on the carpet.

Matson: We've got to stop meeting like this. It's getting to be a habit. You've got to find better playmates; you know you have half of the local and state police looking for people that have tried to kill you in the past few weeks. We've established a new department just to take care of finding your attackers.

Ed: I'm flattered and honored, but believe me is not by choice, I seem to have this magnetic personality that causes this type to be attracted to me. _____**36**

CHAPTER 37
CIRCLE THE WAGONS

𝕸anny suggested they shake up some of the local gangs, in the event that they had gotten the contract. A new Peruvian gang had moved into Hialeah, a Cuban stronghold of Miami, they were very active in drug dealing and had moved into the murder for hire department; the news had spread like wildfire in Hialeah. "A Peruvian gang, huh!" Manny said they would not last long there; "Hialeah may not have the political influence of a Coral Gables, but the neighbors knew how to handle crime without it."

El Indio was the leader of this Peruvian gang sponsored by drug lords back home. When Ed and Manny arrived at their "clubhouse" they asked him politely for information, he then said "Oh yeah! Mamame mi Machu Piccho cabrones puercos. "Roughly, he was very eloquently suggesting, and somewhat poetically too, using a famous ancient Peruvian historical landmark as a metaphor for his member, that we perform an unsavory act that only a few years back would have been considered illegal in several states and territories of the U.S. He had incorrectly assumed that they were cops, hence the use of the words pig bastards.

The gang back home had adapted an ancient Indian ritual used to dispose of bodies. This was done by tying the bodies down near local condor hangouts. The birds would devour the flesh and bones leaving no trace. The gangs however, would some times add a variation or twist to this ritual, and that was that many times the subject was still alive. In Miami, there was a shortage of condors so they just used the many canals with the meandering alligators for the same purpose.

El Indio, the chief … and one other, the biggest Peruvian they had ever seen, were both sitting on the couch watching the Soaps … As The Stomach Turns, I think it was called. His lieutenant's gang name was Pacha, named after Pachacuti-Cusi Yupanqui, a king whose name literally meant "Earth-shaker," it was a befitting moniker as he looked like a cross between a Japanese Sumo Wrestler and the original Kono from the old Hawaii Five-O TV show--one of those big Hawaiian guys that had eaten one-too-many Taro root poi and roasted pork sandwiches.

El Indio: "You think I'm afraid of you guys, huh! " He lifted up his shirt showing unsightly scars all over his stomach, "You see these, they are the bites of the Piranha; they were my initiation rites into the gang." Ed could only hope that a Candiru fish had swum up his urethra too, maybe that would shut him up. After explaining, that they were not cops and Manny lifting him by the neck two feet from the ground, he looked like he would cooperate. Suddenly, his second lieutenant, Pacha, rushed at Manny from the side, Manny tossed El Indio to the side like a rag doll and with a kick to the plexus, the big boy was down, another to the groin and he passed out.

El Indio then said, yes they were approached, but didn't get the gig; word was that an enforcer from Europe had gotten it because of connections here, with a dude from his hometown back in Liverpool.

Ed then said, I don't feel good about any of this, let's get back to Katy's place.

Outside a group of white boys dressed like "wiggers" were playing the typical rap crap on a CD player, the crap that was so prevalent these days throughout Miami, it had the expected lyrics: "I'm gona slap me a white Ho! And shoot me a cop etc, etc."

Manny being an ex-cop and a lover of women, was offended, and jumped in with his own rap verses, pointing at each kid as he rapped.

"You're a stupid white boy; you're a stupid white boy and you're a stupid white boy!
First, I take your money then I take your honey... Why?
'Cause, you're a stupid white boy, you're a stupid white boy.
You wana be a black boy, But all you are, is my dumb white toy... Why?
'Cause, you're a stupid white boy, you're a stupid white boy, and you're a stupid white boy.

Want to hear more? ... and pull up your pants, you look like assholes!

All the skinny white kids could do was to stare with their mouths open.

They arrived at Katy's and asked Coco and the Kid if they had seen anything unusual. They said no. Ed looked at Katy; she had that look of "I know something you don't know."

Katy: Well I did see a black car drive by slowly.

Why didn't you tell Coco or the Kid? Ed said. She then said that they were sleeping and they had been up during the last three nights. Because of this, she didn't want to wake them.

Ed: Why didn't you tell me?

Katy: You know how you get; I didn't want you to worry.

Ed: What the hell! --You didn't want me to worry, are you crazy! ... lets go Manny.

Manny: Where are we going?

Ed and Many dressed up in overalls, slapped a magnetic sign that read, Sears, on Manny's white pickup, Ed went out and bought a new refrigerator for Katy, which she needed badly. They arrived at Katy's and "made" the guy that was watching her house from a block away; they delivered the refrigerator and carried out the old one in the box. They returned that night and stayed with Coco and the Kid on guard duty. That evening around 2:00 AM, they heard the sound of glass breaking down stairs, each of them had taken a position on the four sides of the house, effectively circling it. Manny at the back caught two men entering and shot one blowing him nearly in half with his .44 caliber, he then cold cocked the second. The Kid on the west side shot one six times, a second guy winged him in his right arm, forcing his gun on the floor, the Kid leaped and with a left hook knocked the second guy out cold. He then tied him up with duct tape. They were all packing Uzis.

Manny: Hey Kid, why did you shoot him six times?

Kid: Because the gun only had six bullets.

Ed was on the east side, hiding as two of the guys came in. He was at their back, and hit one hard with a bat on the back of the head, (he had gotten lots of practice lately). The other covered his head, so Ed got him on the side of his leg just above the knee, he buckled, and then Ed caught his head with the bat. Manny had been a cop, and had training in the use of the nightstick or baton. He had taught Ed how to strike at not only the patella or knee cap but also a larger target, the middle of his outer thigh, just above the knee were the vasus lateralis muscle of the quadriceps is found, this will cause temporary motor paralysis. One could make a man buckle and fall on his knee with just one hit. Manny explained how in this area there are nerves with sensitive nerve endings; one good hit in this area feels like an electric current shooting through your leg, it's like being hit by a taser. This causes tremendous pain and momentary paralysis, forcing the leg to buckle. Better yet, if you have an open target, hit his sephenous nerve on the inside of the thigh, this however is a difficult target to strike, and if you're at his back hit him in the gluteral fold, where the sciatic nerve, one of the largest in the body, is found; this will definitely cause great pain and also paralysis.

Manny later said, "You mean to tell me you hit him when he wasn't looking?"

Ed: Just as hard as I could!

Coco was positioned on the south side. It was a very dark night with no moon, and he could not see anything. Suddenly a shadowy figured rushed the house, Coco did not have a clear shot until the guy was within 20 feet of the house, the security perimeter lights came on, they were like a spotlight on the guy, Coco fired one shot that hit him between the eyes. Then they all went outside; he was a big one. It took all of them together to turn the dead guy over...It was Pacha, the second lieutenant of the gang. Ed said, I guess El Indio was not entirely forthcoming with his answers. There had been two contracts, and the gang had gotten one of them.

They called an ambulance for the Kid. The two guys tied in duct tape claimed to be only gang grunts, paid to do all the heavy lifting. They said they were only following orders and didn't know anything... El Indio, who had sat in the car, was the one calling all the shots; they only carried out the deeds. El Indio meantime had already driven off. They then went into a "no comprendo" mode. Manny wasn't s so sure of their bullshit, he had heard this "no comprendo" and "I was just following orders" crap before. He took the two guys in to a side room and began to ask them about any other attempts they were planning, but they continued to stick to their story.

Manny had brought back from the southwest a beautiful but dangerous golden cactus plant that was called the Jumping Cholla, Katy kept it near the window with some other exotic plants and Japanese Bonsai trees. He had noticed the accent of one the guys wasn't Peruvian but more Mexican. He carefully broke a small piece of the cactus with pliers, avoiding touching the prickly needles. He then began telling a little story to the guy. He said that while he was in Arizona he had met this beautiful señorita, her nickname around town was Cholla... jumping Cholla. At first Manny did not know why, but after a few dates he knew why, she turned out to be a stalker, and the most clinging and irritating woman he had ever met, he couldn't even go to the toilet with out her following him. This is how she had acquired her nickname.

Manny then had Coco remove the trousers and underwear of the Mexican guy, and continued, saying, "You're from those parts aren't you? Then you must know what this is, and how it works like hundreds of fishhooks, you know that once they enter the skin it is almost impossible to take them out, causing excruciating pain." He then passed the cactus near the guy's private parts. The guy immediately began telling Manny of a plan B that was to take place if this attack failed, he said El Indio was getting more men and would be waiting for the right moment to attack Ed and Katy.

Manny: You see Ed; there is a method to my madness.

Ed: Yes, there is, and I am glad there is because we are going to have to get to El Indio fast and once and for all, before he gets to us.

They called detective Matson. When he arrived, he immediately showed concern for Katy; he was always very concerned about the safety of women. He asked about her and Ed told him not to worry, she was in New York, staying with her sister, they had taken her out in the refrigerator box just prior to that nights attack. _____37

CHAPTER 38
ATANAS, THE DEVIL INCARNATE
A master of corruption

Musico Atanas was a Greek immigrant who had settled in Brazil. He had accumulated a vast fortune using dirty politics, the diamond trade, as well as real estate schemes of all types. He was also known as a broker who dealt in information and arms. He was suspected of arming terrorists and arranging contacts for those in the market for a contract assassin. He was proud of his underhanded dealings and often bragged that his family name was originally Satanas or Satan, but his great grandfather changed it because it attracted too much attention to their devilish undertakings. Atanas was known as the owner of the Golden Jaguar, the largest yellow diamond in the world. This diamond had been found in the Amazon Golden Diamond mine, the same mine worked by the Guarano brothers and Angel Du Mort. Musico had been a Brazilian senator; the story goes that he had won his Brazilian senate seat by bribing the poor families of the favelas or shantytowns that are scattered about throughout Brazil. He had bought loyalty by offering free milk to the favelas' children in exchange for their parent's votes, not an altogether altruistic gesture, but more of a selfish one, as soon after the election he cut the supply. Atanas later parlayed his power and influence to purchase prime real estate, invest in diamond mines, television, and radio stations. His company had a brochure with hundreds of uncompleted luxury buildings named after American presidents, heroes, sports stars and the like (he was very proud that he had become a naturalized American citizen.) Ed made some inquiries and found out (via Musico's ex-secretary, the former wife of the Brazilian conductor of the orchestra Brazil 66, Sergio Mendes) that the reason these buildings were unfinished and vacant, was that Musico had absconded with all the down payments of every buyer that had pre-purchased a condominium back in Rio. The sum was in the millions of dollars. He got away with it because there were no escrow laws in Brazil to prevent this. Those sums were in turn invested in his Miami properties. The accountant that recently left his employment said that Musico had ordered him to do the same with the collected escrow funds in the USA, but he had refused and quit. Local and federal Brazilian judges tried to intervene, but Musico simply brought out the milk wagons and had the judges replaced for the price of a carton of milk. Once Musico had traveled home to visit Brazil, as he stepped into his limousine, he was promptly fired upon with a high-powered rifle; unfortunately, it was his chauffer that was killed and not him. From then on, he was forced to travel by bulletproof limousine everywhere he went. He took this stolen money and sunk it into two condominium buildings on Collins Avenue, near the Fontainebleau hotel, on Miami Beach. He had named them the Blue and Green Jaguars. The buildings were excessively tall and did not meet local ordinances; their shadows blocked the sun and allowed large amounts of algae to grow on the beach. They were also casting a shadow on the beaches of the buildings next door. The owners of these buildings, one was the Eden Rock hotel, complained to the environmental protection agencies and to the Miami Beach officials, but to no avail, Musico it seemed had gotten to them first, and had managed to bribe them all. He was an extremely ambitious animal and a master of corruption. Other concerned citizens filed petitions to prevent their construction. The buildings went up nonetheless, and still stand as symbols of greed and corruption in the world, to be gazed at by all of Miami citizens and visitors. One of his favorite swindles was to charge a four percent fee for property management, then subcontract it out and charge that expense as an operating expense to the unsuspecting property owners. In effect, double charging for the same service.

He was heavily invested in the Chandler bank and was one of the main stockholders. Police suspected him of having hired Gabriel, as many of his competitors had disappeared and those that had been found were found dead and branded with the infamous consecutive letters. The Police however, could never prove it.

Musico was known to be a large investor in the Amazon Gold Diamond mine, run by the Gaurano brothers. He had managed to get a controlling interest, later buying out the two brothers. Musico was the perfect example of the saying "Steal a little and they throw you in jail steal a lot and they make you king."

Neville's firm was his auditing firm and Neville was the partner in charge of this client; he was in fact the devil's auditor.

A deal with the devil, between two devils.
Gabriel had reached an agreement with Atanas, he would not kill him, if Atanas used his wealth, and influence to help him track the Guarano brothers, and after all, it was partly his money anyways. It was a good deal for Atanas as he owed them a great deal of money, and if they were gone, he would not have to pay them anything. He was making it possible for Gabriel to get leads on his prey and to travel to where they traveled, even if he didn't have an assassination contract at the location.

The Cement tycoon.
Ed had recalled a case were a Greek company president
had been murdered, a case where Neville was also a key
player. Aries Yiocevoc Avontou spelled Υιος ενός
Ανόητου, in Greek. It had been shorten from the original
Greek, ξεγελάσουν γιου ενός ξεγελάσουν.

He was the president of the Kronos of America cement
company, named after Kronos, the titan that had
castrated his father Ouranos with a sickle. Legend has it
he did this while his three titan brothers held the father
down. Befitting name for a company that figuratively
would do the same to their employees, as they were
often fired just before they reached retirement age, in this
manner they would not be entitled to receive their full
retirement benefits. America offers no protection against
this abuse. Aries' advisors had been Neville Fox, Chris
Howell and Larry Perkins or Larry, Moe and Curly, as
they were known. They were the three other titans or
stooges. They hid their incompetence by making sure
Aries never received the true information about the status
of his company. They had been suspected, but it could
never be proven that they had something to do with Aries
murder. Aries was one of the first victims of the Alphabet
Assassin, when it was not suspected that he was a killer
for profit. This initial contract was Gabriel's introduction to
Neville Fox. Atanas had in fact introduced Gabriel to
Neville.

Neville and his cohorts had siphoned off millions of
dollars and then had the CEO murdered; they then
started a fire to hide the evidence, a fire that inadvertently
spread to burn down the company, causing the
unemployment of thousands of employees. None of this

was ever proven. Their arrest would bring some closure and justice to these people.

Ed's reputation, spread by Chandler, had reached the ears of many wealthy and prominent families who had lost relatives to the Alphabet Assassin. They began calling for information and to recruit Ed and Manny in the search for the killer, they all wanted justice, some more than that… they wanted revenge. There were many calls, as the known dead and unresolved murders at the assassin's hands, were estimated at over 27, although only 26 were reported by the press to have been found branded.

One of the families seeking justice was the family of Aries Yiocevoc Avontou, the man Ed had tried to help but could not, because he was "The foolish son of a foolish man," who listened to "las lenguas sueltas,"… "the loose tongues" around the office, rather than the advice of his auditor. The families invited Ed and Manny to visit them on Paros Island, in the Mediterranean. This island was a part of the Cyclades group of islands. The family had a home there. They were to spend a few days and plan a strategy on pursuing Gabriel. The family was very gracious and wanted to make this trip a very pleasant experience, even though it was for a very serious purpose.

The Meltemi, the strong wind coming from the North, hits most of the islands of the Cyclades during the summer months. Paros, one of the main islands attracts thousands of windsurfers every year that concentrate near the New Golden Beach. Here is where the Professional Windsurfers Association (PWA) organizes the annual World Cup. They went to watch and try the sport. The Aegean Sea was full of luxury ships.

Manny asked Ed, "How is the Starship Enterprise like toilet paper."

Ed: How?

Manny: They both circle Uranus in search of Kling-ons.

Ed: You paint a wonderful image Manny.

Ed thought how during an investigation many things about an individual are inadvertently revealed. For instance, during the investigation of Aires' murder, Ed found out several interesting things that he did not know about him. Aries was a proud man that had attended very good schools, but Manny had found out that he wasn't entirely truthful in his Bio. He had said that he had attended Harvard; this was a bit of an exaggeration, the type of exaggeration many hot shot executives make on their resumes. This was not entirely true as all he had done was attend a $20,000 dollar one week seminar. He then casually let it be known around the office that he had "Attended Harvard," all he had to do is let the rumor mill run its course, and by word of mouth ...Tada! he had graduated, not entirely a lie but also not the truth. This is typical to too many U.S. executives and politicians, many of which are currently running our companies and our country.

They traced the last days of Aries. He had traveled from Krono's headquarters in Athens and then to the port of Piraeus where he took a local ferry to the island of Aegina. There had been a planned outing for executives of the Kronos Company at the island. Fox, Howell, and Larry Kline were there, but they all had alibis when he

disappeared. His assistant said that he had received a call and immediately left without an explanation.
The last place Aries was seen alive was on the island of Hydra, a small rocky island in the Argo Saronic Gulf, south east out of the Athens's port of Piraeus and within sight of the southern Peloponnese mainland. His naked body was found tied to a donkey, up by the top of a hill, he was found with his ass prominently exposed.

Tour ships go in and out of the Hydra port every few hours filled with hundreds of tourists. Manny had done some legwork and had narrowed down the ships Gabriel could have taken and passenger's names that matched his description. He had identified a passenger that looked like Carradine. He was traveling under a false Italian passport as Dr. Azreal, the same name he had used when he had traveled to Tahlequah Oklahoma to murder the wives of his enemies.

All they could tell the families at this point was that they were sure who the man was, and then passed on the police artist sketch, as well as the photos taken, as he had walked off the ship, his face however was hidden by a broad rim hat he wore. All they could do was promise them they would continue the search for Angel Du Mort a.k.a. Dr. Azreal a.k.a. Gabriel.

Ed was starting to get a lot of new business generated by this case, via references from Mr. Chandler, Umberto, and Kerrigan. There was a Spanish saying that his mother used to tell him …"Cria fama y echate a la cama," roughly translates to "Create your fame (or your reputation) and you can go to sleep or rest easy, " meaning that once you establish yourself, life becomes a lot easier and success just rolls along on its own inertia.

38

CHAPTER 39
♪ ♫ DIAMONDS ARE A GIRL'S AND A GUY'S BEST FRIEND ♪ ♫

Emil Pantera, known as El Gato, had been a cat burglar and a student and disciple of Jack Murphy, the legendary surfer, beach boy and master thief, known as "Murph the Surf." His moniker came from his acumen as a surfer. He had been named the state's top surfer in 1963, winning the National Hurricane Surfing championship twice. He was said to have a near genius IQ. Murphy was best known for having committed the biggest jewel heist in American history. In late October 1964, thieves stole 22 gems from the JP Morgan Collection of Precious Gems at the New York City's Museum of Natural History. Three of the stones were so famous they would be impossible to sell in their original shape. One of them, the Star of India was recovered, but several of the stones, including the 14-carat Eagle Diamond and the De Long Star Ruby were missing. The De Long Ruby was returned for a ransom of Twenty- five thousand dollars. The Eagle Diamond was never found, at 16.25 carat it was the largest diamond discovered in the continental United States. The word carat came from the Greek word for the carob bean, the bean or seed could vary in weight from 0.1885 grams to approximately 0.215 grams. In ancient times, they were used to weigh precious stones so that a stone that weighed six carob seeds became a six-carat diamond. Overtime the British calculated an average and came up with 0.197 grams, today carats are calculated at five per gram or one per 200 milligrams. The authorities believe the Eagle diamond was cut into smaller stones, and is no longer in existence as one piece. Murph, claimed to know red Chinese fences that would move them. This crime was his most audacious. One of the stones taken, the Star of India, a 563.35-carat star sapphire, and the largest in the world, was the most valuable. Emil had learned his trade while assisting Murphy in many escapes, which included the theft of very exclusive custom-made jewelry stolen from many of Miami and Palm Beach's most wealthy residents. He would use speedboats to access the mansions found on the intracostal. He would then escape through the many canals and waterways of South Florida, leaving no trail and the police baffled. Emil had inherited the skills and connections necessary to continue in the trade. Manny had arrested him ending his career, but had subsequently helped him in going relatively straight. Emil had been one of Manny's many connections to the crime world of South Florida, although now retired he continued to provide detailed information on anything to do with the diamond legal or illegal trade.

Emil called Manny and told him that through the underground grapevine, he had heard that a very big deal was being brokered, a deal worth millions and millions of diamonds. Emil said that one of the reasons the Guarano brothers had been back in Miami was to participate in that deal, he added that another Brazilian, a man well known in the diamond trading circles, a Mr. Atanas, had been competing with them and had gotten the deal after their deaths. The deal was going down soon. It involved high-ranking officers of the Chandler bank. He had only one name, a Madam Du Poi, she was mentioned as a possible buyer, there was also another associate, a man , he did not know his name but sources told him he was a high ranking officer in one of Miami's largest companies. They need the diamonds to launder the cash taken from the bank. The rumor was that they wanted diamonds to avoid recording transactions through the banking system, the talk was that they were going to take the diamonds and smuggle them out of the country soon. There was a lot of traffic on the grapevine. This major deal might also involve lesser players. They would be players, which would be sharing a piece of the pie, in one form or another.

The mastermind and the ultimate culprit.
Neville and Ms Du Poi had known each other since Haiti; they had in fact married. She had soon found out about his sexual inclinations but had decided to stay married for appearances sake. When it was no longer expedient, they divorced. All the while, he mentored and deellied with young boys, whilst she dallied with Matombo. During this time in Haiti, they hatched this scheme. They divorced and then married for convenience, he married the daughter of a partner in the firm, and it was easy as she was a wallflower with no prospects of marriage, while she married the son of the Bank's CEO, a grieving widower. It was a diabolical scheme to steal from the bank millions through the purchase and resale of inflated mortgages. They were selfish, self-centered, ambitious individuals whose avarice knew no bounds, it was easy for them to betray, all they wanted was money and then to go their separate ways. They were preparing to reap what they had stolen. They had forwarded through wire transfer, cash to a Cayman Island numbered account. The islands were a known refuge for tax evaders. They wired in enough funds to aid in their flight from justice, keeping the amount of each wire at just under the $10,000 dollar limit that required reporting it to the US authorities. The plan was to convert the rest of the cash into some form of easily hidden and negotiable item or items of value. They decided on diamonds.

Du Poi and Neville were negotiating with the Guarano brothers to turn their cash, after the sale of their stock, into diamonds and smuggle them out of the country. After the brothers were killed, they ultimately had to deal with señor Atanas. Atanas had blown the cover on the two brothers, who had been hiding from Gabriel under false identities. Atanas had paid his debt to Gabriel, while getting the entire piece of the diamond deal with Neville and Ms. Du Poi. It was a win, win situation for him.

They planned to take the Chandler Bank's corporate jet. First, they stuffed diamonds in the seat cushions, all of them did not fit so they decided to place them elsewhere were the authorities would not think of looking. After they landed and passed customs, they would take them out. They didn't know where they were going yet, but it would be somewhere where there would be no extradition.

They both had married for money. The marriage was also part of the diabolical plan that would enable them to carryout one of the most lucrative and heinous financial crimes of the century. A crime that needed to be kept secret at any cost, they were the ones that masterminded the murders of Armandito, Herbert Afortunado and his AVP Susan Boyl. This was a crime that would strip numerous investors and pension funds of their cash. These funds provided the only security to millions of retired elderly widows and orphans. They could care less.

Neville met with Du Poi in secret.

Du Poi: You get all the diamonds.

Neville: No, but don't worry I'll get them; I need to pay off Medebes and Atanas before they get their goons after me again.

Du Poi: Well get them; we haven't much time! If you hadn't hired that idiot boxer, and those stupid gang kids we wouldn't be under such pressure.

Neville: Hey! Gabriel failed the first attempt, and the second; and he never fails. I had to do something. I'm the one that lured Armando to Gabriel with the pretense that I was going to reveal problems with the acquisition of his bank. It was me who drugged him. All Gabriel had to do was kill him. Your Matombo failed too.

Du Poi: Don't you say anything about Josef; he did succeed and would have succeeded in killing the rest if it wasn't for that damn Castillo ... you hired him!

Neville: I did not, Flannigan did, Old Chandler had gotten suspicious and he wanted someone outside the firm, I had no control over Flannigan, he is not one of my guys. I had that idiot Chris on the job and inexperienced auditors under him, they couldn't find fraud if it bit them in the ass ... If they followed the audit program I wrote, no way could they have found what was going on. They had no imagination or initiative; all they did was follow the program and performed the steps by rote that I approved. Without an original thought in their heads, they could not have found anything, and Chris is just an imbecile ass-kisser who was instructed to approve only positive comments and ignore the negative ones. There was one smart kid on the team, he began finding stuff, and asking questions; but I had him transferred right away. It was a perfect crime if not for that damn Castillo. Old Chandler asked the senior partner, Dewey, directly for an outside consultant. They were poker buddies, so he asked him to have someone from the outside come in, and Flannigan was the one that called Castillo.

Du Poi: Josef's plan was foolproof; it was that damn Castillo, with the help of that traitor Haitian Doctor, who uncovered the truth. That stupid Gabriel … didn't you tell him we didn't want Armando's body to be branded.

Neville: You can't tell Gabriel to do anything; he's insane. He can't control his compulsions; he is useless now as an assassin. He kept branding the men and women we had contracted him to kill, I told him over and over, we need to keep a low profile, and that we didn't want our targets branded, I told him that they must be imperceptible crimes-- make them look like accidents; but he wouldn't listen. He threw that bank officer over the balcony in Finland, attracting even more attention. And how was I to know that … that Armando guy had a brother who was a cop, the bastard is relentless. It was that damn Manuel guy; that Manny that ruined everything, he made the connections that exposed Gabriel. I am sure that damn Castillo had something to do with it; Manny is not that bright. They are even digging up the Aires murder now. When do I get my share? I need to get away and hide for a long time.

Du Poi: Your share? You are lucky if I give you anything. All these years of planning, you did nothing; I am the one who killed Leslie, my first husband. His wealth provided the seed money for my plan, then I poisoned Chandler's son's wife so I could marry him, I influenced Howell's daughter to marry you, it was all my doing. The mortgage scheme would never have worked if it were not for me. You were supposed to help cover it up; instead, you hired that maniac killer and you allowed Castillo to be hired and….we could have completed our plan to murder Old Chandler, his son, and your wife. We could have had it all!

Neville: Hey, it was Atanas who recommended Gabriel. I am the one that got Atanas involved. Without his connections and influence, we would not have been able to sell all those bogus securities around the world. He influenced the financial ministers and heads of the national banks around the world to loosen the securities laws and audit regulations. His lobbyists got the government to loosen regulations here too, and his moles at the SEC and other agencies, made sure we weren't caught. He was the true mastermind. Hell, his plan was foolproof, he had figured-out that once the asshole bank and asshole audit executive's had committed to these mortgage securities there was no way in hell they were going to back track. I mean they had already certified the "Emperor's new clothes" were beautiful and there was no one in the crowd to see the truth and no one with the guts to shout out otherwise. Everything would have gone according to plan if it wasn't for that damn Castillo; he had to stick his nose in it. I offered Gabriel twice his fee if he killed him and Manny by the end of the month. He was so pissed he said he would have done it for nothing, he is committed, said he would be tracking those bastards to the ends of the world.

Neville and Ms. Du Poi's frustration made them sound like those Italian Chefs in the Bertolli TV commercials, you know … Damn Bertolli.

Marta Gutierrez called Ed and told Ed that she had gotten reliable information that Neville Fox and Madam Du Poi had made reservations on the Bank's private jet, the plane she said had the capacity for inter continental flights.

Ed asked how she had gotten that information.

She said, "I am the bank's VP for Public Relations, besides I'm dating the pilot."

Ed: How do you know it's them?

Marta: They did give false names for the flight log, but he described them. They reserved the whole plane and charged it to the bank. You know that bitch would always reserve two seats when she traveled, even when she was told there was a shortage of seats. She would reserve one for herself and one for her fur coat; well she did it again. Two seats for people, one for a fur coat were booked, it has to be her. My boyfriend the pilot was Antonio Medebes's pilot at one time, and he said that Tonio was looking for Neville because Neville had not paid his gambling debt. It looks like Neville and Du Poi are making a run for it.

Ed: I'll call inspector Tradeles. _____**39**

CHAPTER 40
DEAF, DUMB, AND BLIND JUSTICE

They were still loading the plane. Neville said he had to make one more trip to the office, and then they would be done. He was just about to leave to go to his office, as he started his car the FBI swooped in and arrested them. A quick search of the plane, found diamonds in the plane's toilet and sewed into the seats. Inspector Tradeles said they were leaving in a hurry and although there was a lot of money and diamonds, he said there should be more; they already searched their homes and office and found nothing.

They had the jet, a custom-built Citation Sovereign with a range of 3,282 miles and a sitting capacity for 9 passengers ready for take off. The Atlantic's width ranges between 1,770 miles to 4,000 miles in the south. They would have to land in the Azores islands of Portugal, which were 3140 miles or 2729 nautical miles from Miami, at an average mach speed of 0 .77 or 220 mph it would take about 14 hours. The flight plan indicated this; the plane would have to land for refueling there. The next leg of the trip was not logged. They planned to leave no trail that could be followed.

Ed told inspector Tradeles to look again in Neville's office, this time … in the aquarium at the office. Inspector Tradeles went to Neville's office, it turns out that Neville was hiding the remaining loot in plain view; the bottom of the fish tank was full of diamonds that could not be seen, as they blended in the water. Inspector Tradeles also found documentation that Neville was not only acting as

Atanas' auditor, behind the scenes, but also, in violation of several state and federal laws, he was acting as the chief financial officer for Atanas' holdings. He was also linked to the loan shark Tonio Medebes, structuring his financing, managing cash, and setting accounting policy; He was in fact the devil's CFO. Days later Tradeles called Ed about the diamonds and asked, "How did you know?"

Ed: That SOB did not care about one living thing, he seemed too close to those fish for his personality, he never cleaned anything, and if he could, he would hire someone to wipe his ass. He would always stand between you and the large aquarium. He would dissuade you from looking too close; saying the fish were very expensive and sensitive, staring at them in close proximity would cause them to go into shock ...what bullshit! It is a perfect place to hide diamonds, even if you are right next to the aquarium glass it's nearly impossible to make out the diamonds, the water is the perfect camouflage.

Ed thought it is a shame that Florida's infamous electric chair had been decommissioned. He thought that it would have been a just ending for Du Poi, and her voodoo pal Matombo, as well as for Neville and Gabriel. Especially if it malfunctioned, as it was known to do from time to time. When it did, it would first burn the convicted murderer's scalp before it killed him. Ed and Manny were of the opinion, that in the cases where children had been murdered or mass murders, serial killings, torture and mutilation had taken place, the electric chair was just punishment, malfunction would just add to the justice.

The pair could not be tried for the murders because of lack of evidence, as Matombo, the Killer of Afortunado and Susan Boyl, was on the run, and Gabriel, the killer of Armandito and twenty six (perhaps more) others had not been captured. Neville and Du Poi did not know this at the time of their interrogation. The police got them to confess, at least to Manny's brother's death. They said that Armando was getting close to the truth about their lending practices. This came out during the special project he was performing relating to the Florida International bank acquisition. His bank wanted to know the strength of the Chandler bank before considering the sale. Armando was leading the review; he was getting proof of the frauds. They attempted to recruit him but he declined, they then had him killed. The lawyer that Manny was purposely delaying outside the police office got free and stopped the confession before it was signed.

The Federal and state prosecutors told Berto, Kerrigan, and Manny that since there was little evidence to connect them to the murders, and since Matombo could not be found and Gabriel was on the loose, what they had was circumstantial evidence, and the murder charges would probably be dropped; they just could not try them for soliciting murder for hire.

They were accused of masterminding the whole scheme. The case on the civil and criminal fraud charges would proceed; over 20 counts of criminal indictments were filed, including racketeering, fraud, bribery, insider trading, embezzlement, computer crime, identity theft, forgery, mail fraud, investment advisor fraud, falsifying books and records of a bank, conspiracy and a slue of other charges in violation of securities laws and banking laws. Other countries wanted to press charges too, victims hoped that their cells would become their interment tombs. The firm of Dewey Chaney and Howell were accused of obstructing a federal investigation and probably will have to close their doors especially after Chandler sues them for all they've got. His son filed for divorce from Du Poi. The main perpetrator, Atanas, the man behind the scenes, the devil himself, remained free and clear as Neville and Du Poi refused to cooperate; they feared him more than the Law.

Neville had conspired to ensure all audits failed and had falsely testified to the SEC that the bank was in full compliance, a statement so far from the truth as any could be. He had arranged all the murders; he had in fact become the portrait of the Devil's Auditor.

The prosecutors thought it would take over a year to determine the extent of the fraud, as there were hidden assets all over, including apartments in New York, houses in Palm Beach and Key West Florida, even a Chateau near Paris, France. They would be set free on bail but their passports were confiscated, they both had multiple citizenships and passports that made them a flight risk. They even discovered a land-flipping scheme where Neville and Du Poi would buy vacant land in the Caymans for $50 million and later would sell them to the bank for three times as much. Pilots would testify as to numerous trips to Switzerland, and to deposits of large amounts of cash. The victims had been many, including Hollywood directors, producers, and actors. Many pension funds and educational institutions including the one that Professors Redrum, Buteur, and Artimori were teaching at, had been victimized. Ed thought how ironic that Madoff had managed to stay alive and through subterfuge, tricked the feds into thinking his family was not in on it. Thereby saving their hides. While many of his clients including the French aristocrat, Mousier Rene'-Thierry Magon de la Villehuchey, who had lost over a billion of his own money and his family's and friends

money, committed suicide. How many of Neville's and
Ms. Du Poi's victims would suffer the same fate?
Although, only recently it was reported that one of
Madoff's sons had committed suicide, this alone may be
a worst punishment than all the years of jail time that he
received. Also, very sadly for old Chandler, months later,
his son, the president of Chandler bank, feeling guilty and
responsible for the demise of the bank "Fell on his
sword"-- literally, he killed himself by falling on his great
grandfathers civil war sword that had hung proudly over
his mantel.

Ed also marveled that this major incident had caused but
a blip in the earnings of the brokerage firms involved.
Their average salary had actually risen to over $500,000
a year. One writer wrote that they were like legalized
bank robbers, he compared Neville and Du Poi to Bonny
and Clyde taking the money and running. Flannigan had
admitted that Neville, as the partner in charge, had never
seriously audited the bank, Ed thought, "No shit Sherlock
what ever gave you the first clue." The most startling of
all accounts is the fact that all these bankers and brokers
voted themselves huge <u>bonuses at the same time the</u>
<u>government was bailing them out! And then tried to hide</u>
<u>the fact to boot.</u>

The prosecutor said that they would serve over 100 years
in a medium-security federal prison. Neville and Du Poi
could socialize with a coterie of the likes of Franklin C.
Brown former vice chairman of Rite-Aid.

Ed's documented evidence and confessions from
associates of Neville and Ms. Du Poi, her cousin at the
real estate company ,bank officers, appraisers
,investment brokers that had made deals for lighter

sentences as well as mortgage brokers that had done the same, were sufficient to convict them.

Only time will tell if our collective goat, ass and other farm animals were indeed saved.

Ed invited Manny to a large steak at Shula's restaurant, not the one in Ft. Lauderdale by the beach on U.S. one, but the one in Miami Lakes by the golf course. They sat next to the brass plaque that bears the name of several brave and hungry men, many of them football players. There on the second row third from the bottom was Manny's name. To receive this great honor one must eat a 40-ounce steak in one sitting. As a young football player at Florida International University, he had achieved this great feat, a little older now he was still a big eater but didn't want to push himself. They had two large New York Strip steaks, baked potatoes, asparagus, and a couple of Presidente beers. Ed thought this was a long way from the early days in Miami, when they only had "Queso del Refugio" to eat (government surplus cheese for Cuban refugees,) he also thought of the brass plaque at the Chandler bank commemorating Herbert Afortunado and Susan Boyl; two employees who died while doing their duty. ____40

CHAPTER 41

♪   ♫   ♪   ♫

IN A CLEARING ~~STANDS~~ LIES A BOXER

Ed accompanied by Manny visited the firm's office to pick up one last check. As they passed Neville's old office they could see a very large man sitting sideways, Manny saw his right side profile and said. "You know who that is?" Ed said no.

Manny: That guy is Richard Richmond.

Ed: And who is that?

Manny: That's Richie Rich, he was once a contender to the British heavy weight boxing title; he fell on hard times and washed-out as a boxer, what's he doing here?

As they passed, the man stood up; he was massive, he then turned so that the other side of his profile was visible. … He was wearing an eye patch.

Manny: Should we call detective Matson or Tradeles?

Ed: Not just yet ... lets see where he leads us. Ed walked up to him, stared right into the giant " Cyclops " good eye, and asked "Haven't I seen you before?" To which he promptly replied, "No."

Manny tailed the guy all day; he made several stops, including Neville's house and Ms. Du Poi's. Then he drove to the airport where the bank owned jet was hangared. He then drove back to Miami. It was getting dark as Manny followed him to the Peruvian gang hangout, and saw him go in, and then he heard a loud pop, pop. Manny went in, and saw El Indio lying on the ground with two bullet holes to the head. Richie Rich then started to take a shot at him, but Manny knocked the gun from the boxer's hand. The giant just looked up and didn't make an effort to pick up the gun; he just smiled a big smile and came after Manny. He thru a hard punch, Manny ducked and got him with a hard right cross to the chin. The British boxer went down like a sack of potatoes. Apparently, he had a "glass jaw,"... not a good thing for a boxer. If Ed had only known this, he could have saved himself a few swings of the bat.

Manny, looking at his fist, said, "Huh ... I could have been a contender!"

Manny tied him up, called Matson, and went home.

The Boxer was arrested, for attempted murder on Ed and for murdering El Indio. ____41

CHAPTER 42
HE WHO LIVES BY THE POISON....

Ed's phone rang; Little Pierre, the police sergeant from Haiti and Pierre's nephew, was calling Ed and Dr. Pierre from Haiti. He said that although Josef Matombo Mostasa had escaped, he had been able to trace him to Santo Domingo in the Dominican Republic. He was staying at one of Madam Du Poi's homes. He was found in a small shack that had been sealed and bolted from the outside. Hundreds of bites dotted his body, he looked like a well-used dartboard from an Irish pub, there were more pin holes on him than those found on a North Miami police crime map. It could not have happened to a more evil or corrupt man … with the exception perhaps, of a Miami mayor.

A few spiders were found around his body. Ed then remembered Kerrigan's little tale of his pet spiders.

Ed: Let me ask you, did the "stiff" have a "stiffy?"

Little Pierre: What do you mean?

Ed: Did he have an erection?

Little Pierre: Why yes how did you know?

Ed: Just a hunch, Pierre you'd better be very careful, as I am sure these spiders are Banana spiders and have a very toxic bite.

Little Pierre: The examiners suspected that too, they are being examined to see if they are poisonous. But how did you know?

Ed: Just a hunch.

Little Pierre: One more thing, his head was cut off apparently postmortem, and a sign was hung on the head that read "Fate of those who kill with Gu. "

Ed knew that Gu was the Chinese word for poison. It's funny because a new energy drink goes by that name, it probably would not be a big seller in China ... there goes a gazillion loss in new customers. In ancient China, those convicted of poisoning would be executed and a sign containing a similar phrase was hung around their bodies and displayed so as to discourage others. Not a bad practice ... could be used in the U.S. to discourage tampering with over the counter drugs, Ed thought.

Ed called Berto and told him the news. He didn't seem surprised and said he had heard the news a few days earlier, -- but how? Ed had just gotten the news directly from the police. Ed thought about what Kerrigan said about Berto's family and how they do favors for each other.

Little Pierre said, "It looks like someone caught him in time, he was about to escape; the "Pettit Poi," a yacht owned by Ms Du Poi, was by the house with the motor running. Ed thought a better name should have been "The Sea Witch"... well at least justice was carried out.
_____**42**

CHAPTER 43
♪ THE REVELATION, ITS RETRIBUTION TIME ITS RETRIBUTION TIME ♪ 　♫

After the meeting with the two professors at FIU, Ed was left with these nagging doubts. There was something about the comments made when he had visited professor Buteur, something about what was said to the students while he had visited. There was something about the scholarly credentials, and something about other things they had said, but he could not recall why it bothered him. His thoughts went back to Brazil at the dinner table with the captain's wife, the teacher, and the changes she said were coming to the language … to the **alphabet!** Suddenly a flash, a revelation came to him, Ed realized what was bothering him, he headed to a computer to check the questions he had rolling around in his head; with a couple of quick searches he had found the answers he was looking for. He also called Ed Kerrigan, that is Dr. Kerrigan to recheck some terminology and then back to Google.

He then called Manny and told him he had just had a wonderful epiphany.

Manny: When … those were empanadas I brought this morning -- from La Gran Via bakery!

Ed: Never mind.

He then had Manny do a search on all the Alphabet Assassin's victims reported to date, he had him research all domestic and international police reports and had him list all the victims in order, sequenced by the dates they were murdered. He also asked Manny to make a list of all the letters burnt on their necks. They were all there, except three … just as he thought … although the killer wanted to delay the police, he still wanted all of the bodies that were branded found, so he made sure that somehow all branded bodies were found in sequence, only three were missing. The last letter used by the killer was Z but there were only 23 branded bodies. **It all made sense now!** After examining all the information, Ed felt that he now had all the clues he needed to identify the killer.

Ed then asked Inspector Tradeles and Matson to stage a news conference through the Miami's police PIO (public information officer) and had Shauna Gomes deliver the news. A very large crowd had gathered. Ed had situated himself at vantage point where he could see individuals in the crowd. Shauna began by stating that the Alphabet Assassin had been identified and the story headline for the Herald had already been written and was being kept in a vault at the Miami Herald's office, ready to be run in tomorrow morning's paper, after the arrest was made.

She said "The murderer of the 26 identified branded victims, and the others "… she was then abruptly interrupted by a man in the crowd who yelled out "That's not correct it is 23 branded not 26"… she ignored him and continued …"Which included the two victims in Tahlequah, as well as Armando, the brother of then officer Manuel Castillo; would be brought to justice." Ed had now seen the man in the crowd … it was David Carradine, obviously the killer in disguise.

He then arranged a meeting. He asked Chandler to come and Tradeles to bring all suspects of the murders, and all the linguistic professors that were at the Kerrigan party, and to meet him at the bank conference center. Detective Matson and the Miami chief of police were also invited to be present, and to bring several officers to guard every possible exit, as he wanted his "captured audience" to remain as such. He explained that this would be an easy way to expose and capture the killer without alerting suspicion. Ed suspected that the cocky killer would think that there was no possible way they could have identified him, and would attend just so he could laugh at them when they disclosed and publicized the name of the wrong man.

Ed began the meeting by saying, "The killer Gabriel is here right now among us in this room"-- A loud gasp by the attending crowd was heard.

Who is it? Asked Tradeles.

Ed: The man who claims to be an expert.

What do you mean Castillo, these are all experts, so who is it? Exclaimed detective Matson.

Ed: It's quite obvious … elementary my dear Matson, It's the so-called linguistics professor. (You work on this frickin case, gathering boring details for untold number of frickin weeks, without little help or recognition, your damn right your going to drag it out and make it a dramatic ending).

Tradeles: There are a number of them present in this room, who is it?

Ed asked all of the professors to stand, and then asked those with tiepins to step forward. He examined the tiepins, and then asked those that had pins with gems to sit down. Only three professors remained. Professor Redrum, professor Artimori and professor Tueur Buteur where left standing. He then examined their hands.

Ed: The one with the double AA on the pin made of steel, not silver, is the Assassin.

Dr. Artimori: That's ridiculous, he blurted out in his pretentious and obviously affected thick British/Italian accent. I am the brother of one of the victims, and how dare you question my credentials, I am a professional.

Ed: Well you do have some credits to your name, you were an MD wannabe, you were studying to be a doctor but didn't quite make it, you are a former surgical nurse, and you are an expert at professional makeup application, a skill learned at your mother's side. She was not only a makeup artist to the stars but she was also skilled as a special effects artist that applied prostheses to convert the faces of actors, including those who worked as impersonators, into the likeness of others. You are a professional all right –a professional assassin that is. And, is it ridiculous? You call yourself professor and claim to be a linguist, and claim to have a doctorate of letters in English as well as other languages, yet several times you exclaimed, as I recall, "That's not the proper use of the English alphabet."

So? ...The professor exclaimed.

Well, in fact, there is no such thing. There was the use of the Runic alphabet known as Futhorc (or fuþorc), at one time, when Old English was used in England under the Anglo Saxon rulers, but the Latin alphabet has replaced this one for quite some time, since the 7th century to be precise. Although this is not common knowledge to the average individual, someone with a doctorate in the languages would have known this. There are many Alphabets ... Greek, Cyrillic, Arabic, Hebrew, in fact over a dozen, but there is no such thing as the English Alphabet ... the alphabet we use is the English version of the Latin alphabet, and nonetheless it is the Latin alphabet.

Other small facts and idiosyncrasies exposed you, the Portuguese accent ... from Brazil I'd say, specifically south Rio de Janeiro, would slip out when you were overly relaxed or extremely pressured, not Italian as you claim. The silver key chain with the little bell shaped pronged settings cupping only two yellow diamonds in the shape of eyeteeth or cuspeds ... Oh yes I noted as you walked in that you had added the two diamonds to your key chain, while the third remained empty, this is also a "dead" giveaway. What happen? Alligator hunters disrupted your attempts at removing the cusped of señor Alfonso Guarano and you had to stop the tooth extraction and dump the body. These are symbols of the mine you lost to the two brothers. Your obsessive compulsions would not allow you to leave uncompleted tasks, so you later had an accomplice brake into the examiners office to complete the task. You haven't had a chance to mount it on your key chain, but I am sure either it can be found on your person this very moment or it is still in the possession of your accomplice. These are your constant reminders of your success, the revenge you extracted from the two brothers that had betrayed you; they had taken your wealth and even more than that, the love of your life, your fiancée, Francesca; Fernando had taken that too. They had broken you, broken your hand so you could never be a surgeon and broken your heart and had attempted to slit your throat; Alfonso had dumped you and left you for dead back in a Brazil swamp. You went on to repay him in kind. I am also certain your connections in the field of surgery must have provided you the name of an excellent hand surgeon that corrected your malformed hand and the missing tip of your little finger.

The tiepin with the double AA monogram that you referred to as "a tool of the trade," serves a dual purpose it is in fact a branding iron made of steel. By the way, how do you know yours is the only one of steel?

When you corrected the reporter as to the number of murdered branded victims, you were right, as only the police and the murderer could know this to be the actual total count. The police you see never disclosed this to the media. The media simply assumed, based on the last victim branded, Alfonso, who was branded with a letter Z that there were 26 victims, as this letter is the 26th letter of the English version of the Latin alphabet. Not being a genuine professor of linguistics, you were not aware of the English version … or of the revised Brazilian version. You should visit home more often and perhaps take some refresher courses at a grade school so that you familiarize yourself with the current changes to the Brazilian Portuguese alphabet.

You being from South America and Brazilian, however, would use the Brazilian version of the Latin alphabet to account for your victims. In the Latin Brazilian alphabet version, there were only 23 letters until January 1st 2010, when the letters K W and Y were legally added. The Portuguese Language Orthographic Agreement of 1990, had approved these letters for insertion into the alphabet. Brazil being one of the members agreed to abide by the Agreement, but the additional letters were not made official or legally binding until 2010. This is also, why no bodies have been found with the letters **K W Y** on their necks, not because they were not found by the police, but because these letters were never used by you to brand any bodies.

Manny: I think there is a joke somewhere in all this.

Dr. Artimori: That doesn't make any sense, there are many victims by the assassin that were not branded.

Ed: Oh, come on! You and I know that they were just collateral damage, and you never brand them, do you? Don't count them, you don't even think of them as people.

Ed continued: You would not know this, because you are not, and never have been a real professor of linguistics. Oh yes you have a facility with the languages, and can pass for a professor, but you are not, are you? You have been using the common 23-letter version of the Brazilian Latin alphabet to account for your victims; Z being the 23rd letter of the old version, your next victim was to be the AA … and that was to be me.

Had you been using the Spanish version, your next victim would have been branded with U, the 24th letter, as the Spanish alphabet has three additional letters, the Ch, LL and the Ñ," making it a 29-letter alphabet. However, since your choice of alphabet for the murders is pre 2010 Brazilian Portuguese, your native language, you are now using AA for the 24th. The tiepin you now wear, and were going to use on me--by the way, nice cologne, Canoe right? Must be a thing with college professors …Your selfish ego and maniacal personality would not allow an error in the count, so you chose to correct the reporter and at the same time inadvertently revealed yourself. As I mentioned, the police had never revealed that the 23rd victim had been branded with letter Z; the press simply assumed that because it was Z, there must be 26 victims.

Your carefully tailored suit pants are designed to drape beautifully over your shoes, and to hide the orthopedic shoes you wear, the Evenup shoe balancer I believe is your brand. Although designed to hide the higher heel profile, some of it still shows.

You said you had graduated from Oxford and Cambridge with a Suma Cum Laude and a Magna Cum laude, that you held a PhD in Entomology. The British system however, does not follow the American system of awarding Latin honors, their system issues honors degrees that have stated the abbreviation "Hons," after the degree letters in their diplomas. <u>There are no Latin Cum laude, Magna Cum laude or Suma Cum Laude honor designations in the British educational system!</u> Moreover, Entomology is the study of insects while Etymology is the study of words. You incorrectly referred to the first as your field of study.

You would think someone who is as meticulous about his murders, would be more careful in establishing his cover. I also observed during the fund-raiser dinner that you hold your fork like an American, not transferring it from left hand to right after you cut and eat your food, unlike a European born and raised there, who passes it to his right hand.

Artimori: This is all circumstantial evidence, even the witnesses described a different man.

Ed: Your skill with makeup and your connections in the medical field have enabled you to disguise yourself and correct the described scars and other body marks. I am also sure that the inspector will be able to match your thumbprint to the one partial bloody print found in Tahlequah in Francesca's apartment. You also had said that you gave blood to save your brother Felipe; this was not true or possible as he was type O negative.

Artimori: So! That makes him a universal type.

Ed: Now I can see why you did not become a doctor, although you are a sanguinary bastard you weren't paying attention in hematology class, he was a universal "donor," but not a universal recipient, you my sick friend are O positive and as such you could not have donated blood for Felipe's transfusion. I am sure DNA test will match the drop of O positive found at the Bailey's Falls murder site in Tahlequah Oklahoma to yours. And if I may be excused and allowed to use one more bit of potty humor, your ass print will provide positive identification that you were in the basement apartment of the Franklin Castle in Tahlequah when Francesca Guarano was murdered. You know Gabriel or should I call you, Angel Du Mort, you could clear yourself right now –just drop your pants and let the inspector ... well inspect your ass.

Artimori: I will do no such thing!

Ed: You know ... Gabriel, a man has to know his limitations.

Manny had done a background check on professor Artimori, first he tapped into the FBI's National Crime Information Center, there was nothing on Artimori, plenty on Gabriel, most of which had come from him, but no photo. Manny called the Italian police to get a recent picture of Dr. Artimori; it took time, as the Italian police were no different from the French or American. There was the Polizia Municiplale, or municipal police they handled local crimes, then there was the Arma dei Carabinieri, a sort of military police, Polizia di Stato, state police Polzia Provenciale. It was a bureaucratic web, which Manny first had to break through before he could get any answers, and this took lots of time, but he did it; Manny had received a picture, obtained by the Florence police from the university. The photograph was not a picture of the individual that was calling himself Dr. Artimori. It was a photograph of the real Dr. Artimori. The one that had disappeared around the time Gabriel started his killing spree in Europe.

Ed: You killed the real Dr. Artimori and stole his identity and then you killed the only living relative who could identify you … Felipe Artimori his brother, this is why the motive was so confusing to the police as there was no link to his death, no reason to kill him, it was not robbery or a crime of passion it was a deliberate act to hide your identity. They had confirmed that this so-called linguistics doctor was someone else. Ed handed the pictures to Tradeles.

Gabriel: You do not know anything Castillo, none of this proves that I am a murderer and it won't stand up in court.

Ed: I know this; you are Angel Du Mort, better known as Gabriel the redeeming angel, son of a French man that immigrated to Brazil and married a local girl in Rio. You were the third partner in the Amazon's Three Gold Diamonds Mine, and murderer of the Guarano brothers, my cousin and Manny's brother and 20 plus other people around the world that we know of. And this, I am certain of … you are going to burn in hell, you stupid malicious Fuck! _____**43**

CHAPTER 44
JUSTICE DELAYED, JUSTICE ACCELERATED, OR NO JUSTICE AT ALL

At the criminal murder trial Neville and Du Poi were found not guilty. They had been able to post their exorbitant bail, although they had to restrict themselves to their homes. Electronic bracelets were attached to their ankles, a twenty-four hour guard, which they had to pay for, was assigned to their homes. As they were being released at the back of the jailhouse, and stepping out of the building at 8:00 a.m. that morning, two shots rang-out, each one finding its way to and through the hearts of Neville Fox and Madam Du Poi. The police looked around, cordoned the area, and searched around for blocks, no evidence was found. The experts were then called in.

Ed called Berto to tell him the news, Berto said that he had already heard, Ed thought how in the world could he have possibly known, he had just heard only minutes after it happened from the police, and it had yet to be release to the press. Berto ended the conversation by saying "Kerrigan and I do favors for each other." Ed then called the chairman of Chandler bank and he also said that he already knew, but how could they know … unless … he remembered Berto saying how his grandfather was an expert shooter … that little old man?

Several days later Forensics investigators determined that the bullet was a .50 caliber bullet used by sharpshooters in their high powered rifles, the trajectory pointed to a building rooftop about one thousand yards away, no evidence was found on the roof, the only relevant information was that the building belonged to Umberto Afortunado senior.

Ed thought vigilante justice is better than no justice at all. *"Revenge is an act of passion; vengeance of justice. Injuries are revenged; crimes are avenged." (Samuel Johnson quote, English Poet, Critic, and Writer. 1709-1784).* Manny said that he would have preferred a trial and the electric chair, and since the electric chair was not available and killing them with his own hands, his number one choice by the way, was not an option, this was the next best outcome, as justice was attained. He said he would keep his number one option open, if he faced Gabriel once again. Manny thought that this was also best for Neville, as he probably would have gone to jail and ended up as the "cell bitch" of some large black convict named Bubba, then again depending on his preference as a "pitcher" or "catcher" Neville might of looked forward to this experience.

Ed called Kerrigan, he said he already knew and added," As I told you before we do favors for each other," Ed was thinking I guess he means Berto already called him. Kerrigan thanked him profusely, making Ed feel like he was living up to his namesake of Paladino.

Gabriel had been captured. Inspector Tradeles and a team of forensics experts and psychologists went on to interview the captured psychopath and examine evidence at his home. They determined that his IQ was near genius, he was fluent in many languages and had extensive medical training, and he was also an accomplished musician who could play classical violin. It appears that the attack on him by the Guarano brothers and the marriage of his fiancée, Francesca, to Fernando had catapulted his mind over the edge. Ed and Manny had felt that if Angel Du Mort had stopped after killing Fernando and Alfonzo, they would have had no problems accepting his actions; the subsequent murder of even one innocent person however, had made him a villain in their personal book of good and evil.

He admitted freely to killing over 28 people. However, claimed only 23 were planned. He would forge his irons even before he had a contract; he carried a lighter and small torch to heat them up at the scene. He explained how he would not brand the victims of unplanned murders, those he had to commit to cover up his deeds or those to protect him from being discovered, like the teacher and the three students in Tahlequah. He did not even consider them; they were just collateral damage in his mind. He only accounted for the ones he obsessed over, the ones he had used to contradict Shauna's reported number at her press conference, which included contract killings. I guess you could say there was method to his madness.

In his apartment were found fake ID's, driver's licenses, passports from different countries with different names, cash in several denominations, Euros, Dollars, Yen and Rubles. Disguises of all types, wigs, pantyhose filled with cotton stuffing to alter his real weight, makeup and prosthesis; noses, chins and ears. Large amounts of the sedative Triazolam, commonly known as Halcion. And a 9 mm Glock, police matched test rounds from this gun to the one round that was found imbedded in Ed's wall. Every detail that had to be covered to perform a successful murder was there, if the devil is the details, Gabriel was certainly into his. When asked why his hand was not damaged, and the tip of his finger not missing as reported, he just said that he had connections in the

world of orthopedic and plastic surgery; he knew
excellent doctors who had corrected these problems.

He was asked about his David Carradine disguise. He
said he wanted to be remembered, by the witnesses, but
remembered incorrectly as someone else. He added that
he had learned from his mother, the makeup artist, that
the look of certain characters could be best attained if
one has the facial bone structure that is already similar to
the individual one wishes to emulate. He said his facial
structure was very much like David Carradine's and the
other mentioned actors, adding only "I am much more
handsome." A cut of meat that resemble a wedge of
cheese cut from a large ball of gouda was found in a
freezer, later it was determined that several slices had
been cut off, and what remained was less than the
original pound of flesh taken from Fernando's buttocks.
Ed wondered if a cookbook entitled "How to Serve Man"
was also found. A human heart was also found in the
freezer, presumably Alfonzo's. Dr. Pierre asked how he
had accomplished the feat of removing the heart, while
Fernando was still in the grasp of the python. He said it
was simple; he offered the snake a small rabbit, saying
that apparently it wanted an appetizer, an entrée before
the main course, if you will. He then added casually "You
know in Europe an entrée is the term for the dish served
preceding the main course; unlike the improper way the
term is used in the U.S. and Canada." Carefully hidden in
the attic, and only found by using cadaver dogs, was a
string of 23 ears assembled as one would a pearl
necklace, with the desiccated penis and right testicle of
Fernando featured as the centerpiece. Assassination
paid well … in his multi car garage a two thousand
eleven white S600 Mercedes costing over $160,000 was
found.

Gabriel's high priced lawyer (or "liar for hire" as Manny referred to him) told Tradeles that all of this evidence was explainable in court. Identity theft he claimed was not murder, the house was not in his clients name, he actually lived somewhere else, and although his client may have talked, he did not sign a confession, and with Gabriel's state of mind, he was easily going to have everything his client said excluded and made inadmissible. Without more direct and compelling evidence or an eyewitness, he felt he could get his client off, as a last resort he felt that the insanity plea was still an option.

Tradeles called Ed and Manny and asked them to meet him at La Carreta in Little Habana near Calle Ocho. When they arrived, he related his conversation with Gabriel's lawyer, and although he did not let the lawyer suspect, he did agree that if they could not get a confession or stronger evidence, the government would not be able to convict. Ed and Manny looked at each other, and then told Tradeles the good news. They said that those country cops; the sheriff and deputies in Tahlequah, were not the country bumpkins they appeared to be, they had kept some evidence back, but were now ready to disclose it.

Tradeles asked what evidence would that be, and why had they not told the FBI, "We could have used it," he said.

Ed: We only just heard about it today from my cousin, Manny's sister, Dr. Beatriz. In that small town everybody knows each other, and everybody looks out for each other, they just felt that this would be best for all concerned, especially for the community and the victim's family.

Tradeles: Well, what is it?

Ed: The university professor's wife from Tahlequah, Mrs. Lawford, is still alive; she has been in hiding, recuperating from her wounds. She said that she would testify against Gabriel in court, she also said that, she could recognize him with or without makeup. He got so close that she could tell he wore makeup, she also said that she could not be fooled. Only the sheriff and Mr. Lawford knew she was left alive, they kept it quite because they were afraid the killer would come back and finish the job and they would not have been able to protect her, but now that he has been captured, she feels safe to come forward. Her attempted murder was not as random as originally thought to be, it wasn't just a chance encounter. She apparently was well acquainted with both the real Felipe and Seraphim Artimori, as she and her husband had traveled to Florence Italy for a Linguistics forum and there, at a university-sponsored party, met both brothers; they dined at their homes and spent several days with them. She had even met the false Dr. Artimori but he had been introduced to her as Dr. Angelo Morrow. He had made an impression, as he was very handsome. It was obvious that he had tried to murder her because she recognized him in Tahlequah, her husband escaped because he was out of the country. I am sure he would have been attacked as well had he been in Tahlequah at the time. The Italian police had been closing in on his latest identity, so he chose the bachelor brothers who had no other family as good candidates. Seraphim had received an offer to teach in the USA, he was making plans to travel here, and so he was chosen for the identity, his brother had to be killed to cover the identity theft. She immediately recognized Gabriel as being Dr. Morrow from pictures in the newspaper.

The inspector was elated and expressed confidence that with the evidence they had, and now this strong witness, the state and the feds would be able to make a strong case against Gabriel. Tradeles had a big smile on his face, and just said, "He's going down!" _____**44**

CHAPTER 45
CARRIED OF TO JAIL DO NOT PASS GO
♪ ♫ On top of Old Sparky all covered with ash ♪ ♫

Although arrested in Dade County, Angel Du Mort was shipped to a high security prison Upstate; the Raiford State Penitentiary, a Florida State Prison, also known as Starke Prison because it was located near Starke, Florida. This prison houses one of the state's three death row cellblocks and the state's execution chamber. Although the chair was decommissioned, death by lethal injection was still in effect for first-degree murderers, and this prison was one that carried it out.

He would be imprisoned with good company. This prison had held a plethora of noted criminals. After noting the names on the roster of former inmates, Ed was having second thoughts of living in paradise.

A notable former inmate was Theodore Robert "Ted" Bundy; he had been executed there, right on top of "Old Sparky," as the Florida electric chair was nicked named. He had repeatedly denied the murders for over ten years, but finally confessed to over 30 murders, although the actual total number of victims, not unlike Angel's victims, remains unknown, it is estimated that as many as 26 to over 100 died at his hands. He would bludgeon his victims, and then strangle them to death, many times with Hanes stockings, his preferred brand. He also engaged in rape and necrophilia, eek!

Other notables included the likes of John Couey, who died in prison before the sentence of death could be carried out. John Evander Couey was an American sex offender convicted of kidnapping, raping, and murdering nine-year old Jessica Lunsford in February 2005, in Florida.

Paul Jennings Hill, was the first person in the United States to be executed for murdering a doctor who performed abortions.

Danny Rolling, also known as The Gainesville Ripper was executed there after confessing to the murder and mutilation of five students in Gainesville, Florida. Other crimes he confessed to, were the rape of several of his victims, and an additional 1989 triple homicide in Shreveport, Louisiana, he was also accused of attempting to murder his father in May 1990.

Gerard John Schaefer was imprisoned in 1973 for murders he committed as a police officer. He was convicted of two murders, but he was suspected of many others. Schaefer became obsessed with women's panties and also became a peeping tom, spying on a neighbor girl named Leigh Hainline. He later also admitted to killing animals when he was a boy. He even admitted to cross-dressing, although he claimed it was solely to avoid the draft. Schaefer's I.Q. tested at 130, this lies within the very superior range. He was an autodidact and had learned all about all types of police strategies and methods, he was also self-taught on the criminal behavior, and methods of serial killers, skills learned were promptly placed into practice to avoid detection. On December 3, 1995, Schaefer was found stabbed to death in his cell. His killer was a fellow inmate named Vincent Rivera. Rivera was convicted of killing Schaefer; 53 years were added to his life sentence for double murder.

John Arthur Spenkelink, executed in Florida (and the second person to be executed nationwide since the re-introduction of the death penalty in the United States in 1976). The first execution was that of Gary Gilmore in Utah. The last man executed in Florida had been in 1964, and the last execution nationwide had been in Colorado in 1967.

Ottis Elwood Toole (some times misspelled Otis) was an American serial killer and arsonist who died in jail. An accomplice of convicted serial killer Henry Lee Lucas, Toole admitted to many counts of murder, rape, and even cannibalism. He was a person of interest to the police in several unsolved murders, including that of Adam Walsh. On December 16, 2008, police reported to the media that they had identified Toole as the most probable murderer of Adam Walsh. He had recanted a number of confessions, including that of Adam Walsh. Toole was convicted of three counts of murder and confessed to four more murder charges before dying in prison.

Aileen Wuornos was an American serial killer who killed seven men in Florida between 1989 and 1990. She had claimed they raped or attempted to rape her while she was working as a prostitute. She died by lethal injection in 2002. The movie Monster, in which her character was played by Charlize Theron, was based on her crimes.

This was a who's who of some of America's most infamous villains, rivaling Superman's archenemies. Ed felt confident that Gabriel would die here or in a federal prison.

This prison was a maximum-security prison, where escape was thought to be impossible. The warden had assured everyone, including the general public that there would be nothing to fear, as there was no escape. He had taken extra precautions and had isolated the prisoner in a special cellblock reserved for the most dangerous criminals. The prisoner would be kept in solitary confinement in his cell until his trial. So all could rest easy and calmly.

The following morning it was reported that Angel Du Mort had escaped from his prison cell; no one could figure out how. Inspector Tradeles accompanied by Ed Castillo traveled to the location to question the warden, the jail keeper, and the watch sergeant to determine how this could have been possible. Ed asked to be informed on the operational procedures used to secure the prisoner, and walked through every step in the process; a procedure he was well trained to perform as he had done this thousands of times as an auditor.

The warden in a loud indignant voice said, "Heads will roll I assure you," inadvertently using a bad choice of words, as a guard had been murdered and nearly decapitated during the escape.

Castillo then asked to inspect the cell and its contents. There was an unwrapped package; a cake box, sitting on the table used by the prisoner to eat his meals. The table had been pushed against the exterior wall directly under the barred window; he obviously used it to climb up to the high window. Ed noticed the metal shavings that had fallen on the floor and on the table. Ed climbed on the table examining the bars; they had been cleanly sawed away with a very sharp tool. Ed then examined the entire package, the box, the wrapping paper, and that which was left of the ribbon and string. He, rubbed the string between his fingers, looking intently at it, he then examined the fallen particles that had dropped and scattered on the ground.

As Castillo walked around examining the cell, he asked the warden to relay in detail the events preceding the escape. The warden went on to describe them. He indicated that a visitor had come to see Angel Du Mort that day, a woman; she had been carrying a box wrapped in a festive holiday paper with a shiny sparkling string and ribbon. She said it was a present, a gift of cake, as it was Du Mort's birthday. The warden proudly said that he had made sure the package and the woman had passed through the metal detector, he then personally had unwrapped the package, and had sifted diligently through the cake. It was he, himself, who delivered it to the prisoner, ensuring that no tools of any kind were hidden inside. He assured the inspector and Ed that it would be impossible for anyone to smuggle contraband of any kind into his prison.

Ed Castillo looked down at his hand and the slightly raw skinned, almost bleeding fingers, then exclaimed "Well that's how he did it. "

How? Asked the warden in a huff, how can you possibly know how he did it. "Yes, how?" Inspector Tradeles asked.

Ed Castillo, in his best Sherlock Holmes like voice said "Elementary my dear Inspector." You see, the string and ribbon are not what they seem to be. They are not made of a decorative fiber, but rather they are made of a very thin synthetic strand of spun carbon graphite, coated with epoxy, and covered with industrial diamond dust. Totally undetectable by your metal detectors.

The string is in fact a very strong and highly sharpened saw blade, capable of cutting through the hardest of tempered steel and easily through the substandard steel of the bars in this cell. This tool in fact can also be used as a garrote; a very effective weapon for strangulation or for cutting, as it can easily sever a man's head."

Guard: Yes, we know, the sentinel guard stationed at the back entrance to the prison had been killed a la OJ Simpson or Symsonized as the inmates refer to it.

Inspector: His throat had been cleanly severed through, almost all the way, nearly decapitated the man, just as the poor victims, Nicole Simpson and Ron Goldman are known to have died. The depth of the wound was very much like that of Fernando Guarano's.

Manny said to the guard, I like OJ'ed better. You know— "'He was OJ'ed"… it's catchier.

Ed gave Manny a disapproving look .

Ed then added, "Well warden, you literally, single-handedly handed over the means of escape to the prisoner."

Ed: Can you describe the visitor warden?

Warden: How can I forget, she looked just like Bo Derek.

It sounds like Catalina Calor, Ed said. "No wonder she was asking all those questions about where I lived and my schedule, Gabriel had put her up to this too, he uses his charm to manipulate women."

Detective Matson: We were able to arrest Gabriel's accomplice, goes by Catalina Calor, this individual was arrested at the Miami International airport. The accomplice was boarding a plane to Chile, we were lucky because we put out a BOLO (Be on the look out) immediately for an individual with the last name of Calor, and an alert ticket agent saw the name and alerted security; he was promptly arrested.

Ed: He?

Detective Matson: Yes, she it turns out is a he, his real name is Carlos Calor, a.k.a. Little Caca, a female impersonator that was a member of the cast of the "Sunday Drag Brunch", a drag queen show at the Palace hotel in South Beach, you could say Pussy Calor didn't have one.

Ed: So you could say the member had a member.

Detective Matson: That's right ... She ain't no woman! ... She's a man, baby!

Ed: I guess we should stop this, we could go on all night with this, -- you win.

Detective Matson: You are right it's somewhat silly and immature, certainly not politically correct --and you are right ... I won. Oh, yes, before I forget, in a hidden compartment of his luggage we found a large golden diamond fashioned in the shape of a tooth, most likely the one stolen from the coroner's office.

Matson had never expressed the slightest sense of humor, but here he was ... one of he guys.

Thinking back on Manny's date with Pussy, Ed came up with this limerick, that he would début at the next Lucky Leprechaun get-together, to commemorate Manny's date with Pussy:

> *The lass my cousin brought home was a prize.*
> *With breasts of unusual size*
> *They were plump and firm*
> *As he would confirm*
> *But her penis was quite a surprise.*

Ed: Good god and I wanted her held against me … eek!

Manny: Ed you are such a prude!

Ed: Huh?

Manny: He-she fooled all of us, haven't you seen all those pictures in the Internet of beautiful half dressed women who in the final picture take off the bottom of their string bikinis, and surprise!--It's not a landing strip it's a rocket launch site. I thank my lucky stars it went no further than it did.

Ed: No, I don't look for those sites.

Manny: Sure you don't.

Ed called Kerrigan with the bad news; he thanked Ed and said, "Ok then you're still on the clock. You were great in tracking the SOB, but the incompetent cops let him get away, I want you back on his trail, this isn't over yet." Again, he added, we, that is Berto, Chandler and myself are very grateful for what you've done. Chandler also wants you to look into the death of his daughter in law, he always suspected Madame Du Poi, but he wants confirmation. Oh, and Mr. Howell wants you to see what you can dig up on Neville, he feels that he married his daughter so he could get an influential position in the Chandler bank audits, so he could cover up the fraud. The only one who seems happy and excited by all this, is Berto's grandfather, he said he has been practicing and would like a "shot" at Gabriel.

By now, Ed thought Gabriel had boarded one of Atana's jets, one of two Hawker 4000 Beachcrafts, with a range of 3,400 miles, it could cruse non-stop to Europe or South America and at average speed of over 220 mph, it could be in Europe within 14 hours. But he hadn't, he actually was at the Key West marina the same day of Ed's cousin's wedding, Gabriel had been stalking Ed and Manny, unable to find an opportune moment to make his move he chartered one of the 60 foot catamarans. Several days later it was found near a port in Punta Can in the Dominican Republic, the crew could not be found, the captain however had been strangled and his body hanged with the mooring line tied to one of the ship's cleats. His body was hung over the side; sharks had repeatedly bitten his feet, which had been dangling in the water. Little Pierre and the local police suspected he was planning to rendezvous with Matombo, to form an unholy alliance of assassins and then flee to some unknown destination.

Inspector Tradeles had put out a BOLO for Gabriel, a task force of several domestic and international agencies was formed, his profile and description was issued, although, because of his mastery of disguises, the beat cops were instructed to treat him as an "Unsub" or unidentified subject and not rely on the description. Beside his physical description and possible limp, he was described as an unsociable criminal that expressed no remorse or guilt, and took no responsibilities for his actions, a perfectionist that used many aliases, and could be found working in many professional fields. One who had many fake identities and documents, many had been found at his apartment, but knowing how clever he was it was determined that he must have more, hidden away in "safe houses." _____**45**

EPILOGUE

Ed's aunt Edwina had invited him and Katy to spend a few weeks with her in Arizona, and Ed was seriously considering visiting her. In Phoenix Arizona there was a neighborhood made up primarily of retired elderly couples, widows and widowers. Edna had moved next door to Ed's aunt Edwina. Edna appeared to be in her late seventies, she had a matronly figure with gray hair worn in a bun on the back of her head, rather old-fashioned Edwina thought, as it made Edna appear older than her age. She wore bifocals, and although old, she was nonetheless a strong tall woman. She told Edwina she was from Scandinavian descendants, from Holland; she said that the people there were known to be very tall. They were classified as some of the tallest in the world.

She had moved in only recently, and hit it off right away. Edna could be quite charming, they had laughed about how their names were so alike. Edna was a widow; she had one son that she rarely saw, as he traveled extensively. She told Edwina that he would pay for her to visit him often. She often traveled and was gone for several weeks a time and would ask Edwina to keep an eye on her place while she was gone. She would some times bring souvenirs from far a way places. Edwina noticed that Edna could be very moody before and after her trips.

She was slightly bent over, as though she suffered from scoliosis or calcium deficiency, an affliction Edwina thought was common to the elderly, not that she was so much younger than Edna was. Although Edna was hunched over, she did not appear at all frail for her age.

Edna at times did chores around the house, on one occasion; she picked up this box and put it on the porch.

Later, Edwina stopped over with some coffeecake and noticing the box, tried to bring it in for Edna, but when she went to pick it up, she could not, the box was unusually heavy, and though Edna was a large woman, Edwina thought, "How can a woman that age lift such a heavy object."

At times, she moved slow and deliberately, as one would expect from a woman that age, but then at other times she moved quickly and very limber. Edwina noticed also that at times, she didn't seem to need her glasses or her cane, and her limp and stiffness would come and go; Edna attributed it to her arthritis. Although Edna wore a thick makeup, it didn't seem to hide her wrinkles.

The news about Gabriel's escape was on all the stations, his picture with and without makeup was displayed prominently on TV, and the fact that he was a master of disguises was mentioned several times. Edwina then had her morning coffee and then walked her dog, picked up the mail and newspaper, and sat down to a second cup of coffee.

Edna had come over and said she would be gone to visit her son, but this time she would be gone for quite sometime, so she told Edwina not to worry, and asked if Edwina could watch the house. Edna noticed how Edwina was looking up at her, and then down at the newspapers, intermittently and somewhat nervously Edwina would talk, look up at Edna, and then down at the newspaper. For some reason Edwina noticed Edna's hands for the first time, they seemed larger, she also noticed that her shoulders were broad. She was walking very briskly and not stooped at all, her voice was more youthful sounding; her limp however was more pronounced. What earlier had seemed to Edwina the walk and talk of an elderly woman, had now taken on the more youthful attributes of a younger woman. This youthful exhilaration and appearance could have just been the happiness Edna was feeling, at the thought of visiting her son. Edwina put down the paper and asked, "Would you like some more coffeecake and coffee or tea," as she walked towards the kitchen, at the back of the house to fetch the refreshments.

Edna: Why yes, some coffee please, thank you.

Some time had passed; Edna could not hear Edwina in the kitchen. Edna then yelled out "Edwina?" but got no answer, Edna had noticed Edwina's somewhat nervous behavior while she was reading, she walked over to the side table and picked up the newspaper, as she looked over at the page Edwina was reading, she yelled out towards the kitchen saying casually "What ya reading." Again no answer ... It was the story of Gabriel's escape, included was a large prominent picture of Gabriel, with and without makeup. Edna's face turned pale, then red then purple, she frowned and squinted her eyes, her face turned angry, and then she became enraged, she began running towards the kitchen, as she approached she noticed Edwina was gone, Edwina had left suddenly and unexpectedly. Then Edna heard a car starting up by the front of the house, she grabbed a butcher knife from the kitchen and ran like a sprinter towards the front of the house, only to see Edwina driving away.

Edna was not what she pretended to be, Edna was not the elderly hunched over little old lady neighbor of Edwina ... Edna was not a woman at all ... Edna was Gabriel.

Gabriel had moved next to Edwina, shortly after encountering Ed and failing to murder him. This was to be another of his hideouts; he had figured that Ed would never suspect it. He had also figured that Edwina could serve as a hostage in the future, if he found himself in a tight circumstance; he would use her as leverage against Ed. After his identification and arrest, she was just going to serve him as victim of his revenge. Gabriel would have to run and hide at another of his hideouts, The frustration and anger at failing to hurt Ed again was driving him more insane,(if that were possible). Fortunately, for Edwina she also had apparently inherited the Castillo trait of observation, a trait that had saved her life. She called Ed and he then called inspector Tradeles, a posse was soon formed to pursue him, but as always he was too fast and had left little to trace.

Katy was back from visiting her sister, the scare had brought them closer together, the thought of being separated made life seem more valuable and shorter, they wanted to ensure that every moment they spent together from then on would be as full as they could make it.

At the wedding's special dinner in Key West, Ed and Katy relaxed by the pier, readying to savor the chef's signature dish, the famous Florida Red Snapper Flambé ala Appétit, suddenly there was a commotion in the kitchen. Chef Phillip Gaston Pépin Appétit, was lying dead on the kitchen floor, at the end of his extended hand was written several scrawled words, using ketchup, "Poisson rouge est po…" the last word was incomplete. His assistants Jack Strape and Jean Appétit his brother were gasping, but still alive.

The manager said, what could that mean, were they poisoned?

Ed: The chef wrote his last words in French; they were a warning, I believe what he was trying to say is that the red fish, that's "Poisson rouge" in French, is poisoned.

Gabriel had been in Key West, and at the wedding; he had now appropriated the killing method of Matombo. He was not finished yet, as he had tried to act on his threat.

Ed was not going to let this man rule his life, he would take reasonable precautions but he was not going to succumb to fear.

Ed and Katy decided to stay in Key West for a while, and attempt to unwind, but just as Ed started relaxing again, a lawyer acquaintance called him, he said he had a job for Ed, performing an audit of a client's assets. The clients were the owners of a well-known historical estate in Miami. He failed to tell Ed at that time that the clients had been missing for over six years, they had disappeared under suspicious circumstances and were presumed dead, killed by the hand of a killer or killers unknown.

TO BE CONTINUED....

CHAPTER INDEX

THE DEVIL'S AUDITOR

There is poetry in them thar... Prose.
Prose can be just as emotionally moving, spiritually uplifting and passion evoking as any musical melodious rhapsody, and it can be written, not only with the same cadence of music, but also with the subtle heart warming rhythm of poetry; without the reader even being aware that there is poetry in the prose. (Hot-Damn, that's poetic ... too bad this novel had none of it)
...Me

ABOUT THE AUTHOR

Born in Havana Cuba, Ed now lives in Coral Springs Florida. His experience as an auditor has spanned over 20 years. He has conducted numerous audits and fraud investigations of many types of companies, in many industries, in several countries. He audited banks during the commercial loan failures of the seventies and now he has had a ringside seat during the mortgage industry's recent debacle, leading to the current mass unbridled foreclosures.

His profession requires him to relate to individuals at all levels of the hierarchy. "The people one meets during these encounters run the gamut of human personalities. The combinations and permutations of physical, emotional, and mental characteristics of these individuals provide a never ending pallet of characters."

His work requires a thorough knowledge of each business' operating processes and the economic and financial environment in which they flourish or fail. He has traveled to many international locations and has dealt with all kinds of financial situations, providing a myriad of experiences, from which Ed has drawn on for inspiration for his stories. You can find Ed's published essays "Tell It like It Is," and "The C-level Auditor" on the internet. He has created numerous "what if" scenarios, and has devised plans identifying the existence of fraud. It turns out that this same process has proven to be very suitable and adaptable to fiction writing.

BOOKS
BY
AUTHOR

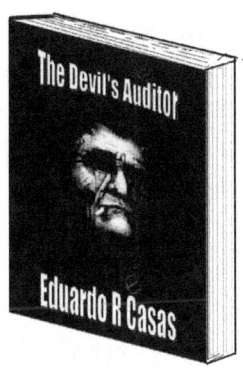

SOON TO BE RELEASED